Leaving Lana'i

Edie Claire

second of the Pacific Horizons novels

Dedication

To everyone who has ever felt a special connection with Lana'i,
whether you are one of the many who have visited briefly
or one of the few privileged to call it home,
may the island whisper in your ear
always.

Chapter 1

Maddie looked across the blue waters of the Au'au Channel, her gaze riveted on the greenish-brown mound of earth that rose from the ocean some nine miles before her. Propelled into existence practically overnight by some angry ancient volcano, the island of Lana'i had ever since, and ever so slowly, been sinking and eroding back into the sea. The island had filled her memories and spun her dreams since childhood, yet only rarely had she seen such a view of it. Standing on the wharf in Lahaina, Maui, she could take in the entire profile of Lana'i at a glance. But the rocky shores and windswept peaks visible to her now bore no evidence of either the luxurious resorts or the friendly, humble town she remembered.

She drew in a deep breath of the warm, moist air, enjoying the feel of the morning sun on her face. Mynas chattered around her; the ocean breeze was stiff. She stood still and silent on the dock, content to do nothing but absorb the feel of the islands. She had been waiting fifteen years for this day. For a woman of twenty-five, it seemed a lifetime.

"Everybody headed to Lana'i, step right up!" a man's voice rang out pleasantly. Maddie looked over toward the catamaran she was planning to board to see a tall, handsome redhead standing by the gangplank holding a clipboard. Several dozen people rose from the shade of the trees nearby and headed toward him to check in. Maddie took her time and joined the end of the line.

Taking a day cruise with the tourist set was a splurge for her, but it was a calculated one. In the nearly five years Maddie had lived on the island of Lana'i as a child, she had seen the distant spouts of humpback whales many times, and she had watched with glee whenever their sleek dark backs and black and white flukes breached the surface of the water near shore. She had even managed a few closer views when she rode the ferry to Maui. But never had she been fortunate enough to ride on one of the dashing catamarans she and her playmates used to watch dock at the small boat harbor in Manele Bay — sailing cats whose sole purpose was to take their passengers up close and personal to the giant whales who shared the islands' warm, blue waters.

Today, she would fulfill that dream.

That one, and perhaps a few others.

She readjusted the wide brim of her sun hat, surveyed the crowd, and then quickly dropped her chin. All of the passengers she had seen waiting before were either couples or families, but the trio of single twenty-something guys who had just walked up set off her alarm bells. The distinctive scent of stale beer lingered around them, and each hid what were most likely bloodshot eyes behind high-end sunglasses. Two out of three had wet hair from last-minute showers; the third looked like he had been asleep five minutes ago. All wore expensive beachwear that appeared newly purchased. One wore a Rolex watch along with Volcom boardshorts and a matching rashguard, never mind that his pale skin and flabby limbs made him look about as much like a surfer as Maddie did a professional jockey.

She stepped out of the men's line of sight. Predictably, the trio did not walk to the end of the line but cut in front of the family ahead of her instead, sparing her their dubious company — at least for the time being. She was glad she had braided her hair this morning and that she was wearing her wind jacket. Her height and profile made her stand out in any crowd, but she had learned ways to minimize the effect. And today especially, her "effect" was something she preferred not to deal with.

"Don't tell me," the man with the clipboard ordered as she approached. She was the last passenger remaining on the dock, and he raised a palm to forestall her as he scanned the roster on his clipboard. "Madalyn Westover?"

"That's me," Maddie replied.

"Well, that's a relief," he said playfully. "If you weren't, I was going to ask if you could fake it, because we're running ten minutes behind already. You the one-way?"

Maddie shifted her backpack, her attention having been subconsciously directed to its weight on her shoulders. She planned to spend tonight on the island. This particular excursion company didn't usually do one-way trips to Lana'i, but she had worked it out with the management over the phone already. She would be dropped off at Manele Bay and would finagle her own accommodations from there. Tomorrow afternoon she would meet the crew back at the harbor for a separate return voyage.

No problem. Surely someone who remembered her would still be living on the island and would be willing to take her in. If not? Well, it would be an adventure.

"Yes, I'm the one-way," she confirmed.

"Awesome," the man said affably, shaking her hand. "Ben Parker. I'll be your captain today. Always happy to meet another ginger. Nice shade, too. Are we related?"

Maddie smiled. Although her hair was always a popular target for pick-up lines, she didn't think the boat captain was flirting with her. He did indeed sport the same unusual shade of dark red-gold as her own, and pick-up lines didn't usually reference a shared gene pool. Besides which, his eyes had yet to stray below her chin. "I doubt it," she replied. "Unless you have relatives in central Ohio."

He looked thoughtful. "Seems unlikely. The Parkers have been a West Coast clan for a while now. Maybe back in Scotland?" He gestured for her to precede him onto the boat.

Maddie did so with a laugh. "Maybe."

As soon as everyone was on board, the passengers received their initial orientation and Maddie found a spot in the cabin to stow her backpack for the journey. She climbed the steps back up to the deck and began scouting out an available place to sit. The ocean swells would be choppy in January, and the passengers were advised to remain seated during the first part of the journey. The bow of the boat had the most space, but the up-front crowd was boisterous, and Maddie kept moving down the side rail. She spied the perfect stretch of empty cushion next to a friendly-looking family of four, but before she could claim it, the group scooted down to make room for someone else at the other end. Maddie searched on, but apparently the boat was near capacity, and when she saw that the benches across the stern, inside the cabin, and up the far side were also now full, she realized she would have to return to the bow.

She was not the only passenger still hunting for a seat, and as the retired couple ahead of her also picked their way slowly back up to the front she shucked her jacket and relaxed at the rail a moment, stretching her arms into the sun and looking longingly at the island ahead of her.

Lana'i.

I've missed you so. Have you missed me?

Her heart gave a little leap. She knew she was being melodramatic. She knew she was being childish. But she *had* been a child when she'd left the island before. And she had certainly not left by choice.

"Hey," a husky voice sounded.

Maddie straightened and faced the stranger. "Yes?"

The guy with the Rolex pulled his shades from his eyes and perched them on top of his artificially highlighted brown hair. He leaned over the rail beside her and slid in so close that if she had not taken a step back, his shoulder would have collided with her chest. Maddie studied his bloodshot eyes and reassessed her earlier opinion. The man had not just awakened from last night's bender. He was still on it. "I'm Cory," he said smoothly, waggling his eyebrows like something from a *Saturday Night Live* sketch. "And I think I've been waiting for this moment my entire life."

Maddie chastised herself. She had forgotten about the men; let her guard slip. It was enough that they were half drunk and she was the only unaccompanied woman on the boat. That alone should have made her keep her jacket zipped for the duration. But no — she just *had* to feel the sun on her skin. And to make matters worse, she'd worn a tank top.

She took another step away and leveled a cool gaze back at him, even though his eyes weren't focused on her face. "Oh?" she said politely. "You study baleen whales?"

Cory's eyes glazed over. They moved slowly upward until focusing somewhere in the vicinity of her nose. His head bobbed on his neck as the boat began to move.

"Could everyone take a seat please?" the captain announced.

Whatever Maddie had said that Cory couldn't process, he quickly forgot. "We saved a spot for you," he said instead, smiling.

Maddie looked over his shoulder to see his two companions standing over prime seats along the bow. They were gesturing to her wildly and grinning like idiots. There were indeed several unoccupied spaces next to them, no doubt because the other passengers had given all three men a wide berth. Unfortunately, those seats were the only ones available.

Cory put his hand on Maddie's upper arm. "Come on, beautiful," he cajoled, rubbing his thumb along her biceps. "God, I've never seen a face like yours." He was no longer looking at her face. "You've got to be a model. Are you a model?"

Maddie silently weighed her options. He wouldn't have his hands on her at all if they weren't in a public place in front of children, several of whom might be disturbed at the sight of a grown man doubled over with groin pain. She would have to dissuade him in a more civilized manner, even if it was likely to take longer. That said, if his thumb moved one more centimeter toward second base, both the dude and his Rolex would be going for a swim.

She pulled her arm back. "I have a seat in the cabin below deck," she said dispassionately. She'd long since gotten over the temptation to get smart-mouthed with drunks. The SOBs could get angry quickly, and though she was five-feet-ten and no shrinking violet, keeping the element of surprise was more important than the satisfaction of a verbal burn. Furthermore, under the circumstances she really didn't want things to get ugly, despite the blow to her pride. "Thanks, though," she forced out.

She turned to move toward the steps leading below deck, knowing the cabin was already full but willing to sit on the floor if she had to, when Cory snatched her arm and spun her around to face him again.

"Hey, Sis!" a loud voice called from the bridge. "There's room up here, if you want to keep me company!"

Both Cory and Maddie looked upward. The captain was leaning out from behind the ship's wheel, watching them intently. Both his voice and expression were calm, but Cory was not too drunk to read the unspoken — but painfully clear — subtext of the message.

Don't make me come down there.

Cory dropped Maddie's arm.

"Cool! Thanks!" she called back brightly, her tone belying the vigorous thumping of her heart as, without looking back, she moved away from the pesky drunk and across the deck toward the bridge.

Sheesh! Could she not go anywhere alone?

She grabbed hold of the handrail, climbed the few steps up to the bridge, and sat down on the cushioned bench seat beside where the captain stood. "Hey, Bro," she greeted. "Thanks for that."

Ben smiled at her, but given the twitch of his jaw muscles as he watched Cory and his degenerate friends settle into their seats along the bow, she suspected that if the captain were not on the job, he might also have preferred the swimming-Rolex scenario. "No problem," he answered evenly. "Sorry it happened. We'll try not to let them spoil the rest of your day."

The boat chugged out of the harbor and, with all the passengers finally seated, it kicked into high speed. The ocean wind hit Maddie square in the face, and as the bench seat began to bounce with the rhythm of the waves, her spirits buoyed. "Spoiling my day would be impossible," she said gaily, pulling off her hat and sitting on it instead. "Jerks come along every day. The chance to see Lana'i again... not so much."

She was aware that her voice had become wistful, despite the need to shout above the wind. So be it. She *was* wistful.

"You've been to Lana'i before?" Ben asked.

The images played in Maddie's mind like something between a movie and a fairy tale. High cliffs and crashing waves. Grassy fields with starry skies above. Tall pines dripping with foggy dew. A boy's laughter; the twinkle in his eyes. Loving brown arms enfolding her in a hug as soft as a featherbed.

"I grew up there," she answered.

"Really?" Ben exclaimed with surprise. "How long has it been since you've been home?"

A less welcome image intruded into Maddie's reverie. A dark house in a gloomy town in the middle of the mainland. She had thought it would never stop raining. *This is your home now, Maddie. You're going to live here with us for a while.*

"Lana'i hasn't been home for a long time," she explained. "We moved there when I was six years old, and we left when I was not quite eleven. I haven't been back since."

"Wow," Ben said after a moment. "This must be quite an event for you, then."

"It is," Maddie acknowledged. "I've been trying to get back to Hawaii ever since, but it's so expensive, particularly when you're coming from the East." She smiled to herself. "The way to do it, you see, is to plan your entire educational path so that the only logical place to do your post-doctoral fellowship is on the island of Maui."

Ben's eyes lit up. "What area?" he asked, his interest obviously genuine. "I mean, your graduate work?"

Nice... and smart, too. Maddie found her gaze straying toward the captain's left hand. *Dammit.* He was already married. Of course. "I just finished up a PhD in ecology. Specifically, ecological processes — studying species interactions in changing environments. For my thesis, I studied a feral cat colony in rural Alabama."

She studied Ben's reaction. This was usually the part of the conversation where, if she liked the person, she took mercy on them and shut up. Or, if she didn't like them, she went on to elaborate about population dynamics and host-microbiome network interactions.

"Are you going to study feral cats on Maui, too?" he asked hopefully, his hazel eyes practically dancing with delight.

Maddie did a double take. "As a matter of fact, I am. Specifically, I'm going to be tracking patterns of parasite shed, looking at how—"

"Please tell me you're studying toxoplasmosis," Ben broke in.

The enraptured look on his face rendered Maddie momentarily speechless. "Um," she responded finally, laughing a little, "I am studying *Toxoplasma gondii*, yes."

"That's fabulous!" he exclaimed, his voice so exuberant that two of his crew members turned to stare, probably wondering if he had sighted a whale already. "And way overdue! You know we could be losing monk seals because of all the contaminated runoff? Spinner dolphins, too."

"I am aware," Maddie replied, laughing out loud now. Nobody, short of other grad students in the exact same field, ever gave a damn about her work. Talking about it with a cute boat captain while sailing through the Au'au Channel was pure delight, even if he was already taken. "And how is it that you know so much about toxo?"

Over the next twenty minutes, she learned that Captain Ben Parker had a master's degree in oceanography but was interested in pretty much everything that had anything to do with the natural world. She also learned that he spent his summers running similar whale-watching tours in Alaska, that he was a happily married newlywed, and that — unfortunately — he had no brother.

Being no slouch in the art of conversation, Ben also managed to get her to divulge that she had been born in Dayton, Ohio and had lived in Sandusky, Ohio until her father landed a middle-management job with the two five-star resorts on Lana'i. She told Ben that her family had left the island because her father was offered a better position managing several state park resorts in Kentucky, but in that explanation she had been less than truthful. For one thing, the new job wasn't better. For another, not all of the family had returned to the mainland. Her mother had died on Lana'i.

But Maddie didn't want to talk about that.

"Nick!" Ben called out suddenly, gesturing to one of the younger crewmen, "Code green, starboard."

"Got it!" Nick answered. He slid down from his position near the mast to assist the stumbling Cory, who had left his place near the bow and was attempting to move to the back of the boat. The waves had become increasingly choppy farther from shore, and as the boat pitched more and more Maddie could see why walking steadily on the deck would take some experience, even for a sober person. The agile Nick had no trouble reaching Cory, but the overgrown frat boy would never have made it to the rear corner of the boat if not for the ship's rail on one side and Nick on the other.

"Whoa, take it easy, man," Ben called out as Cory hurled what was left of his breakfast into the churning wake. "Don't worry. Happens all the time." Ben's voice was suitably sympathetic, but as he turned toward Maddie with a muttered, "What a shame," he made no effort to hide a grin.

The next hour flew by in a happy haze of blue ocean, white sea spray, and the giant, gleaming backs and fins of several obliging whales. The weather was a perfect seventy-five degrees, drifting clouds were few and far between, and as the boat neared the sheer cliffs of the southern edge of Lana'i, Maddie's voyage felt increasingly surreal. When the catamaran pulled within sight of Pu'u Pehe, the Sweetheart Rock, she felt sure she must be dreaming.

She had seen countless photographs of the landmark since adulthood, but none of those images had ever come close to the ones that burned so brightly in her memory. The colors were never as vivid, the angles never as sharp. Photographs could show nothing more than a slant-topped chunk of reddish rock rising from the ocean to form a sea tower. Videos did a better job of showing the tower's dramatic placement, sitting like a punctuation mark a hundred fifty feet out from the highest point of the cliff that separated the Manele boat harbor from the Hulopo'e swimming beach. Travel books could gush about how, by catching the trailhead at the beach and walking along the cliffside path, one could reach the overlook a hundred twenty feet above the ocean and gaze over at the surface of the sea tower to see the burial mound of Pehe.

But none of the above could create the feelings that rushed through Maddie now. It was not only the sights she was seeing. It was the warmth of the sun on her face, the movement of her hair in the wind, the taste of the salty spray on her lips. Her eyes could see only one side of the Sweetheart Rock, but her senses remembered so much more. In a flash she was again standing high atop the cliff, half her hair still braided while the other half flapped around her eyes trying to blind her, her bare toes caked with the powdery red dirt, her mouth dry with thirst from the climb. There was no guardrail before her, no paved path, no warning sign. Just a couple more feet of flat dirt, then a straight drop clear to the ocean. She was with a half-dozen other rowdy, school-aged children whose parents had only the vaguest idea where they were and wouldn't have cared if they did know. No other adults were around.

She was fine.

She was sure, in fact, that life held nothing better. Far below her feet, the ocean crashed into the rocks, sending up a curtain of white spray that looked tantalizingly cool. It was one memory. It was a hundred. She was seven years old. Ten. Eight. The rocks, the ocean, and the red dirt never changed. The curious rectangular arrangement of dark stones atop the sea tower never changed, either. Though an obvious product of human hands, it had stood there, looking just as it did now, for hundreds of years.

I think there's bones in it, she had insisted.

There's not, Kai had contradicted.

Nobody knows for sure.

They do, too!

Do not!

It could have been one argument. It could have been fifty. From what she remembered of her childhood charms, it was probably closer to the latter.

Maddie snapped back to the present. Ben was entertaining the other passengers by telling them the traditional legend of Pu'u Pehe, which involved two lovers, a sea cave, an unexpected storm, and a Romeo and Juliet ending complete with tomb. He was a good storyteller, but Maddie could not keep her mind from drifting. She was back at the top of the cliff again. And it was a boy who was talking.

There's nothing WRONG with the story, Kai had explained. *I just get tired of it. Why does everybody always have to tell the same story over and over again? If it's not true anyway, why can't I make up new ones?*

"There were no human remains found at the site," Ben finished. "But archeologists do believe the structure was a form of Hawaiian temple, or *heiau.*"

Maddie chuckled, and Ben looked at her curiously.

"Sorry," she said. "I just realized I owe somebody an apology. A rather long-overdue one." *Too bad he won't be here to apologize to,* she thought with a sudden pang.

She shook off the feeling as quickly as it had come over her. Kai Nakama would be twenty-five years old now, the same as her, and he was no more likely to have stayed on Lana'i than she was to have stayed in Paducah, Kentucky. She knew that. She hadn't expected to find him here, or any of her other childhood friends. She knew that most if not all of them would be gone.

Just please, God, let Nana still be okay, and be here. And Mr. and Mrs.

Nakama. And old Mr. Li and Mr. Kalaw...

Several passengers in the bow of the boat cried out with delight and pointed forward.

"Spinner dolphins!" Ben announced. He launched into a description of the familiar marine mammals as they frolicked at the mouth of the bay.

Maddie looked eagerly toward the sleek gray fins, but found her eyes drawn beyond them to the road past the marina that headed uphill towards Lana'i City. She felt a sudden and unexpected chill as she remembered something else.

But Dad, can't I even say goodbye? Won't everyone wonder where I've gone to?

I'm sorry, honey, but there isn't time. Your grandparents are waiting. I'll make sure everyone knows what's happened and pass along your goodbyes for you, okay?

No. It was not okay. It was not okay at all.

Tell them I still want to go to the mountains, just as soon as I get back. Okay?

She couldn't remember her father's expression when she'd said that. Most likely, he had paused before answering. Perhaps even fought back a tear. He had to feel guilty for deceiving her, but she realized now what the poor man must have been going through himself. His wife was dead. His only child needed family, who lived thousands of miles away. He had no idea what tomorrow would bring.

She had not come back. Ten-year-old Maddie Westover had simply disappeared one day, never to be heard from again.

Well, almost never. She had written Kai a letter once. Mailed from her grandparents' house in Dayton.

He hadn't written her back.

The stinking rat.

"Maddie?" Ben was looking at her with concern. "You okay? If you're getting cold feet about this little adventure of yours, you're more than welcome to come back with us later today."

Maddie stood up. The catamaran had pulled into the harbor and the water was calm. "Thank you," she said genuinely, flashing him one of her better smiles. "But I'm fine. Just momentarily overwhelmed with a rush of childhood memories, that's all."

He smiled back at her. "Good ones, I hope."

"With few exceptions, they were the absolute best," she said honestly. A lump formed in her throat as she spoke, and she fought back the fear that gnawed at her gut.

Her recollections of the island had always been glorious. Idyllic. Warm, wonderful, and carefree. They were a child's memories, true.

From a child's perspective. But with every fiber of her being, she longed for what she'd left behind here. For goodbyes left unsaid, for hugs not given, for endings never written.

She *had* to come back.

She was not naive. She knew that her memories could have become tainted with time. Whitewashed, slanted, perhaps some even wholly fabricated. Even if most of what she remembered was accurate, both the place and the people could have changed by now, at least as much as she herself had changed — which was a whole hell of a lot.

She knew that. She also knew that, as a child, her memory was likely to contain certain omissions. Omissions that could prove much more relevant to her experience of the island as an adult. What if nothing was as she remembered? What if all the people she had loved were gone? What if they were all still here, but were not the people she believed them to be? What if all those years of built-up hope and dreamy anticipation had done nothing but set her up for one colossal fall?

"We're here!" Ben called out merrily once the catamaran was secured to the dock. "Welcome to Lana'i, everyone!"

A strong gust of wind blew across the bank ahead of them, jostling green fronds of palm and threatening to lift off the hat Maddie had replaced mere seconds before. She raised a hand and clamped down on it, her heart leaping with joy as another of her senses awakened to memory. It was the scent on the air — the scent of Lana'i. Exactly what that aroma consisted of, she had no idea. The volcanic earth, its microflora, the peculiar Cook Island pines... a blend of all of the above? She could not describe it; she had no words to do so. She hadn't realized that such a scent existed, much less that she would recognize it.

But here it was.

And here she was.

Welcome back, Maddie, the island whispered.

Chapter 2

Maddie set her backpack down by her feet near one of the benches at the marina's portico. The next item on the passengers' itineraries was snorkeling at the nearby Hulopo'e beach, and the assembled company had been milling around for several minutes now, deciding how best to get there. Some groups opted to walk up the road and around the bend themselves, while others decided to wait for the promised vans which could deliver them there in a matter of seconds. Ordinarily, Maddie would walk. But snorkeling at Hulopo'e was not on her agenda, at least not today. What she needed was a ride further inland into Lana'i City, and she was hoping to hitch with one of the van drivers.

"Beautiful trip so far, huh?" a man said politely as he stepped up beside her into the shade.

"Gorgeous," she replied. The man appeared to be in his late forties, and he dressed with the meticulous look of a businessman who took vacation only when he had to. Maddie had seen him sitting on the boat earlier with his wife and teenaged son; she had noticed the family because they barely talked to each other. At the moment, he was alone.

"Gorgeous, indeed," he said more quietly, edging closer. He looked her up and down. "You staying somewhere in Ka'anapali tonight?"

Oh, God. Not again. She really didn't want to put the jacket back on.

Maddie picked up her backpack. "No." She swung it over her shoulders, walked to the opposite end of the waiting crowd, and set it down again. She dug out an oversized tee and finished donning it just as two white vans pulled up.

"Aloha!" a friendly woman's voice called as she hopped out of the van nearest Maddie and walked around in front of it to open the passenger doors. "Welcome to Lana'i, everyone! You ready for the beach?"

Maddie studied the woman eagerly, taking in her broad face, light brown skin, and straight dark hair, but nothing in the picture stirred recognition. It was possible that Maddie had seen the woman before. She might even have known her name once. But it was also possible they had never met.

"Aloha! Welcome!"

Maddie froze. The driver of the other van had now also disembarked and was standing a mere twenty feet away. Her voice drifted through Maddie's brain like a song, bringing with it an unexpectedly powerful wave of emotion.

Mrs. Nakama! Maddie sucked in a breath, overwhelmed. All she could do was stare at the mildly plump, strikingly attractive forty-something woman who opened the side doors of the far shuttle van. She looked almost exactly the same as Maddie remembered her. And she was still giving tours. After fifteen years. Why shouldn't she? She had always been good at it.

Maddie was still standing, still staring, after all the other passengers had been seated. "You coming with me, dear?" the unfamiliar driver asked.

Maddie shook herself and picked up her pack. "No, I... I'd like to ride with Mrs. Nakama. If there's still room?"

The woman looked at Maddie curiously. "Malaya?" she called over. "Can you fit one more?"

Mrs. Nakama threw Maddie only the briefest of glances. "Sure! You can sit up front." She closed the side doors behind her other guests, popped open the front passenger door, then walked around the hood and back to her driver's seat.

Maddie called out her thanks to both drivers, hurried to the other van, and jumped in. Her pulse pounded as Mrs. Nakama threw her a superficial smile, started up the van, and began the usual line of tour-guide small talk on the short ride up the hill and around to the beach. Maddie herself didn't speak. Her thoughts were elsewhere.

So, she thought with amusement, "Malaya" was Mrs. Nakama's first name? It was musical, which suited her. Had Maddie known it before? Probably, but children weren't interested in such things. What she remembered most about Kai's mother was that she laughed a lot, enjoyed singing, and was always full of life. Although, Maddie recalled with a vague sense of chagrin, the woman was definitely capable of anger — under certain unfortunate circumstances.

Maddie also didn't remember her as being so pretty, no doubt because she had only seen her as someone else's mother. But Mrs. Nakama was indeed a beauty, and Maddie found herself wondering what ethnic makeup had created such a pleasing blend of features. As a child Maddie had given little thought to race, except when reminded that she herself was a *haole* — white — and therefore a second-class islander. Almost all the other children at her school were some shade of brown, and they were the true Lana'ians. They might also be Filipino or Japanese or Chinese, and how all those terms fit together with being Lana'ian or Hawaiian she had never been quite sure, but it had never particularly mattered to her.

Looking at Mrs. Nakama now, Maddie couldn't help but wonder. She was fairly certain that Kai's father's people were Japanese, while his mother's side of the family were Filipino. Mrs. Nakama's smooth skin was a medium shade of brown, and her glossy black hair spread in rippling waves over her shoulders, framing an oval face with high cheekbones, a pert chin, large dark eyes, and lashes to kill for. Her son Kai had had the same pretty bone structure, not to mention the same overlong, perfectly curled eyelashes. Eyelashes no boy had any right being born with.

The stinking rat!

Maddie smiled to herself. Kai's little sister had been cute, too. But Chika had looked more like their father.

Mrs. Nakama turned to look at Maddie periodically as they drove, but her gaze never lingered for long, and as the van pulled up to the drop-off spot at the beach, a fluttering began in Maddie's stomach. Kai's mother didn't recognize her.

In another minute, Mrs. Nakama would unload the van and drive away.

"Here you go, everybody!" Mrs. Nakama announced, hopping out again to release her passengers promptly. The van was theoretically air conditioned, but no conversion van packed with people shoulder to shoulder could ever be called comfortable. Maddie opened her own door, but after stepping down, declined to close it. She still needed a ride into town.

She took a deep breath and plucked up some courage. It wasn't Mrs. Nakama's fault. God knew Maddie looked different, and her being here now was completely unexpected. She stood still, holding the door, waiting for the other passengers to unload and walk away. At last she was the only one left.

Mrs. Nakama turned. She studied her remaining passenger for a moment with her head cocked slightly to the side, and Maddie felt a flicker of hope. "Is there..." the van driver began uncertainly, "something I can help you with?"

"Mrs.—" Maddie stammered. She felt every bit the child again. "Mrs. Nakama?"

The woman's eyes widened slightly.

Maddie's heart leapt. "Picture me a foot and a half shorter and a whole lot chubbier," she blurted. "At least in most places. Other places, I'm a bit... wider now."

Mrs. Nakama blinked. Her chest swelled suddenly with breath. "*Maddie*," she exclaimed on the exhale. "Holy— You're *Maddie!*"

Maddie nodded enthusiastically. Hot tears sprang unexpectedly to her eyes, embarrassing her thoroughly until Mrs. Nakama gave a loud and merry laugh and enfolded her in a hug.

"I can't believe it!" Mrs. Nakama gushed over her shoulder. "I wouldn't have guessed it in a million years, but now that I know, it's as plain as—" She pulled back and gave Maddie an approving once over. "Girl, you have turned out *well*, can I say it? What a beauty you are!"

Maddie smiled genuinely at the compliment. Despite being "a friend's mom," Malaya Nakama was a youthful forty-something, and the girlfriendy vibe she radiated now seemed a natural evolution.

"I can't believe you're back! After all these years! Does anybody else know you're coming?"

Maddie shook her head. "I know I probably should have called. But I just flew into Maui for grad school two days ago, and I couldn't wait to come over and see... well, everything! But I'm almost afraid to know what's changed."

Mrs. Nakama's eyes searched hers. "Things always change. But I suspect less has changed here than most places!" She paused a moment, then smiled gently. "I never had a chance to tell you how sorry we all were about your mother."

A quick stab of guilt flitted through Maddie's middle. She never knew what to say to such comments. Of course it had hurt to lose her mother, but she would never get over the queer feeling that the loss hadn't wounded her as much as it was supposed to. She had loved her mother, but the sad truth was that she felt like she had barely known her. Although she had cried into her pillow for months that rainy spring in Ohio, missing her mother had accounted for only a fraction of her grief.

"Thank you," Maddie replied. "It was a shock to everyone in the family, her having a heart attack as young as she was; they say she didn't have any signs beforehand. I'll confess I was angry at my father for a long time, whisking me away like he did. But I understand now how hard the circumstances must have been for him. I know he did the best he could."

Crow's feet appeared at the corners of Mrs. Nakama's almond-shaped eyes, and for several seconds, frown lines marred her brow. But then a soft smile returned, making her look years younger again. "It was a very hard time for your father, I'm sure," she said soothingly. "No doubt he thought you needed your grandparents, and the sooner the better."

"I wrote to Kai, you know," Maddie blurted, regretting the words immediately. They sounded almost petulant. Well, hell. It still bothered her, didn't it? Poor little girl that she was, her mother dies suddenly, she's dragged thousands of miles from home, and her supposed best friend can't take the time to answer one lousy letter?

Mrs. Nakama's eyebrows lifted slightly.

Maddie cringed at her blunder. Nothing was more endearing to a mother than having veiled insults flung at her only son. Maddie backtracked quickly. "I mean, he never answered, but that's not surprising. Boys that age hate to write, right? It's my fault, really. I feel bad that I didn't call Nana. I don't know why I didn't. I didn't even think about it. Maybe because I wasn't used to talking to her on the phone — or any of you. Maybe if my grandparents had suggested it — but they didn't understand. They tell me now that at the time, I rambled on so much about everybody else on Lana'i *but* my mother, they thought it must be some kind of defense mechanism—"

Maddie shut her mouth. Her emotions were running away with her. *Too much, too soon.* "I'm sorry," she added, laughing at herself a little. "You're very unlucky to be the first person I've run into here. There's just so much stuff I've been waiting forever to say, and to ask. But I know you're busy working. Is there any chance you could give me a ride into town? If not, I'll be happy to pay anybody with four wheels to drive out and pick me up."

Mrs. Nakama looked unsettled as she waved off the suggestion. She pulled out her phone and checked the time. "Of course we'll get you into town! I can't hijack the van that long, but Gloria's out of school now. She can come get you."

"Gloria?" Maddie repeated. "*Baby* Gloria?"

Mrs. Nakama smirked. "She's seventeen now, God help us."

Maddie blew out a breath. She herself might have grown up in the last fifteen years, but for Kai's youngest sister, who had been born when they were eight, to do likewise seemed preposterous. "I don't want to put her to any trouble. I can wait and go in with the tour later if I have to."

Mrs. Nakama was already calling. "It's no trouble. *She's* trouble, but not you. You have someplace to stay already? How long are you going to be here?"

Maddie's heart warmed. She was so damned lucky. "Just overnight. But no, I haven't found anyplace to stay yet."

"You'll stay with Nana," Mrs. Nakama announced. "She's got room. She'll be so happy. Should I tell her, or you want to surprise her yourself? She— *Gloria?*" Mrs. Nakama's voice turned scary-mom in an instant. "Who's that I hear talking? Where are you?"

Maddie hugged herself. *Nana.* Her precious, precious Nana was alive and well... and she was going to stay with her tonight! As it became clear that Gloria was in trouble with her mother for reasons unrelated to the requested ride, Maddie left her pack on the ground near the van and stepped away to give the mother and daughter some privacy.

The beach park at Hulopo'e looked different. There had been a parking lot, restrooms, and picnic benches when she left, but the whole park area was larger and fancier now, and there were more people both on the beach and in the water. But the changes were only superficial, and as she caught sight of the same stretch of sand on which she'd spent so many joyful hours splashing and playing, her feet began to itch abominably. The urge to kick off her flip-flops and go running straight out into the clear blue water was so strong it was almost overwhelming. "Patience, Maddie," she begged. "Patience."

She had never been very good at patience. In her mind she saw the same bay as it had appeared fifteen years ago. Kai was standing in the shallow water near the reefs, poised with a handmade spear. He could stand there motionless, just like that, seemingly forever.

Don't you get bored? Maddie had whined.

No.

I don't believe you.

No answer.

I'm not that hungry. Can't we just go home and eat?

I'm hungry. Be patient! Sheesh.

There's one.

I see it.

So go get it!

Don't move! he ordered.

But if you stepped over there you could—

I'm fine.

She groaned. *Will you just—*

And then, always, he would spear a fish.

"Maddie?" Mrs. Nakama called.

Maddie whirled around, embarrassed. Exactly why she was embarrassed, she wasn't sure. "Yes?" she replied.

"Gloria will be here in a couple minutes," Mrs. Nakama said. "Keep an eye out for a red truck. She'll take you to Nana's house and then Nana will bring you over for dinner tonight." She stepped in closer and her eyes grew suddenly moist. "I still can't believe our little Maddie grew up into *you*," she said fondly, leaning in to deliver another quick hug. "And that you came back to us. I'm sorry I can't chat more now. I have to go; I have to run some people back over to the harbor to look for something they lost. But we'll catch up over dinner. Okay?"

"That sounds fabulous," Maddie agreed. "Thank you so much."

Mrs. Nakama snorted out a laugh. In most women, any sort of snort would be unattractive, but her particularly merry take on the art could only make one smile. "Don't thank me yet. Gloria's in a mood — I caught her hanging out with that guy at the golf course again. Just don't pay any attention to her. She's doing that high school senior thing where the parents go from 'Wah, my baby's leaving home,' to 'God, get this child out of my house!' You know what I mean?"

Maddie chuckled. "That bad, huh?"

Mrs. Nakama swore. "Worse than that. Chika was bad. Gloria's..." She waved a hand in the air and shook her head. "There's no words."

Chika. Maddie did some quick math in her head. The Nakamas' middle child would be 22 now. Maybe out of college, if she had gone to college. "How is Chika?" Maddie asked tentatively. The older sister was just three years younger than Kai, and although Maddie had known her well and even played with her sometimes, Chika had her own set of friends.

Mrs. Nakama smiled. "She's good. She's working in Honolulu now, but she visits every couple of months."

"That's nice." Maddie hesitated. This was the perfect time to ask about Kai. It would almost be strange if she didn't.

"Well, it looks like my passengers are ready," Mrs. Nakama said, moving back toward the van where a flustered-looking young couple were being led by one of the boat crew. "I've got to go, but we'll talk more tonight, all right? See you then!"

"See you!" Maddie called, her gay tone belying her disappointment at the missed opportunity. She watched as the passengers loaded up and the van drove away.

Patience, Maddie. All her questions would be answered soon enough.

She was tempted to run to the beach now and at least dip her toes in the water, but if Gloria had been "caught" at the nearby golf course at Manele, the Nakamas' truck could roll up any second, and it would be foolish to prevail on Gloria's good nature to wait around. Maddie's memories of "the baby," who had been all of two when she left, were positive. She remembered a sleeping infant and a cute, placid toddler who didn't talk much, but was always ready with a smile. How difficult could the teenager be?

An engine roared. Maddie looked up to see a bright red four-door pickup tearing down the lane towards the park. Kicking up a storm of dust on either side, it made a wide turn in the parking lot and came to stop with a jerk six feet short of Maddie's toes. The passenger window was half rolled down, and as the dust slowly cleared, the angry face of a very short teenaged girl became visible behind the steering wheel. The girl said nothing, merely glared, and Maddie stood silent a moment, watching her.

"So?" the driver bellowed finally. "If you don't know who I am, go away! If you're this chick I'm supposed to take to Nana's house, then *get the hell in!*"

Chapter 3

Maddie got in. The truck started up with a fury before her seatbelt was fastened, and Maddie had only just managed to secure it when another truck came into view, at which point Gloria immediately slammed on the brakes, launching Maddie into said belt like a crash-test dummy.

"Sorry," the girl mumbled, moderating the vehicle to a respectable speed. As they passed the oncoming truck and the drivers exchanged a wave, Maddie suppressed a chuckle. For Gloria, being rude to a stranger was a relatively minor infraction for which she willing to bear the consequences. Having another Lana'ian catch her driving recklessly in her dad's truck was another matter entirely.

Maddie studied her young chauffeur and decided the girl looked very much like her older sister Chika. She was tiny in stature, with a delicate bone structure and fine, straight black hair. Both girls resembled their father, but whereas Chika had inherited their mother's smile, Gloria had Mrs. Nakama's spirit. You could see it in the spark of fire behind her eyes.

Maddie remembered well when Mrs. Nakama had been pregnant with Gloria. Maddie and Chika had been tremendously excited about the upcoming birth, and so had Kai, although in boyish fashion, he had attempted to hide his feelings. For some unfathomable reason the Nakamas had promised to let Chika name the baby if it was a girl and Kai if it was a boy. The family had been less than enthusiastic with the outcome, but five-year-old Chika was certain that her baby sister had the most beautiful name in the world.

Wordlessly, Gloria drove them from the beach up the long slope of cliff and onto the high, flat plateau that formed the center of the island. The wide, windswept plains of the plateau, from which the ocean was no longer visible, were a different world from the shorelines that surrounded them. The one paved road that meandered through the country was bordered on each side by a single line of Cook Island pine trees, which stood tall and unflinching despite their obviously artificial placement in a rolling, arid landscape covered with bunches of green grass, scraggy bushes, and short, scrubby trees.

For most of the last century, Maddie knew, these fields had been covered with pineapple plants. For almost seventy years, "The Pineapple Island" had been the largest pineapple plantation in the world. Before James Dole came on the scene in the nineteen twenties, "outsiders" had tried using the island for other things, like a ranch, and a mission outpost, and a sugar plantation; but nothing else ever seemed to work out very well. And eventually, neither did the pineapples.

Maddie looked out at the red dirt to see torn remnants of the old weed-choking black groundcover still sticking up from the earth as far as the eye could see. When pineapple farming ceased to be profitable, the island's owners had turned to tourism instead — building the resorts that had employed her father — and the fields had been left to go fallow. The ecosystem had filled the void, as ecosystems did, with a variety of resilient wild plants. But although the available pickings might be acceptable to the imported axis deer and mouflon sheep that roamed the island, the leftover, torn-up, half-buried groundcover material made the land forever useless for grazing livestock.

It was a beautiful sight, nevertheless, to watch the wind rippling through the pale green grass with the darker mist-topped mountains beyond. Maddie had always wondered, as a child, why the later newcomers had so much trouble making the island work for them, when long before the first haoles arrived Lana'i was already home to twice as many as people as lived here now. Not that the island's original inhabitants didn't have their own problems — like humans everywhere, the Hawaiians on the various islands couldn't resist fighting with each other. But without power, refrigeration, airplanes, or container ships, the first Lana'ians still managed to fish and grow their own food, build houses, raise families...

"So how do you know Nana?" the girl barked, breaking Maddie out of her reverie.

Maddie cleared her throat, which had become dry with the stirred-up dust. Gloria was talking to her. It was progress. "I used to live down the street from her."

Gloria's thin eyebrows rose. "Seriously?"

Maddie smiled. "I went to Lana'i Elementary for first grade through most of fifth. I spent a lot of time at Nana's after school, and sometimes in the evenings, too, when my father worked late. Nana was always so kind to me. She took care of other people's kids all day, and as far as I know, my parents never paid her a dime, but when I showed up on her doorstep lonely and—"

Maddie stopped. She was about to say "starving," but that wasn't true. She had never been starving. It was just that her mother wasn't the greatest about remembering to keep food in the house, much less cook it, and when her dad worked evenings Maddie often did go hungry for a while. Nana must have opened her door dozens of times, at all hours of the evening, to find a little girl with an unkempt mass of red hair standing there looking embarrassed, fidgeting as she tried to come up with a new excuse for coming over. Always, Nana would usher her in with a smile and a hug, then chit chat with her as if she'd been waiting and hoping for Maddie to appear. No matter what Maddie actually said, Nana could always ascertain the real reason for the visit, which usually meant that Maddie soon found herself in the house's tiny kitchen, wolfing down vienna sausages and eggs. After a while, Maddie stopped bothering with the excuses. Nana's home became an extension of her own. *Nana* became her own.

"So you were one of Nana's strays?" Gloria concluded, not unkindly.

"Yep," Maddie confirmed. "Fleas and all." Gloria's use of the plural sent another ripple of worry through her. Of course Nana would be attached to many children. She had run a home day care center for decades. Maddie liked to think that she was special, but she needed to be realistic. Even if it hurt. "It's been fifteen years since I've seen her," she admitted sadly. "I'm afraid she may not remember me."

Gloria snorted. Unlike her mother, her snort was in no way appealing. "Nana remembers everything," she said somewhat spitefully. "She's not *that* old."

Maddie sensed there was a story behind the teenager's tone. Perhaps one involving certain deeds that were witnessed by certain grandmothers and relayed to certain parents. Given the frown on Gloria's face, Maddie declined to pursue it, and instead went back to looking out the window. The outskirts of the city were coming into view.

"So, you knew my mom and dad, too, then?" Gloria asked.

"Sure," Maddie replied happily. Despite Gloria's desire to be unpleasant, she was evidently enough of an extrovert to dislike long silences. "I knew your family very well. In fact" — Maddie weighed her options and decided to risk it — "I was at your house the day your parents brought you home from the hospital."

Gloria's face screwed up awkwardly. She said nothing.

"You were unbelievably tiny," Maddie continued, "and you were wearing a little knit cap with a pink tassel on top. Your mom had you wrapped up in a bright yellow blanket, and your dad carried in that little stuffed dog he bought on Maui. I thought it was so funny that he'd gotten you a poodle, of all things! A white, fluffy poodle with a turquoise blue collar around its neck."

"Puffles," Gloria murmured. "Okay, that's just creepy."

Maddie laughed and gave a shrug. "Sorry. I'm afraid it was a pretty memorable day for me. There were never any babies in my family. My stepbrothers were preschoolers when we met."

"So," Gloria continued, sounding a little freaked out, "you were a friend of Chika's?"

"Chika was three years younger than me," Maddie answered. "I was more a friend of Kai's. He and I were in the same grade."

Buildings popped into view over the horizon, and Maddie could barely contain her excitement. A tingling warmth spread over her as she realized that Mrs. Nakama had been right. Very few small towns went fifteen years with no changes at all, but it seemed that Lana'i City, with its population of around three thousand people, had come pretty close. So far, everything looked wonderfully familiar. The city had been built in the nineteen-twenties to be a model plantation town, and as such it had been intentionally laid out with a rectangular green space in the middle and neat grids of residential blocks to either side, all nestled comfortably within the curve of the mountain ridge. Although the town had continued to expand throughout the plantation boom, the outskirts which they were approaching now, Maddie noted with glee, were in essentially the same place she remembered, with no signs of random sprawl.

She sensed that Gloria was staring at her. She turned.

"You," the girl said heavily, "were a friend of *Kai's?"*

Maddie blinked at the bizarre reaction. "Um... yeah. When we were kids. Why?"

"Like, what kind of friends?" Gloria demanded.

Maddie's lips twisted. Why had Gloria said Kai's name in such a weird way? "Like, how many kinds of elementary-school-age friends are there?" she asked in return.

"What I *mean,*" Gloria said with exasperation, "is were you, like, *close?* Would he even remember you, now?"

Maddie's teeth gnashed. She didn't know the answer to the last question, as much as she would like to. But she had no reason to lie about the first one. Heck yes, they'd been close. They had been best friends! That had been no easy feat, either, considering that they were of opposite genders in the height of the "cootie" years, and that she was a haole besides. Kai could have been teased for hanging out with her; he probably had been. But she had never heard him complain about it. Kai had always been one to do what he wanted, just like her. They'd spent time together because they enjoyed each other's company; it was as simple as that. And yet, it wasn't. Maddie had felt convinced they shared a special connection — like she understood him better than anyone else. That's why she had been so certain that he would write back to her after she left Lana'i, certain that *he* would understand, if no one else did, how much she missed the island, and how upset she was at the way she had been made to leave it.

Clearly, she had been wrong about the cosmic connection thing. She had created expectations for an ongoing, long-distance friendship that Kai had obviously not shared. But that didn't mean they what they *had* shared wasn't special at the time.

"We were close," Maddie admitted. "We were best buds, actually." She looked out the window again, her spirits oddly diminished. The Buddhist temple looked just the same. That was nice.

"Has he *seen* you since you were ten?" Gloria pressed.

"No." The houses were all very small, by mainland standards, but to Maddie they looked wonderfully normal. They passed an unkempt hovel with hoarded debris piled up waist-high in the yard, tumbled against a partially caved-in fence covered with "No Trespassing" signs. The house immediately next door, an otherwise identical cottage, was in pristine condition and surrounded by a finely manicured flower garden. Maddie's spirits picked up a little.

"Not even a picture?" Gloria asked.

Maddie struggled to figure out the question. Had Kai seen any recent pictures of her? "No!" she replied shortly. "Why would he? We haven't been in touch."

"Not *at all?*"

Maddie turned and exhaled with impatience. "No!"

An evil-looking smile broke out on Gloria's lips and spread slowly up her cheeks. "Oh," she said in a low voice. "This is good. This is *soo* good!" She squealed with glee, kicked her feet on the floorboards, and pounded her palms on the steering wheel. The truck swerved sharply to the left into the path of an oncoming jeep.

"Gloria!" Maddie cried, leaning over to grab the wheel.

"I got it, I got it!" Gloria protested, righting the wheel and safely passing. She threw a dismissive wave in the direction of the jeep. "It's a rental. They don't know who I am." She chortled again. "Oh, Kai is *so* screwed!"

"Excuse me?" Maddie was getting annoyed. If there was a joke involved, she wanted in on it. "Explain, please."

But Gloria would only smile that annoying smile of hers. "Let's just say it's complicated. I don't know what Kai was like when he was ten, but I think it's safe to say he's changed since you knew him. *A lot.*"

Maddie felt a pang of disappointment on top of her annoyance. Everybody changed when they grew up. She couldn't expect Kai not to change at all. But "a lot" didn't sound good. She had liked him the way he was. "Oh?"

"Yeah," Gloria continued. "I mean, I was pretty little when he still lived at home, but I remember he was more laid back then. After he went to the mainland for college he got all stuffed up, you know?"

Maddie did not know. "All... 'stuffed up?' Like... snobby?"

"No, no," Gloria corrected. "Not stuffy-snobby like 'I'm better than you.' More like 'I know better than you.'"

Maddie considered, then breathed a little easier. "Well, he was always like that."

Maddeningly, Gloria shook her head. "No, it's different. It's the whole *morality* thing. His grandparents screwed him up. They're all super-religious and everything."

Maddie was confused. "What grandparents?" Nana's husband had died ages ago. Kai's father's parents had always lived on the island and, as far as Maddie could remember, were not particularly religious.

"The ones in Utah," Gloria said impatiently. "That's where he went to college."

Maddie's head spun. Kai had relatives in *Utah?* Deep in the back of her brain, a lone bell began to chime. Actually, she knew that. Kai had mentioned family on the mainland more than once. She didn't remember his calling them "grandparents," but his family was multi-faceted and vast, they used all sorts of relational terms in ways that made no sense to her, and she'd had little interest in the topic at the time. She was jealous enough of the plethora of aunts, uncles, and cousins he had spread all over the islands — to know that he also had relatives on the mainland, when her own tribe was so sparse and unworldly by comparison, was just plain annoying.

"When did he come back?" Maddie asked, her heart racing suddenly. "Is he here now?"

Gloria looked at her as if she were stupid. "He doesn't live here.

He's a lawyer. There's no jobs. But he comes over pretty often." She grinned again. "And I would really like to be there when he gets a load of you."

Maddie relaxed a little, but as she sensed a theme to Gloria's comments, she frowned. "And what exactly does his relatives in Utah being super religious have to do with me?"

Gloria squirmed a bit. "Well, no offense or anything. It's just that you're... well, you know. Like, *hot.* And he's got this... well..."

As her voice trailed off to nothing, Maddie resisted a strong urge to scream. "This what?" she prompted finally.

"Oh, crap!" Gloria spouted, removing her foot from the accelerator. "What day is it?"

Now Maddie really wanted to scream. "Tuesday," she forced out.

"Crap!" Gloria repeated. She slowed the truck to a crawl, which wasn't difficult, since she had been driving slowly ever since they reached town. City drivers were rarely in a hurry. "I totally forgot!" she wailed. "Dad got off early from the lodge today! He probably went over to Nana's to work on her yard, and I was supposed to clean up the truck!"

They coasted slowly through the last block before reaching the park, and Maddie was once again distracted by the happy familiarity of her surroundings. Some things had changed, but far more things were beautifully, fantastically, the same. "That's new," she murmured, pointing at the police station, which was across the street from the one she remembered.

"No, it's not!" Gloria argued absently, pulling the truck into the first empty spot near the grassy side of the town's central park. She turned off the engine, flipped herself around, and threw her top half over the seatback. *"Crap!"* she said for the third time.

Maddie twisted around to look at the back seat, and was not surprised to see mounds of trash, plenty of red dust, some wet beach towels, flip-flops, and at least two empty beer bottles. With the wind no longer blowing, the vehicle had a distinct aroma as well.

"It was bad enough before," Gloria lamented, her upside-down face completely obscured by a curtain of dangling black hair as she thrashed around in the mess. "But then Dylan had to invite his stupid friend to come along! They even left their damn bottles!"

"It smells like marijuana, too, by the way," Maddie offered.

Gloria stopped in mid thrash. One thin hand rose and pulled her hair away from her eyes. "Seriously?" she squeaked.

"Seriously."

A string of increasingly unpleasant words poured from Gloria's mouth.

Maddie reached for her backpack. "Look, I can just walk to Nana's from here, okay?" she offered, getting out of the truck. "You do whatever you need to do. I'll see you at dinner."

Gloria plopped back down in the front seat. "You're coming to dinner?" she asked sullenly.

Maddie nodded.

Gloria's eyes met hers, the question within them unspoken, but painfully obvious. Was Maddie on her side, or was she a stinking narc? In a flash, Maddie felt some possible insight into Gloria's seeming resentment of her big brother. Kai was, no doubt, disapproving of some of his little sister's "moral choices." And for that, Maddie could hardly blame him. If she ever caught her own twin stepbrothers, who were also seventeen, driving around with open beer bottles in a truck that reeked of pot, her reaction would be no more endearing.

But Gloria wasn't her sister.

"I'm anxious to see Puffles," Maddie added.

Gloria's shoulders relaxed a little. Her lips curved into a smile. "He'll be there."

Chapter 4

Maddie walked out into the open green space of the park, took in a deep lungful of the cool, fragrant air, and smiled from ear to ear. *Home.* Lana'i City looked, smelled, and felt absolutely heavenly. She bent down and picked up a fallen "leaf" from one of the Cook Island pine trees. The structure looked as bizarre as she remembered, consisting of multiple leathery needles twisted into a length of braid the width of a child's finger. The leaves burst out of each branch in clusters like nests of snakes, all the way up and down the tall trunks. She twisted the now-brown, leathery segment in her hands, trying to tie it in a knot, as she had done so many times before. As always, it bent nicely but would break when pushed too far. She never had managed to make a necklace or bracelet of them, although if memory served, she did make a passable Christmas wreath once.

She raised her eyes and studied the view. The old plantation-style buildings along the long sides of the park looked much the same, although they had all gotten a facelift and fresh landscaping. There was a new ice cream shop near the corner, but the gym and the church across the street were just as she remembered. The children's playground inside the park had been completely replaced and updated and— *Oh, my.* The "old man" bench!

Maddie stared at the distant, seated figures for only a second, then averted her eyes. She couldn't bear to look. She knew that many of the men she remembered likely would not be there anymore. How many times had she skipped up to the old man bench, eager for a smile — and possibly a quarter — from old Mr. Li or Mr. Kalaw? How many times had old Mr. Hiraga bellowed out his grand greeting: *"Akage-chan!"* which meant "little red-headed girl?" They had considered her a horrible pest, no doubt, but Maddie had loved them all anyway, with the possible exception of Mr. Puyat, who smelled like fish and never smiled or said a word to her. But in her child's mind, even he had been a part of her family. She wouldn't look now, but she would ask Nana about them. And then she would be back.

She turned and walked toward the recreational complex across the street. One of the perks of living in a planned community was having a variety of wholesome amusements centrally located, including a baseball field, pool, library, and movie theater, and — at various points in the past — a bowling alley and live playhouse. Maddie glanced in the direction of the baseball field with a smile. Kai had been good at baseball. He was getting very good around the time she left, which was a frustration because it took up so much of his time. She herself was a fast runner and could hold her own at anything that required brute strength, but fine motor skills had never been her forte, and connecting a skinny bat with a ball had been beyond her even if she had the patience to stand around in an outfield, which she did not.

She reached the far corner of the park, and her heart skipped a beat. Here it was. *Lana'i Elementary and High School.* A silly grin spread across her face, and her feet slowed. The K-12 facility was no architectural wonder: it consisted of a series of unremarkable long, narrow one-story buildings scattered across a grassy lawn. School was out and the campus was quiet, but Maddie's mind easily recreated the sounds of children talking and laughing as she walked, and she found herself whisked back in time to a memory of her first day at school.

This is Madalyn, her first grade teacher had said, standing her in front of the class. Mrs. Eda had been a tiny woman with a beautiful voice like a tinkling bell which the children had to strain to hear, but she managed to keep control of the class with — ironically enough — an actual cow bell that she would clang loudly whenever she needed to get everyone's attention. *She prefers to be called Maddie. She comes from the mainland, from the state of Ohio. Her father works at the resorts. Would everyone please say hello to Maddie?* The children repeated the greeting like robots, their faces neither welcoming nor hostile. Well, a couple of the boys looked hostile, but Maddie thought most of her new classmates seemed more curious than anything. *Is there anything anyone would like to ask Maddie?* the teacher prompted.

A half-dozen girls had raised their hands. *Do you dye your hair?* the first asked.

Maddie remembered being confused by the question. She didn't know any six-year-olds who dyed their hair. *Dye it what color?* she had asked.

The girl had frowned at her. *THAT color!*

Oh, Maddie had replied, understanding. *No. It just grows this way.*

There had been no more questions for Maddie.

Do you have any questions you would like to ask your classmates, Maddie? The teacher had offered politely. The children appeared to be done with her. They were already getting out their notebooks for their first class. But Maddie had not been done with them.

Grown-up Maddie let out a giggle. How much of what she was remembering was accurate and how much had she unintentionally editorialized over time, she had no way of knowing. But the memory, such as it was, was etched quite clearly in her brain.

The teacher probably hadn't expected Maddie to have any questions. Particularly after such a lukewarm reception by her classmates. But Mrs. Eda hadn't known whom she was dealing with. Miss Madalyn Westover from the Buckeye State hadn't a shy bone in her husky, oversized, tomboyish body, she had been waiting for this moment for months, and once given her golden opportunity for the floor, she had not shut up for at least half an hour. She asked about the school, the town, and the houses. She wanted to know about the beaches, the fish, and the dolphins. She wondered what was up in the mountains, what plants you could eat, which insects might kill you, and whether any of the other kids had ever seen a ghost. She wanted to know if it was true that it never snowed, and if they worried about the volcano erupting again, and if any of the trees on the island were good for climbing. Once the class actually started answering her questions, the discussion got so lively it might have gone on all day if Mrs. Eda hadn't tactfully put a stop to it.

Maddie reached the street corner at the far edge of the school and looked up. *Her neighborhood.* Nothing in Lana'i City was very far from anything else, but she could have literally crawled to school if necessary, which was nice. As she contemplated crossing the street she was struck by another memory of that day, this one equally suspect. On her way home there had been a boy from her class crossing in front of her, heading the same direction she intended to go. He was a little guy, and he was terribly cute. She had noticed him earlier because he seemed smart, especially in math. He hadn't said anything when she was asking all the questions, but he had almost smiled back at her once, and that was all the encouragement she had needed.

She had barreled across the street and run right up to him. *Hi. Do you live on this street, too?*

He had seemed surprised by her boldness and didn't answer her. She had been surprised by his surprise, and figured he must be shy. *What's your name?*

Kai, he had answered in a deadpan, not really looking at her. In fact, he had looked back over his shoulder, as if concerned they might be seen.

Shy Kai, Maddie had thought to herself, not realizing that the nickname was well-entrenched already. *Do you like Sabina?* she babbled. Sabina was the only other haole in their class. There were two haole boys in the other first grade class, but Maddie hadn't met them yet. She had only met Sabina, whom she had pegged as a snob within five minutes and had come to dislike intensely within an hour. Sabina spoke with a funny accent, acted like she was better than everybody else because of whatever stupid job her dad had, and derived pleasure solely from making fun of other girls' hair and clothing.

Kai had looked at Maddie when she'd asked that question. He looked at her like she was a puzzle he was trying to figure out. *No,* he had replied.

I don't either, Maddie agreed. *Do you like math?*

Yes, he had answered more quickly, almost defiantly. Maddie noted an intriguing flash of rebelliousness in his pretty brown eyes.

Me too! she had gushed. *Do you like me?*

There had been a long, long pause. As well there should have been, Maddie thought in retrospect. What a pushy little brat she was!

I don't know yet, Kai had answered.

Which was, no doubt, the truth. They reached Maddie's house. *Do you want to come in and have a double chocolate chunk cookie?* she had asked. *My grandma made them. We brought them with us from Ohio.*

Kai had considered through another long pause before rendering his final decision, which he delivered in the same serious, steady voice.

Yes.

Maddie chuckled at the memory only to realize, with a start, that she actually *was* standing in front of her old house. She raised her eyes to take in the small, squarish, clapboard building with its center-peaked metal roof, wide eaves, and tiny cut-out-of-the-corner front porch just big enough for one person to get out of the rain. The cottage had been built to house workers on the pineapple plantation and had no more living space than a single-wide trailer, but Maddie had been comfortable here. She and her parents had shared a kitchen, a living area, and one bathroom, and there was one small bedroom for them and one very small one for her. The house sat on stilts to keep out the damp and the bugs, and though it was painted a dull beige color now, in Maddie's day it had been a cheerful pastel blue.

She stood still, staring at it. She felt like she was waiting for something to happen, but when she quizzed herself, she could not determine what. Of the ten short years she had lived with her mother, the five she should remember best had happened here.

And yet, oddly, she felt very little. There was no sentimentality. No sadness. No fear. Not even a bittersweetness. She remembered a woman with auburn hair and a warm smile who was always kind to her daughter and never raised her voice. A woman who enjoyed birthdays and Christmases. A mother who was always there when Maddie came home. And when Maddie's father returned from work, the three of them would eat dinner together and talk about the day. But if her father worked late, Maddie would go to Nana's, because her mother didn't cook.

Maddie frowned. She was remembering Nana again. And her father. Why? She had always assumed that she remembered so little about her mother because she had been so young. But standing here now, thinking of Kai and Nana and the other places and people who had been equally absent from her life for the last fifteen years, the fallacy of that assumption hit her square in the face. While her other memories of the island played before her eyes in brilliant color, those of her mother remained in sepia tones. They were little more than a series of vague, semi-warm vignettes, blurry and devoid of any real emotion.

And almost every one of them had occurred within these four walls. Why *did* her mother always seem to be at home? Why would any mother not make dinner for just herself and her daughter? Why could Maddie remember no family events at school? No fun trips out and about on the island? What did her mother do all day?

Maddie felt a sudden sick feeling in her middle. Could her mother have had some illness that both her parents had hidden from her? If so, she could understand their motivations at the time, but surely her father would have explained in the years since. It would be irresponsible of him not to let her know her own mother's medical history, particularly if it involved cancer or some other chronic disease.

She pondered the disturbing thought for some time, but finally shook her head in dismissal. No, that could not be the answer. *Everyone* had been shocked by her mother's sudden death — that much even a ten-year-old could perceive with certainty. And although Maddie's observation of her mother's health was probably not that all that astute, she was sure there had been no progression. In terms of attitude and energy, at least, her mother had seemed no different in the last few weeks or months than at any other time in Maddie's life.

A shadow moved at the house's front window, and Maddie stepped away. She had been staring too long and was creeping out the current residents. She knew that the polite thing to do would be to stop and introduce herself, but she didn't care to see the inside of the house. At least not now. Later, she would drop back by. Later, she would figure out why she felt so apathetic about the place.

But for now, she should hurry. Nana might very well be waiting for her.

Maddie's steps quickened as she moved down the street. She wondered if Mrs. Nakama had forewarned Nana of the rather drastic change in Maddie's appearance, sparing Nana the embarrassment of not recognizing her. Maybe Nana had to be reminded who she was, period. Maybe Nana, even now, was struggling to put a face to the unfamiliar name...

Maddie walked around the curve to where she could see Nana's house. She took a few steps more, lifted her head, and stopped short. Kai's grandmother was sitting outside on her front steps, waiting. The second the older woman saw Maddie, she grabbed onto her stair railing and struggled up.

Maddie gulped in a breath. "Nana!" she cried, feeling no more than six again as she tore up the street and through the little gate in the toddler fence that had been left open for her.

The woman whose arms opened to her embrace was short and pear-shaped, with weathered brown skin, wavy gray hair, and a perfectly round face with apple cheeks, merry brown eyes, and a splash of dark freckles across her nose. But although Nana's smile was as warm, wide, and welcoming as ever, Maddie's larger-than-life savior had shrunk to elfin proportions. How could Nana possibly have gotten so *small?* Maddie had to bend nearly double to hug her, but she managed the awkwardness with determination, surprised but not embarrassed by the stream of tears that flowed down her cheeks. "Oh, Nana," she said raggedly. "You didn't forget!"

Nana chuckled as the embrace ended at last. "Well now, how old do you think I am?" she chastised mildly, setting Maddie a step away and looking her over. "I course I haven't forgotten you, but I can't say I would have recognized you, either. You look like some mermaid princess, risen out of the sea!"

Maddie laughed out loud. Unbeknownst to Nana, she'd actually heard that line before. But it didn't matter. Nothing mattered except that Nana remembered her. Maddie could see it in her eyes: that same, warm glow of unconditional love that had never failed to brighten a little girl's world. "Oh, Nana," she gushed, hugging her again. "I'm so happy to see you again."

Maddie pulled back, wiped her eyes, and looked around the little porch. Nana's house was larger than Maddie's own family's had been, and better kept, with a fresh coat of yellow paint, crisp white trim, and a well-tended garden. A hand-painted sign near the door bore the image of a rocking horse and the words "Nana's House," which Maddie knew to be an inside joke. Nana's daycare was a strictly informal affair, but if it were a registered business, it could certainly have no other title. "Nana" was a pet name for grandmother, not her given name, but she had been Nana to so many kids for so long that even her own children referred to her by the moniker.

Maddie smiled. "Do you still keep kids?"

Nana chuckled. "Not like I did, no. The arthritis is getting to me. But somehow they're always around anyway." She turned and opened her door. "Come in, come in! Just set down that pack of yours anywhere."

Maddie went. The cozy front room seemed dark compared with the bright sun outside, even though no shades covered the windows. As Maddie's eyes adjusted, another round of tears threatened. With the exception of the fact that everything, including Nana, had been miniaturized, it all looked just the same. The living room walls from five feet down were a nearly solid mass of colored crayon, a "mural" to which Maddie herself had contributed. The furniture was sparse, consisting of a few comfy chairs and various cubbies for holding toys and books. The kitchen/dining area held the same rectangular metal table with the bright red top that was chipped on the corner. Four chairs matched the table, two extras did not. Wall hangings in the house came in two varieties: children's drawings and Catholic art. Both were plentiful.

"Sit down," Nana insisted, gesturing toward the table. "I'm hungry. We'll have a little snack."

Maddie was drowning in deja vu. Nana never had asked Maddie if she was hungry back then. What a clever woman she was, and how sensitive to a child's pride!

Maddie watched as Nana moved around her small kitchen, first filling two plastic cups with water from the tap, then pulling a package from her cabinet. Though Maddie guessed that Nana was probably no more than seventy, she shuffled as if her hips ached, and the creases in her face seemed to have deepened. Nana sat down, removed a chip clip from the package top, and held the bag out toward Maddie. The joints of her fingers looked uncomfortably swollen. "Yum," she offered proudly.

Maddie was careful to present a smile as she reached out for a handful of the tiny dried shrimp. A lot of kids on the island ate them like popcorn, but she had always loathed the things. She didn't mind eating them if it would make Nana happy, though. She would do anything to make Nana happy.

"Just look at you, child," Nana remarked, studying her. "What's happened to my little fireball, eh? Still making trouble for the boys?"

Maddie gulped down her shrimp. Nana was nothing if not perceptive. "Always," she answered. "Just trouble of a different kind, now."

"Mmm hmmm," Nana responded, nodding. "Don't you take no crap from those boys now either, Maddie girl."

Maddie smiled. "Have I ever?"

Nana smiled back knowingly. "Well, don't keep me waiting, now. You have to tell me what you've been up to all this time! Where have you been? What have you been doing? And don't say behaving yourself and being all ladylike, because no matter what you look like, I won't be believing that."

"You *do* remember me," Maddie chuckled. With sudden inspiration, she rose from her chair and walked to the low bookcase under the front window. Slid behind it, as always, was an oversized children's atlas. She brought the book back to the table and opened it up to a very simplified map of the mainland, which did not outline the states but showed cartoon illustrations of various icons and landmarks.

Nana straightened her back and fiddled with her glasses in anticipation. For a woman who, to Maddie's knowledge, had never ventured further from home than Kauai, she had always showed a keen interest in other places and other people — an interest she had managed to instill in many of her young charges. "At first, I went to live with my grandparents, here," Maddie said, pointing to the approximate area of Dayton, Ohio, which appeared just above a racehorse in Kentucky. "Then my dad got a job at a resort area called Land Between the Lakes, and we moved here, to Paducah, Kentucky." She moved the tip of her finger to a point midway between the St. Louis arch and a sparkly guitar, which she presumed to represent Nashville. "That's where my dad met Lisa, my stepmother. They got married when I was twelve, and I have twin stepbrothers, and I adore them all. When it came time for college I wanted desperately to come back to Hawaii, but my father was worried about the money, and I wound up getting a full scholarship to Murray State, so that's where I went. The only problem was, it's right *here*." Maddie moved her fingernail a fraction of a millimeter closer to the guitar.

"Oh, Maddie, girl," Nana clucked sympathetically, studying the map. "So far from the ocean!"

Maddie's feet started to itch again. She just *had* to dip her toes in the Pacific soon! "I know," she lamented. "I was wilting on the vine, Nana, I swear. Everyone else thought I was crazy, but I knew you would understand."

Nana's brown eyes smiled at hers, and Maddie swallowed another lump in her throat. *Fifteen years.* What had she been thinking? How could she go so long without calling? Without writing? She loved this woman! What the hell had been wrong with her?

Nana's gaze broke away suddenly. She stared at the map again. "Was it cold in the winter in Kentucky?"

Maddie got the feeling that Nana was avoiding too much gush. She pulled herself together. "Freezing. We had ice storms. And the summers were awful too, crazy hot and sticky humid — you'd have hated it! I had a good time in college, despite the weather, but I was restless. I wanted to move on. I got my bachelor's in three years and started looking for someplace to start my PhD, because by then I knew exactly what I wanted to do with my life. I found the perfect program in ecology, just a couple hours away from the Gulf Coast, in Alabama." She pointed to an empty spot halfway between a shrimp and an orange. "And I had a plan for how I could eventually land a real job back here."

Nana's eyes lit up. "Did you do it?"

"Not yet," Maddie admitted. "But I'm close. I arranged for a post-doctoral fellowship through the University of Hawaii, doing research on Maui. I'll be staying at the Haleakala Field Station for at least a year. After that, who knows? My plan is to make myself so indispensable, someone somewhere on the islands will *have* to hire me."

"You're on Maui? That's wonderful!" Nana exclaimed. She paused a beat. "Kai is on Maui now, too. Did you know?"

Maddie's breath caught. "Kai's on Maui?" she squeaked.

"Since last summer, yes," Nana nodded. She started to say something else, then seemed troubled. Her gaze drifted elsewhere and she extended the bag of shrimp again. "More?"

Maddie pulled out two more of the dried crustaceans. "Gloria said he was a lawyer?" she prompted.

"That's right. Have you seen Aki yet?"

Maddie nearly choked on her second shrimp. Nana herself had brought up the subject of Kai, only to abandon it almost immediately. Why? Both she and Gloria were acting strangely where Kai was concerned. And who was Aki, anyway? Maddie quickly realized that Nana must be speaking of Mr. Nakama. Of course: Malaya and Aki Nakama. "No, I haven't seen him yet," Maddie answered. "I'm afraid my memory for first names isn't the best, seeing as how I didn't use them when I was a child. I can't even remember yours. I'm sorry."

Nana laughed. "Oh, my. I'm not sure anyone else can, either. It's Caliso. Caliso Jangcan."

"Caliso's a pretty name."

"Yes, it is. Call me Nana."

Now Maddie laughed. She looked into the twinkling brown eyes again, which hadn't seemed to age at all in fifteen years, and another wave of emotion overcame her. "I'm so sorry, Nana," she whispered. "I don't know why I didn't try to keep in touch. I missed you so much. But I was so self-absorbed... I never even thought that you might wonder what happened to me, that you might not even know my address. I just felt sorry for myself."

Nana shook her head and reached for Maddie's hand across the table. "No, lamb. You were just a child. And we... we wanted to respect your father's wishes." She looked uncomfortable. "You made a clean break, Maddie, moving someplace new, starting a whole new life. Maybe that was best for you."

Nana patted Maddie's hand, then tried to attach the clip back to the top of the bag of shrimp. Her swollen fingers struggled with the task.

"Here," Maddie offered, taking the bag. "Let me. I want one more anyway." She pulled out another of the despicable snacks and crunched away, careful not to wince. Then she replaced the clip and returned the bag to its place in the cabinet.

"I know that my father did what he thought was best," she said quietly, looking away. "And I don't mean to complain. I had a perfectly wonderful life on the mainland. Things were a bit grim for a while, but all that changed when my father met Lisa. She's a wonderful person, Nana. You'd like her. I couldn't have asked for a better stepmother, and I love being a big sister. I wouldn't trade any of that. But..."

Maddie turned. Nana was watching her expectantly.

"But no matter how well things were going, a part of me always felt like I was living in exile," Maddie finished. She sat down again. "I *need* my ocean. I need the mountains and the red dirt and the open air and the mists and the breezes and all the shades of green. No matter what anyone else thinks, *I* feel like this island is my home. And I can't tell you how happy I am to be back again."

Maddie studied Nana's patiently smiling face, and guilt pummeled her. She felt like the prodigal daughter, taking off without a care, then returning one day and expecting a party. Nana owed her nothing, after all. Neither did any of the Nakamas. It was she who owed them, for being kind enough to treat her like a member of their family all those years.

She looked around the little house, which was clean but shabby. Nana had always had what she needed, but rarely anything more. Unfortunately, as much as Maddie would like to buy her something nice, extra cash was something she herself was also lacking — and would continue to lack for the foreseeable future. Still, there had to be something she could do for Nana, and for Mr. and Mrs. Nakama. She would not just show up after fifteen years, partake of their hospitality, and disappear again.

"Tell me more about your family," Nana asked politely, taking a sip of water.

Maddie grinned at her. Politeness be darned. She knew what Nana really liked to talk about. "I will. But first, you have to tell me about everybody here. I'm dying to know everything I've missed! Marriages, births, any juicy little bits of gossip. Bad news first, please, and then the good. I've been... well, afraid to ask about the old men."

Nana grinned. "Ack! Those ornery things! Most of them are still kicking, don't you worry."

"Old Mr. Kalaw?"

"Oh, yes."

"And Mr. Li?"

Nana nodded. "Let's see, fifteen years, eh?" She thought a moment, then told Maddie about all the Lana'ians who had passed away in that time. As Nana ran through a mental catalogue of the years, Maddie could see that Gloria had not been exaggerating. Nana *did* remember everything. Her mind was as sharp as it had ever been, which was far sharper than Maddie the child had given her credit for.

To Maddie's relief, although she remembered several of the people who had passed away, none of her nearest and dearest "old men" were on the list. "Oh, we have to go over to the park and see them!" she said excitedly. "Maybe we can run up there on the way to the Nakamas' later?"

To her surprise, Nana exploded with laughter. "Oh, I don't know about that."

Maddie's smile disappeared. "Why not?"

Nana continued to chuckle. After a moment she removed her glasses and wiped her eyes. "Maddie girl, you know Nana always tells it like it is, right?"

Maddie nodded warily.

"At least two of those old geezers died because their hearts gave out," Nana explained, fixing Maddie with a maternal look as she gently squeezed her hand. "You go running up to that bench with a body like that and start giving out hugs?" She shook her head sadly. "Sweet Jesus, child. We'd lose every one of them."

Chapter 5

"Ta-da!" Malaya Nakama sat the steaming dish down on the table in front of Maddie. Kai's mother, father, and grandmother all grinned at her expectantly. Gloria fidgeted, looking bored.

"Oh, my," Maddie murmured, her eyes threatening tears again. "I can't believe you remembered. Spam-ghetti!"

Aki Nakama served a heaping spoonful of the casserole onto Maddie's plate, and she beamed at him with thanks. Kai's father was a master gardener and landscaper who had worked his way up through the ranks at the resorts, but the substantial cred he had built up in Lana'i City was based entirely on his character. Besides being level-headed, wise, and the soul of integrity, Aki was just plain likable.

"How could we forget our *tomato-chan* and her skill with chopsticks?" he said affectionately, using his own pet name for her, which meant something like "little tomato." He shook his head with a sigh. "No child on the planet was more hopeless!"

Everyone except Gloria broke into laughter. Maddie had no idea how she had wangled her first invitation to the Nakamas' dinner table, but she did remember that she had refused all offers of a fork. If Kai was eating with chopsticks, she had been determined to do the same. Unfortunately, well... the fine motor skills thing. At some point Kai's mother must have gotten tired of picking noodles up off the floor, because one night she concocted a special dish just for Maddie: cooked spaghetti chopped up and tossed with chunks of Spam and shredded cheese, then baked in the oven. The result was a sticky, gooey mixture that even Maddie could get to her mouth with two sticks. And she had loved the taste of it besides.

"Oh, Malaya," she said gratefully, calling Kai's mother by her first name as requested, which seemed more natural to say. "This is wonderful. Thank you!" Maddie rose and delivered a quick hug, which Malaya returned before sitting down to eat herself.

The Nakamas' house was a two-bedroom cottage similar in size to Nana's, and the eating area felt full with just the five of them. Throughout Kai's childhood he had shared the second bedroom with his sister Chika, while Baby Gloria had slept in their parents' room.

Maddie wondered if Gloria had later been squeezed into the kids' room on Chika's side of the curtain, or if Kai had been banished to the couch. The house would have been cramped with all three kids at home, but thankfully, with weather as beautiful as Lana'i's, they needn't spend much time inside.

She smiled her thanks at Aki once more before digging in, but she knew better than to try and hug him. Though he had greeted her warmly upon her arrival, whatever his wife had told him about Maddie had seemed insufficient to prepare him for the shock of her appearance. When he had opened the door to her, his jaw had literally dropped. Maddie could have handled that; she understood that it must be tough for a man to see someone he knew as an unkempt brat magically transform into a grown woman. What made the meeting excruciatingly awkward, however, was the fact that Aki was considerably shorter than Maddie. And as a polite man who meant no disrespect, he found it difficult to interact with her without getting a kink in his neck.

Sitting at the table was better.

As the family began eating, Malaya asked Maddie to catch them up on her life on the mainland, which she did happily, between bites. The Spam-ghetti was fabulous, but even if it hadn't been, she was famished. There were foods she liked and foods she didn't — anything fishy came to mind — but she had long since learned to eat either without complaint. Before coming to the island she had existed on peanut butter and jelly sandwiches and things that came in boxes with cartoon characters. The diet that awaited her on the island, far from the prototypical pork- and beef-laden experience of a tourist, consisted of whatever meat could be shipped in an unrefrigerated can and a bunch of Asian foods she'd never heard of. But Maddie was always hungry. So Maddie ate whatever was offered her.

As a starving graduate student, she still did.

"We don't have many stray cats wandering around on Lana'i anymore," Aki offered, responding to Maddie's explanation of her upcoming work on the effect of feral cats on island ecosystems. "If anyone traps one, they take it to the refuge. Seems to work pretty well."

"I know about the refuge," Maddie said eagerly. "That's one of the things I want to do while I'm here — go see how it works." She smiled to herself. The feline refuge hadn't existed when she lived here; for the first such experiment of its kind to pop up on Lana'i was too fortuitous for words. The concept of feline "group homes" as an alternative to traditional shelters or trap-neuter-release programs fit in wonderfully with her research, and if she played her cards right, "field trips" to Lana'i could someday become a work expense.

"Gloria's got one more day of school break; she can drive you out there tomorrow," Aki offered pleasantly. Gloria shot him a resentful look, but he ignored it. "What time would you like to go?" he asked Maddie.

"Any time tomorrow is fine," she replied. "I just have to be back at the boat harbor by five."

"The most important thing for you to see is the cultural center," Malaya insisted. "You absolutely must make time while you're here!"

"I will. I'm looking forward to it," Maddie said sincerely.

Aki's face lit up. "Ah! And as soon as you get back to Maui, you'll have to go and see Kai. It'll be quite a surprise for him, eh?"

Gloria let out a snort. Malaya and Nana exchanged a worried look.

Maddie watched the three women in puzzlement. Gloria's reaction she could halfway understand, insulting as the implication might be. Apparently, in Gloria's mind, Maddie's appearance deemed her as morally suspect, and Kai — now under the influence of religious crazies — would somehow be either offended or upset by the very sight of her. The source of the older women's angst was impossible to guess. Why had Nana avoided talking about Kai earlier? Was there something about him they didn't want her to know?

If so, Kai's father seemed oblivious to it. "You should just show up at his office," Aki chuckled. "See how long it takes him to recognize you!"

Maddie grinned. "I was thinking of doing just that, actually," she confessed. "It would be cruel, but fun!"

Aki laughed merrily. "Do it! We won't tell him."

Maddie felt movement under the table. Malaya had dropped down in her seat. Aki jerked and looked at his wife questioningly. Malaya stared back at him.

What the heck?

"Can I go?" Gloria interjected. "I *so* want that moment on video."

No one replied. Awkward silence prevailed as Malaya and Aki kept up an animated conversation with no words and Nana stared down at her hands in her lap.

Maddie tried to translate, but gave up. "So," she asked gaily, "I understand Kai is a lawyer now. What kind of work does he do?"

Aki's attention turned back to Maddie. "He just graduated from law school last summer," the proud father announced. *"Summa cum laude."*

"Impressive," Maddie congratulated.

Aki nodded at her. "He's doing an internship now. With a nonprofit environmental group. They're national, but he snagged a spot at their office in Kahului." Aki grinned. "We were all so happy to have him home again. He'd been gone for so long."

"Like *forever*," Gloria added sourly.

"He'd like to keep working for them after the year's up, but they don't hire very many interns on," Aki continued. "We keep our fingers crossed, though."

Maddie mulled the information. "I'm not surprised Kai went into law," she commented. "He was always making a case for something or other, wasn't he?"

Malaya laughed. "His teachers used to call him 'the crusader.' He could be so shy and quiet, but when he got all worked up about something, he'd argue with a rock!"

"The boy believes in justice," Aki praised.

"But he's never been judgmental, and that's what's important," Nana chimed in.

Gloria snorted again. She leaned toward Maddie and rolled her eyes. "What they're all thinking, but don't want to say, is that he's turned into a damned prig."

"Gloria!" Malaya chastised hotly.

"Well, he has!" the teen shot back.

"Define 'prig,'" Maddie said.

Gloria opened her mouth, but Aki was quicker. He silenced his daughter with a stern stare — one with which Maddie was disturbingly familiar. "In this house," he began in a decisive tone, "we allow everyone to choose their own religion. Or not. And we do not—" his dark eyes shot a withering look at his daughter, who crumpled under the weight of it, "under any circumstances, mock what anyone else believes. *Understood?*"

Gloria's eyes remained downcast. She made the tiniest of nods. Aki's thunderous look evaporated and he smiled at Maddie again. "More Spam-ghetti?"

Maddie accepted the offer, pondering as she did so. This was the second time religion had been mentioned in reference to Kai, which was curious. Her own parents were nominally Presbyterian but hadn't gone to church at all when they lived on the island, and so far as she could remember neither had Kai or either of his parents. Nana, on the other hand, had walked to Sacred Hearts every single Sunday for mass. But she had always gone by herself.

"Forgive me if this is a stupid question," Maddie asked, bold as usual. "But how did it come about that you have different religions? I suppose I should know all this already, but when I was a kid I never paid any attention to the different families' backgrounds."

Maddie knew now that only a fraction of the individuals currently living on Lana'i were direct descendants of the original Polynesians. Most were the descendants of immigrants who came over in the last century to work on the pineapple plantation. The majority had come from Asian countries across the Pacific — Japan, the Philippines, China, and Korea; but some came from the opposite direction — from Portugal and Puerto Rico. And since most of the island was controlled by American businessmen during that time, haoles had mixed into the fray as well.

"My family is Japanese, and we were Buddhists," Aki explained. "Nana is Filipino and a Catholic. Most of the Catholics here are Filipino."

"I am *three-quarters* Filipino," Nana corrected.

"That's right," Malaya declared. "Nana's *hapa* Hawaiian. Her maternal grandmother was full Hawaiian. She was here before the plantation started, back in the nineteen-twenties."

Nana nodded. She smiled at Maddie, and her brown eyes glowed with pride. "You know, there were only about a hundred or so native Hawaiians living on the island then, but my grandmother was one of them. She married a Filipino man who came to work in the fields. They had my mother and six other children. My father was full Filipino also. But he didn't come over until after World War II."

"Then Nana married a Lana'ian who was half Filipino and half Puerto Rican," Malaya added with a chuckle. "Just to give us kids a little more variety, you know."

"You?" Gloria said with derision. "I'm all that and half Japanese!"

"You're one lucky girl, then," Aki admonished. He looked at Maddie. "The Nakamas built Lana'i City. My great-great grandfather came over nearly a hundred years ago with two of his grown sons and their families. They were carpenters. Went right to work building all the old city."

Malaya chuckled. "And they were fruitful and multiplied."

Aki chuckled back. "Oh, yes they were."

Maddie smirked. Nakamas were everywhere on the island. There had been three of them in her grade alone.

"Dad, can I take the truck out tonight?" Gloria blurted.

Silence descended. The request had come awkwardly out of the blue, and Gloria sensed her own faux pas. She shrank a bit and avoided direct eye contact with her father.

Aki studied his daughter, seemingly in no hurry to answer. "Ah, that's right," he said eventually. "You were supposed to clean the truck today, weren't you?"

Gloria nodded emphatically. "I did! It's all done. I even used upholstery cleaner! And air freshener. It smells like 'country lilacs' now." She smiled thinly, her eyes flickering toward Maddie for the briefest of seconds.

Air freshener, indeed, Maddie thought wryly. She turned her gaze to Aki. Kai's father was no fool. Then again, many men had blinders on when it came to their daughters, especially their youngest ones.

Aki stared at Gloria for a long moment, during which the girl suddenly developed a renewed interest in her Spam-ghetti. He exchanged a long look with his wife. Then he turned back to his daughter again. "Was Dylan Karl in my truck today?" he asked, his deep voice low and deadly calm.

Gloria's small frame shrank in her chair. She didn't answer for a very long time. Then she gave one short, sharp nod.

"Give me the keys," Aki replied.

Gloria fidgeted. She looked at her mother and opened her mouth as if to speak, then her eyes flashed with venom and she shut her mouth again. She got up from her chair, pulled a set of keys from her pocket and slammed them down on the table in front of her father.

Aki stood, and Gloria bolted for the door. "I still have feet!" she shrieked as she flung herself outside. "You can't take them away!"

The door slammed behind her.

The room went quiet again.

Malaya cleared her throat loudly. "Well, that was pleasant," she said with cheerful sarcasm. "Would you like some dessert, Maddie?"

"Don't worry about me," Maddie said quickly. "I have two seventeen-year-old brothers, remember? And yes, I would." She kept her tone upbeat, trying to lighten the mood, but she could see it wasn't working. The expression on Aki's face was distressing. It was anger and frustration and hurt, but there was a great deal more emotion churning in his kind, dark eyes. There was helplessness. And rage. And fear.

"Excuse me," he said politely, rising. With slow, measured steps, he walked out.

Malaya watched with distress as the front door closed behind him, and Nana reached across the table and patted her hand. "Let him go, Malaya," she said gently. "He needs to be alone. The situation... it's so hard on his pride."

Malaya sank her face in her hands a moment, then gave herself a shake. "I know, I know." She turned back to Maddie. "I would apologize again, but hey — welcome to life. I should explain, though. This guy, Dylan. Gloria isn't allowed to see him. I know how useless it is to say that to a seventeen-year-old, but we don't know what else to do. We've all talked to her. Chika's talked to her. Kai's talked to her. But she refuses to see how he's using her."

Nana nodded knowingly. "Gloria's a smart girl, Maddie. Usually. Everybody here knows what goes on... some of the young men that pass through here — they go looking for the local girls. They want to get set up with drugs and... other things. All the girls know to watch for this. Gloria knows. But this one... he's been living here a while. He works at the golf courses. She's got herself convinced he's... different."

"He's not," Malaya added bitterly. "He's a shiftless, spoiled party boy. A rich little haole brat who—" She cut herself off and turned to Maddie. "No offense."

"None taken," Maddie murmured. "How old is he?"

Malaya growled beneath her breath. "Twenty-four."

"Twenty-four!" Maddie cried, scooting her chair back with surprise. "Are you kidding me?"

"I wish," Malaya replied. "Word is that his family over on the mainland is filthy rich, but he's dead broke, which tells you something. He's mowing grass and washing carts, and he wouldn't have that job if his sweet Uncle Jim hadn't pulled strings for him. That's where Gloria comes in. Dylan doesn't have a car, so he gets her to drive him places. To introduce him to people. To help him buy... things. He manipulates her emotions, jerks her around, then tells her he loves her. He 'borrows' money from her — gets her to borrow more from her friends. I don't even want to know what else he's talked her into. A high school girl!"

"But," Maddie stammered, disgusted, "Aki's a manager in landscaping! Can't he get this guy reprimanded? Or maimed or stun-gunned or deported or *something?*"

Malaya looked thoroughly miserable.

Nana spoke up. "That's the problem, child. 'Uncle Jim' is Aki's boss's boss. He can't say a word against the boy. Not on a personal matter like that. Not when Gloria's above the age of consent and making her own foolish choices."

"Oh, my," Maddie exclaimed, feeling miserable herself. She was about to say, "I had no idea," but bit back the comment just in time. Earlier today, the idea of tattling on Gloria had seemed overzealous and intrusive. Now she felt like a traitor to Malaya and Aki.

"I'm so sorry," she said helplessly.

Malaya scooped the truck keys off the table and extended them to Maddie. "Gloria won't be needing these for a while. Why don't you just drive yourself to the refuge tomorrow? In fact, why not take the truck all day? Explore the island grown-up style?"

Maddie looked at the dangling keys. She felt terrible about Gloria. She had no idea what she might be able to do to help the situation, but if she came up with anything, she would certainly give it a try. It was the least she could do to repay the kindness of her favorite family on Lana'i.

In the meantime... She extended her hand, and her fingers closed firmly over the jagged metal of the keys.

Oh, yeah.

Chapter 6

Kai Nakama stared at the legal brief in front of him, fixed his eyes on the first sentence of the third paragraph, and started to read. Several seconds later, he reached the last sentence. Once again, he had absolutely no idea what came in between.

He sat back in his chair with a groan. Why was he even here? He couldn't concentrate. He was accomplishing nothing. Except, perhaps, for appearing contrite. Showing dedication.

Begging for mercy.

He closed his eyes and rubbed his face with his hands.

He wasn't used to failure. Up until today, everything about his internship with EarthDefense had been going fabulously. He was used to things going fabulously, because he was used to working hard for what he wanted. There were obstacles, certainly, but he always found ways around them. As long as he was willing to put forth the effort, the reward had been his for the taking. Never before had he given a task everything he had — only to be shoved flat on his backside.

Today's disaster at the negotiating table had been humiliating. His team had failed, utterly and completely. And the fault was his alone.

His desk phone rang.

Kai separated his fingers around one eye just enough to peer at the caller ID. He cocked an eyebrow. His *mother*? Seriously?

He let it ring once more before guilty visions of an ill family member propelled him to whisk the handset to his ear. "Hi, Mom. Is everything all right?"

"Kai!" Malaya exclaimed with relief. "What are you doing at work, still? I've been calling your cell all day! Didn't you get my messages?"

Kai sat up. "No. Sorry about that. We were in negotiations — I turned the ringer off. Is something wrong?"

"No, no," Malaya said quickly, although her voice sounded less than convincing. "Listen, I guess it's just as well. Don't bother listening to the messages now. Just delete them. All I wanted to tell you is that you may be running into somebody you used to know in the next couple days. If you do, please try and remember not to bring up anything... unpleasant. Then afterwards, give me a call and we'll talk about it.

Okay?"

Kai closed his eyes again. His head ached. "Mom. What are you talking about?"

"You'll understand when you see... him. Or her. Now, is everything okay with you? You sound tired."

Kai heard a door opening somewhere else in the previously empty office. He stiffened. Maybe this was it. Maybe his boss had come back to fire him. "It's been a long day. Listen, Mom. I'm sorry, but I have to go. We'll talk another time, okay?"

Malaya reluctantly agreed. They hung up.

Kai listened for more noise, but instead of the expected interior doors opening and closing, all he heard were muffled whispers and the occasional odd bump. He was about to get up and investigate when a light knock sounded on his door.

"Yes?" he called, sounding several hundred times more self-assured than he felt. He would not quit this internship early. If anyone suggested it, he would plead his case, fight for another chance. He could do this. He knew he could. Still. Even if he wasn't sure quite how.

The knob turned. Kai held his breath as he waited to see which attorney's head popped into view. To his surprise, the door was opened by someone with no head at all. Or at least, without a head in the usual location. He leaned out over his desk to see a tiny toddler, just over two feet tall, standing in the narrow opening grinning at him. She was an unusually beautiful child with wavy light blond hair, giant blue eyes, creamy skin, and chubby red cheeks, and she would have looked like a cherub straight out of a painting if it weren't for the bright-green plastic turtle sunglasses on her head and the sticky note on her chest which bore a giant smiley face and the words "Hi, Mr. Kai!"

A small ray of warmth penetrated Kai's gloom. He smiled.

"Well, hello to you, too!" he greeted. "You must be Miss Sophia."

The little girl smiled even more broadly. She giggled. Then she grabbed the door, turned around, and toddled back out. An explosion of adult female giggles followed.

"Hello, Haley," Kai called.

His door opened the rest of the way to reveal two very attractive women, one of whom he knew, and one of whom he had only heard about. The one he knew, a tall, lean brunette with sharp green eyes, now carried the toddler in her arms. "Hello, Kai," she replied. "And you are correct. This is Sophie, the most wonderful niece in the world."

She planted a kiss on the child's temple with an indulgent smile, then gestured to the woman beside her. "And this is my sister, Micah."

Kai exchanged a greeting with the shorter sister, a lovely blue-eyed blonde who was unquestionably the child's mother. "So, how are you liking Maui?" he inquired.

Micah grinned. "Oh, I may never leave Maui. We're only supposed to stay a week, though, so things may get ugly soon."

Haley laughed. "I warned them this could happen."

Micah sighed. "Yes, well. Reality will win out in the end, I'm sure." She reached out her arms and retrieved her daughter. "It was nice to meet you, Kai. Haley, we'll see you back at the condo later?"

"You will," Haley assured.

As Micah and the toddler departed with a wave, Kai's temporarily suspended sense of doom returned. If Haley wasn't leaving with her sister, that meant she had actually come to see him.

At the sound of the front door closing, Kai turned to face her fully, his shoulders squared. You could put Haley in a backless sundress, give her a visor and sandals, even let her kiss a baby and introduce you to her sister, but if you let all that lull you into a false sense of security, you'd be making a serious mistake. Haley Olson, Esq., was nobody's gal pal. At least, she was no gal pal to the likes of a lowly intern like him. She wasn't even one of the staff attorneys; she was a consultant who worked with the nonprofit only on an occasional basis. Haley had made a name for herself before she was thirty as a corporate shark, then had shocked all concerned by "retiring" to a quieter, saner life of legal research for the opposing side. Gamesmanship was still in her blood, however, and whenever she needed the hit of adrenaline that only face-to-face confrontation could provide, she would pop over to EarthDefense and lend a hand, pro bono.

Recently, Haley had taken on the challenge of coaching Kai and the rest of the staff on negotiating tactics. The topic itself was nothing new for any of them, but what Haley Olson brought to the table could not be found in the usual textbook or seminar. Haley knew how the for-profit interests operated in the real world — dirty tricks and all.

Kai respected her talent as an attorney immensely. He also liked her as a person, because she was fair, reasonably good-natured, and had a sharp wit. But never, *ever* would he underestimate her. No matter what she was wearing.

He studied her green eyes closely. She studied him right back. After a long moment, she smiled a little. "If we're having a staring contest," she said with amusement, "you're supposed to warn me first. I think I blinked already."

Kai dropped into his chair with a sigh. "I'm sorry. Please, have a seat, Haley. I was just trying to read you. But I can't. Your eyes are like a stone wall."

She smirked. "Thank you. I wasn't born with that ability, you know. It took work." She relaxed into the chair opposite him. "So what is it you're trying to determine?"

He drew a breath and steeled himself. "You haven't been in the office all day today. Yet here you are. Did Candace call you?"

"Yes," Haley said evenly.

Kai's teeth gritted. *Show no emotion. Show no emotion.* This was bad. This was very bad. Candace was the top attorney in the Maui branch office. Her input would undoubtedly be key to determining who got hired at the end of the contract year. And he had screwed up so horrifically today that Candace had evidently called in reinforcements to berate him. As if being yelled at by two staff attorneys hadn't demoralized him enough already.

Haley shook her head. "Wrong reaction, Kai. Think about it. If Candace had given up on you, if you were toast and she'd set her sights elsewhere already, why the hell would she interrupt *me* in the middle of a perfectly lovely family outing, ranting and raving for twenty minutes about how incredibly aggravating it is to watch someone with as much potential as *you* stagger so spectacularly over such a potentially fixable flaw?"

Kai was silent for a moment, attempting to process the rather complicated sentence.

Haley smiled at him. "Everything's fixable if you want it bad enough, Kai. Just tell me what happened."

He released a breath and relaxed a little. Haley was being terribly nice about all this. His respect for her climbed an additional notch. "Didn't Candace already do that?"

"More or less. But I want to hear it from your perspective."

Kai felt a glimmer of hope. He took a moment to collect his thoughts, then spoke. "I was asking for three concessions, and we only needed one. I wanted all three. I really thought I had a shot at that. But two would have been acceptable to the team; no one would have faulted me. The last time I tried the same methods it went brilliantly. But this time, it fell apart. *I* fell apart."

"Why?" Haley prompted. "What was different this time?"

Kai frowned. "You know what was different. I was negotiating with a woman. A woman my mother's age. It's not like I haven't dealt with female lawyers before — you know I have. I thought I could turn the gender thing off altogether. But it didn't play out like that. She walked in and shook my hand and—" he faltered.

"And what?" Haley prompted again.

Kai exhaled with frustration. "And she smiled at me. A nice, pleasant, maternal smile. Like you'd get from a friend of your mother's at the grocery store."

Haley sat up. "Right there, Kai! Right there. It's your tell. She had it already!"

Kai looked back at Haley with disbelief. "But that's not possible! I didn't do anything! I hadn't said a word; my facial expression did *not* change as they walked in. I made sure of it!"

"But she did see something," Haley insisted. "Something that convinced her a maternal approach was the way to go. I've told you before, Kai. It's in your eyes."

His shoulders sagged with frustration.

"Look," Haley continued. "It's not all your fault. You can't help that you have gorgeous big brown puppy-dog eyes with ridiculously long lashes. Seriously, women see that, and they're primally *drawn* to take a closer look at you. And when they do look deeper into your eyes, they connect with that inner... well, *sparkle* of yours. And then they've got you, my friend. They know that no matter how much of a hardass you're trying to come off as, deep down, you're a total sweetheart."

Kai growled under his breath. "Do you have any idea how much I do *not* want to hear that?"

Haley laughed. "Hey, don't knock it. It's not a bad trait to have, in other contexts."

Kai could take issue with that statement. But he kept his mouth shut.

"As a negotiator, however," Haley continued, "it is the absolute kiss of death. Which is why you've got to own it, right now. Let's start at the beginning again, with the opposing team walking into the room. You believe that you greeted them with a straight face and gave nothing away. But the woman in the group, at least, took one look at you and saw a nice, polite boy who is respectful of his elders."

Kai winced.

"So she smiled at you in a maternal fashion," Haley pressed. "And how did you respond?"

"I smiled back."

Haley shook her head sadly. "It was all over then. You know that, don't you?"

Kai nodded miserably. "Now, I do. Then I just thought, 'Oh, what a nice lady! This will be easy!'"

Haley made a face.

"I know, I know!" Kai admitted, running a hand through his already-mussed hair. "Whatever they see, they'll use."

"Without a twinge of conscience," Haley finished. "You have to operate in one mode and one mode only: strategic thinking. Personal codes of conduct get in the way of that. By presenting herself as someone you were obliged to treat politely, maybe even chivalrously, she was able to usurp your strategic thinking. Just like a little bird chirping in your ear: 'Be nice to this lady! Your mother would want you to!'"

"I could see it happening," Kai lamented. "I realized after we lost the first concession that I hadn't fought it hard enough, and I knew she'd derailed me. I tried to get back on track, but..."

He couldn't seem to finish the sentence. Haley finished it for him. "She switched tactics? Let me guess. If I were her, and you called my bluff on the maternal thing, I'd respond with some funky I'm-offended-at-your-inappropriate-behavior-you-young-whipper-snapper-and-besides-did-you-know-I'm-a-psycho-bitch routine."

Kai stared. "Um, yeah. I guess you could call it that. Sheesh, is that an actual tactic? I thought the woman was unbalanced!"

"So what happened?"

"I fell apart," he confessed. "I couldn't string a coherent sentence together. We lost the second concession, they begrudgingly tabled the third, and then off they merrily went. When she calmed back down so quickly and turned normal again, I couldn't believe it. I really thought there was something wrong with her."

"I assure you, she's yucking it up in a bar somewhere even as we speak. The flip is very effective when someone is already rattled. I believe I've mentioned that before."

Kai looked away, embarrassed. "Yes, you did. But in the heat of the moment... it's different."

"Yes, it is," Haley agreed. "Which is why you need practice. You've got to work on getting rid of that tell and you've got to prepare yourself for a whole range of different situations, until the correct responses become second nature." She stood up. "I'll be honest with you, Kai. You handle yourself very well when you're dealing with other men. You're already ahead of the game there. But women are a problem. Maybe it's because where you went to law school there weren't enough women to practice with; maybe it's because you're a born gentleman and you can't shake the Lancelot thing. I don't know. But it's a problem we've got to fix."

Kai stood up with her. His heart pounded. He didn't like hearing his shortcomings described so bluntly. But there was something in Haley's words that encouraged him. "What are you saying, exactly?"

"I'm saying that Candace asked me if I could help," Haley replied. "She wants me to work with you one on one, to see if I can take the world's sweetest intern and mold him into an inflexible, arrogant jerk. I think I'm up to it. That is, if you're game."

Kai stared at her speechlessly for a moment. "Candace is... paying you to coach me?"

Haley smirked. "Candace doesn't pay me anything. But I agreed to do it, because she's right. You have a brilliant mind, Kai. You have all the right instincts. You've shown more potential for this work than any intern they've had here in a very long time. Candace wants to see you succeed. And so do I."

She started towards his door, then turned around. "I was just kidding about changing you. Changing you would be a crime against humanity. There are too few men like you in the world as it is. All you need to do is learn how to role-play, how to act — and react — on the job. You *can* learn how to separate that mode of action from who you are off the job. Some attorneys don't. They're the unhappy ones."

Kai smiled. In that respect, he couldn't have a better teacher. Haley was the happiest attorney he knew.

She pulled some car keys out of her bag. "Now, if you'll excuse me, I have a family party to return to. I'll be back in the office Monday and we can work out a schedule for some extra practice sessions then. Unless, of course, you're not interested?"

Kai blinked. "Haley," he said breathlessly. "I don't know what to say. 'Thank you' doesn't begin to cut it. Of course I want your help. I'd give anything for that kind of opportunity. I do want to stay on with EarthDefense. I'll do whatever I have to do to make that happen."

"Good to hear." Haley opened the door to leave. "Oh, and by the way," she called back with a grin. "Your eyes are sparkling."

Chapter 7

Maddie felt like a pup on a leash. Nana moved so slowly as they made their way up to the park the next morning, it was all Maddie could do not to run in circles around her feet and jump up and down. *Hurry! Hurry!* Instead, she contented herself with bouncing on her toes a little. Waking up to the sounds of the island, with myriad birds calling and relatively few cars stirring, had been invigorating. The morning air was moist and cool, heavy with the scent of pine and earth, and Nana's guava juice was just as watered down and tasteless as ever. Maddie had enjoyed her overnight immensely and was looking forward to today's agenda even more. Nana had insisted they wait a suitable amount of time for the old men to take up their customary stations, but now the two women were finally headed off to the bench.

Nana smiled slyly at her. "You always were an impatient little thing."

"I'm not little anymore," Maddie countered. "One out of two isn't bad."

Nana laughed. "You'd better stop that bouncing before we get there. I warned you about that once already."

"Yes, Nana. I know," Maddie said affectionately. Her honorary grandmother had been doling out all sorts of unsolicited sage advice, and Maddie had been loving every minute of it. Her own grandmothers were lovely women, but neither were as humorously pragmatic as Nana — and they certainly were never as candid.

They walked past the school again and turned at the corner to walk up the sidewalk across from the park. Maddie smiled as they strolled in front of the art center she remembered and the launderette she and her father used to haul their clothes up to. She was standing in front of it, thinking that the building itself had looked shabbier in her day, when some of the same troublesome thoughts that had plagued her yesterday returned.

Why was it always her father that she pictured herself with? She did come here with her mother, too. She could remember her mother being here. Putting the wash in. Walking with Maddie back to the house. The memories just weren't as clear.

"Looks better, doesn't it?" Nana asked, catching up to her. "New owner fixed it up a bit."

Maddie nodded absently. She and Nana had talked about many people and many things last night, but the one topic that neither of them had broached was Jill Westover, Maddie's mother. As many questions as Maddie's newly refreshed memories — or lack thereof — were raising in her mind, the sad truth was, she didn't *want* to think about her mother right now. She wanted to enjoy the present.

"Well, there they are," Nana announced, turning toward the center of the park and gesturing in the direction of the old man bench, which held nearly a dozen occupants. "Now, you let me walk up first and do the talking. And *no* bouncing!"

Maddie laughed. "I promised, didn't I?" Her pulse raced as they walked across the grassy lawn. Nana moved unhurriedly on hips that had carried her around the city her entire life and — she was bound and determined — would continue to do so until the day she was buried. Maddie kept half a pace behind, her own long legs needing to stop altogether every now and then to avoid a collision. The men on the bench noticed them at a distance and by the time the women were twenty feet away every man in the group was focused intently upon them.

One of them called out to Nana, speaking to her in a flurry of words that Maddie tried to understand and couldn't. She frowned to herself with disappointment. "What did he say?" she asked Nana with frustration. "I guess I've gotten rusty. I didn't catch a word of that."

Nana eyed her strangely. "Just as well," she mumbled. She lifted her head and called something back, the result of which was an embarrassed look on the face of the man who had spoken and peals of laughter from everyone else.

Maddie, who had been forced to stop walking again, planted her hands on her hips with annoyance. "Now what did *you* say?" she asked. "I should be able to understand *you*, for God's sake! It hasn't been that long."

Nana looked up at her with a mischievous smile. "Not if I don't want you to."

Maddie's lips twisted. She hated not being able to understand. The official language of all Hawaii was English, of course. It was spoken everywhere, it was written everywhere, everyone understood it. But there was a second language unique to the islands known as Hawaiian Pidgin, which was reserved for casual conversation. It had come about during the plantation days when the different groups of laborers, all of whom were in the process of learning English, wanted to communicate with each other ASAP. Pidgin became a middle ground, a simplified form of English peppered with words from other languages — whatever vocabulary worked.

Maddie's classmates had all spoken "standard" English to her and to their teachers, but outside of class they dropped into Pidgin. Maddie had resolved immediately to learn it and join them, but she found that her efforts were not appreciated.

Haole girls don't talk Pidgin! Kai had informed her sternly.

Says who? she had demanded.

Says everybody!

Why not?

Because... I don't know. They just don't. Kai had looked mildly disturbed then, Maddie remembered. Probably because he knew his argument was shaky.

I don't have to speak it! she had countered, seeing her opening and pushing it. *I just want to understand it. Can't you teach me? I won't tell anybody. I promise. Please, Kai?*

She could remember exactly how he had looked, then. Why could she remember the look on his face so well, even now? She couldn't picture her own mother's face at the launderette, but she could see Kai's dark eyes as clear as day, studying her, sympathizing with her, weighing his options, considering the risk to himself in aggravating his friends, yet feeling for her predicament, perhaps even wanting to make her happy, just because...

Yeah, okay, fine. But you have to just listen and don't go around trying to act like—

I won't! I swear!

Maddie smiled. Then and now. "You give it your best shot, Nana," she said teasingly. "I'm an island girl again. And I intend to get back in practice."

They reached the old men and Nana stopped short, causing Maddie to nearly trip over her.

"I've brought an old friend of yours," Nana announced, even as Maddie struggled to regain her balance, feeling like an idiot. "Someone who used to live here when she was a child. Any guesses who this might be?"

The old men studied her, and Maddie studied them back. Her eyes lighted on Mr. Li immediately, and she smiled broadly. The Chinese great-grandfather had looked a hundred when she knew him; he looked a hundred now. Had he added another "great" to his title? The eyes that squinted back at her were cloudy, and she realized that he couldn't see her, and perhaps not much else. "Aloha, Mr. Li," she called. His face wrinkled with concentration, and the man next to him, whom Maddie recognized as Mr. Kalaw, whispered something into his ear. The kindly Filipino man had aged considerably, and Maddie felt a twang of fear as she noted his sunken cheeks and shriveled limbs. Would he know her? "Aloha, Mr. Kalaw," she added softly.

Her eyes surveyed the rest of the men, all of whom stared at her practically without blinking, until one of them pulled hastily to his feet. *"Akage no Maddie chan!"* he called out in amazement.

Maddie grinned, her heart leaping with joy. She recognized the phrase. It was Japanese for *Maddie who has red hair.* "Yes, it's me!" she acknowledged. "Maddie Westover. Aloha, Mr. Hiraga! Mr. Puyat. Mr. Yokota..."

The men burst into an explosion of Pidgin, which Maddie tried in vain to follow. Only after several moments of chaos did the men oblige her by switching into standard speech.

"Maddie, child," Mr. Kalaw said, rising slowly and extending his hand. "Is it really you? After all this time? How old are you?"

"I'm twenty-five," Maddie replied, stepping forward. She extended her own hand and he pressed it gently in both of his.

"You are bigger now," he said matter-of-factly.

"Yes," Maddie agreed. "But I still need money."

Mr. Kalaw's shrunken lips drew up at the corners. He leaned down and spoke in Pidgin into Mr. Li's ear, after which both men laughed aloud. Mr. Li then answered back in a mumbled Pidgin even Mr. Kalaw seemed to have a hard time hearing. But after a moment he nodded and raised his head back to Maddie with a smirk.

"Mr. Li says he can't chew popcorn anymore. But he'll lick off the butter and salt."

Maddie cracked up laughing. As she looked into Mr. Li's unseeing eyes, tears sprang into the corners of her own. He *did* remember her. They both did!

So many afternoons Maddie had come to the park for much the same reason the old men did — she was bored and looking for conversation. Or, as they put it, to "talk story." They seemed to find her amusing, as she did them, and although at first she couldn't understand their words with each other, over time she came to understand far more of their conversation than they suspected, which made her time at the bench all the more entertaining. Many of the children came to chat and beg for quarters, as was the custom of bored and broke children everywhere, but whereas most came and went, Maddie was far more likely to stay a while, bringing a book to read or simply hanging out on the grassy lawn nearby. She begged her fair share of quarters too, running across the street with glee to purchase something chocolate from one of the markets. There was rarely any spare money around her house for such things, and she was always craving chocolate. She did feel a certain compunction about the begging, however; and so whenever her father gave her money to spend on a weekend matinee at the movie theater, she made a point of sharing. She would buy a giant box of popcorn and then take it, untouched, straight to the old man bench, where old Mr. Li, especially, would be waiting. He loved popcorn. Every time a new movie would come out, he would tease Maddie about looking forward to his treat. As far as she could remember, she had never disappointed him.

"I can't tell you how good it is to see you again," Maddie said, bending down and speaking loudly enough that Mr. Li could hear her. "All of you," she repeated, straightening.

Some of the men began to talk among themselves, and Maddie got the idea that several of them didn't remember her, and others were trying to jog their memories. She saw a hand held three feet off the ground (she had never been that short!) and then she heard — or thought she heard — something Pidgin which meant "wife of Westover."

She jumped as Nana barked out a command in a tone that brooked no dissent. The words weren't clear to Maddie, but she could perceive the gist. *Don't talk about that! Do you hear me?*

The same ill-at-ease feeling that had bothered Maddie at the launderette resurfaced. Is that really what Nana had said? Or was Maddie just imagining it? Regardless, why *had* she spent so many idle hours here, hanging with the old men, when her own house and her own mother were just a few blocks away?

Maddie's head snapped up. One of the men had mentioned Kai.

"No, no," Nana replied. "She hasn't even seen Kai yet. But she's going back to Maui today, so I'm sure they'll run into each other again soon."

More unintelligible Pidgin followed. The men all laughed merrily, and Maddie sighed. She had a feeling she knew that joke.

"Tell us, Maddie!" Mr. Kalaw said pleadingly. "Tell us where you've been all these years! What have you been doing?"

Maddie looked out at the faces of the men, all of whom — with the predictable exception of grouchy old Mr. Puyat — were now smiling at her. Mr. Yokota rose and gestured for everyone to scoot around and make room on the bench for her and Nana. The women sat, and Maddie started talking.

Nearly an hour later, after Maddie's creatively edited recap of her life had been well received and the men had reciprocated by sharing their own family highlights, Nana rose from the bench and announced that it was time to move on. Maddie departed with a light heart, knowing that this time "See you again soon!" was a promise she was fully capable of keeping.

"Oh, Nana," she gushed as they walked through the thick grove of Cook Island pines that filled the far half of the park opposite the school, "I'm so excited to be living so close! The ferry's not cheap, but I should be able to afford to come over at least once a month now."

Nana smiled at her. "Well, you save your money for the ferry, then. You know you can stay with me anytime."

"Thank you," Maddie replied sincerely. Nana was walking slower than ever. The long period of inactivity on the hard bench seemed to have taken its toll. Maddie slowed her own steps further and studied the sights. The restaurants on this side were both still open, although the Tanigawa had changed its name, and the buildings all had a fresh coat of paint and colorful landscaping. The little store where she and Kai had once rented videos was now an art gallery with beautiful paintings in its windows, and the front of the old theater had been completely renovated. Maddie smiled. It was good to see the historic structures being taken care of. God forbid anyone should ever turn such a charismatic piece of history into generica.

"What was it they asked about Kai?" she inquired, trying to sound matter-of-fact. In reality, she had been forcing herself to wait at least five minutes before asking the question. She could have sworn she heard a certain Korean word in the same sentence whose meaning one did not easily forget.

Nana waved the question away. "Oh, one of the men was just confused. They saw you with me and thought you were Kai's wife from the mainland."

Maddie's heart came to a full stop. Then it started again. "Kai is married?"

Nana made a face at her. "No, of course he isn't married. Did I say that? Somebody said you were Kai's friend before — how do I know? They're old."

"It's just that I thought I heard—" Maddie sensed she was treading on delicate territory. Then again, there was nothing delicate about Nana. "I mean, what were they laughing about?"

Nana rolled her eyes. "They're men. What else do they have to think about?"

Maddie decided not to pursue it. But she could not shake the feeling that both Nana and Malaya had some problem or other with Maddie's getting in touch with Kai again. And since she might not see either one of them again before she went back to Maui...

"Nana," she asked. "Is there some reason you think I shouldn't go see Kai when I get back to Maui? I mean, just to say hello?"

Nana's face flickered with discomfort. "No," she said evenly. "I'm sure Kai would love to see you. He was always very fond of you. Here we are." She stopped walking. "The cultural center is in the old administration building, where the court used to be."

Maddie exhaled a frustrated breath. Whatever the issue was, she would not be getting any explanation out of Nana. At least not today. She looked around. "The post office is gone," she commented, remembering a small building that used to stand beneath their feet. Then she looked across the street to where Nana pointed. The long, low building looked just as it always had, rather like a camp headquarters.

Nana chuckled. "You have been gone a while. Well, if you don't mind, child, I'll leave you here. I need to get to the market, and you'll want to spend some time at the center. Malaya worked so hard to get it up and running. All the volunteers did. She's bound to quiz you all about it next time you drop by. If I were you, I wouldn't miss a single exhibit."

"I won't," Maddie agreed. She reached out and hugged Nana gratefully. "Thank you again, so much," she gushed, her eyes moistening. "I will be back in no more than three weeks. I promise. I'll get those ferry tickets if I have to eat nothing but peanut butter and ramen the entire time."

"You do that," Nana replied, her own dark eyes watering. "I'll save you some shrimp."

Chapter 8

Maddie opened the Nakamas' refrigerator and unloaded the groceries she had bought. She had no intention of freeloading as an adult after everything Malaya and Aki had done for her as a child. Her available funds were nothing to brag about, but she'd managed to pick out a few treats for the family as well as leave a little cash behind in Nana's whatnot drawer.

She took a quick, guilty snoop around the main room, hoping to see a recent picture of Kai hanging about that she had missed before, but she was disappointed. She saw no framed photos anywhere. She closed the door and walked outside to the truck, then hopped in with a surge of glee. She liked driving trucks. Her department at Auburn had one they called "the Humpty," a once-white Ford four-door that had been in so many fender benders it looked like a cracked boiled egg. How she had loved traveling solo, bouncing it about the Alabama countryside! She revved up the engine of the Nakamas' much nicer vehicle and her eyes alighted on a slight figure leaning against the side of the house.

Maddie leaned out her window and smiled, but Gloria shot her a sullen look and turned away.

Maddie drummed her fingers thoughtfully along the dashboard for a moment. "Hey, Gloria!" she called cheerfully. "Want to come see the kitties?"

The girl made no response.

"Well," Maddie said playfully, "it's not like you're doing anything better right now, is it?"

Silence.

Maddie itched to get going. She wanted to see the refuge, and she wanted to get to the beach. She still had time to do both before catching her boat back to Maui, but only just barely. She'd spent far longer than anticipated at the cultural center, pinpointing the places in her memory on the 3-D map, poring over the pictures and histories of the old Lana'i City families, and pondering what life was like for the ancient Hawaiians who had thrived for a full six hundred years before smallpox and colonialism had ended their way of life forever. She'd had trouble dragging herself away, and now time was of the essence. Still, this was important. She waited.

She waited longer.

Finally, without a word, Gloria got up, walked over, and got in the truck.

Maddie suppressed a smile and pulled out. She said nothing, and neither did Gloria, all the way through the city. They were well out into the countryside, tooling along between the single rows of Cook Island pines, when Maddie first heard the small but defiant voice.

"I don't smoke pot, by the way," Gloria announced.

Maddie kept her eyes on the road. She decided to say nothing.

"Well, I don't!" Gloria repeated. "I tried it once, but I didn't like it. It made me feel weird."

Still, Maddie said nothing.

Gloria slouched in her seat. "Just because of Dylan, my parents, like — they think I'm doing all this stuff, and I'm not. Maybe he is — but he's older. He can do what he wants. That's his business."

Maddie turned her head sharply to look out the side window. A Hawaiian owl, or *pueo*, was flapping silently over the fallow fields. She smiled to herself. Most owls didn't fly around in plain sight in the middle of the day, but for whatever reason, the *pueos* didn't seem to have a problem with it.

"So what's so great about him?" Maddie asked casually. She really didn't want to screw this up.

Gloria didn't answer immediately. Maddie tried not to seem too interested and kept her gaze out the window.

"I don't know," Gloria answered finally. "He's different. He's been a lot of places."

"How long's he staying on Lana'i?" Maddie asked offhandedly. She flashed at quick look at Gloria, and saw that the girl was scowling.

"Till whenever he gets bored of it, I guess," Gloria said.

Maddie made no response. *Right,* she thought to herself. *Let that sink in.*

Gloria whipped around in her seat, facing Maddie. "I mean, like, *you* drank when you were my age, didn't you?"

Maddie suppressed the urge to squirm. "Actually, no. And I don't drink now, either. I can't afford to."

Gloria regarded her skeptically. "It doesn't cost *that* much."

"No, I don't mean the money." Maddie hesitated, but only briefly. Gloria might as well hear the unvarnished truth. "What I mean is that I can't afford to slack off and get so relaxed that I lose my better judgment, not around men who are drinking, anyway. It's in my best interests to stay sharp and be on guard, if you get what I'm saying."

Gloria was staring at her. "You do get what I'm saying, don't you?" Maddie repeated uncertainly.

Gloria swore under her breath. At least, Maddie thought they were swear words. They weren't English, but one convenient thing about having so many languages blend together is that there were always plenty of swear words to choose from. "Seriously?" Gloria said with unexpected sympathy. "It's that bad? I mean, you actually get grabbed and stuff?"

"All the time," Maddie said quietly. She really didn't enjoy discussing the topic. "People make assumptions based on my appearance. They look at the way I'm built and jump to the conclusion that I must have had a boob job."

"You mean you didn't?" Gloria blurted, wide-eyed. "They're real?"

Maddie tried not to sigh. "Yep. This is just the way I am. My mother was built similarly, but I'm a bit more extreme."

"But your arms are so skinny!"

"No, they're not!" Maddie protested. She held the steering wheel with her left hand and flexed her right arm, displaying nicely toned biceps. "That's all muscle, I'll have you know. I lift free weights!"

"Okay, okay," Gloria giggled. "Sorry. I guess they're not really skinny. It's just that you're... well, you're not fat anywhere else!"

"I am what I am. The problem is that once people assume I paid money and suffered through elective surgery to look like this, they assume I must have done it because I *want* to attract attention. Specifically, because I must *want* men I've never met coming up to me in public places and making lewd advances. Therefore, it's perfectly okay for them to do so. After all, I *asked* for it."

Gloria stared. "Oh, wow," she said after a moment. "I never thought about it like that. But you're right. I thought the same thing. I thought you had a boob job because you were a model. Or maybe a porn star."

Maddie's teeth gritted. "You are not the only one."

"Well, that sucks, then," Gloria declared, turning to face forward again. "You could always get a bust reduction, you know."

Maddie made no reply. She was no stranger to that particular nugget of advice, either. She had tired of explaining to people that insurance wouldn't cover such a thing unless it was medically necessary, which in her case it was not. She had never even attempted to explain her deeper aversion to such a solution — her fundamental resistance to the idea that *she* should undergo elective surgery to correct for other people's mistaken presumptions.

"Is this it?" she asked, pointing to a turnoff.

"Yeah," Gloria replied "It's up there and off to the right."

Maddie turned. They were in an open area of the plateau, where once they would have been surrounded by thousands of pineapple plants. Now they drove down a red dirt road flanked by red dirt fields peppered with wild scrubby green grass, bushes, and low trees. Maddie caught sight of a sign for the Palawai Feline Refuge and pulled off into a red dirt lot. She parked the truck and looked through the windshield.

"Wow," she said with surprise. She was not sure what she had to expected to see. She was hoping it was not just an ordinary cat shelter with a bunch of outdoor cages like a zoo. She was also hoping it was not just another colony of feral cats that were supposed to be living under controlled conditions but were in fact suffering from ill health while still managing both to multiply and devastate the local ecosystem.

What she saw was an actual refuge, an outdoor space that was physically bounded and enclosed with fencing on its borders, but whose interior was still vast, airy, and open. In its center was a grove of shade trees, surrounded by a sprawling array of variously shaped wooden shelters, feeding stations, perches, climbing obstacles, grassy lawn, and dense brush. There was not a "cage" in sight. Furthermore, from where Maddie sat, she saw very few cats.

"It's cool, isn't it?" Gloria agreed. "I volunteered out here all last summer. Me and my friend Ellery would come out and help with—" Her eyes fixed on something that caused her brow to crease and a small, disgusted sigh to escape her lips.

Maddie followed her gaze to see a very tall, lanky man step out of the green-painted clapboard building next to the gate.

"You go on," Gloria finished, slouching in her seat again. "I'll stay in the truck."

Maddie took another look. The man seemed familiar. "It's Kenny!" she cried.

"Yeah," Gloria confirmed without enthusiasm. "He works here."

Maddie jumped out of the truck. She watched as the expression on the man's face changed from friendly anticipation to confusion to male appreciation. She supposed she could understand the progression. Kenny Nakama would certainly recognize the truck. He probably expected to see Gloria or someone else he knew. He was definitely not expecting Maddie.

"Aloha," he said uncertainly, smiling at her politely. "Welcome to the Palawai Feline Refuge. Is this your first visit?"

Maddie's heart sank a little. Her erstwhile classmate and somehow-or-other cousin of Kai and Gloria obviously didn't recognize her. But that was okay. She really should stop expecting otherwise.

"Yes, it is," she replied, trying to catch his eyes. More often than not, she and Kai had hung out alone. But when she was allowed to tag along on group adventures, like one of the many daytrips up into the mountains she had enjoyed so much, Kenny was always one of the half-dozen in the crowd. One of the few kids her age who was taller than she was, Kenny had always been an awkward child, skinny as a stick and poorly coordinated. He had very light brown skin, a thick mop of bushy black hair, and large dark eyes that never missed a thing going on around him. He wasn't the brightest of the bunch academically and had always lacked ambition, but he was good-hearted and funny and easy to be around, and Maddie had always liked him.

"Well, come on in and have a look around," Kenny said formally as he moved to open the front gate. He gave her a rehearsed spiel explaining the mission of the refuge and its importance to preserving the birds and other wildlife of the island as well as the welfare of the cats, then let her into the double-gated entrance area and asked her to sign the guestbook. He also tripped twice while walking backwards, fumbled with the lock, forgot the word for "pen," and knocked over a display of brochures.

Maddie sighed to herself as she followed him into the main part of the refuge. She had made a point of printing her name legibly in the guestbook, but he hadn't even glanced at it. No sooner did he step into the enclosure than three wonderfully healthy-looking cats circled his feet and another practically jumped into his arms. Two more came up to investigate Maddie, one particularly bold orange tabby giving her only the briefest of sniffs before rubbing up against her shin. "I thought these cats were supposed to be feral!" she exclaimed.

Kenny gave her a goofy smile. "They were at one time or other. But we socialize any who are willing, and some eat it up. Isn't that right, Jazz?" He caressed the black cat in his arms behind the ears, making the gray tabby at his feet whine with jealousy. "We adopt out as many as we can. The wilder ones live out their lives here. But they're all spayed or neutered and seen by a vet regularly."

Maddie walked away a bit, investigating. Everywhere she looked, now that she was looking more closely, she saw cats. Cats sleeping, nibbling, wandering, lounging. The natural landscape of tall grass and bushes as well as the man-made shelters seemed to provide a near infinite amount of hidey-holes and lookouts. "How many cats are in here?" she asked incredulously.

"Almost three hundred," Kenny answered.

Maddie was amazed. "Don't they fight?"

Kenny shrugged. "Nah. They've got enough room to keep to themselves if they want. That grassy field over there is like a maze. They make their own nests, multi-layered even, like condos!"

"Wow," Maddie remarked. A breeze kicked up and the tall grass fluttered, along with the leaves on the shade trees. The sun was shining, clouds were few, and the weather was typical Lana'i — pleasantly warm but not too hot. She couldn't smell a thing except red dirt and countryside, and with the exception of the brown tabby who was currently mewing at her ankles to be petted, there was nothing to hear but the peaceful hum of the wind. These cats didn't look like prisoners. They looked like friggin' tourists.

"So, how long are you visiting for?" Kenny asked, his tone of voice changing again.

Maddie noted the hopeful glimmer in his eyes and felt another pang of disappointment. He'd been nervous around her, then gotten more comfortable. Now he was going to try his luck. And still, not a hint of recognition.

"Why?" she asked casually, scooping up the tabby. "Were you planning on pulling my hair again, Kenny? Mrs. Eda frowns on that sort of thing, you know."

Kenny's eyes widened. He stared at her for several long, painfully awkward seconds. Then he swore. "Maddie?"

She smiled broadly. "Yeah. About time."

He swore again, smiling back. "Aw, man. You look different, you know? It's been a while."

"Yeah, well. I'm back now." Maddie placed the cat on a nearby perch. She turned around to find Kenny still staring at her, his dark eyes dancing. "You aren't going to pull my hair again, are you?" she teased, trying to shake him out of his stupor. "Because you remember what happened the last time."

He shook his head slowly, his eyes dazed.

This was bad. "I pulled your hair right back," Maddie reminded. The sooner he thought of her as a freakish brute of a child again, the better for both of them. "You whined like a girl and told me never to do that again or your brother would beat me up."

She watched with satisfaction as his face crinkled with laughter. "Oh, yeah," he admitted. "I do remember that. You were a hostile little thing, weren't you?"

"I wasn't the one who started it."

He laughed again. "Ah, that was probably true. And if I said that about my brother, I was lying. If I'd ever come home and told him I let a girl pull my hair, the sonuvabitch would have beat *me* up."

Maddie laughed. She'd had no trouble with Kenny after that first unfortunate incident, and she hadn't held it against him. There was something about pulling her hair that most boys under the age of eleven couldn't seem to resist, and it was a problem for which she'd had a standard remedy since preschool. Anyone who pulled her hair got their own hair pulled back — immediately and twice as hard. She could still remember how delighted she'd been, on her first introduction to Mrs. Eda's class, to see how many of her male classmates wore their own locks long and shaggy.

"So, seriously," he continued, the telltale lights back in his eyes again. "What are you doing back here? And how long are you staying?"

Maddie relaxed and explained her situation, all the while trying to subtly dissuade his interest in her person. But she quickly realized that she was failing. Without the benefit of being able to drop a definitive "my boyfriend this or that" into the conversation, her polite options for saying "not interested" were limited, and no matter what tone or body language she used, she could see that her every friendly reminiscence was being willfully interpreted as flirtation. When she realized that at some point Gloria had slipped out of the truck and joined them, she turned to the girl with relief. "I think they like you," she teased, referring to the two cats Gloria was cuddling while she reclined against a climbing ladder.

Gloria grinned lazily. "This is Yuki, and this is Chigger," she introduced. "They love me."

"Hey, Gloria," Kenny called to his younger cousin. "How's loser-man?"

Maddie felt the air spike with tension. If Gloria were feline, her hair would have bristled. *"Just fine,"* she said acidly.

A tense silence followed. Maddie decided to cut her losses. "Well, it's good to see you, Kenny, but we'd better get moving. I've got a boat to catch."

"Well, hey," he said to Maddie. "Give me a call next time you come over. We can hang out or something. Or maybe I can look you up next time I'm on Maui?"

Gloria snorted loudly.

Kenny shot her a glare.

"It's funny that Kai's back on Maui now too, isn't it?" Gloria said pointedly, glaring back at him.

Kenny frowned. Then he stepped away and gestured for Maddie to follow him to the gate. He smiled at her pleasantly again. "Our little Kai's a big lawyer man, now," he offered.

"So I hear," Maddie replied. There was no mistaking the note of resentment in Kenny's voice. "Little Kai" certainly did engender strange feelings these days.

Kenny took a brochure from the rack, scribbled something on it, and handed it to Maddie. "Call me," he begged, his eyes twinkling at her again.

"Gotta go! We're late!" Gloria shouted, bursting in between them. Once she and Maddie were both back outside and getting in the truck, she called over to him in a sing-song. "By the way, Kenny, tell Anissa I said hi!"

Maddie waved goodbye and pulled out, trying not notice the irritated look on Kenny's face or the gleam of wicked satisfaction in Gloria's eyes.

"Oh, he is such a damn hypocrite!" Gloria cried with disgust as soon as they were out on the road. "Acting like he knows so much better than me. Calling Dylan a loser, like he's some kind of prize! One look at you and he's got his tongue hanging out like a dog! Did you know he's like, practically engaged?"

"Good for him," Maddie deadpanned, feeling lousy. She wished she could have stayed longer at the refuge. She would even have liked to spend more time catching up with Kenny.

Gloria was quiet for a moment. "I've got to ask," she said finally. "Having all these guys hit on you... I know it gets old, but surely you've got to enjoy it a little. I mean, come on! You could go out with any guy you wanted to!"

"I'd rather have friends," Maddie said bitterly. She knew she should shut up and let it go, but she couldn't seem to help herself.

Gloria's face screwed up with confusion. "So? You can have both!"

"No, I can't!" Maddie protested. "All my friends are gay."

Gloria laughed. But when Maddie didn't laugh with her, she

sobered. "Wait, you mean, seriously?"

"Seriously," Maddie replied. "I do not have a single close male friend who is straight. I can't even remember the last one. The last one that lasted, I mean."

"Well, why not?" Gloria asked.

Maddie gritted her teeth. She tried to avoid talking to people like this, because it usually just made them see her as an ungrateful whiner, and she was not by nature a complainer. But once in a while, dammit, it really did help to vent. "Because the ones who are taken already don't seem to feel much need for outside companionship, and if they do, their significant others tend to have a problem with me," she explained. "The ones who aren't taken, the ones who say they're cool with just being friends, are usually only sticking around because they're hoping I'll change my mind. And when they realize I won't, they're gone."

"Come on," Gloria said skeptically. "It can't be that bad."

Maddie's shoulders drooped with disappointment. No one ever understood. "Believe me or not," she said tonelessly.

Gloria frowned. "You have to have *some* guy friends."

"I have acquaintances, comrades, study buddies," Maddie agreed. "It's just that we can only get so close. There's an invisible line somewhere, and once we cross it — however innocently or accidentally — things get weird. A switch flips in the guy's brain, and from then on, being around me just irritates him."

Gloria stared. "That's... wow. Never thought about it."

Maddie shrugged. She shouldn't have brought it up. "There are worse fates in life than being me," she said dismissively, trying to regain her earlier cheer.

Gloria continued to stare. "I wonder what Kai will do."

Maddie felt a flicker of panic. "Do? About what?"

Gloria grinned. "About you, of course. You're going to rock his righteous little world, you know that?"

Maddie's brow furrowed. "Define 'righteous.'"

Gloria exploded with laughter, then shook her head. "Oh, no. No no no. You're going to have to find that out all by yourself."

Maddie exhaled loudly. She would indeed find out for herself. Possibly tomorrow afternoon. She knew it was pure selfishness, but she really, *really* wanted to know if Kai would recognize her. Aki had promised her they wouldn't forewarn him of her visit, but as many people as she'd run into on the island, including Kenny now, it was only a matter of time before someone else did.

She would be lying through her teeth if she said she wasn't nervous about seeing Kai again. If she said she didn't have expectations, if she said that failure wouldn't crush her to the bone. People misunderstood, though. Clearly, they thought that Kai would be shocked by her adult appearance. No one bothered to wonder how she might feel upon seeing him again, but the unspoken assumption was that romantic attraction would be in the air. After all, they had been childhood sweethearts, hadn't they?

Maddie's fingers clenched the steering wheel. *No, they had not.* They had been children, for God's sake. Their little minds had never gone there, not even close. They were friends. Not *just* friends, but *real* friends. As real as it got, with no romantic or physical anything to get in the way. What they had was a meeting of the souls that was pure and natural and meaningful and easy...

And she wanted it back again.

She had lied when she told Gloria she couldn't remember her last straight male friend. She could remember, because Kai had been it. Assuming he *was* straight, which she didn't know. It could actually make things easier if he wasn't. Either way, she was certainly glad he wasn't married. If he was straight and married, there would be no hope for her. His wife wouldn't let Maddie get close enough. Wives never did.

"You okay?" Gloria asked.

Maddie's mind was elsewhere. "Fine."

She knew she shouldn't pin so much hope on becoming Kai's friend again. She hadn't intended to, but from the second her plane had touched down and the memories had started bubbling up, what started out as a fanciful quest had turned into a burning mission. She remembered "her Kai" so clearly now. Throughout her manic girlhood, he had been her rock. His cool reason and unending patience had kept her grounded — and in one piece — while his stories had ignited her imagination and his crazy dreams had warmed her heart. Maybe she had no reason to believe that he would be any different from any other man, now. No reason to place her faith on his thin brown shoulders. And yet... she couldn't let it go.

"Where to next?" Gloria asked.

"Taking you home," Maddie answered. She would not get to the beach on this trip, after all. Malaya had told her to leave the truck at the marina, and she had forgotten that asking Gloria along meant she would have to deliver her back to town first. But that was okay. She felt better about Gloria. The teen had fallen for the wrong guy, but it wouldn't last forever. All the family could do was wait it out. "I've got a boat to catch," she said again, lightening her tone.

"Kai really will be happy to see you," Gloria said thoughtfully, smiling at her.

Maddie smiled back, but the ever-so-slightly wicked sparkle in Gloria's eyes set her nerves on edge. What if Kai *did* want more than friendship, just like Kenny? Of course it was a risk. But she consoled herself in thinking it was not a great one. Physically, she and Kai were an obvious mismatch. Not that Maddie had a problem, in general, with couples where the woman was taller. But as shallow as it made her sound, she doubted she could ever have romantic feelings about a man who made her look and feel like a giantess, and Kai must surely feel the same about a woman who made him feel like an elf. Fifteen years might make for some significant changes, but there was no way around Kai's gene pool. Even if he'd miraculously grown two inches taller than either of his parents, he'd still be nearly half a foot shorter than she was.

Which wouldn't matter in the slightest, if only they could get back to that warm, comfortably deep connection they'd felt once before — and nothing more.

But he had to want the same thing.

"I hope so," Maddie replied.

Chapter 9

The light rapping on his door made Kai tense with frustration. Between the phone and other people popping in, he had been interrupted at least twenty times today. It was quitting time now; he had hoped that at least the regular staff would go home and the office would quiet down. But no. He wasn't behind exactly, but he wanted to stay on top of things so that he had plenty of time and space to work with Haley next week.

"Come in," he called absently, flipping through the brief in front of him.

A figure slipped in the door and stood still, saying nothing. He finished the paragraph he was reading before looking up.

One glance told him he wouldn't be interrupted for long. Clearly, there had been a mistake.

"I'm sorry," he said distantly, still thinking about the brief. "Was there no one at the front desk? You're at EarthDefense. If you're looking for the Regus Agency, it's at the other end of the building, around the corner." He pointed his visitor in the right direction.

Now go away, please, he thought uncharitably, trying not to look at the vision of femininity that stood not six feet away from him. How anyone had mistaken his law office for the modeling agency was beyond him, but clearly, this woman had. He hated to be rude, but he really had no wish to stop and escort her out; if he did, he would never get his mind back on his work.

He buried his nose in his papers again and began flipping pages. To his surprise, the woman didn't move.

"I was looking for *you*, Kai."

His hands stopped shuffling. The voice was unfamiliar, yet oddly intriguing. He looked up.

He saw what he had seen the first time. An impossibly beautiful woman around his own age, both her face and figure exquisite. But this time, he looked closer. She was tall and lithe, with a mane of wavy red-gold hair that began by framing the face of a goddess, then went on to curl lazily around the most perfectly proportioned torso known to mankind. Her eyes were an unusual shade of grayish blue, light in the center, but darker around the edges, striking in their contrast both internally and to the reddish hue of her hair. Her cheekbones were high, her facial features proud and strong rather than delicate, with the exception of an ever-so-slightly tipped nose, which cast a vague look of mischief about her.

Mischief?

Good God.

It can't be.

"M... Maddie?" he stammered stupidly.

No, seriously. It can't be.

A brilliant smile spread across her face, and her eyes lit up so brightly Kai wheeled himself backward several inches in his chair.

Impossible.

"I was hoping you would recognize me!" the stranger replied happily. "I'm so glad you did, even if it did take you a couple seconds. Everyone else has needed a hint first!"

Kai knew he should reply. Or get up from his chair. Or something. But he couldn't seem to move. This woman was not his Maddie. She couldn't be, no matter what she said. His Maddie was heavyset, and brutish, and pushy, and impatient—

"Well, geez, Kai, aren't you even going to talk to me?" the woman demanded, planting her hands on her hips and glaring at him playfully. "I don't look that horrifying, do I?"

Well, damn.

It *was* her.

Kai studied her another moment. He had never been one to speak before he thought. Then slowly, he rose. "I'm sorry," he said in a more normal voice. "If you were trying to surprise me... you can count this as a win." He caught her amazing eyes and smiled at her, a budding warmth quickly replacing the shock that had derailed him. "Hello again, Maddie. It's... really, really good to see you."

He didn't know what to do. A handshake seemed too formal for the occasion, but a hug didn't seem right either. They had never hugged before. They weren't the hugging kind of friends back then. And hugging her now would be... awkward. But it didn't matter; the desk was conveniently between them.

His thoughts were interrupted by the sudden change of expression on her face. No sooner had he stood up than her smile disappeared, replaced with a look of confusion.

"Kai!" she cried, distressed. "What happened to you?"

He looked down at his now thoroughly rumpled cheap-as-I can-get-away-with dress shirt and slacks and held up his palms. "Excuse me?"

Maddie was staring at him as if he had morphed into another species. "How did you get so *tall?*" she demanded.

Kai lifted an eyebrow. "I'm six-one. I don't think the NBA is interested. Besides, who's talking? What are you, five-nine?"

"Five-ten," Maddie murmured, "But I've always been taller than you."

"We were kids!"

"Yeah, but still..." she mumbled something unintelligible.

Memories tumbled through Kai's brain, alternately delighting and confusing him. The tone and inflection of her voice, if not its tenor, were warmly, wonderfully familiar. Every gesture of her hands, every twist of her lips and slant of her eyebrows must have been unknowingly archived all this time, because he knew them. As drastically as her body had changed, her mannerisms, at least, were all just as they had been, and if he allowed his mind to overrule his eyes, myriad pictures of the past filed before his vision in vivid color.

Maddie. Maddie at school, standing up to the bullies, pulling their hair. Maddie swinging on the Tarzan trees, yelling like a maniac. Maddie yelling at him for taking too long to fish. Maddie goofing around with Kenny on the trail to Pu'u Pehe and nearly tumbling into Shark's Cove. Maddie eating her own dinner and half of his. Maddie calling him a wimp. Maddie telling Sabina in front of the entire class that Kai was way smarter than Sabina's father. Maddie giving him a piggyback ride home from the baseball field — the long way through the brush so that no one would see them — when his bruised shin was too painful to walk on and he didn't want to admit it. Maddie laughing at the crazy stories he made up. Maddie not laughing when he shared his dreams... and his fears.

So many scenes, so many memories long untapped... all of it tumbled forward in one giant rush. He felt like he needed a time-out to breathe.

"I know this is terribly unfair," Maddie said, smiling at him again. "I've had all this time to prepare, and you get zero. Rude of me, I know. But I couldn't resist trying to surprise you. I made your parents promise not to tell."

"My parents?" With a start, Kai remembered his mother's phone call. So Maddie was the person he "used to know." Indeed. But what was the other part of it? Don't bring up anything "unpleasant?"

Oh. *That.* Why on earth would he? It was the last thing he wanted to talk about, with Maddie or anyone else.

"You've been to Lana'i already?" he surmised.

Maddie nodded. A healthy blush rose in her cheeks, and Kai could see that thinking about the island made her bloom with happiness. Had she missed it so badly?

"I had a lovely time," she gushed. "I stayed over the night before last, with Nana. And I saw the old men again. And I had dinner with your family, and I met Gloria. Oh my, is she grown up!"

A flicker of worry intruded on Kai's high. He exhaled roughly. "In a manner of speaking."

Maddie's eyes turned sympathetic. She took a half step toward him. "She'll be all right. I don't think she's quite as confused as you think she is. We had a good talk yesterday."

Even as she moved toward him, Kai reflexively moved backwards. This mature, genuinely-concerned-for-his-sister Maddie put him further out of sorts. As long as she was teasing and quirking with her little quirks he could see her as the Maddie he knew, but if he saw her as a woman at the same time he thought of his child-friend his brain would explode. Either way, he had to block out the raw effect of the visuals or he'd be no better than a starving wolf faced with a steaming rack of lamb.

Think child-friend. Think child-friend.

He could do this. He was good at self-denial. He'd had enough damn experience at it, hadn't he?

"Um..." she said uncertainly, studying him. Then she smiled again. "I would apologize for the surprise, but you know I'm not really sorry. It was too much fun to see the look on your face. But I'll take mercy on you and leave now. It's obvious you were working. I just wanted to tell you that I'll be living here on Maui for the next year, working on my post-doc in ecology at the Haleakala Field Station. And I'd love to have dinner some time and catch up."

Kai processed her words slowly. This visit was not a one-off. She was living on Maui now. She was back.

She was *staying.*

His mind spun with chaos. *Maddie.* He could remember her so very well now, even though, if you'd asked him an hour ago, there's no telling what he might or might not have recalled about her. If he said that he had missed her every day of the last fifteen years he would be lying; he had been a child when she had left, and his own life had taken several drastic and unforeseeable turns since then. He had never expected to see her again and had put no effort into keeping her memory alive. In fact, there had been a time when he had devoted some effort to the opposite. But when he looked in her eyes he could sense it: that old connection, buried deep yet holding on, with a mountainload of covertly entrenched memories to shore it up.

She most certainly could not leave him now. Where had she been all this time? What had driven her to come back? He had a million questions to ask her, and he wanted to lose himself in those eyes — and stare at the gorgeous rest of her, tolerance permitting — while he was asking them.

"How about now?" he suggested.

She looked pleasantly surprised. "Are you sure you can? I mean, that would be great. But don't get in trouble with 'the man' on my account."

Kai smiled and began to straighten up his desk. "'The man' is a woman. And she expects me to eat dinner. Just give me five minutes."

"Okay, then. I'll wait outside."

Kai stopped to watch as she turned and walked out his door. His heart beat like a jackhammer. He was dreaming all this, wasn't he?

Cut it out. If nothing else, she's bound to be taken already.

Kai forced his breathing to slow. He wasn't used to this much excitement in his life. And if he was smart, he wouldn't get used to it now. Of course Maddie was already spoken for. When was a woman like her ever not? All she'd said was that she wanted to have dinner and catch up. With an old friend.

Chill, bruddah.

Kai blew out a breath, pocketed his wallet, and shut off his computer. He was okay. Everything was good.

He finished packing up and walked out of the office to find her standing beneath a palm tree in a grassy area at the edge of the parking lot. His heart sank to see that she was not alone. Evidently, he had invited himself to a dinner for three. The man standing opposite her appeared to be in his forties, dressed in the pricey style of casual reserved for tourist golfers, and as Kai studied the couple his head spun yet again. His Maddie had had many and varied aspirations for her life, but "trophy wife" had never been among them. Kai could not see her expression because she was facing away from him, but as he watched, the man's confident, smirking face turned beet red. Kai began to walk towards them, having no idea what was going on, but by the time he reached the palm tree Maddie had turned around to smile at Kai and the man in question was moving rapidly in the opposite direction.

"Where would you like to eat?" she called out pleasantly.

The wind lifted her red mane and tousled it about her shoulders. Most of her hair was hanging freely down her back, but the front part she had swept away from her face and pinned up. Kai's breath nearly caught at the sight of it. She had never worn her hair down as a child. At least not intentionally, although bushy clumps of tangles were always escaping from her braids and ponytails. The clothing she wore was unremarkable, consisting of a solid-colored, loose cotton shirt and shorts with nothing cut too low or too high. Maddie had never cared a fig what she looked like when she was child, but somehow Kai didn't think that this particular modest, nondescript outfit was an oversight. He suspected she was making a conscious effort not to attract attention.

She was failing miserably.

"Wherever you like," he answered.

"Actually, I had my eye on the Mexican place around the corner," she replied, pointing. "I was going to eat there after I saw you, anyway. I'm starving."

Kai chuckled. "Still starving all the time, huh?"

Maddie grinned. "Always. I can't get away with eating quite so much anymore, though."

No way was Kai making any comment on her figure. "Mexican sounds great."

They began walking towards the restaurant side by side, and Kai felt an odd prickling of deja vu. It was as if he had suddenly reclaimed a lost appendage.

Then he realized that she was looking at him strangely.

"I'm not sure I like looking *up* at you," she exclaimed. "It's too weird. I still don't see how you got so tall. I mean, everyone else in your family is so short! How is this possible?"

Kai's eyes left hers. *Oh, right. She didn't know.* And why would she? He certainly wouldn't have spelled it out for her, not back then. His family situation was nothing to be ashamed of, but neither did he want to stop and explain it all right this second. There would be time later. "Worried you can't push me around anymore?" he teased. "Maybe an arm wrestling rematch is in order."

Maddie grinned. "Don't be so sure of yourself." Her gaze settled on his biceps, at which point her smirk faded. "You work out?"

Kai smirked back. "No. I just work."

His cell phone rang. He groaned and stopped walking. "Hang on a second. If this is anyone from the office, I'll have to take it." He pulled out his phone and checked the number. "It's one of the staff attorneys," he reported glumly.

"No problem," Maddie said gaily. "I'll go ahead and order. What do you want?"

"Fish tacos?" Kai called out as she began walking ahead.

Maddie smiled over her shoulder. "You got it!"

Kai indulged in the view of her departing form for another second before answering.

The call did not please him. It was nothing but unnecessary blather, a request for him to repeat a bunch of information he had already passed on earlier in the day. The garrulous attorney on the other end of the line not only had nothing better to do than talk on the phone but also had no qualms about obliging a powerless intern to listen, and even Kai, who ordinarily prided himself on his patience, was about to lie and claim signal failure when the man finally relented and let him go. Kai hastened around the corner and looked for Maddie. She should be through the counter line by now, and if he knew her tastes she would have headed for the outdoor seating area. He located her red head immediately, but was discouraged to see that she was sitting with another man. This time, a twenty-something one.

His phone rang again.

Dammit!

He paused and looked at the number. It was his mother. The man sitting with Maddie was laughing and smiling at her. Once again, Kai couldn't see her face. Had Maddie arranged earlier to meet him here?

He answered the phone. "Hi, Mom."

"Kai!" Malaya's excited voice replied. She was quiet a moment. "Well?"

"Yes, I've seen Maddie," he confirmed. "She showed up at my office a little while ago."

"And..." Malaya prompted. "She's turned out somewhat... *attractive*, wouldn't you say?"

Kai made no response.

Malaya chuckled. "I knew you'd say that."

"Look, Mom," Kai suggested. "Can I call you back? We're meeting for dinner now."

"I see," Malaya said, her voice quickly turning anxious. "Kai, the reason I called..."

"Yes?" Kai kept his eyes glued to the scene at the table. The man sitting with Maddie had acquired a more serious expression.

"Listen," Malaya continued. "Maddie thinks her mother had a heart attack."

Kai's gaze dropped. He gave his head a shake. "Wait. What did you say?"

"I said that Maddie seems to believe her mother died of a heart attack. Nana and I figure that's what her father must have told her back then. You know, to make things easier. And I guess he never told her otherwise."

Kai felt a cold, prickling sensation inching up his limbs.

Oh, for God's sake! he chastised himself. *Stop it! That was ages ago!*

He forced the black images to the rear of his mind. "But that's ridiculous!" he said hotly, regretting his tone even as he spoke, knowing that whatever he was upset about was hardly his mother's fault. "She's not a child anymore!"

"I agree with you!" Malaya replied with equal ardor. "But it's not our business, is it? I'm only telling you so you can keep from putting your foot in your mouth. She's so happy to be back on the islands, Kai. Let's just let her enjoy herself. All right?"

The man at the table leaned in closer to Maddie, touching off a flare of angry heat within Kai's chest.

"Kai," Malaya continued, her tone anxious again. "I know you don't want to hear this from me, but I'm going to say it anyway. I can't help worrying about what seeing her again is going to do to you. I mean... catch up, yes, have a nice time. Just don't let yourself go back *there*. Okay?"

Kai didn't answer. His attention was fixed on Maddie. Her body language seemed tense.

Malaya sighed. "Look, I'm just going to say this. I know you're... *looking* right now. And I know Maddie isn't attached either because she told Nana she doesn't have a boyfriend."

Kai watched, frozen in place, as Maddie calmly scooted her chair back, collected her trays, moved to another table, and sat back down again.

"But I really don't think—" Malaya continued.

"Mom," Kai interrupted, "I have to go. We'll talk later. Thanks."

He hung up and started moving toward Maddie, watching in

disbelief as the man pursued her to the next table, came up directly behind her, laid an arm across her back, and began to caress her shoulder.

Kai doubled his steps, but by the time he reached the table several things had already happened. First, Maddie shoved her chair backward with such force the man nearly toppled onto the patrons behind him. Second she stood up and faced him eye to eye, fixing him with the one and only Maddie Westover freeze-glare, which Kai knew from personal experience usually preceded violence. Third, other customers turned and stared at them. Fourth, the man's face turned purple, he straightened his shoulders, and he walked away.

"There you are!" Maddie called out cheerfully to Kai as he approached. She sat back down and slid a tray in his direction. "I ordered the plate with three tacos and got some Maui onion chips on the side. Hope it's what you wanted."

Kai fell into a chair and stared at her. He was breathing heavily, thoroughly rattled. Maddie seemed unaffected. "What just happened here?" he demanded, albeit in a hushed tone.

Maddie shrugged as she lifted one of her own tacos and took a bite. She chewed it a moment, then took a sip of tea. "The kalua pig's good. Do you eat here often?"

"Yes. What just happened here?"

She sighed. "Nothing out of the ordinary. Can we move on? Talk to me. Tell me about your job."

"No!" Kai retorted, feeling ten years old again. Why, he couldn't fathom, but it was as if they'd both just sunk two feet lower at the table. Grown-up Maddie had disappeared and he was once again staring at that forever disheveled, mule-headed little girl who refused to believe there was a single thing on earth she couldn't handle.

"What about the guy I saw you with in the parking lot? Was he just some stranger, too?" Kai could feel his blood pulsing in his veins. He couldn't remember the last time he'd been so angry. Indignant over what was right, yes, but not angry. That wasn't like him. The fact that men could behave like asses was no newsflash, but to see his Maddie looking so... like *that*... and then within the space of twenty minutes to have two other men take one look at her and feel like *they* had some God-given right to—

"Kai," Maddie protested, seeming suddenly more self-conscious. "Stop looking like that. I'm used to it. It's no big deal."

He begged to differ. "You didn't know either one of them, did you?"

She shook her head.

"They were just hitting on you out of nowhere."

She shrugged again. "I can handle it. You saw that."

"Why do you tolerate it?"

Her perfect eyebrows lifted wryly. "And your alternative suggestion is..."

Kai felt like an idiot. What *was* she supposed to do? She wasn't dressed inappropriately. She hadn't been acting provocatively in any way. "I'm sorry," he said genuinely. "I don't know what I'm saying." He reached out for his taco and took a bite. They ate in silence for a while as he collected himself.

The quiet could have been nerve wracking, but for Kai it had the opposite effect, and he suspected that Maddie felt the same. They had often eaten together in silence when enjoying one of their childhood picnic spots, every one of which had a drop-dead gorgeous view of some combination of fields, mountains, ocean, or cliffs. The commercial district of Kahului, Maui's largest city, bore no resemblance to anywhere on Lana'i, but with a warm breeze rustling the fronds of the planted palms nearby, their imaginations were able to make do.

Kai stole a look at Maddie and realized she was grinning at him slyly.

"What?"

She grinned more, and her gray eyes danced impishly. She didn't even look ten years old. At that moment, she looked about eight. "You got all protective there for a minute, didn't you? If you think about it, that's really cute."

His teeth gritted. She always did know how to get to him. "Cute?" he repeated with annoyance.

She chuckled. "Totally. You used to do the same thing when the other kids tried to bully me. Even though I was bigger than you were. It was sweet."

Kai smothered a groan. After his recent debacle in negotiation, he didn't care if he ever heard the words "sweet" or "cute" again.

"You don't really even know me anymore," Maddie continued. "But when you thought I was in trouble, you jumped right back into protective mode, just like you used to. Just like time had stood still." She pursed her perfect pink lips around her straw and took another sip of tea. "There's some funky psychology behind that, for sure."

Kai diverted his gaze back to what was left of his taco. "How about the fact that you went right back to baiting me?"

"I did?" Maddie asked innocently.

Kai arched his eyebrows at her. "You know perfectly well I despise being called 'cute.'"

Maddie grinned at him again. "Touché."

Now she looked twenty-five. And she had told Nana that she was single.

His thoughts were all over the place.

"Thanks, by the way," she said softly, her gray eyes glittering at him so intently it made his knees weaken. He was glad he was sitting down.

"Thanks for what?" he asked.

"For being protective," she answered. "And for getting through an entire fast food meal now without once laying a hand on me or suggesting how much you'd like to. Forgive my bluntness, but that's a rare treat for me. I suggest we celebrate. With dessert." She leaned out and looked up and down the block. "Are there any ice cream places within walking distance? Or shave ice?"

Kai didn't answer. He could hardly accept such credit from her, when the mere act of her leaning out from the table, stretching her torso, and letting her long ginger locks drape softly over her shoulder nearly undid him. His thoughts were anything but pure, and as far as his actions went, if she was giving out awards for a man's being able to go a mere thirty minutes without pouncing on her, she was setting the bar pathetically low.

But if the last half hour was any indication of the frequency with which she got badgered for casual sex, her low expectations were no wonder. It would also be no wonder if any kind of flirtation repulsed her. In which case, her "thank you for not pawing me" line was probably not a spontaneous thought so much as a carefully calculated, preemptive declaration.

Please make a note of it.

"Oh!" she cried, bouncing in her seat a little. "I see a shave ice place. You want to try it?"

Kai took a slow, deep breath. Then, without really thinking, he answered her the exact same way he had answered her a thousand times before.

He shrugged. "Sure."

Chapter 10

Maddie dug her spoon into the passion fruit section of her shave ice, shoveled the cool, tangy-sweet slivers onto her tongue, and closed her eyes with delight.

"Bliss," she murmured.

Kai chuckled.

Her eyes remained closed, and it occurred to her that if she didn't know who he was, his voice wouldn't help in the slightest. It was so much deeper now. And as embarrassing as it was to admit, for all her guesses about what he might look like now, the truth was that if she had passed him randomly on the street she wouldn't have recognized him.

She opened her eyes to find him laughing at her as he dug into his own shave ice.

"I'm guessing you haven't had one of these in a while," he said.

Maddie shook her head, then spooned in some of the mango flavored section. The rounded mound of shave ice had three stripes: mango, passion fruit, and coconut cream, with vanilla ice cream filling the paper cone beneath. "There was a place in Gulf Shores that claimed they had Hawaiian *shaved* ice," she said derisively, rolling her eyes. "Really, like who says, 'iced cream?' And it wasn't shave ice at all, it was crushed ice like a snow cone."

"Gulf Shores?" he repeated. "Where's that?"

Maddie met his eyes, albeit with a certain, ill-defined reluctance. Dear God, the man was gorgeous. He had always been coo-out-loud cute — with those liquid dark eyes and long lashes, not to mention the high cheekbones and killer smile — but when you added tall and broad-shouldered to cute, the effect really was over the top. His appearance was not at all what she had expected, and it was throwing her off balance in a major way. Grown-up Kai Nakama was, in two words, totally hot. And totally hot guys were used to getting what they wanted.

Which messed up her plans entirely.

"Gulf Shores is in Alabama," she explained. "I got my doctorate in ecology at Auburn University, also in Alabama." She searched his face for genuine interest in the topic and found some, which relaxed her a little. But although she was doing her best to appear calm, inside she was a tempest. She wanted so much for Kai to enjoy her company again. But although his actions thus far had been nothing short of gallant, his eyes were hot with desire.

She shouldn't have worn her hair down. She had debated with herself for nearly an hour over the issue, finally deciding that the outfit she'd chosen was already so lame that if she wore braids or a ponytail she might as well carry around a giant lollipop. But striking the right tone on this first meeting was too important. She should have swallowed her pride, braided her hair, and carried around a damn lollipop besides.

She offered Kai a summary of her graduate work as she ate, along with the briefest of bios in terms of where she had spent her time over the years. She left out huge chunks of her life, events that were really important to her, and even to her own ears her voice sounded increasingly distant and stiff. Her frustration mounted. There was so much that she had been dying to share with him. But now there was a six-foot-one-inch wall between them. She didn't know this Kai.

She didn't trust him.

"So I hear you've been living in Utah?" she asked, tacking the question onto the end of her spiel before he could ask her anything else about herself. She dropped her eyes and focused on a mynah bird that was pecking the ground nearby. It cocked its head and looked up at her hopefully. Mynahs, which were ubiquitous in the islands, looked something like robins but were shameless trash scavengers.

"That's right," he answered. "For undergrad and law school."

"Both at the same place?"

"Yes. I have family there, and I got a nice scholarship."

Maddie started to ask something else, something about his grandparents that weren't really grandparents. But she wasn't feeling it. In fact, a part of her felt a sudden, inexplicable urge to cry. Their previous selves would have shared everything. They would have taken one look at the bland mass of generic box stores and strip malls around them, run until they reached a grassy field or mountainside somewhere, huddled up against a tree trunk, and talked all night and all the next day.

A flicker of ire shot through her as she lamented how different their reunion could be if time had stood still. If they could meet each other again in their happily simplified, ten-year-old bodies. She would take one look at that short, skinny Kai and hug him until his bones cracked.

This one, she was afraid to even smile at.

She dug her spoon deeper into her cone, aiming for the ice cream. The thin neck of the spoon promptly cracked, and she swore under her breath with annoyance.

To her surprise, Kai exploded with laughter.

"What's so funny?" she challenged irritably. Why couldn't anyone manufacture a decent plastic spoon?

The look on her face seemed only to amuse him further, and it took several seconds for him to sober enough to answer her. He seemed more familiar when he laughed. She was tempted to throw the handle stub at him.

"Don't you remember?" he asked, chuckling still. "Those little strawberry ice cream cups, at the market? The paddle spoons?"

Maddie's brow furrowed. She really had no idea what he was talking about. "I remember getting ice cream cups. Kind of."

"You broke those spoons every time!" he accused, his eyes still dancing with amusement. "You'd hold the thing like a spear and jab at the ice cream like it was trying to escape. And then you'd blame the company. Said they weren't made right!"

Maddie felt her cheeks redden. "You must be remembering somebody else."

Kai laughed again. "There was nobody else like you, Maddie. Hang on. I'll get you another spoon." He straightened from the wall against which they'd been leaning and headed back toward the concession window.

Maddie shook her head in confusion. How could he remember something like that when she couldn't?

A bright yellow bird fluttered through her field of vision and into a nearby cluster of trees. Grateful for the distraction, she turned and followed. It landed on a branch bordering the outdoor seating area of the barbecue place next door, and as Maddie leaned out to get a better look, the smell of smoked meat made her hungry again. "Hello, little white eye," she whispered to the bird with a smile. "Haven't seen one of you in a long, long time."

She was absorbed with watching the bird's quick, anxious movements when a man walked up from the barbecue place and stood, smiling, just opposite her. "Bird watching?" he asked, his tone mocking.

Maddie looked over long enough to see a man in his fifties, well dressed, wearing a wedding ring and making no effort not to leer.

"You look more like a swimsuit model to me," he pronounced, smirking.

Maddie was in the process of running through her library of responses and had decided on the smiting turn-around-and-walk-off-with-no-acknowledgment strategy when the man's facial expression changed. She stood still and watched as his smirk melted first to a look of uncertainty, then to sheepishness, then rapidly to alarm. He said nothing else but turned from her and moved away.

A plastic spoon appeared over her shoulder. "If you break this one, too," Kai instructed, "maybe you should consider packing stainless steel."

Maddie whirled and looked at him.

He looked innocently back at her.

His eyes were the same, she thought. Housed in a different package, perhaps, but the same. They could be inscrutable on occasion, when he tried really hard, but most of the time she could see right through him.

"Kai Nakama!" she chastised. "You gave that man the stink eye! Didn't you?"

A sly grin played on his lips. "What man, now?"

Maddie felt a welcome flush of warmth in her veins, and she laughed out loud. The "stink eye" was local lingo for a dirty look, which could be employed in various ways for various reasons. In Kai's case it was rarely employed at all. But when the boy Kai did get riled — which usually happened only after a particularly egregious miscarriage of justice — his execution of stink eye had been so potent it had scared *her* witless.

She felt a strong impulse to hug him, but as always with men, she squelched it. "Thanks," she said instead. "That was sweet of you."

He threw her a feigned look of disgust.

She chuckled. "Oh, right. Sorry. That was... very considerate of you."

They walked back towards the concession window, found an open table this time, and sat down. "It wasn't necessary, though," she continued. "As I said, I can handle these things."

She wasn't sure why it was so important to her to point that out, but it was. Maybe because so many guys had turned the issue against her in the past, setting themselves up as bodyguards when they were the ones she had to protect against.

He studied her a moment. "I can see that," he praised. "But you shouldn't have to."

His eyes flickered with unmistakable desire again, and Maddie dropped her gaze. Dear God, this was confusing. She wanted to get close to him again. But not that kind of close. Not now.

That kind of close would ruin everything.

Not that she wasn't interested in men. Of course she was. She was twenty-five years old, she was lonely as hell, and she was getting lonelier. But was it so much to ask that once, just *once*, a guy could want her for *her*? Did it always have to be about sex, and did it always have to be about sex *so soon*? It's not that she was holding out for marriage... necessarily... but was it so much to ask that a guy actually be in love with her first? Really care about and be committed to her?

She didn't think so. But she was beginning to wonder.

No guy had wanted Meggie, that's for sure. And Meggie was exactly like her. Meggie had been her online persona, her dating profile, her "out there" self. She had poured every ounce of her wit and charm and zing and zest into Meggie's quest for the perfect man. The only thing Maddie hadn't shared with Meggie was a profile picture. Meggie's picture, doctored with a friend's software, showed a woman who was multiracial, flat-chested, and had an overbite.

In eighteen solid months, Meggie hadn't scored a single date.

Except, of course, for the dozens of men who wanted casual sex.

"Is it as good as you remember?" Kai asked.

Maddie jumped. "Excuse me?"

He looked confused. "The shave ice?"

"Oh," she breathed out heavily. "It's fabulous. Especially the passion fruit. I miss passion fruit."

Crap! Was that too suggestive?

Maddie felt her cheeks flaming. Perhaps she had made a mistake. She had multiple reasons for wanting to come back to Hawaii besides the possibility of reconnecting with Kai Nakama, but she had wanted to find him again, and she did have an ulterior motive. What she sought, embarrassingly enough, was reassurance that some man somewhere was capable of caring for the woman *inside* her body, and she had fixated on Kai as the perfect candidate. After all, he had genuinely liked her for herself once before, hadn't he? She had set out with fond hopes of rekindling a platonic, adult friendship with him — a goal that had seemed both simple and reasonable at the time.

Now, suddenly, it seemed neither. Because he was available. And she was available. If he *was* attracted to her, what then? She could hardly blame the man for not passing some arbitrary test she had set up in her mind.

She hadn't thought this through.

"Did you like Utah?" she blurted.

He nodded, seemingly unaware of her inner turmoil "It was beautiful there. The mountains were awe inspiring. And I liked the wide-open spaces. But I don't miss the weather. Winter was so cold. And sometimes the air would get smoggy. I hated that. And it was always very dry. Coming back to Lana'i in the summers, I felt like the air was soup."

"Ha!" Maddie chortled. "You don't know from humid till you've lived in Southern Alabama, my friend. We *swim* through the air in summer, and we don't stop till October."

Kai smiled back at her. She wasn't sure, but she liked to think that he, too, liked the sound of the words that had just rolled so easily off her lips.

My friend.

Perhaps there was hope.

She needed to be polite, nothing more. Maybe she could even be herself, seeing as how she was never a flirt anyway. *Relax.*

"Did you get to swim at Hulopo'e while you were on Lana'i?" he asked, finishing off his shave ice and propelling the paper cone into a nearby trashcan.

Maddie shook her head. Her own treat was almost gone as well. "I didn't have time. There's a million things I still want to do there, but they'll have to wait a while." In retrospect, she wished she had stayed on Lana'i a few more days, since she didn't officially start her post-doc until Monday, and getting settled in at the field station hadn't taken nearly as long as she thought it might. She didn't regret cruising on the catamaran — meeting the captain had been a delight and the whale watching had been spectacular — but it hadn't come cheap.

"I'd go back every weekend if I could," she admitted, "but the truth is, I'm pretty broke. I'll have to wait until my stipend kicks in, then I'll hop on the ferry."

Kai watched her for a moment, then stood abruptly. He held out his hand for her empty cone and spoon and then tossed them into the can for her. "I'm afraid I've got to get back to the office," he said.

"Oh," Maddie replied, rising also. "Sorry. Don't get fired on my account."

He smiled shyly. The sight gave Maddie a bizarre twinge in her middle. Kai might have been shy with every other girl on the planet, but he had never been shy with her, not after that first day of first grade, anyway. He had never treated her like a girl. Nor had he treated her like one of the boys. She had always occupied some nether space in between.

"I was planning on taking the ferry home this weekend," he told her. "Why don't you come along? You can stay at Nana's again. I usually stay there myself, but I can crash on the couch at home. I have a feeling this will be my last chance for a while. I've got to start doing some overtime with one of the consultants; I'm only getting away this weekend because she's got family visiting."

Maddie's heart skipped. Back to Lana'i? Tomorrow? She would love nothing better. *But.* "I already told you, I don't have ferry money right now."

"It'll be my treat," he offered. "Consider it a homecoming gift."

Maddie frowned. "Aren't legal interns poor, too?"

He shrugged. "Not as poor as I would be if I wasn't renting a room on the cheap at my uncle's house."

Still, Maddie hesitated. She didn't want to be indebted. Debt could be used as leverage. *Had* been used as leverage. Many times.

Kai shrugged and started walking. "Forget it. It was just an idea. I know. I don't like to take handouts, either."

She watched him as he walked away. His added height hadn't changed the distinctive way he carried himself. That weird way he swung his left arm to the side, particularly when he was upset...

You'd take a quarter from the old men! Her own, younger voice argued from somewhere in her brain. *But you won't take money from me? Why not?*

Kai had been upset with her. Even as a girl, Maddie could see that his pride was hurt, but she still thought he was being ridiculous. She'd just gotten money for her birthday, and she didn't need it and Kai did... for what? She couldn't remember. But he had refused her.

I don't need your stinking money!

But I want to give it to you!

I don't care!

But he *had* needed that money, whatever it was for. Maddie remembered sneaking into the tiny bedroom he shared with Chika and shoving the dollar bills under his pillow. She also remembered finding the same amount, several months later, tucked beneath her own.

He had never said a word about it. And neither had she.

"Kai?" she called.

He stopped and turned around.

"If we call it a loan, you're on," she offered.

He smiled back at her.

He nodded.

Chapter 11

Kai followed Maddie as she filed along with the other waiting passengers into the lower cabin of the ferry. He exchanged nods with the folks he knew, but declined to engage in conversation. Maddie spied two seats by a window and hustled forward to claim them.

Kai knew she would have preferred to climb up top and ride in the open by the railing; but it was raining both hard and steadily, a relatively unusual circumstance for which neither of them had come prepared. Kai sat down beside her, being careful to leave a polite distance between them. They had spoken little since dinner the evening before. With neither of them having a car, Maddie had been happy to take him up on his offer of a ride to the ferry dock in Lahaina via his cousin's dilapidated SUV, but Risa's chatter about her gigs as a wedding florist at the Ka'anapali resorts had left zero space for other conversation.

"Darn this rain," Maddie grumbled, frowning at the spattered window. "I was hoping to do some more whale watching." She cast a disparaging glance at her lightweight jacket, which did not appear to be waterproof. "I couldn't care less if I get soaked, but it would be rude to show up at Nana's dripping wet."

"You could reminisce over a dryer cycle at the launderette first," Kai teased, recalling a litany of childhood complaints about laundry days. He didn't remember Maddie as a complainer in general, but she had always bored easily.

Maddie threw him a strange look he couldn't decipher. "I suppose so." She drummed her fingers anxiously on the back of the seat in front of her, then slumped into her own. "Never mind. I'm sure it will clear up soon enough."

She turned her gaze out the spattered window again. Kai perceived that she was uptight, and her discomfort had a mirrored effect on him. Why the angst?

He did a quick analysis of her body language. His skills at the art had improved since Haley had begun working with the firm, but it didn't take an expert to read the message Maddie was sending now. If she had dressed to avoid undue attention last night, today she had dressed one step short of a nun. Her hair was tightly swept into braids on either side of her head, and much of her face was concealed by the brim of a floppy hat. Whatever shirt she wore was completely covered by the jacket, and her legs were obscured to her shins by baggy cargo-style capris. The attempt to hide her assets was so blatant it was almost laughable, because short of putting a bag over her head and suspending a barrel from her shoulders, the quest was hopeless. Her attempt, however, spoke volumes.

Don't hit on me, okay? Don't even look at me that way.

Kai found the message disheartening, to say the least. But he also found it sad. Beauty like Maddie's should be allowed to shine, no matter whom it drove to distraction.

He was definitely among that number. The fact that he had extensive experience in gentlemanly behavior was not helpful in the slightest, because the strictures that had bound him for the last seven years happily no longer applied. He'd been looking forward to his freedom for a very long time now, and thus far, he'd had precious little chance to exercise it.

Still, she had made her wishes clear, and that was that. If there was ever to be anything more between them — and he reserved the right not to lock that door, even if he did agree to close it — the first move would have to come from her. He wanted to tell her that she had nothing to worry about, but they weren't at a place where that was possible. Despite their shared history, they were still virtual strangers, feeling each other out. Getting back to a place of comfort — and of genuine trust — would take time.

He relaxed into his own seat, careful not to touch her. He could handle this. Really, he could. But *why* did she have to turn out so ridiculously sexy? Under the circumstances, he felt like the butt of somebody's joke.

"Was Nana okay with me coming back again so soon?" she asked.

"Of course," he assured. "She loves having company. You and I aren't the only ones making use of her spare room. She could charge rent for it."

"She probably should," Maddie agreed thoughtfully.

Kai watched what portion of her face he could actually see and wondered what she was thinking. He wondered if she was aware that Nana was one of the few Lana'ians who actually owned her own house. It had been purchased by a prudent ancestor during a brief window in time when doing so was actually possible, and for Nana to own it outright now and be able to live alone was a rare privilege. Over a hundred years ago, one wealthy rancher from Kauai had bought up almost all the land on the island, and it had been concentrated into one parcel ever since. Most Lana'ians were renters, and housing space was at a premium. If Nana hadn't owned her little house, odds were she would have been displaced from it years ago.

Another silence ensued, and Kai exhaled with frustration. The awkwardness between them, in and of itself, was awkward. Their childhood friendship had been anything but polite. Maddie was just as likely to punch him in the shoulder to get his attention as she was to say hello. They'd had mud fights after a rain. She thought nothing of wearing the same shirt three days in a row and her toenails were always too long. He honestly never even thought of her as female. Good God, they used to go swimming together in their underwear!

Back then he could have told her anything, said something stupid, done something rude, and it wouldn't have mattered; they would still be friends. He would give anything to be even half so comfortable with her now, but that happy past seemed light years away. Perhaps it would put them both more at ease if they continued talking about their childhoods?

"Tell me more about Kentucky," he suggested. "What was it like starting middle school there after being on Lana'i? Did the other kids find you exotic?"

Kai could just see Maddie's lovely gray eyes underneath the brim of her hat. They were swimming with emotion. "I had to finish the fifth grade in Ohio first. That was pretty awful. I remember it seemed so dark all the time. No green anywhere. Just shades of brown and gray. And cold. And wet."

Kai cursed under his breath. He hadn't meant to take her *that* far back. The first few months after her mother died must have been sheer misery, no matter what her father told her.

"I was pretty depressed," she confirmed. Then she tilted her head and looked him fully in the face. "I wrote you a letter once. Did you get it?"

Kai's pulse quickened. *Her letter.* Memory flickered, a stab of guilt. A sense of failure. Of weakness.

Knock it off.

"Yes, I got it." He cleared his throat. "I'm sorry I didn't respond." He was sorry, but he was not going to beat himself up over it. He was past all that now.

Yet Maddie's accusing gaze would not let go. "Why didn't you?" she demanded.

A sick feeling surged. *Dammit!* He was not going to do this. "I was a kid," he answered, somewhat more flippantly than intended. "I guess I didn't know what to say."

Maddie's face flashed with hurt. She turned to the window.

"It wasn't that I didn't care," Kai amended. "I did miss you. I missed you a lot, actually."

Maddie turned back around. "Really?" she said skeptically.

"Yes!" he said firmly. He smiled at her. "Who else would sneak out at midnight to stare at the sky with me?"

She huffed. "Nobody sane. I got bit by so many bugs!"

He laughed. "Nobody thinks Lana'i has a lot of mosquitos except you."

"They never bit anybody on Lana'i except me!" she protested. "If there was one mosquito on the whole damn island, it would fly the length of it to sniff me out! Speaking of which, I haven't even been on Maui a week yet, and I've got half a dozen bites already, in the middle of winter. I wonder if I could tattoo myself with DEET?"

She lifted her foot and slid up her capris to expose a calf and knee, then suddenly thought better of it. Her reversal of action was just as well, since whatever bites she had intended to show Kai were eclipsed by the shapeliness of her leg.

"I have to admit, though, the bugs were even worse in Kentucky, at least in the summer," she continued. "And in Alabama. What about Utah? Oh, wait. I forgot. Bugs don't like you."

Kai smiled smugly. "Guess I'm just lucky."

Maddie scowled at him. She looked cute when she scowled. She always had. Her gaze dropped to his arms, and she studied him with a wistful look that made him restless. When she was a child, she used to tell him how much she envied the color of his skin. How smooth and attractive it was, unmarked by the myriad bug bites, scratches, and bruises that stood out so obviously on her own. He wondered if she still felt that way.

He doubted it.

She seemed about to say something, but thought better of it. Her mouth closed and she turned around to pretend to stare out a window obscured by raindrops.

Why was this so difficult?

"You never did tell me about your job," she blurted suddenly, turning around again. "You asked me all about my life last night, but I didn't have time to return the favor. So do you like being a lawyer? Living the high life in Kahului?"

Kai had to chuckle at that. "If you call living at my uncle's house and working like a dog 'the high life,' then I guess I like it fine."

She studied him again. "You never said you wanted to be a lawyer. All I remember you saying you wanted to be was an astronaut."

"What ten-year-old wants to be a lawyer?" he replied. "Wanting to be an astronaut made me seem weird enough, as you recall. Kind of retro for the nineties."

Maddie considered. "I don't even remember what I said I wanted to be."

"That's because you kept changing it."

"Ah, right," she agreed. "I just knew it would be something exciting. Still, how could I ever have dreamed that one day I would spend weeks at a time staking out dumpsters in rural Alabama waiting for feral cats to come paw through the trash?"

Kai grinned. "At least one of us got to live the high life."

She grinned back, then stared at him thoughtfully. "You might have said you wanted to be an astronaut, but what you always wanted to *do* was help the people of Lana'i. You wanted to do something that meant something. You just weren't sure what. Is that why you went to law school? To find out how to make things happen?"

Kai felt an odd, fluttering sensation in his gut. She remembered that? Not only had she remembered, but she had just effortlessly pieced together what had taken him ages to figure out for himself. He felt laid bare — by a woman he barely knew. The sensation was disconcerting, yet at the same time, it gave him a peculiar feeling of elation.

"Yes," he confirmed. "Exactly. I knew that politics wasn't for me, but law seemed to be a good fit. I wanted to make life better for the people of Lana'i and all the islands. Economic opportunity. Social justice. That's what I focused on most in law school, public policy. I had a couple of prospects for work in Honolulu that would have been more along those lines, but then the opportunity came up with EarthDefense on Maui."

"And you couldn't resist," Maddie suggested.

He smiled at her. "No, I couldn't. I've never wanted to live in Honolulu, and both those jobs had other drawbacks besides. But I really liked the people and the whole mission at EarthDefense, and after being so far away from home for so long it's great being able to hop on the ferry whenever I want. Environmental law wasn't my first choice, but it's growing on me."

"Oh?" Maddie beamed at him approvingly. "As an ecologist, I heartily approve. Somebody has to preserve the natural resources of the islands, or the economic issues will be a moot point. And if we don't stop climate change, so will social justice. Get to work, Nakama!"

"Hey, this is the first whole weekend I've taken off in a month!" Kai protested. "I usually only get one night in, and lately I've spent most of my downtime trying to straighten Gloria out."

His mind flashed with an unwelcome image of his beloved baby sister screaming profanities at him, and his insides roiled with the sick sense of worry that had become second nature. He shouldn't have mentioned the topic — he had wrecked his own mood just when he and Maddie were finally getting a light-hearted vibe going. But Gloria was never far from his thoughts.

When he'd first come home last summer she'd treated him like her hero, just as she always had. So when the trouble started and his parents had asked for his help, he'd been certain he could fix everything.

Wrong.

Oh, the carnage.

God help him. He'd made things so much worse. Whatever Gloria thought of him now, he was definitely no longer her hero. They'd been apart for so long, and she'd grown up so much, he had no idea how to relate to her, how to deal with the changes in her. Now his ordinarily happy family was spiraling into chaos. Last weekend his grandmother, whom *everybody* respected, had seen Gloria's paramour pawing up another girl behind a neighbor's house, and Nana had reported the incident to her granddaughter only to be screamed at and called a liar.

"Gloria's not stupid," Maddie assured him, looking absurdly confident of the fact.

Kai felt himself bristling. What could Maddie possibly know about the situation? She had been around his teen sister for what, one day? Of course Gloria wasn't stupid, but that didn't mean her judgment wasn't pathologically impaired. Growing up was one thing, but for his sweet baby sister to go straight from wearing frilly princess outfits to being possessed by multiple demons couldn't possibly be normal! He frowned. "Do you have any idea what a piece of work this guy is that she's so crazy about?"

Maddie had the nerve to smile slightly. "Love can be blind."

"It's not love!" he pronounced. "I don't know what it is, but it's not *that!* She's going to get herself hurt." He felt his face growing hot. He drew in a deep, slow breath to calm himself. "You know, I could count on one hand the number of times I seriously thought about resorting to physical violence. And every time had something to do with one of my sisters."

Maddie laughed. But her expression soon turned serious again. "I believe the cracks in this guy's armor are starting to show, Kai, but you can't speed that up. You can only slow it down by forcing her to defend him. I realize nobody asked me, but if you *did* ask me, I'd say just drop the subject. She'll break up with him soon enough."

Kai kept his mouth shut. Similar points had been made and rebutted across his family's dinner table for weeks now. Nana agreed with Maddie, believing that Gloria needed the space to learn from her own mistakes. Kai was more sympathetic with his father, seeing a simpler solution in encouraging the guy to surf solo at Polihua beach, then waiting for his corpse to wash up. Malaya's views alternated with the wind, but lately she'd been leaning toward the corpse idea.

Maddie turned to the window and rubbed at the condensation on the glass with her forearm. Now that the boat was moving at a faster clip, the raindrops on the outside were being whisked away by the wind, permitting a poor to marginal view of the Au'au Channel in the dimming light of sunset. After a few moments of what was probably a fruitless search for a whale spout, she pivoted back to face him.

"I keep thinking about our conversation last night," she said in an unexpectedly playful tone. "And I can't believe how many things I'm dying to know about you that I didn't ask. So now that I have you captive for a while, I'm determined to run through the list." Her gray eyes glinted at him with a hint of their old mischief, and he felt an instant pang in his chest that surprised him. Her ability to attract him physically was one thing. But the direct pull she could exercise so effortlessly over his heartstrings was another. How could she be so deeply entangled in his emotions after having been absent from his mind for so long? He wasn't entirely sure *what* he had felt for her back then, but whatever it was, it had obviously been strong.

"Knock yourself out," he challenged.

She smiled. "First of all, where exactly did you go to college? You just keep saying Utah."

Kai braced himself. Here it came.

He knew that answering even the most basic questions about his life on the mainland would require an extensive explanation, more so to Maddie than to most people, because she was starting out with a false presumption about him. That was entirely his fault, and he was expecting to have to set the record straight — and to suffer the consequences. He just wished he'd put a little more effort, in the last twenty-four hours, into planning how best to do that.

"BYU," he answered. "Brigham Young University."

Maddie blinked. "Oh. So, you're Mormon? Or part of your family is?"

She sounded surprised, but not scandalized. That was encouraging. "No, and yes," he replied, measuring his words like any good attorney. "That branch of the family are all LDS: Latter Day Saints. I wasn't raised that way, as you know. The Nakamas are Buddhist and Nana is Catholic and my parents never attended any particular church on Lana'i that I can remember." *All true,* he praised himself, *technically.*

He paused a moment, debating with his conscience. He wasn't ashamed of the truth. It wasn't even a secret. Any random adult on Lana'i could probably tell Maddie his entire family history. The truth wasn't the problem. The problem was that he'd kept it from her before, when it might actually have mattered to her. The more he thought about his selfishness, the more unforgivable it seemed. But he couldn't bear the thought of making her angry with him now, just as they were on the brink of reconnecting again. And although he had no way of knowing how this Maddie might react to the revelation, he knew damned well that *that* Maddie would not only have his head on a platter, she'd put the platter on a pike, put the pike in the ground, and then stand there stamping her feet and screaming at his severed head...

Surely it could wait.

"Are we talking about your mother's side of the family or your father's?" this perfectly reasonable-looking Maddie asked.

Kai answered evenly and without hesitation, as per his legal training. "My father's." Then he added, smoothly linking two unrelated topics, "There are LDS churches all over the islands. They were the first missionaries on Lana'i, you know."

"I know," Maddie replied, still looking thoughtful. "So, you said you got a scholarship, and you went to BYU for undergrad and law school. But you don't consider yourself LDS?"

He shook his head. He couldn't tell what she was thinking. Growing up in Lana'i City, he hadn't thought of the small number of Latter Day

Saints in town as being any different than any other church or temple-goers. However, if growing up on a 141-square-mile island was as close as one could get to growing up inside a bubble, spending seven straight years in Provo, Utah ranked a close second. It was not until he had been unleashed onto the secular island playground of Maui a mere six months ago that he had begun to see his family's religion as others saw it.

He could only assume that Maddie's having spent most of her life in the Midwest and South would not bode well for him. But he wasn't going to lie.

"They first invited me to fly out and spend the summer with them when I was thirteen," he explained. "I have a lot of extended family in Provo, and they were all very warm and welcoming. I really bonded with a few of my cousins, and so I kept going back. When it came time to look at colleges, BYU seemed like a no-brainer. I had the chance to go to school on the mainland at hardly any cost to my parents, and I had plenty of family and friends close by."

"Weren't they hoping to convert you?" Maddie asked.

Kai smiled a little. Maturity had changed many things about Maddie. Lack of subtlety wasn't one of them.

"Well, *duh*," he replied in kind. "Of course they were. It's an evangelical faith, and it's not like I had anything else going on in that department. Nothing would make them happier than my joining their church, and I did try to keep an open mind. But in the end, I just couldn't make myself believe everything I was supposed to believe."

He braved a deeper look at her. She didn't seem to have drawn any conclusions about him yet, but her interest was definitely piqued. He wondered if she professed any particular religion herself. She didn't use to, but that could be either good or bad for him.

He took a breath. He might as well get it over with. If she was going to dismiss him as a weirdo, so be it. That would be her problem.

"That said," he continued, strengthening his voice. "I do admire the way they live. There's so much strength and support in the LDS community, and the people have a certain zest for life and capacity for joy that's hard to explain. After a while I realized that the lifestyle suited me better than I would have guessed. If it hadn't, I wouldn't have stayed in Provo as long as I did." *Although*, he added silently, *the last three years were definitely pushing it.*

Maddie sat up straighter. Behind her out the window, Kai saw the distinctive spray of a whale plume in the distance.

"So you don't have to be an LDS member to go to BYU?" she asked. "Can you be any religion?"

Kai chose his words carefully. "There's no requirement to profess any certain religion, no. But you do have to agree to abide by the honor code, which follows some of the basic LDS principles about lifestyle and values."

Kai looked hopefully for any signs of disinterest on Maddie's part, as now seemed an excellent time to change the subject. Unfortunately, she appeared fascinated.

"Like, not drinking alcohol? Caffeine?" she asked.

"That's right."

"So, you went along with that? The whole time?"

"Yes."

Maddie's eyes widened slightly. He couldn't tell if she was impressed or merely amused.

"I didn't really need to ask that," she said, flashing him a knowing look. "Your sense of justice would never allow otherwise, would it? If you agreed to it, you'd do it. If you didn't agree, you wouldn't sign on and cheat — you'd more likely lead some official protest."

Kai felt that "laid bare" feeling again. That is, in fact, exactly what he would do.

"So what else was in the honor code?" Maddie pressed. "What else couldn't you do?"

"Whale!" Kai cried, pointing.

Maddie whirled around. "Where?" she asked with frustration. "I don't see anything."

The last traces of white spray had long since floated back into the sea, but under the circumstances, Kai felt no guilt. After all, there was a good chance they'd see another one. In any event, she had forgotten her question. "Keep looking that way," he advised.

Maddie sat quietly, staring, and he sent up fervent hopes the whale would reappear. It was a lousy time to whale watch. The sinking sun had left both the sky and the waves a dull grayish color, and although the rain had let up, the surface of the water was etched with white chop, making the spouts harder to distinguish on the horizon.

"Oh, there it is!" she cried happily, pointing herself.

Kai looked in the direction she indicated. "I see it!" he replied, gratified. But the whale had moved farther away, and even though Maddie kept her eyes glued to the window for some time, she saw nothing more. Finally, with a sigh of disappointment, she turned back to him.

"What were we saying now?" she asked.

"I was thinking about the whale game," he answered, launching into the first on a list of diversions he had come up with while she was preoccupied. But when he faced her, he did a double-take. At some point while looking out the window, she had removed her hat. That one small change was enough to make his brain play tricks on him — to convince him for an instant that she was someone he'd never seen before. Even with her hair bound up tight in the juvenile-looking braids, the raw beauty of her adult face was jaw-dropping. Yet if asked last week, he would not describe the Maddie he remembered as pretty, even though he remembered other girls as seeming pretty at the same age. How could he possibly fail to see the potential in her? It had to be there, albeit hidden beneath a rat's nest of red tangles and perpetually smeared dirt. Was he freakin' blind?

"I used to win the whale game," he continued, speaking by rote while his mind wandered, "And you used to accuse me of lying."

Maddie looked confused for only a second. Then her lips drew slowly into a wide smile.

Such full, sumptuous, rosy lips...

Kai made a concerted effort to redirect his thoughts.

"I remember the whale game," she said devilishly.

Kai smiled back at her. They would climb to the top of a good lookout during the winter months, most often the cliff across from Pu'u Pehe. She would claim the ocean to one side of the rock, and he would take the other. Every spout sighted was worth five points. A tail fluke or other body part counted ten, and grand prize — a full breach — snagged twenty. *But* the sighting only counted if verified by someone else, which was a problem if there were only two of you and your opponent refused to look, which Maddie sometimes did when she was in a mood. And if she didn't see it herself, she refused to acknowledge it, even though she knew Kai wouldn't lie.

Thinking back on it now, the dynamic seemed bizarre. If Kenny or one of the other guys had accused Kai of lying, he would have been angry, and they would have regretted it. But Maddie *did* believe him, and he knew that.

"*Were* you lying?" asked the incredibly kissable grown-up lips which were inches away from his and bore no resemblance whatsoever to anything from his childhood memory.

He swallowed and regrouped. "What do you think?"

The woman smirked. "I knew you wouldn't lie to me," she answered. Her gray eyes held his, and for a moment he thought he sensed a message in them, almost a plea. It was as if she wanted something, but didn't know how to ask. Her look of longing was so piercing it nearly drove him to speak, but before he could open his mouth, her expression changed abruptly. She straightened in her seat and replaced the wide-brimmed hat on her head. "But I hated how you always won the damn game," she finished, scowling at him playfully again.

Kai's mind spun with confusion. What the hell *was* that? What did she want?

He had no idea. The only thing he knew for sure was that her agenda did not include any scenario whereby he would derive any benefit from her newly gorgeous body, which was unfortunate in the extreme.

Because he wasn't at BYU anymore.

"We've got to get back to Hulopo'e Beach sometime this weekend," Maddie suggested brightly. "Maybe we can have a rematch. I'm dying to get my feet wet again. And swim with the dolphins! Do they still come around when people are in the water?"

Kai tried not to imagine grown-up Maddie swimming in the ocean. He failed.

God help him.

Chapter 12

Maddie stepped out of the ferry and onto the dock, enjoying the rather spooky feel of the Manele boat harbor after dark, with the lights of the marina glimmering over the water and the palm trees bending in the brisk, wet wind. Everyone in the small crowd seemed to know exactly where they were going, including Kai, and Maddie followed him wordlessly through the misty rain up the hill to the parking lot. Malaya was waiting for them in the Nakamas' red truck, and after getting out and delivering an enthusiastic hug to them both, she jumped back into the driver's seat and hastened to be among the first in line to pull out on the road towards town.

"I'm making dinner for everybody at our house," she explained, driving one-handed with only the occasional glance at the road, as was customary in her profession. "But I hope you're not starving, because it may be a while. Kai, I'm taking you to your Uncle Shin's house. Your cousin Riku's just got in from the Big Island, and he needs help. Your dad's already there."

Maddie watched as Kai stiffened in the passenger seat in front of her. She couldn't recall a cousin Riku, but Kai had a million cousins. When she lived on Lana'i he had at least three uncles in Lana'i City alone, and they were all married with kids.

"What's happened?" Kai asked, his voice grim with concern. "Something with his wife?"

Malaya sighed. "She's taken the kids somewhere. He's afraid she might have gotten them to the mainland."

Kai's eyes widened with horror. "Oh, God, let's hope not. Could she afford that?"

Malaya shook her head. "Not by herself. But she has family there. Riku thinks she might have borrowed the money."

Kai ran a hand through his hair. He seemed genuinely upset, and Maddie tried again to remember someone named Riku. She could not.

"Can she do that?" Malaya asked fearfully. "Could she keep them there?"

Kai shook his head. "It depends on so many things, Mom. What's so unfair is that working through custody arrangements can take time, and if the burden of travel falls on Riku..." He blew out a frustrated breath. "He loves those kids. It's not right."

Malaya's lovely dark eyes moistened. "They're so little. They won't understand, either." She looked at her son. "What can we do?"

"We can help him find a good family lawyer, like *now*," Kai replied. "And we can help him pay for it. And for plane tickets, if he needs them."

"That may not be easy," Malaya said dully.

"No," Kai conceded. "It won't."

They rode the rest of the way into the city in sober silence, and when Malaya pulled up beside a house not far from the Buddhist temple, Kai made apologies to Maddie and hopped out.

"He's a good boy, that one," Malaya said proudly as she pulled the truck back onto the street. "If he got paid for all the legal advice he doles out around here, he'd be a rich man already. But he's always just happy to help. He claims he's not qualified to do anything in particular and that everything he says is really just common sense."

Maddie considered. "I'm guessing he downplays his value."

Malaya laughed. "I think you're right. People know better, though. They respect my Kai, young as he is."

Maddie's thoughts drifted back to the BYU honor code. She could not get it off her mind. No caffeine or alcohol. For seven straight years. And he wasn't even a Mormon! The alcohol thing wasn't that big a deal. She didn't drink either, after all, and no honor code was stopping her. But life without diet cola or iced tea? No thank you. She tried to recall more specifics about the LDS lifestyle, but could not. Where she lived, Mormon churches were few and far between.

"Home sweet home," Malaya called in a sing-song a few moments later. She parked the truck in the driveway and grabbed Kai's overnight bag for him. Maddie picked up her own pack, hopped out of the back seat of the truck, and followed Malaya into the house. Her thoughts were still swirling around Kai's life in Utah, with some lingering sense of confusion, when she realized that Malaya seemed agitated.

"What's wrong?" Maddie asked.

Malaya ceased her pacing and exhaled roughly. "It's Gloria. Of course. And there's nothing necessarily wrong. It's just that I don't know where she is. I thought she'd be here."

Maddie felt awkward. "I'm sorry about my timing. You guys obviously have enough to deal with without putting up with a houseguest. Is there anything I can do to help?"

Malaya smiled and extended her hands for Maddie's. "You're no bother, girl. If you were, I would have dropped you off at Nana's and made her feed you."

Maddie laughed.

"You believe me, don't you?" Malaya asked, giving her hands a squeeze.

Maddie nodded. "Yes."

"All right, then," Malaya replied. "So here's the answer to your question. You can help me by trying to conjure up enough clean dishes for six people to eat off by the time the noodles are ready."

Maddie grinned. "Done."

Her hands were deep in the midst of a pile of suds when the muddle of uncertainty in her brain finally crystallized into an askable question. "Malaya," she began casually, as she and Kai's mother stood practically shoulder to shoulder in the small kitchen. "Kai told me about going to school in Utah, and how all the family there were LDS, although he never became a member himself."

"Oh?" Malaya replied offhandedly, her dark eyes flashing with more interest than her tone would indicate.

"But I still don't completely get it. Where's the link? I mean, is anybody in the family here LDS?"

"Well, I guess I am," Malaya answered. "Technically."

Maddie stopped scrubbing the dishes. Now she was really confused. "You?"

Malaya shrugged. "I joined before I got married. But I haven't been active in so long, I'm not sure it still counts anymore."

That explanation didn't help in the slightest. "But Kai said it was his father's family," Maddie repeated. "The family he actually lived with, were they his godparents or what?"

"No, he lived with his grandparents, my first husband's parents," Malaya answered, stirring something. "When he wasn't on campus, anyway. He moved on and off. He shared a place with one of his cousins for law school."

Maddie found her eyes fixating on a small, floating island of white suds. It was rapidly popping itself into oblivion. Her brain felt the same. *My first husband's parents.* Malaya had been married before she married Aki? Kai had never said one word to Maddie about that. He sure as hell hadn't said a word about considering some other couple in Utah his *grandparents.* Gloria had used the word. But not Kai.

"Maddie?" Malaya said softly. "Something wrong?"

The island of suds dissolved to a flat, thin film. Maddie blew on it and finished it off. "No, of course not," she replied cheerfully, resuming washing the dishes. "I shouldn't be asking you any of this, anyway. It's none of my business."

Malaya snorted her pretty snort and returned to the stove. "Since when has that ever stopped anyone from asking me anything? I'm sorry if I said something that surprised you. I assumed you would know already, but I guess there's no reason you would, being so young when you were here and then leaving when you did."

Maddie said nothing. She scrubbed vigorously at a melamine plate with a rooster on it.

"I was widowed when Kai was just a baby," Malaya continued. "Aki adopted him after we got married. I'm guessing Kai never told you he was adopted?"

Maddie shook her head. Her eyes felt hot. The intensity of emotion she felt was unfathomable. *No, he hadn't told her.* But what did it matter? Why did she care? What possible, freakin' difference did it make? It wasn't her business!

"There's something you have to understand," Malaya continued gently. "Aki was the only father Kai ever knew. Lana'i was the only home he ever knew. I never kept anything a secret from him, but it's hard to explain to a toddler, you know? His birth father was just a face in some pictures, but he loved Aki and Aki loved him. We were a family and Chika was his sister. When he started school he came home in tears because the teacher had called him by another name. He wanted to be a Nakama like the rest of us. He wanted to be Aki's son."

Maddie's own eyes threatened to tear up, and she cursed her ragged emotions. "I can see how he would feel that way."

Malaya nodded. "Kai asked Aki to adopt him, and of course Aki wanted nothing more. It was a hard thing for Kai's grandparents to accept, but bless them, they're such good people — I know they were hurt when he changed his name, but they said they understood and that it was the best thing for him."

Maddie finished scrubbing the dishes. She felt like a heel. If Kai hadn't wanted to share all this stuff with her way back then, so what? He was a boy. He didn't want to talk about it.

"Anyway," Malaya continued. "Everyone knows that Kai isn't Aki's biological son, but nobody goes on about it, out of respect, you understand?"

"Of course I understand," Maddie agreed. She gave the dishes a final rinse. While she was in the midst of stacking them, a long-buried memory bubbled up in her mind. "Did Kai's grandparents ever visit him here?" she asked.

"As often as they could afford to," Malaya answered. "Which was only every three or four years, when he was small. Why? Did they come when you were here?"

"I think so," Maddie answered, frustrated at the scantness of the memory. "I remember him having 'relatives' come from Utah for a visit, but I can't remember meeting them. Which is kind of funny, if you think about it. Considering how often I was over here."

"Well, that might not have been an accident," Malaya replied. "There was a time when Kai was pretty sensitive about the situation. He didn't want everybody reminded that he's half haole."

Maddie dropped a knife in the sink with a clatter and whirled around. "He is not!"

Malaya stopped what she was doing and smiled with amusement. "You know something I don't, Maddie girl?"

Maddie stood perfectly still. Her limbs felt cold. "But—" she stammered. "He doesn't look half haole!"

Malaya cocked an eyebrow. "You think he looks half Japanese?"

Maddie swallowed. It couldn't be. It just couldn't. Kai's skin wasn't quite as dark as Malaya's, but it was darker than either of his sisters' or Aki's. Besides, he would have told her *that*. "Yes?" she answered uncertainly.

Malaya chuckled. "Chika and Gloria are half Japanese. Not Kai. Come here, look at this." She turned down the stove burner and led Maddie out of the kitchen and over to a bookcase in a corner of the main room, from which she pulled out a thin photo album. She flipped through some pages of snapshots of herself as a high school girl, stopping when she reached a full-page studio portrait.

"Here," she said fondly, turning the album so Maddie could see better. "This is our wedding picture, me and Kevin. Ack! We were babies, weren't we?"

Maddie was not going to say anything. But the familiar young girl in the picture did indeed look no older than Gloria. Fantastically pretty and brimming with life, she hung onto her husband's arm with a wide smile and a devil-may-care glint in her eye.

"Don't ask," Malaya grumbled. "I was eighteen. And yes, I was pregnant."

Maddie's heart beat quickly as her eyes moved to the boy, who looked little older than Malaya. He was tall. Of course. How many other clues had she missed all this time? He was "white," albeit dark-complected, with curly black hair and vivid blue eyes. His face was roguish with a strong, square jaw, and his smile was easy, if ever so slightly crooked. To describe him as 'tall, dark, and handsome' would be technically correct, but to Maddie's mind 'wickedly dashing' was far more apt. The couple looked picture-perfect, star-struck, and ready to take on the world — or knock over a bank, depending on their mood. "The two of you look like a movie poster," she said honestly.

Malaya laughed a bit ruefully. "Yes, *well*. We thought so, anyway."

Maddie studied the boy's image again. She could easily see some of Kai's features in him. Kai had Kevin's forehead and jaw, his height, his build. But he had Malaya's eyes and her cheekbones, not to mention her softer, gentler smile. "How did you meet?"

Malaya sucked in a breath. She put the album down, led Maddie back to the kitchen, and returned to her work at the stove. "The summer after I graduated from high school, I went to work on Maui, doing housekeeping. I was living with an auntie, trying to make some money before starting community college in the fall. Kevin and his cousin were working in the same hotel. Kevin was living with relatives too, just for the summer, because he was supposed to start his mission later that year. You know, his mission for the church."

Maddie nodded. She picked up a towel and began to dry the dishes she'd washed.

Malaya stirred the noodles and smiled to herself. "I have no excuse. I was young, irresponsible, thrilled to be someplace besides Lana'i for the first time in my life, and head over heels in love. Kevin was almost nineteen and from the mainland, which as far as I was concerned made him the most worldly man alive. His cousin Rich, now *there* was a wild child — something Kevin's parents didn't know when they sent him to Maui, or Kai never would have been conceived, I can promise you that. But Kevin wasn't like Rich. He might have gotten a little carried away with *aloha*, but when we found out I was pregnant he never thought twice about it — he called his parents right up, told them he was sorry to disappoint them but could they please send some extra money so he could bring his pregnant fiance home and marry her?"

Maddie's eyebrows lifted. "And they did? They were okay with that?"

Malaya grinned. "Well, I wouldn't say they were *okay* with it. Kevin did break the church's rules, and his mission was cancelled, and it changed all their plans for his education. But as I said before, the Fords are good people. They sent the money, they took us both into their home in Provo, and they welcomed me into their family with open arms. I've never felt anything but love from Stan and Amy, and they'd do anything for Kai."

Maddie was quiet a moment. "Wow."

"You're telling me," Malaya agreed. "I honestly believe they would have adopted me right along with Kai after Kevin died, if I'd been willing. They always treated me like I was their own daughter." Her eyes brightened with moisture. "Kevin's death was a horrible shock to all of us. He was killed in a bicycle accident with a car at a city intersection. He wasn't wearing a helmet. It probably shouldn't have surprised us as much as it did because he was always so reckless... at everything. But at the same time, he just seemed too full of life to die."

She buried her face in her cooking. "I hated to upset the Fords even more, but I couldn't stay in Utah. It was so cold and bleak that winter... and as good as everyone was to me, I was just so lonely for Nana and everyone back here. I needed my family and I wanted to bring my baby back home. I wanted to raise him in the sunshine."

"And they were okay with that, too," Maddie surmised.

"They were heartbroken," Malaya replied. "But they didn't argue with me. Amy even confessed that if she were me, she would feel exactly the same way. Even though they'd just lost their son, and they knew it meant I'd be taking their grandson thousands of miles away from them."

"Wow," Maddie said again.

Malaya smiled. "You know, people ask me sometimes if it doesn't bother me that they 'stole Kai away' after high school. Tempted him out there for summer vacations, then offered him money for college." She chuckled to herself. "I'll tell you this, Miss Maddie. You'll never hear one bad word come out of my mouth about Stan and Amy Ford. *Ever.* And that's the truth."

The front door opened. Malaya dropped her spoon and hastened into the front room, and Maddie followed.

Aki and Kai — who, Maddie noted, looked like a giant standing next to his father — greeted them with guarded smiles. Nana was with them also, and her soft brown eyes twinkled at Maddie with welcome.

"Well?" Malaya prompted.

"We'll get him a lawyer," Aki said softly. "My brothers have some contacts in Hilo, and so does Kai. We'll start making calls first thing tomorrow." He bowed to Maddie with a smile. "Lovely to see you again so soon, *Tomato Chan.*"

She returned the gesture. "Likewise."

He looked up, then glanced around the remainder of the small house with a frown. "Where is Gloria?"

Malaya's forehead creased. "I... don't know. I thought she'd be home by now. You haven't heard from her?"

Aki's face paled. His entire body stiffened with tension, and he muttered a Japanese word Maddie had never heard him use before, but which she remembered was one of old Mr. Hiraga's favorites. She didn't know its translation but could guess its intent.

Aki sprang into motion and dashed through the door into Gloria's room.

Malaya followed. "What is it?" she demanded.

"Has she taken anything?" his voice rang out from the small chamber.

"Who can tell in this mess?" Malaya shrieked. "What's happened? Tell me!"

"Is this her purse? Her wallet?"

"Yes! Why?"

Aki reappeared in the main room with his wife close on his heels. He paused for breath, seemingly to calm himself. "I am upsetting you all for nothing. I apologize."

"What is it, Dad?" Kai echoed. "You might as well tell us."

Aki rubbed his face with his hands, then smoothed them over his nearly bald head. He had always been such an incredibly patient and even-tempered father, Maddie couldn't help but sympathize with his current misery. He had always doted on baby Gloria, especially. "One of the men told me that Dylan's been talking about moving on," he explained quietly. "He's bored of Lana'i and wants to live someplace with a little more 'action.'"

"Well, amen and hallelujah, Jesus!" Nana exclaimed. "That's *good* news!"

Aki's face turned grim. "This man also overheard Dylan telling Gloria that he would take her with him."

The room went silent.

"But she wouldn't go," Kai pronounced, looking to his mother for confirmation. "Would she?"

Malaya exhaled loudly. She closed her eyes and shook her head. "I don't know, I don't know. That girl's head these days... Who knows?"

"It doesn't matter!" Nana proclaimed with certainty.

Malaya opened her eyes and looked at her mother, as did everyone else.

Nana drew up to her full, diminutive height. "Think sense. This boy doesn't need her. There's girls everywhere! He tells her what she wants to hear. If he leaves, he leaves alone." Her voice lowered. "Most likely, without her even knowing when he goes."

"But Nana," Kai argued. "What if he does care enough to take her with him?" He turned to his father. "Did Dylan say where he wanted to go?"

Aki's face turned even grimmer. "He's asked for a company transfer to the resort in Mexico. Or Costa Rica."

"*Costa Rica!*" Malaya shrieked.

"No, Mom," Kai assured, although his voice sounded equally horrified. "She's still a minor. She couldn't get there without a passport and papers."

"There are fakes!" Malaya cried. "If she left the country she might never get back in!"

Nana sighed and shook her head.

Gloria popped open the front door and slipped inside.

All heads turned to stare at her.

The teen surveyed the now-silent assembly with a puzzled look. "What?" she said petulantly. "Did somebody die or something?"

Chapter 13

Malaya growled like a lion. If she could have breathed fire, she would have. *"Where have you been?"*

"At Ellery's!" Gloria shot back. "I told you that!"

"That was hours ago!"

"Well, you said dinner would be late, didn't you? You texted; I adjusted!" Gloria cast a glance toward the kitchen table. "And I obviously didn't miss it! So what's the big deal?"

Everyone including Maddie let out a collective sigh of relief.

"There's no big deal," Kai answered, stepping over and sweeping his little sister into a sideways bear hug. "We're just happy to see you, that's all." He dropped an affectionate kiss on the top of her head, and even as Gloria made a show of stiffening in response, Maddie could see that she was hiding a smile.

"Let's just eat," Malaya snapped.

Maddie decided to make herself useful. She headed into the kitchen and set the table as best she could without getting in Malaya's way. The task was not particularly easy. Six adults made for a tight fit around the table, and that was with two people on stools instead of chairs. Maddie took one of the stools and regretted the choice immediately. Not only did the seat sit her higher than anyone else at the table, but it wobbled her like a drunkard besides, and she felt awkward enough already. Since Kai had returned to the house with his father, she hadn't once been able to look him in the eyes.

"Oh, crap!" Gloria said loudly, breaking a lengthy silence as they all dug into their noodles.

Maddie looked over to find the girl's gaze fixed on her as if noting her presence for the first time.

"I forgot!" Gloria continued, her face beaming with mischief as she looked at Kai, then at Maddie again. "I missed the big reveal! How did it go?"

Maddie's face reddened.

"What are you talking about?" Kai asked.

Gloria rolled her eyes. "I *mean*, give me a play-by-play! Did Maddie surprise you at your office? Did you recognize her?"

Maddie couldn't look at Kai, so she looked at Nana instead. Then she looked at Malaya. Then Aki. Every one of them appeared far too interested in the topic for comfort.

"Yes, she did surprise me," Kai answered. "And yes, of course I recognized her."

"I don't believe you," Gloria teased. She turned to Maddie. "Did he really?"

Maddie's cheeks were on fire. "Yes, he recognized me."

"Well?" Gloria prompted. "*Then* what happened?"

"Nothing," Maddie answered.

"Oh, come on," Gloria wheedled suggestively. "*Something* had to—"

"Well, it didn't!" Maddie retorted, a little too sharply.

Gloria rolled her eyes again. "Kai!" the girl chastised. "What is wrong with you? Is there no hope whatsoever?"

Kai glared at her, but didn't speak.

"Gloria," Aki warned in a low voice.

"What?" Gloria protested. "I'm only pointing out what everybody's already thinking, aren't I? I mean seriously, look at her!"

All eyes darted involuntarily to Maddie, who had just managed to pick up a full load on her chopsticks.

"He's twenty-five years old!" Gloria continued. "What else is he waiting for?"

Maddie's noodles fell off.

"Gloria!" Aki said louder.

Maddie scooted her stool back and dove down under the table. She'd made a considerable mess. How convenient.

"I'm only asking the question," Gloria protested.

Nana cleared her throat. "Seems like a reasonable enough thing to talk about to me."

Maddie's heart fell as she plucked the wayward strands off her leg and the floor. *Et tu, Brute?*

"You have some advice on healthy relationships you'd like to share with everyone, Gloria, child?" Nana continued pleasantly.

Silence. Maddie straightened up and raised her head. Gloria was now staring at her own noodles. Nana, who was sitting close on Maddie's left, winked slyly. "Didn't think so," she mumbled.

Maddie smiled at her weakly and rose to carry her dirty noodles to the trashcan. Her thoughts were in a muddle. There was more to her frazzled nerves than a little embarrassment, innuendo having been her constant companion since puberty. The real problem was that she was angry with Kai. Never mind that she had no good reason, no logical right to feel that way. The emotion consumed her nevertheless.

She stepped on the trashcan opener and the lid flew up. Kai's taunting six-year-old voice rang in her ear. *Haole girls don't talk Pidgin!*

She flicked the noodles into the liner and lifted her foot. The lid slammed closed again.

The stinking little rat!

She sat back down at the table. The family were discussing something about someone Maddie didn't know. She tried to focus, but her thoughts kept drifting.

Just because other haoles did bad stuff ages ago doesn't make it MY fault! Maddie had defended after a particularly bad day at school. Her status as a perpetual "outsider" was something she had always accepted without argument, but when Sammy or one of the other truly spiteful kids in her class framed their jabs in more personal terms, she could not deny that it got to her.

Forget them, Kai would say calmly. *They're idiots. You want to go over after school and see the horses?*

Someone at the Nakama table said something funny, and everybody laughed. Maddie faked a smile, but when her gaze accidentally caught Kai's, she felt nothing but ire. She looked away.

Forget them? She thought to herself, her teeth gnashing. That was the best he could do? Not *Gee, I know just how you feel, Maddie?* Or, *wow, guess what we have in common?* No, indeed. He'd kept his little lips zipped tight, hadn't he? For almost *five years.*

The table went quiet. Maddie looked up to find five expectant faces staring at her. "Um... Excuse me?"

"I asked how you were planning on spending your weekend," Aki said politely.

"Oh, I'm sorry," Maddie apologized. "Well, there are a lot of people I'd like to visit with eventually, especially some of my teachers. And I'd like to drive everywhere I couldn't go when I couldn't drive. And I definitely want to get to the beach for a swim and a hike up to the Sweetheart Rock—"

Maddie stumbled over the last few words, but managed to get them out. She grabbed for her glass and took a drink of water. The chaos such a simple statement spurred in her mind was ridiculous, and her face reddened all over again at the thought of anyone reading her mind. She'd had so much fun at that beach with Kai when they were kids, and she'd secretly been looking forward to reliving a healthy chunk of it this weekend, but now...

Her eyes involuntarily locked with his across the table. He looked back at her with undisguised concern. She set her glass down and cleared her throat. "But I don't know if I'll have time for everything," she finished shortly, stabbing her chopsticks at what was left of her noodles.

"Well, we've only got the one truck, but we'll be happy to offer a ride wherever we can," Aki said pleasantly.

Maddie cringed with shame. "Oh, no, I hadn't meant to assume. I'll beg, borrow, or steal rides from somewhere. Or I'll walk. Don't worry about me."

She dropped another load of noodles. This time they landed on top of her cleavage.

This time they stuck there.

Malaya and Nana promptly covered their mouths with a hand, smothering snickers. Aki and Kai politely averted their eyes. Gloria just stared at her.

"Oh, for God's sake!" Maddie said with a good-natured groan. "Just go ahead and laugh, will you?"

The Nakama family obliged.

Maddie finished the rest of her meal, which proved blissfully uneventful, with a fork. And when a tired-looking Nana announced immediately after the table had been cleared that she was ready to head home, Maddie's relief was undoubtedly visible. She grabbed her pack and headed for the door. "An early night sounds good to me too, Nana," she agreed.

"I'll drive you," Kai said, pulling the keys off the peg where his mother had hung them. "It's still raining a little."

"Thanks, love," Nana said warmly, throwing an arm around her grandson's waist as he passed by.

Maddie followed them out, trying not to let her continuing inner turmoil show as she thanked Malaya and Aki for their hospitality.

It wasn't that big a deal. What was her problem?

You're a haole.

Kids had called her lots of names when she was growing up, both here and on the mainland. So what?

Haole girl!

Kai had never made fun of her for being a haole. Kai never made fun of anybody. It wasn't his fault.

Look at the haole, thinking she's so hot. Thinking she belongs here.

What had Kai said all those times? What had he been thinking when they taunted her?

Kai's hanging out with the haole again!

I'll hang out with whoever I want to hang out with! Get over it!

Within three minutes, the truck had reached Nana's house and Kai was outside and opening Nana's door for her. He helped Nana step out and onto her walk, but when Maddie got out, he blocked her path. "Wait," he said firmly, making sure to catch her eyes. He held open the front door of the truck for her. "Can you hop in the front seat a minute? There's something I want to show you." Then without giving her a chance to reply, he bounded off to help Nana up her front steps and into her house. "I'll have Maddie back before too long," he assured.

Nana threw him an approving, knowing look. Thoroughly irked, but seeing no less socially awkward option, Maddie jumped into the truck's front seat and slammed the door behind her. She didn't look at Kai as he restarted the engine. He said nothing, and neither did she. But when she realized he was headed north out of town, she could hold her temper in check no more.

"Where are you going?" she asked sharply.

"Somewhere you can yell at me without half of Lana'i overhearing every word you say," he replied.

Maddie decided to look at him. He seemed even taller driving a truck, something which she'd never seen him do before. In the dim glow of the console's lights he also seemed even better looking, which was especially galling when she was furious. How *dare* he turn out to be so damned hot? None of the other girls were interested in the old Kai. He was short and shrimpy and shy and didn't even like the girly girls, and she'd had his attention all to herself. She didn't even want to think about how many women had woken up in *this* Kai's bedroom.

"What makes you think I want to yell at you?" she asked, attempting a neutral tone.

He threw her a look and shook his head.

They reached the pastures by the Lodge at Ko'ele. Kai pulled the truck off to the side of the road near the fence and parked. There were no horses visible now, probably because they were sheltering in the rain. But she and the old Kai used to come here often. She had never ridden one of the horses and never particularly wanted to, but there was something about sitting quietly in the grass and watching the regal beasts toss their heads and twitch their tails that had always soothed her.

Had he remembered that?

He turned in his seat and faced her. "Maddie," he said heavily, his brown eyes beseeching. "I'm sorry I never told you that I was half haole."

She sucked in a breath. How could he know that? He and Malaya hadn't been alone for a second!

He exhaled roughly. "I saw the album open on the couch. You've been staring daggers at me all evening. Come on. I was going to tell you the whole story this weekend. And I was getting to that part. I swear. I was just... taking it one chunk at a time."

He looked so earnest. So sincere. Adult Kai was being perfectly rational. And what else should she expect? Even child Kai had been rational most of the time, rarely letting his emotions override his common sense, at least with other people. Well, she was just as mature, was she not? Just as above it all? "There's no reason you should have to tell me anything," she said evenly. "It's none of my business."

"But you're mad at me anyway," he asserted, the smallest of smiles playing on his lips.

"No, I'm not," she lied. "It was ages ago. It doesn't matter now."

Kai's smile faded. "I would understand if you were upset," he said softly. "We did share a lot, and it is a big thing to keep from you, particularly when so many other people knew."

"I told you," she repeated stiffly. "It doesn't matter."

He was quiet a moment. "Are you sure?"

"Of course I'm sure," she snapped. She had thought that she was special, dammit. That the kids they'd been had had a connection. A bond. Something that maybe, just maybe, could translate into adulthood. But he'd *lied* to her. She thought she'd known him so well — better than anybody. She was sure that he would never lie to her. She was positive of it.

Molten lava bubbled up in her chest.

"Right," he said sarcastically. "And you think I believe—"

The volcano blew.

"You are such a liar!" Maddie accused hotly, whirling in her seat to face him. "Were you lying in the whale game too? How many of those lobs and spy hops did you fake? Once you had me fooled, how many other things did you lie about? How many times did you get me to defend you to everybody else? Oh, no, *Kai* would never lie! Kai would never lie to *me!"*

Her voice escalated to a near screech, and she watched as his eyes widened in surprise.

"I didn't lie to you," he insisted. "I left a lot of things unsaid and unexplained, but I never lied."

"Are you kidding me?" Maddie railed. "What kind of legal hair-splitting is that?"

He bit his lip in frustration, and Maddie felt a sharp pang of... something. Child Kai had bit his lip, too. Not very often. Only when he was really upset.

"Listen to me, Maddie," he said calmly. "I honestly cannot remember ever lying to you. You never asked me anything about being adopted. You never asked me anything about my relatives in Utah, and I did mention them. You never even asked if I was Japanese or Filipino or whatever. You never seemed to care. And if you didn't ask, I wasn't going to bring it up, because I didn't want to talk about it."

"You intentionally didn't let me meet your grandparents!" Maddie accused.

Kai's eyes flickered with guilt. He breathed out heavily. "I didn't let anybody meet my grandparents. I had some issues back then. I'll admit it. I didn't like being half haole, and I didn't want everybody in town reminded of it. I wanted to be a Nakama. I wanted to be Aki's son."

Maddie's blood heated again. "You stood there while the other kids gave me all kinds of grief and you *knew* you were half haole and *they* knew you were half haole and you never said a word to me!"

"That is *so* not fair!" Kai fired back, his own voice rising for the first time. "I never just stood by! I always defended you! I always defended anybody when the kids were piling on like that!"

"But I didn't *know!*" Maddie cried, her voice reaching a crescendo as her eyes welled up with tears.

"Why did it matter?"

"It mattered because it would have made me *feel* better to know that it was something we shared, you miserable rat!" Maddie shouted. Her arms flew up from her sides, and in a gesture practiced countless times before, she laid her hands on his chest and delivered a playful shove.

Maddie froze and sucked in a breath. She looked at him in horror. *So much for mature and rational.* "Oh, my God. I'm so sorry. I can't believe I just did that." She looked down at her hands, which were still resting lightly on his shoulders. She couldn't seem to move.

Kai's chest shook suddenly beneath her fingers.

He was laughing.

Maddie searched his face. It was close to hers, and the brown eyes that twinkled back at her looked, for the first time, like the eyes of the boy she knew — despite their modified packaging. Her next apology died abruptly on her lips.

"Oh, shut up!" she groused, delivering another shove as she righted herself. "You deserved that and you know it."

He kept on laughing. "Now, there's the Maddie I remember!"

In a blink, the myriad images in her memory overlaid themselves on the adult face before her. "Is that what it takes for us to feel like old friends again?" she asked, still reeling a little. "Violence?"

He smiled and shook his head. "Don't be silly," the deeper voice said. "You never hurt me. You were merely... an expressive child."

Maddie raised an eyebrow. "Are you saying you liked me *better* when I pushed you around and yelled at you all the time?"

"Well, not exactly," he chuckled. "I'm just saying that... well, at least we kept it real. Right?"

Maddie was quiet for a moment, and so was he. It was tough to put into words, but they both knew that some invisible barrier had been broken. Whatever they were to each other now, at least they were no longer strangers.

They sure as hell would no longer be polite.

"Well, Nakama, I hope you weren't too attached to this veneer of mature sophistication," Maddie said flippantly, slumping down in her seat. "Because unfortunately, real Maddie is just as impatient and impulsive as she ever was."

"Surely not," Kai mocked. "And does she still hate to lose?"

Maddie slid her eyes slowly toward his. She smirked.

"Try me."

Chapter 14

Maddie sank into the less stable of the two wicker chairs on Nana's porch and swished her guava juice around in her plastic tumbler. She smiled serenely. She had never liked guava juice. Its flavor was bland and its texture did not appeal. But ever since she had left Lana'i, the beverage's taste and smell had become inextricably bound with warm memories of her time in Nana's house. Therefore, she loved it. She had sought out its soothing powers at some of the lowest points in her life, and it had always comforted her.

She looked up to see a promising stretch of blue sky gaining ground on a patchwork of dissipating clouds. Her feet started to itch again. She was dying to get in the ocean. Only a little more time to kill, and she could walk up to the Nakamas' house. Kai had promised to take her to the beach this morning, and Kai always kept his promises. Her smile broadened.

She couldn't wait.

"I found it!" Nana crowed, pushing open her screen door and coming to join Maddie on the porch. "I knew I had it. Just had to look in the right box."

Maddie leaned forward and took the dog-eared snapshot from Nana's hands. It was a photograph of several children taken on the porch they currently occupied. Three little ones sat on the steps, licking at bright yellow popsicles. Nana stood behind them, holding a baby. A toddler, its face turned away from the camera, clung to her leg. One older girl rode the porch railing like a rodeo bull, her own popsicle held high in one hand.

Maddie squinted, taking a closer look. "Holy crap," she murmured.

The chubby little girl on the railing appeared to be seven or eight years old. Her voluminous red hair had presumably been tied back in a ponytail, or a braid, or something, at some previous point. But when the picture was taken the hair consisted of three frizzy, tangled clods, one at the base of her neck, and one roughly on either side of her head. Her faded shirt was too small and showed her midriff. Her shorts looked like men's track shorts and were baggy and ill-fitting. Both her face and her legs looked dirty.

Maddie felt a twinge in the pit of her stomach.

"Something wrong, child?" Nana asked. She had settled herself into the other chair and now watched Maddie with concern.

"I just..." Maddie stammered. "I didn't..." She drew in a breath and blew it out again. "I don't know. I'm sure I never paid any attention to what I wore or what I looked like. And I did pretty much run wild all over the island. I shouldn't be surprised. Still, I look awful. I look like something social services needs to come investigate, you know?"

Maddie ended her statement on a laugh. She was a willful child. It was hardly her parents' fault if she got dirty all the time. At least it looked like she'd been made to wash her hands before she ate! But when no answering chuckle came from Nana, Maddie's stomach suffered yet another twinge.

She looked up from the photograph to find Nana's expression not only serious, but sympathetic. "I didn't mean to upset you, child. But I'm pretty sure it's the only picture I have."

"Oh, no, of course!" Maddie said quickly. She had asked about pictures, had wanted to see what she looked like, and to remind herself what Kai had looked like, since she had never had a picture of him. Her years on Lana'i were greatly underrepresented in her own family's album, a fact that had always bothered her, and she was hoping that Nana or the Nakamas might have some pictures she could make copies of. Maybe even a picture of her and Kai together.

But the girl in the photograph was not the Maddie she expected to see.

She said nothing for a moment. She tried to think of other things, but neither her mind — nor her stomach — would settle.

"Nana," she asked finally. "Did I always look like that? I mean, did I always look so... unkempt?"

Silence.

Maddie's heart began to pound. "Nana?" she repeated, the squeak in her voice betraying her angst.

The older woman smiled gently. "Well now, I suppose that's the Maddie I remember. What do you remember, child?"

Maddie's face reddened, and she quickly lowered her head to stare at the picture again. Her hair looked as if it had not been brushed in days. She tried frantically to remember a time when her mother had brushed her hair. She could remember her father doing it. Nana. Herself.

And if you want a French braid, you do it like this, see?

A woman's voice arose in Maddie's mind, soft and sweet. Her touch was gentle, her smile kind. She had not only brushed Maddie's hair, she had taught her how to shampoo and condition it. She had taken her out shopping for nice-smelling soaps and girly deodorant and comfortable underwear and bright-colored new clothes. She had understood what Maddie needed without her having to ask. Without Maddie even knowing herself.

Lisa. Her stepmother.

Maddie could remember being puzzled by all the attention.

Good God. Clothes that fit and basic hygiene were attention?

Maddie handed the picture back to Nana. "Thanks for finding it for me," she said, attempting to infuse some cheer back into her voice. "I'm so anxious to get to the beach! I think I might take a walk through the park before I go. Is there anything you need me to do around here first? Did we get all the dishes?"

Nana smiled and waved a hand dismissively. "Everything's done. Off with you. Have a good day."

Maddie intended to. She grabbed her bag, jogged down the steps, waved goodbye to Nana, and took off around the corner.

Don't think about it. What does it matter now?

Her feet carried her down the street in front of her old house. They stopped and left her there. She still didn't want to think about it. But her body wouldn't move.

Her father was a giant of a man, well over six feet tall with flaming orange hair, a full beard, and a deep, rumbling laugh that made everyone around him smile. He was good-natured and fun-loving and kind. Her mother had been a tall, willowy woman with soft brown curls, luminous blue eyes, and delicate features that had always made Maddie liken her to a flower. As it happened, Jill Westover loved flowers, and Maddie brought her loads of them, keeping a plastic cup full of some blossom or other on the kitchen table whenever she could.

That's lovely, sweetheart. Thank you.

Maddie could picture her mother lying on the couch in the main room, smiling her beautiful smile. She had loved her daughter. She just... didn't have a lot of energy. And as daughters go, Maddie was about as tractable as one of the refuge's more feral cats. Surely keeping her hair neat as she roamed loose about a tropical island would be difficult for any mother?

The little house looked empty. Unwelcoming. Neutral. For a moment it seemed almost defiant in its refusal to agree or disagree with that hypothesis.

It would only make her feel guilty!

Maddie's limbs went numb. The voice in her head hadn't come from the house. Not now and not then. She had heard it at the resort, from her father. On the single worst day of her life.

She had been waiting in one of the guest rooms. Kai's aunt had brought her there, one of Malaya's sisters-in-law who worked in the same division as Bill Westover. Maddie couldn't remember her name. The woman had come to one of Maddie's classmates' houses, where Maddie was working on a project after school, and told Maddie her father wanted to see her. Maddie had waited at the resort a very long time, not understanding what was taking so long, or why Kai's aunt looked so sad.

Maddie's memory of what happened after her father told her that her mother was gone was less clear. She remembered a doctor visiting, and her father coming and going, and Kai's aunt staying with her. And she remembered asking for Nana, only Nana hadn't come. She had been told that her own grandparents were coming, and that they would be with her soon. Kai's aunt had been outside the door talking to her father, and Maddie had put her ear to the door, because it had sounded like they were arguing. The words were too muffled to make out, except for one phrase that her father had shouted, and those words she had definitely heard.

It would only make her feel guilty!

Maddie's feet started moving again. Why did she have to remember that now? It made no difference to anything. She didn't want to think about it.

She jogged at a steady pace up to and past the school, but at the corner by the park, she stopped again. The green lawn and shady grove of pines beyond it looked cool and inviting, but the old men had begun to gather already. Any other time Maddie would have headed over for a chat, but at the moment she was out of sorts. She needed to think. Or something.

She jogged up along the park only a little ways before veering off into an alley and wandering deeper into the neighborhoods surrounding, where she slowed her steps to a walk. A small boy exercising a large — and thankfully friendly — dog on a leash looked up at her with surprise, and Maddie patted the dog's head and moved on. She knew why the boy was surprised. She looked like a tourist, and tourists didn't usually wander around solo in the back streets by the trashcans. But she wasn't in the mood to talk to anyone.

Maddie continued to walk, weaving amongst an assortment of homes that varied widely both in architecture and in upkeep. Most were rented out by the same entity that owned both resorts and most of the rest of the island, but a few houses sprinkled here and there were privately owned. Such had been the case with her own house, although she hadn't been aware of it at the time. The young Westover family had owned a house in Ohio since shortly before Maddie was born, and her father had been determined to continue as a homeowner on Lana'i, even though the only property available at the time was in dubious condition. Maddie had seen "for-sale" pictures of their house in the family album: the photos showed a collapsed porch and a bright blue tarp on the roof. Her father had had to work on the house extensively before they moved in, and she could still remember a drip bucket that had occupied one corner of her bedroom for months.

She had never considered how her mother might have felt about that. Moving to a tropical paradise certainly had its upside, but was Jill Westover upset about having to downsize into such a small, dilapidated house? Was she unhappy to be moving to a place as isolated as Lana'i, away from all her family and friends?

Maddie frowned. As a child, the condition of the house had never mattered to her. Of course, she was never there anyway, was she?

It would only make her feel guilty!

Another pang hit Maddie square in her middle. Had her mother been horribly lonely all those years? Had Maddie neglected *her*?

A horn honked.

Maddie looked up, hoping to see a vehicle driven by a Lana'ian she knew. She was disappointed to see one of the brightly colored rental jeeps, driven by a handsome man in his thirties.

"Hallo! Need a ride somewhere, then?" he asked in a cheerful Australian accent.

"No, thank you. I'm good," Maddie answered. She ran down her mental checklist of contributing factors, but couldn't identify any. Her hair was in a ponytail, and although she wasn't wearing a jacket, her shirt covered her shoulders and it wasn't tight. Of course, she wasn't wearing either a hat or sunglasses.

The man shifted the jeep into park. In the middle of the street. He leaned out his window. "Aw, now. You must be going somewhere. We're all going somewhere, aren't we? Or at least we'd like to." He grinned broadly.

Maddie looked around. One house up, a man was emerging from

his back door carrying what looked like a bag of trash. He was dark-skinned, probably in his late 60s, and heavyset. "I'm going right here," Maddie answered. She walked up to the house, smiled a greeting at its resident, and joined him on his steps. Then she called back to the man in the jeep with a wave. "Hope you have a nice visit on the island. Goodbye!"

The Aussie threw her a puzzled smirk. Then he shifted the jeep into gear and drove on.

Maddie smiled sheepishly at the man beside her. He was, predictably, looking at her like she was insane. But he hadn't said a word. "Sorry about that," she apologized, stepping off his porch. "I owe you one. Maddie Westover. I'm staying with Nana over on Caldwell. Thanks!"

The man did not answer her. But he did look mildly amused.

Maddie jogged off, determined to keep her mind on happier thoughts. She passed by one of the smaller churches in town, one which occupied a house like any other house and was distinguishable as a church only by the sign in its yard. Ordinarily such a sign would be of little interest, but this morning it stopped her. *Church of Jesus Christ of Latter Day Saints.*

She pondered a moment. Had Malaya ever attended here? Did Kai find it at all interesting that there was a congregation right here on the island, or had he left all that behind when he graduated? And what else was in that BYU honor code, anyway? She had meant to look that up. Curious, she pulled out her phone. But before she could start a search, the time caught her eye. She jumped with glee, tossed the phone back in her pack, and made a sharp turn toward the Nakamas' house.

To the beach!

She was jogging toward the house on a side street when she caught sight of Gloria alone in the yard. The teen was slouched against the clapboard siding with her arms crossed over her chest, looking miserable. Maddie could only assume that the family's latest efforts to circle round and protect its youngest had not gone over well.

"Hey!" Maddie greeted, slowing to a walk and approaching her. "You going to the beach with us?"

Gloria's eyes flickered up only briefly. She uttered something between a sniff and a snort.

"Oh, come on," Maddie cajoled, undeterred. "When was the last time you went to Hulopo'e just to splash around in the water and goof off like a *keiki* again? I'm twenty-five — if I can do it, so can you."

Maddie really did want Gloria to come with them. She wanted to help the family out somehow, and although she had no plan, she knew that getting closer to the teen was a good first step. "It'll only be for a couple hours," she added.

Throughout Maddie's speech, muffled voices could be heard inside the house. Now the volume of the other conversation doubled, and Gloria rolled her eyes skyward. "Mom doesn't think she's loud," she explained, almost apologetically.

Maddie knew she shouldn't try to listen, but it was difficult to resist. Malaya's voice became more shrill, and the deeper tones that alternated with it were clearly Kai's. His voice wasn't heated like his mother's, but there was a passion behind his rumbles.

"They think I'm an idiot," Gloria said in a matter-of-fact tone. "The whole family thinks I'm an idiot. Did you not pick up on that last night?"

Maddie caught a few of Malaya's words. "Nana says... no business... bad for you!"

"They're fighting over whether I'm more likely to get dumped, get pregnant, get stuck in Costa Rica with a fake passport, or I don't know... maybe stand in the rain with my mouth open until I drown," Gloria speculated. "You know, like a lobotomized chicken. Which are you betting on?"

Malaya screeched louder. "You are *not* going to say anything!"

Gloria and Maddie looked at each other. Then they looked at the wall of the house. Gloria banged on it with a fist. "Yo!" she shouted. "We can *hear* you, geniuses!"

The sounds in the house went quiet, and Gloria rolled her eyes again. "And they think *I'm* an idiot."

Everything went silent for a moment. Even the breeze stopped. A few birds chirped. In the distance Maddie heard some slow-moving traffic and a child playing. But she suspected that all their nearest neighbors had gone quiet in order to hear the rest of the exchange.

The noise that struck her loudest was her own pulse pounding in her ears. Gloria seemed certain that her own adolescent drama was the cause of all the fireworks, and Maddie had no reason to think otherwise.

And yet.

The front door banged open and closed. A second later Kai appeared around the corner of the house. "There you are," he said to Maddie pleasantly, though the faint sheen of sweat on his forehead betrayed his recent angst. "You ready to go?"

"I am," Maddie said with equally fake cheer. "But we have to wait for Gloria to change. She's decided to go with us."

Kai's face brightened instantly. "Really?" he replied, smiling at his sister. "Awesome!"

Maddie held her breath. From the guttural sound Gloria had made when Maddie began her announcement, she was certain the girl was about to refuse. But Kai's enthusiastic response seemed to affect her.

Gloria pushed past Maddie and around Kai. "Just give me a minute," she grumbled, heading for the house.

Maddie beamed.

"How did you do that?" Kai whispered, his brown eyes twinkling. "She's barely even talking to me right now."

Maddie studied him and felt a tug at her heartstrings. Poor guy. She had come to Lana'i this weekend for nothing more than reminiscing and fun in the sun. What had he come for? She wasn't sure, but all he had gotten so far was hit up for free legal advice, shoved around by his erstwhile best friend, mocked and abused by his baby sister, and now yelled at by his mother. Sheesh.

"Don't take it personally, Nakama," Maddie chided with a smile. "Teenagers always strike out at the ones they love best. I ought to know. I did it myself." She shrugged her pack off her shoulders and pulled out her hat and sunglasses. "Now, what's on our agenda for this morning? Are you going to spear me a fish?"

Kai grinned, and Maddie noted again what a looker he'd grown into. He was wearing a tank shirt that showed his shoulders, and he definitely wasn't "shrimpy" anymore. "There's no spearfishing allowed at Hulopo'e. It's a conservation zone." He looked at her sharply. "Which you should know full well, Dr. Ecologist person."

Maddie laughed out loud. "Didn't stop you when you were eight."

"I got away with a lot of things when I was eight," he replied smugly. "You want to spearfish, I'll take you to Red Tank sometime."

Maddie felt a jolt of elation. *Sometime.* This weekend was only one weekend. She would be back another time, and so would he. The possibilities were endless.

All her questions and doubts and paranoia of the morning disappeared in an instant, and she was suddenly so excited she couldn't stand it. *She and Kai were going to the beach!*

It took ages for Gloria to reappear. It took forever before the truck left the city behind, and it took an eternity to cross the old pineapple fields. Maddie's feet fidgeted on the floorboards the whole way, and when at last they began their descent to the beach on the southern edge of the island, her hand fixed itself to the door handle.

"I hope you're planning to wait to open that until we actually stop," Kai teased.

"We'll see," Maddie mumbled. "Why does everybody drive so damn *slow* around here?"

Gloria hooted.

"Maybe we should go golfing instead," Kai teased.

Maddie narrowed her eyes at him. She hated golfing. Although Lana'i was famous for its two excellent upscale courses, it also had a very nice public course, which was free. Like most kids, she had given the sport a shot, but found its required brute-strength-to-finesse ratio not to be in her favor. The first time she swung a club she had hit the ground and dug up a giant clod of dirt. The second time she had swung high and accidentally let go, whereupon her club had winged its way into a tree and knocked off a coconut. Kai had laughed so hard he'd had stomach pains.

"I'll need a hardhat, though," he continued wryly.

"Yuck it up," Maddie retorted as they pulled into the beach lot. "Just for that, Nakama, I'm not waiting on you."

Kai chuckled as he shifted the truck into park.

Maddie jumped out and headed for the water.

Chapter 15

There it was. Her ocean. Her beautiful, beautiful bay!

The weather could not be more perfect. The temperature was somewhere in the seventies, with a mild, equally warm breeze. The sky was cerulean blue; the only clouds remaining now were puffy white and widely scattered. The sandy beach stretched out in a u-shape around the bay, one arm of which led to the sprawling luxury of the Resort at Manele Bay, the other arm of which was alive with coral reefs and bordered by sheer cliffs of volcanic rock. The water within the bay sparkled as blue as the sky, and rolling waves broke gently on its shore, the fury of the churning ocean beyond having been blunted by the bay's loose confines. Cradled in the center of the beach were the sunbathing, picnicking, and camping areas, which were playing host this Saturday morning to a few dozen assorted locals and tourists. And in the center of them all stood Madalyn Westover.

She kicked off her shoes by a tree, dropped her pack, and started running.

The warm sand squished between her toes, and she giggled in delight as the dry ground first turned wet, then the cool sensation of frothy ocean water splashed around her ankles.

Yes!

Maddie kept going. The crashing waves overwhelmed her calves, her knees, her thighs. Just as it covered her waistline, she threw her hands out in front of her and plunged underwater.

Bliss.

The world transformed into a cool, heavy paradise. She moved instinctively past the chaos of the tumbling shorebreak, and her watery world went silent. Her hair floated around her; her limbs felt light. If only she had a decent mask or goggles, she could probably see a zillion fish.

She pulled her head up out of the water, opened her eyes, and tasted the salt on her lips. The water she had reached was around chest deep. She lifted her feet and treaded water with her arms. The feel of the bay was just as she remembered it. Coolish, but pleasantly so. The waves lifted and dropped her in a gentle rhythm.

Her annoying shirt billowed around her like a balloon. She flattened
it. Someday she would find a swim shirt that could breathe, but wasn't
see-through. Right now this was the best she had. Wearing it over an
industrial-strength running bra with a pair of women's boardshorts, she
could almost swim in comfort without attracting attention. She cast a
glance back at the beach to see Kai and Gloria stripping off their own
shirts.

Lucky dogs.

A bright yellow fish caught her eye, and she watched it from above
the water, following it among the rolling waves. She had always liked
watching the yellow ones. She'd gotten angry if Kai had tried to spear
one.

Maddie's spirits were so high she practically giggled as she half
walked, half swam around in pursuit of the bright yellow tang. It led
her on a merry chase — or perhaps, it and a few of its identical friends
did — until she found herself near the east side of the bay, within
earshot of a young couple who were wading in the shallows with a
baby.

They were speaking quietly to each other in Pidgin, and they took
no notice of Maddie as she continued to stroll about, staring at various
fish. Maddie had been working on her Pidgin all week, trying to
eavesdrop whenever she could, getting used to the rhythm of it again.
It wasn't coming along as quickly as she would like, but her
comprehension was improving. The woman spoke too fast for her to
follow much, but the man seemed to be a natural slow-talker, which
helped. They had mainly been talking about the baby, and about how
early some people were teaching their babies to swim.

Maddie tried not to grin as she pretended not to listen. There was
something about Pidgin that made outsiders think whatever comments
they couldn't understand must necessarily be crass or rude. Pidgin
could be crass *and* rude, but it could also be anything else anyone
wanted to say. It was no different from any other language whose sole
purpose was social communication. In this case, communication about
what awful parents such-and-such neighbors were because they fed
their four-month-old baby ice cream from a spoon.

Maddie's eyes strayed back to the beach. Why hadn't Gloria and Kai
joined her yet? Surely they weren't just going to stand around all
morning?

She spotted them and understood the delay. They had met up with
friends. The tallest one looked like Kenny Nakama, but she didn't

recognize either of the other two guys, at least not from this distance. She dropped her gaze back down to look for another yellow fish. Whoever the newcomers were, if they wanted to say hello to her, they could come in the water.

She was busy.

"Riku..."

Maddie stiffened. The couple with the baby had seen the same group of people on the beach, and now they were talking about Kai's cousin. Keeping her head down, Maddie moved slightly closer. She couldn't catch much from the woman, but she did note her use of the word *lolo*, which meant foolish or crazy and which appeared to be lobbed at Riku's AWOL wife. But the man's words were clearer, and they made Maddie smile. Loosely translated, his response to the woman's spiel was, "Kai Nakama will help him. He's smart as they come, and he's a good guy. The best."

Maddie was still smiling as she moved off down the beach out of earshot, her conscience having finally caught up to her. Listening in on random conversations between strangers on Maui was one thing, but sooner or later, here on Lana'i, she would get herself into trouble. For all she knew, she could run into this very couple over at Nana's this afternoon.

She waded into knee-high water and turned to look for dolphins at the mouth of the bay. They weren't terribly hard to spot if they were in the mood to play — spinner dolphins were born acrobats and loved to leap. But even if they weren't feeling quite so frisky, they showed their presence with random little spouts and splashes and the occasional dark back or fin arcing out of the water. Maddie stared hard, but could see no activity. The dolphins traveled in pods; either they were around or they weren't.

"Looking for whales?"

Maddie sighed to herself. She did not need to lower her eyes from the horizon to know that the voice she heard had most likely come from the same middle-aged man who'd been circling her like a great white shark ever since she hit the water. She'd been hoping he was one of the "admire from afar" types who wouldn't actually approach her. Or perhaps he had a woman waiting for him on the beach somewhere already, but was merely bored. At least the latter was still possible.

Realizing that her shirt was plastered to her torso, she made as subtle an effort as possible to grab the hem and release it with a shake. *Drat.* She'd lost her ponytail band as well. "No whales, no dolphins," she replied in a practiced tone. Not rude, but not overly friendly, either. If the man really did want to talk, as opposed to flirt, he should be open to academic conversation. "But the coral reefs here are lovely. You can see tangs and parrotfish even without snorkeling gear."

"Are you a model?"

Maddie gave up. She was trying to decide whether to exit the conversation via land or water when she realized that Kai and the others had begun to walk toward her. She smiled broadly. "Yo, guys!" she called loudly, waving a hand above her head. "You going to get wet, or what?"

Kai smiled and waved back to her, as did Kenny. She still didn't recognize the other two men, although she noticed that Gloria was tagging along closely with the skinnier of the two. The other guy was quite heavy. All were in their twenties. Maddie looked over her shoulder and chuckled to herself as "great white" melted back into the ocean.

Maddie waded deeper into the water, deciding to make the crowd come to her. As they neared, the heavier of the two new guys began to look familiar.

"Yo, Maddie!" Kenny cried loudly, flinging himself into the waves so as to create the largest, messiest splash possible. He always had been a goofball. "What happened to your haole friend?"

"He was scared of you," Maddie said with a grin. "But not of me. Imagine that."

Kenny laughed. "Fool! I'm afraid of you!"

"Thank you," Maddie replied.

The others soon joined them in the water. "You remember Sam?" Kenny asked, nodding his head to the heavy guy.

Maddie turned and looked closer. "Sammy?"

Holy crap! The boy had practically been her nemesis. He was the only kid her age who had been both taller and bulkier than she was, and he had always despised her. He'd started on day one giving her the typical "haole girl" grief, but unlike most of the others, he'd never let up. The two of them had never actually rolled around in the dirt trading punches, but she never doubted for a moment that he would like to, if circumstances were different. But besides her own strength and tendency to fight dirty, Maddie had one thing going for her that Sammy couldn't get around. Too many of his guy friends, including Kai and Kenny, liked her just fine.

"You're in trouble now, brah!" Kenny squealed. "She does

remember you!"

Maddie watched in shock as the once-jeering face before her cringed with embarrassment. "Aw, man," he said sheepishly, unable to meet her eyes.

Are you freakin' kidding me? Maddie did a double take. Yes, it was the same Sammy. Fifteen years later he'd wound up exactly the same height as she was. But while she had slimmed down, he'd packed on the pounds till his face was hardly recognizable. Even less recognizable was his attitude. Sheepish? Shy? Sammy?

"Why's he in trouble?" Gloria piped up suddenly. She had been hanging back looking bored, but now her interest was piqued. "What did he do?"

Kenny merely laughed. The last unknown member of the group, who looked a lot like Kenny and who Maddie suspected was his younger brother, looked as confused as Gloria.

"I was kind of an ass," Sammy said in a low voice, still hanging his head. He couldn't seem to look at her, but the ghost of a smile on his face made him look childishly hopeful. "Sorry about that."

Maddie could swear the guy was sincere. She threw a "what the hell?" look at Kai, who had been standing silently in the water throughout the exchange, and he lifted his shoulders with a shrug. Kai had always been big on wordless shrugs, and as Maddie stood there watching him it occurred to her that despite a fifteen-year hiatus she could read his body language as easily as the day she had left Lana'i. Which, if you thought about it, was pretty darn cool. Translation: *Seems legit to me.*

Maddie felt an urge to shake herself. The scene was surreal. Here she was, standing chest deep in beautiful Hulopo'e Bay with a blue sky above, a balmy breeze ruffling her hair, her oldest and once-dearest friend back at her side, and yellow tangs darting around her legs — and Sammy "the cyclone" Santos was apologizing to her for being an ass.

Life didn't get any better than this.

"Apology accepted," she said with a smile.

Sammy's brown eyes twinkled as he responded with something halfway between a grin and a smirk.

"Group hug!" Kenny yelled.

Maddie dove underwater. She reemerged a few feet away between Gloria and the new guy, who nodded at her and introduced himself. He looked older than Gloria, but still several years younger than Kenny or herself. "I'm Dan. Kenny's brother. You wouldn't remember me, but I kind of remember you."

"He says you were a beast on the Tarzan trees," Gloria chipped in.

The older guys all laughed, and Maddie grinned smugly. "I," she proclaimed, looking back at them, "was the undisputed *king* of the Tarzan trees, and don't any of you losers forget it!"

The guys all cracked up again, and Kenny bowed with his arms extended in homage. The "Tarzan trees" were banyan trees covered with long, strong vines that had grown on the hill behind the historic Hotel Lana'i, at the opposite end of the park from the school. At least, most of the vines had been strong — strong enough to let a grade-schooler swing a good distance without falling and breaking something. When it worked, it was tremendous fun, and Maddie had loved it. The old men told her they could hear her Tarzan yells from all the way down on the bench. She was always Tarzan. Woe be unto anyone who called her Jane.

"She *was* a beast, man," Kenny continued playfully, talking to his brother. "Not just on the trees, either. She nearly threw me off the cliff into Shark's Cove one time."

"Oh, I did not," Maddie argued. "You were always nearly falling off of cliffs."

"So were you!" Kenny argued back.

"It's a miracle either one of you lived to adulthood," Kai said wryly.

"Who's an adult?" Kenny teased, splashing him.

"Good point," Kai returned.

"Hey," Sammy said to Kai, "I haven't seen you out here since forever, man. You going to catch us some fish?"

"Yeah, man!" Kenny agreed. "We'll have us a barbecue, just like old times!"

Maddie's heart leapt with joy at the mere mention. They used to build the most wonderful cooking fires, made with sticks gathered from the nearby mesquite trees. The alternately raw or charred fish was never that great, but she loved the smell of the smoke. And the thrill of being able to fend for themselves for the day. Or rather — letting Kai fend for them.

"Hey," Kai protested lightly, "if you people haven't learned how to feed yourselves by now, it's not my problem!"

Kenny laughed. "Aw, but you were so good at fishing, brah!"

Maddie treaded water and enjoyed the irony as a particularly large parrotfish swam a few feet behind Kenny and Sam without their noticing. They'd been every bit as lousy at spearfishing as she had been.

Too restless, too loud, too impatient. It was always Kai who'd been the master. They would hitch a ride to the beach on a Saturday morning, sometimes just her and Kai, sometimes a half dozen kids or more, and everybody else would splash around and goof off while Kai caught enough lunch for everybody. They weren't supposed to spearfish in the reserve, of course, but as local children with every intention of consuming their spoils they felt entitled to an exemption, and no one ever bothered them about it. Maddie herself preferred to hunt for the local variety of lobster, which conveniently had no pincers and required more quickness to catch than patience. She rarely caught sight of one, however, no doubt because the creatures weren't dumb enough to show themselves in her obvious presence.

"Maybe we could sneak into the pool!" Sammy jested.

They all laughed, including Maddie, even as the memory gave her a sharp pang of melancholy. She shot a glance at Kai, knowing that the memory bothered him too, although for a different reason. Kai had always been both naturally cautious and a deep thinker, and whenever he disapproved of something the other kids were doing — like when Maddie attempted a particularly stupid leap off the Tarzan trees — she always knew, even if he didn't say anything. She knew because he got a tiny furrow right between his eyebrows.

He had it now. Even as he smiled.

Kai had *never* wanted to sneak into the pool.

The resort had been sold and completely remodeled since they were kids, and Maddie was sure the pool was magnificent now, but even back then, it was a thing of beauty. So pristine and clear... such a fabulous fantasy of a play place... and with such a view! Of course no child could resist it. Of course it was reserved for guests only. And of course that didn't stop any of them.

Except Kai.

Kai, much to Maddie's annoyance, had always been the moral compass of the universe. He didn't see why they wanted to sneak in the pool and risk the embarrassment of getting publicly thrown out when the ocean was... well, *the ocean*. He thought they were being stupid and he wanted no part in it, and no amount of peer pressure could make him change his mind. Kai could reason away the no-fishing sign, and he even turned a blind eye when the other kids sneaked toilet paper out of the restrooms to help kindle their cooking fire, but he would *not* sneak into the pool.

So Maddie had sneaked in without him. Many times. And in all those years of keeping watch and laughing and screaming and making quick retreats and dodging close calls, they had only technically gotten caught once. That was the time the manager on duty had locked all the gates before calling them out one by one and threatening to fine their parents if he ever caught them there again. It was also one of the most mortifying days of Maddie's life. Because while every other kid in the group had gotten yelled at and thrown out, the manager had looked Maddie right in the eyes — and then looked the other way. And it wasn't because her father worked for the resort. All of them had parents who worked for the resort. He had let her stay in the pool because she was a haole.

Maddie's gaze found Sammy's. He'd been a spiteful little jerk, but that didn't mean his resentment of her was entirely without cause. As his dark eyes looked back at hers without any strong sentiment one way or the other — except, perhaps, the usual involuntary male appreciation — she appreciated his willingness to forget the childhood baggage and move on. "Nah," she said loudly, smiling back at him. "Screw the pool. The ocean's better. I miss my waves." She picked her feet up again, drew in a full breath, and floated on her back.

She looked up, watching the occasional fluff of cloud move across the sky. Ocean water covered her ears on and off as her head bobbed, blurring the words of the others' conversation into muted blips. For several long, blissful moments, Maddie felt as if time were standing still. She was back on the islands and back in the ocean doing nothing more than enjoying life and the planet. She had a group of friends to enjoy it with, and her best bud Kai was at her side. She was officially at one with the universe. She had come full circle; she was a kid again. Life was good.

"Yo, Maddie!"

Kenny's call jerked her rudely back to reality. She turned to find all four guys staring with various levels of surreptitiousness at her chest, which by necessity when floating on one's back was visible above the surface.

Crap. So much for being a kid again.

Maddie put her feet down and stood up. "What?"

"Sammy wants to know why you came back to Lana'i now, after you'd been gone so long. Like, did you really just show up, without even, like, talking to Nana or anybody at all since you left?"

Maddie resisted an urge to look at Kai. She had to stop blaming his non-response to her letter for her own failure to keep in contact with anyone else. She should have pressed her father harder, made her grandparents understand that it wasn't just her friends at school that she was missing. Instead she had accepted vague redirections like "you need to concentrate on making new friends here."

Why couldn't she explain herself back then? Surely her father must have understood, even if her grandparents did not, that her feelings for her second family could not just be erased. Nana had *raised* her, dammit!

"Maddie!" Kenny prompted again, splashing her in the face.

She splashed him back with twice the volume. "I just showed up," she answered. "I thought it would be more fun to freak everybody out. Worked on you."

Kenny cackled, and in her peripheral vision, Maddie noticed Gloria grinning at Kai, though there was nothing about Kai's neutral expression that would seem to warrant it.

"Besides," Maddie continued lightly, suspicious that she was missing something, "it's fun going around incognito, eavesdropping on people who think I can't understand Pidgin."

"Nah, man!" Kenny protested good-naturedly. "That's not right."

Maddie smirked, having no intention of confessing her loss of skill. She had always liked Kenny, but she had never completely trusted him. He was a good-hearted soul overall, but he lacked something in the empathy department, as evidenced by his shameless flirting with Maddie despite the existence of an almost-fiance somewhere.

"I can't get away with it forever, though," Maddie laughed, thinking of the couple with the baby and how likely she was to meet up with them again. "I keep forgetting how small Lana'i City is. Twice now I've stopped and stared at my old house, and of course the people living there now have no idea who I am and think I'm some psycho stalker tourist. And you know some day Nana's bound to introduce us!"

"You went back to your house?" Sammy asked incredulously.

Maddie stared at him. As little as he'd said to her so far, this seemed like an odd time to jump in. "Well, sure. Why not?"

His dark eyes widened. He blinked at her. "Well, it's just, I mean... I'm surprised you'd want to, that's all. After what happened with your mother and everything."

Maddie was confused. Her mother?

Of course her mother's death at such a young age was a tragedy. But what did that have to do with Maddie's memories of her childhood home?

Kenny had gone oddly quiet. So had Dan and Gloria. Maddie shot a questioning look at Kai.

He looked horrified.

Chapter 16

Maddie was baffled. "Oh," she said finally. "You mean, because she died there?"

The temperature of the ocean seemed to have dropped a few degrees. All of the others stood stone-faced. As if they were afraid to speak. Afraid, even, to move.

Maddie struggled to clarify. "I guess I can see why you'd think it would be upsetting, but I don't have any memories of... that particular event. The memories I have of my mother in our house are all happy ones."

She felt guilty as she said it. And feeling guilty annoyed her, because what she said was true. They *were* happy memories. Maybe there weren't as many of them as she would like, but she didn't have any bad ones either. Did she?

She checked her memory. No, she did not. Jill Westover had never raised her voice to her daughter, much less been abusive in any way. She was always sweet and smiling.

Why the hell *wouldn't* Maddie want to go back and see their house again?

A sudden spurt of fear shot through her. Both as a child and as an adolescent she had worried that there was something wrong with her, that she must have some innate deficiency if her mother's loss hadn't torn a deeper wound. Perhaps if she had felt the kind of pain she was supposed to have felt then, she wouldn't be able to look at the family's house now without falling apart. Is that what Sammy meant?

"Hey," Kai interrupted smoothly, "did they ever find out how that fire started behind the house on Kamoku Street? Was it arson?"

"No, man!" Kenny's brother Dan answered enthusiastically. "It was the baby!"

"The baby?" Kai repeated.

"A two-year-old!" Dan explained. "They didn't think he could strike a match or anything, but he'd been watching TV, and he did the thing with the magnifying glass, you know? And the grass was dry, and poof! Lucky he ran away and nobody got hurt, but can you believe that, man? Burned the whole yard up! Nobody could believe it, but they found the glass and..."

Maddie's mind wandered. Nana had told her all about the fire already. Kai was behind the times.

Various uncomfortable thoughts refused to settle as the group's conversation drifted, and she found her participation dwindling. When the topic turned to people she didn't know, she excused herself and walked up the beach to the restroom.

When she emerged from the remodeled — and amazingly plush — public bathroom, she did not return to the ocean, but instead got a drink of water, pulled her phone out of her bag, and wandered into a nearby grove of trees. She leaned against one of them, closed her eyes, and smelled the breeze.

Saltwater. Pines. Red dirt. Maybe just a touch of diesel exhaust — but that would be gone in a minute. She needed to think. She had been hearing, seeing, and feeling all sorts of vaguely disturbing things ever since she returned to the island, and she had been willfully ignoring all of them. But the cumulative total was getting to her.

She needed to talk to her dad.

Maddie looked down at her phone and was relieved to see four bars. Lana'i City was well covered, but the rest of the island was spotty. She was lucky here only because the resort was close. She tapped on her father's number and put the phone to her ear.

After three rings, a woman's voice answered. "Maddie, honey?"

It was her stepmother. "Hi, Lisa."

"Hey there! Your dad's driving, but we'll be getting where we're going in a minute. How are you? Is everything okay?"

Maddie felt herself tense. The words could easily be taken as idle greeting from a concerned parent whose daughter has just moved thousands of miles away. But there was more to Lisa's words than that. Maddie could hear it in her tone. Her stepmother was genuinely worried.

Why would she be?

"Everything is fine," Maddie replied, albeit without her usual cheer.

"Obviously not," Lisa countered. Maddie could hear a hand covering the phone, then a muffled, "Pull over, Bill."

Maddie got a sick feeling in her stomach again.

"What's up, honey?" Lisa continued.

Maddie stifled a sudden urge to cry. Lisa's motherly concern had always had that effect on her. "There's nothing *wrong* wrong," Maddie insisted. "Things have been going great, actually. I'm back on Lana'i again right now. I went to surprise Kai at his office like I said I was going to, and we really hit it off again, just like old times. He loaned me some money for the ferry so we could come back for the weekend, and at this very moment, we're at the beach."

"Well, that sounds delightful!" Lisa enthused. But her chipper Southern accent couldn't hide her angst from Maddie's practiced ears.

"But the thing is," Maddie began, "I'm picking up on something, and I don't know what to make of it. Something about Mom. And I just want to know if—"

"Hang on, honey," Lisa interrupted. "Here's your dad."

"Hello, Mads!" Bill's loud voice boomed into her ear. "You still having a good time?"

Maddie blew out a small breath of frustration. Her father's unstoppable good humor had always made him a joy to be around. It also made him extremely difficult to talk with about anything more serious than a shortage of laundry detergent.

"I am having a good time," Maddie answered. "But I need to ask you something."

"Oh?" he replied, managing to infuse the single syllable with an overtone of reluctance.

"I know I was a difficult child, in a lot of ways," she forced out quickly. "But I'm getting the idea that Mom might have been a bit, well... neglectful, maybe? Was that true?"

She heard a pause. Then, uneasy laughter.

"Oh, Mads! That's hardly fair. You were a little tornado — that's what your mom used to call you, her 'little tornado!' Nobody could keep your hair tidy and you got dirty the second you walked out the door. Your grandmother couldn't do a thing with you, either. Lisa had better luck, but you were older, then. You never gave a hoot what you looked like, not until you started wanting a little more attention from the boys. Isn't that right, babe?" He laughed again.

Maddie did not hear Lisa laughing with him.

Her mind swam with confusion. Everything he said sounded perfectly reasonable. At no time while she was living on Lana'i had she cared one whit what she looked like. And after her mother had died and Maddie had gone back to Ohio, she had pitched a fit when her grandmother tried to brush her hair. But that was because Grandma hadn't known how to do it without pulling. Grandma meant well during those months, but she had no idea how to take care of a distraught little girl. The poor woman was out of practice, and she had only raised boys, besides.

If Lisa wasn't laughing over Maddie's previous tendency for dishevelment, it was because the story she told had always been a little different. Lisa had noticed Maddie tagging along with her father to the state resort offices over that first summer and, knowing something of the family's recent tragedy, had gone out on a limb and offered to help her boss by taking his daughter shopping for the new school year. Apparently Maddie's wardrobe at the time consisted partly of what she had brought from Lana'i and partly of what her grandmother had allowed her to pick out at the Goodwill store in Ohio, since which time Maddie had grown at least an inch. And Lisa, understanding all too well the nature of sixth-grade girls at the Paducah Middle School, could not in good conscience allow that coming apocalypse. Although others accused Lisa of using Maddie to cozy up to Bill, she insisted — and Maddie believed her — that the opposite was true. Lisa hadn't been interested in Bill at first precisely because she was so annoyed by his disregard for Maddie's social wellbeing. Only later did Lisa realize he wasn't uncaring so much as blind.

Blind.

Maddie had to wonder.

"Dad, just listen to me, okay?" she said earnestly. "I'm getting strange vibes from some of the people here, and I don't understand them. I only have happy memories of Lana'i. Of Mom. Of the house. And... it keeps seeming like this surprises people. Like they would expect me not to."

She paused a moment.

Silence.

"Dad?"

"Yeah?"

More silence. Her pulse pounded.

"Well, what do you make of that?" she tried again. "I mean, I was *there.* I know Mom was never abusive or anything. But do you think maybe some people here might have a different impression for some reason?"

"Um..." Maddie heard a scratching sound. She could picture him fussing with his beard. He was nervous and trying to think of what to say. "Yeah, that could be. You know how gossip gets going in small towns."

"But it would be just gossip, wouldn't it?" Maddie pressed. "Mom never got, like... really angry with me, or violent—"

"God, no!" Bill protested hotly. "Mads, you have to remember your mother better than that! She was the sweetest, gentlest thing! Don't you remember how she used to smile so pretty... whenever you brought her flowers..."

Without warning, his voice cracked. For several seconds all Maddie could hear were muffled sounds.

She closed her eyes and exhaled with frustration. Her father was a mountain of a man physically, and a tower of strength in many ways. But he had always been a crier.

"Dad?" she called quietly after a moment. "Dad? Are you there?"

"Maddie, hun," Lisa's voice returned softly, "It's me. Can your Daddy call you back in a bit?"

Maddie hesitated. She doubted there was much point. It made no sense that she would remember her own childhood wrong, but it made plenty of sense that gossip would spread about the family after her mother's unexpected death and their precipitous departure. "Never mind," Maddie assured. "I don't want to torture him if he doesn't want to talk about it. It's just that he never wants to talk about Mom. Or Lana'i."

"No," Lisa agreed soberly. "He doesn't. But that doesn't mean he shouldn't. Not if you want to. He'll call you back tonight. I'll make sure of it."

Maddie didn't answer. She wasn't sure she did want to talk to him anymore, at least not about Lana'i. The family's time here couldn't have left them with more radically different feelings about the island. To her, Lana'i was sunshine and ocean and warmth and laughter. To him, it meant sadness and heartache. Maddie was hoping that he and Lisa would come to visit her on Maui at some point. But she knew that he would never return to Lana'i.

"How long will you be there before you go back to Maui?" Lisa asked.

"We're taking the late ferry out on Sunday," Maddie answered, thinking even as she spoke that she was wasting valuable seconds at one of her favorite places in the world. "But I'll probably come back as many weekends as I can. I love it here." She lightened her voice, insisted that she was perfectly fine and that her worries were undoubtedly nonsense, apologized again for upsetting her father, and wrapped up the conversation.

She turned off the phone and smiled to herself. Despite the drama of the call, she did feel a little better. Until she took her first steps back toward the beach.

"Hel-lo," said the great white shark, stepping out from behind the tree against which he'd been leaning. "Did you lose your friends?"

"Only temporarily," Maddie assured. Although, at a glance, she could no longer see any of them.

"No offense to them," he continued politely, "but how would you like to join me for dinner at the resort tonight? Just you and me." He flashed her an orthodontically perfected smile, then blew a breath on his sunglasses to wipe out a smudge with the corner of his Hawaiian silk shirt. "I hear the desserts are incredible."

Maddie had wasted enough time on this particular individual. "No thanks," she replied with a half smile, walking away.

But he wouldn't let it go. "Wait!" He rushed up to her side, grabbed her by the wrist, and leaned close to growl into her ear. "What do you want? Just tell me."

Maddie stopped walking. How she hated having to do this! She flicked her wrist quickly and violently, twisting herself away. Then she turned and faced the man down. *"Don't. Touch. Me,"* she ordered, her voice a deathly whisper.

She became aware of someone standing fairly close to them. Someone small. She hoped it wasn't a child. Her gaze remained locked on her pursuer. *Please, you damned idiot. Just go away!*

The man glared back at her, his eyes fiery with rage. It always happened that way when they rejected her "polite no" and forced her to use a "hell no" instead — they got angry at *her* for humiliating them.

She really hated when it got this far.

She tried hard to keep her gaze level and cool, not at all challenging or baiting — if she could manage it. It wouldn't do for him to see what she was really thinking.

We have an audience, moron! Be a man. Go away.

The person standing near them stepped up close to Maddie. Gloria swung around to face the man and flashed him her most innocent smile. "Hey there!" she said cheerfully. And very, *very* loudly. "Haven't we met? I think I babysat your kids at the resort earlier!"

Maddie watched, and tried not to laugh, as the crimson anger in the man's face dissolved into a dull puce of embarrassed confusion.

"Um..." he mumbled uncertainly. "I don't... think so. Well... Later." He cast a last, disappointed glance at Maddie. Then he whirled and walked away.

Gloria turned to Maddie with a smirk. "You know, you can tell the ones who actually *have* a wife and kids by how long they hesitate. It's pretty hysterical, really. They can't seem to decide whether I'm serious or not, even though you think they'd remember if they'd actually met a babysitter!" She cackled with laughter.

Maddie laughed with her. "Thanks. You use that line often?"

Gloria nodded. "The older girls are always getting hit on. Not me so much. I look like jail bait. But that makes me good for 'protection.'" She chuckled again, then looked at Maddie sympathetically. "Didn't you already ditch that guy once?"

Maddie started walking back toward the water. "Yep."

"That's crazy. And you're wearing that... well, *that!* Don't you ever wear a real swimsuit? I mean, what would happen if you did?"

Maddie's eyes scoured the ocean. She didn't see any of the guys. Where were they? "I don't wear swimsuits."

"Seriously? Like, ever?"

"Nope," Maddie confirmed, ready to change the subject. "Where did everyone go?"

"I'm here," Kai said from behind her.

Maddie turned to find him walking up alone.

"The others had to leave," he explained. "Sammy's got work, and Kenny was driving him. We saw you talking on your phone earlier. They said to say goodbye."

"So, you've *never* worn a bikini?" Gloria continued incredulously, oblivious to her brother's arrival.

Maddie squelched a strong desire to throw Gloria in the ocean. Only seconds ago, she had wanted to hug her. "Can we talk about something else?"

"Do you ever wear, like, camis and tank tops and stuff?" Gloria pressed.

"Why don't we walk up to Pu'u Pehe?" Kai suggested. "Have lunch up there?"

"Sounds fab," Maddie agreed quickly.

"But seriously," Gloria insisted. "What's the worst that could happen? In a public place?"

Kai groaned. "Gloria, will you—"

"That question, I'll answer," Maddie said sharply, turning to face his little sister. Sheesh, one minute the girl seemed thirty years old, the next she seemed about twelve. Maddie planted her hands squarely on her hips and fixed Gloria in the eyes. "How about my getting arrested for assault?"

Chapter 17

Kai tried not to look as thunderstruck as he felt. He wasn't sure how much more he could take. It wasn't even noon yet, and the day had already produced an endless stream of bizarre events that seemed specifically designed to stress him the hell out.

It was working beautifully.

"Please tell me you're joking," he said to Maddie, his voice demanding. She *had* to be joking. Never in a million years would he admit how irked he had been when she plunged into the water in that pathetic getup. Women's board shorts? Seriously? Who even manufactured such a thing? And she wouldn't even take her shirt off? In the ocean?

He realized he had no rational right whatsoever to be disappointed, particularly given her crystal-clear signals regarding the nature of their relationship. It was none of his business what she was wearing underneath that dripping wet shirt and what she would look like in a perfectly decent, normal swimsuit that showed a healthy amount of upper thigh. She didn't owe him or any other man on that beach a peek at a damn thing.

He didn't care. He was still disappointed.

And the fact that she might have a valid reason for ruining all his perfectly innocent fun irked him all the more.

"I am not joking," Maddie replied in complete seriousness. She located her pack, picked it up, and slipped on her sandals. Kai and Gloria followed in silence. "I am exaggerating," she admitted as they all moved off towards the trailhead. "But only slightly."

"Well, you have to tell us now!" Gloria pestered, walking close by her side. Kai followed a pace behind.

Maddie sighed. "Fine. It happened a couple years ago, when I was at a hotel in downtown Atlanta for an ecology conference. The last night, one of the other grad students and I decided to go out and have a nice dinner somewhere, just for fun. So I dressed up. Nothing excessive, just your standard little black dress and some makeup. But then he met a guy he was interested in, so I came back alone. No big deal. I hadn't been drinking; we just said goodnight and I took a cab. Everything was perfectly fine until I got into the elevator at the hotel. Just as the doors were closing, some man stumbles up and pulls them open again. He's falling down drunk, of course."

She rolled her eyes in disgust, and Kai found his core temperature climbing. Feeling protective of Maddie was indeed second nature to him.

"So at first he was too drunk to even notice me," she continued as they started up the trail through the trees beside the beach. "His eyes weren't focused. He forgot to push a button. He just leaned against the far wall looking seasick. He was obviously a businessman, in his late forties maybe, wearing a tailored suit. I thought about getting out and taking another elevator, but he looked pretty harmless, so I just ignored him."

The trail angled up sharply as they climbed along the volcanic rock ledge that formed the east end of the bay. Down and to their right, the lava rocks swept out to sea in a variety of elaborate curls, creating a series of smaller pools whose depth varied with the tide. Concrete steps led down to one particularly appealing, protected *keiki* pool where many Lana'ian toddlers, including Kai himself, had first learned to swim.

"We'd gone up maybe three floors out of twenty-something when I realized he was looking at me," Maddie continued. "He gave no more warning than that. He didn't say a word. The next thing I knew, he had launched himself across the elevator and was crushing me against the wall, groping me and pulling at my dress."

Kai felt fine drops of sweat break out on his forehead. He must also have made some sort of noise, because Maddie glanced over her shoulder at him. He wiped his face of emotion as quickly as possible and blinked back at her.

"So," Gloria prompted, her own voice furious with contempt. "What did you do? Me, I'd *bus' hees ala-alas!*"

Maddie smirked. Kai wasn't sure how much Pidgin she could remember, but the meaning of that particular phrase wasn't hard to guess. "It really wasn't necessary," she said calmly. "My response is always the same: do whatever I have to do to get the guy off me, then exit the situation. In this case, though, there was a complication."

Maddie paused a moment to stop and look at the view. Kai knew how much she loved this place. Here, the red dirt and scrubby tufts of grass that were usually under their feet met the swirling volcanic rock that separated the earth from the ocean. From this height they could see all the way across Hulopo'e Bay, past the sprawling resort on its opposite shore and up the far hill to the new and mysterious private construction beyond. At the mouth of the bay, a reef break created striking lines of pure white spray that fell upon the dark blue water. Straight ahead was the open Pacific.

As fabulous as the view was, Kai couldn't stir himself to look at it. He was focused entirely on Maddie, and on maintaining the necessary facade of calm when he so desperately wanted to break something.

"What complication?" Gloria prompted.

Kai noted with chagrin that the natural beauty surrounding them seemed to have no effect on his little sister, either now or at any other point during the morning. It was a blindness that could happen when you knew nothing else, and he wished he could afford to take her to the mainland in February.

"I gave him one good shove," Maddie said flatly. "That's all it took to get away from him, since he was so drunk he could barely stand. But because he was so drunk, the shove made him fall backward, and when he fell, he hit his head on the handrail on the far side of the elevator."

Kai stifled a low noise in his throat. He did not like where her story was going and he hated that she was reliving it through the telling. But doing so was her choice, and he supposed she was making a point for Gloria's sake.

"My plan was to hit the emergency stop and get out, then report him to the hotel desk," Maddie explained. "I was going to do that regardless, but when he slumped to the floor unconscious, I added a request for medical assistance. I explained everything to the hotel staff, their security guy took a statement, and I went to bed."

She stopped suddenly, bent down to examine some sort of nest in a clump of grass, and then moved on. "Five o'clock the next morning, somebody's banging on my door, yelling 'police.' I barely have time to throw on a shirt before they break the thing down. So I answer it, wearing sleep shorts and a tee and my hair all over the place, and these two men look at me like *I've* got a lot of nerve, showing up to a police interview dressed so inappropriately."

"Oh, that is *so* wrong!" Gloria sympathized.

"So they start right in, asking me all kinds of questions about what happened last night, and I tell them the exact same story, except it's clear they don't believe a word of it. And of course I have no clue why, until finally they decide to tell me. Turns out Mr. Romeo is a high-level exec of some company in Phoenix, and he can't remember a damned thing that happened to him after he and his buds headed to the bar. He regained consciousness at the hospital, was diagnosed with a mild concussion, demanded to see his personal effects, and discovered a couple hundred dollars in cash missing from his wallet. He called the police, the police called hotel security, and their collective genius derived the only possible conclusion — he'd been lured by a prostitute who'd then assaulted him and taken off with his money."

Kai's steps stopped. So did Gloria's.

"Are you freakin' kidding me?" his sister protested. "That's nuts! You were staying in the hotel! You called security yourself! What would make them think you were a prostitute?"

Maddie stopped and turned around. Her perfectly shaped lips drew up into a rueful smile. She looked first at Gloria, then at Kai. For a moment it seemed as if she would say something. Then she seemed to think better of it. She turned around and started walking again.

Gloria swore.

Kai opened his mouth to chastise his sister's word choice, purely out of habit. But no words came out. She was only saying what was on his own mind.

Gloria caught up to Maddie. "What happened?"

"They asked me a bunch more insulting questions, and then they searched my room," Maddie answered. "They seemed pretty surprised to turn up exactly twenty-seven dollars and some change — and nothing stronger than a Tylenol. Still, they were acting like I must be guilty of something. Turns out the businessman in question was not only used to throwing his weight around in Phoenix, but he was pretty well-connected in Atlanta, too. He was respectable, you know. I was just some chick with big boobs."

The slow burn in Kai's gut ratcheted up another notch, and he realized that his sisters were not, in fact, the only women who could stir his ordinarily peaceable soul to thoughts of violence. He stepped up beside Maddie. "They didn't actually charge you with anything, did they?" he demanded.

Her lovely gray eyes looked up at his, not seeming offended so much as curious. Then the corners of her mouth turned up, ever so slightly, into a smile.

A flush of warmth crept over him. He liked all of Maddie's smiles, even the gigantic cheesy ones she used to make when she was teasing him. But this subtle, sly one was his favorite. At least it was now. There was something excitingly intimate about it.

I know what you're thinking, it proclaimed. *You're getting all protective again. You lawyer, you.*

"No," she answered. "But I believe they would have, if it weren't for the camera in the elevator."

Gloria moved in closer, and the three of them stood together for a moment, sheltering their eyes from the red dust as a large gust of wind kicked up from the ocean. They were near enough to the crest of the ridge now that they could see over its other side. Far below them to the east, waves rolled onto the salt and pepper beach of Shark's Cove, and across that body of water another ridge jutted out toward Pu'u Pehe, the Sweetheart Rock.

Kai could not take his eyes off Maddie as the wind lifted her still-wet hair and tousled it about her shoulders. Her locks were tangled with seawater, her shirt was modest and now dry, and she wore absolutely no makeup.

She was the most beautiful creature he'd ever seen.

"There was a camera?" Gloria repeated when the wind died down. "Well, thank God. So, it cleared you?"

Maddie nodded. "They just had to get the head of security in to access the tapes. Once he showed up and took a look, it was obvious what had happened. I'm pretty sure the police got a call to that effect while they were still in my room. They just up and left. With no explanation."

Gloria swore again. This time she did not use the exact words Kai was thinking, but silently, he conceded that hers were better.

"Did they ever apologize to you?" Gloria asked. "Or anything?"

A dark look passed over Maddie's face, and with it, the air surrounding Kai turned colder. "One of them called me, actually," she said. "The younger of the two. He said he wanted to apologize to me." Her voice had changed. Her steady, slightly defiant tone now smacked of despair. "He invited me over to his place for a beer."

Her shoulders shivered. The movement was slight, so slight that only a person watching her closely was likely to notice.

Kai was such a person. Even as his eyes registered the gesture, his memory reminded him of one of the few times he'd seen it before. A group of them had gone on a day hike up into the mountains, and his middle sister had gone with them. Chika had been only seven or so at the time, and she had gotten suddenly and violently sick to her stomach. The episode left Chika so miserable and weak she had dropped down in the woods, seemingly unable to walk. Maddie felt

awful because she had been the one to convince Chika to come, and
Maddie stayed beside her and held her hand, yelling at Kai to run back
for help. He did not, of course, having witnessed such melodrama on
countless occasions before and knowing that Chika would be perfectly
fine in ten minutes. But Maddie had been truly worried that something
horrible had happened. She was miserable because she thought it was
her fault. And her shoulders had been shaking. Just like now.

Kai didn't think. He just reacted. His arm reached out and circled
grown-up Maddie's shoulders, pulling her to his side and giving her a
squeeze. "I'm sorry," he said gently. "No one should have to go
through that."

Only then did he remember his promise to himself not to touch her.
For a second he was paralyzed, afraid he had offended her. But his
fears quickly proved unfounded. Not only did Maddie relax into his
embrace, but for one long and glorious second, she leaned her head
lazily onto his shoulder.

Then she was up again.

Maddie took a couple steps away from them both and faced the
ocean for a moment. Then she summoned up a smile and turned back
to them. "So anyway, Gloria," she said with her usual strong, confident
tone of voice. "That's why when I go to the beach I wear some crap
outfit like this instead of a swimsuit. There are jerks everywhere, and
I'm perfectly capable of dealing with them. But I don't invite trouble.
Wearing a bikini would never be worth it to me."

Kai's teeth clenched. So this was the moral of the story? It was her
fault after all?

"I see your point," Gloria said begrudgingly. "But it's not right."

"Nope," Maddie agreed. Then she turned and started walking up
the trail again.

Kai said nothing. It wasn't like he had any business giving the
woman advice. She had lived with the problem since puberty; she had
found a way to deal with it. As long as roaches survived to crawl the
earth, so too would men looking for sex. Those men were going to
notice Maddie, and she was correct that every subconscious message
she sent — the way she dressed, how much makeup she wore, even the
way she moved — would affect their decision on whether to approach
her.

He could see her as a child in his mind's eye, splashing about in the
one navy-colored tank suit she had worn for two years straight when
she first came to island. The suit had started out so big it hung in

wrinkles around her middle and it had wound up so tight it dug red marks into her shoulders. At neither end of the spectrum was it entirely decent, but Maddie could not have cared less, and Kai was certain that if schoolyard law and common decency had permitted, she would have happily chucked the thing and cavorted in the buff. Feeling free and unencumbered — enjoying the world and being real — was a part of Maddie's indomitable spirit.

How indomitable was it now?

Kai's jaws clenched tighter. It wasn't right that Maddie had to hide herself away, that she was forced to feel so self-conscious. *It just wasn't right.*

"Oh, look!" Maddie called out gleefully. "There they are!"

Kai looked out over the rippling blue waters of Shark's Cove to see tiny white blows of spray and glints of sleek dark backs breaking above the surface. The spinner dolphin pod was passing through, and it looked like they were sleeping. The dolphins had the bizarre ability to turn off half their brain and rest, even as the other half allowed them to cruise along at the water's surface, blowing gently and making smooth arcs with their unconscious bodies.

Maddie stopped to watch. To his surprise, Gloria joined her. *Gloria,* who to his knowledge had not expressed enthusiasm over anything so ordinary as a dolphin since the age of five. Kai stopped a pace behind them, but his interest was reserved for Maddie. He could not seem to take his eyes off her.

And that really wasn't good.

He was already having one of the most emotionally insane days of his life. He hadn't gotten to sleep on his parents' too-short couch until the wee hours of the morning, and then he was awakened almost immediately by Gloria trying to sneak the truck keys off the peg by the door. He got the keys and told her they would discuss it with their parents in the morning, but Aki was up in a flash, and then Malaya went wild. Sleeping in had not been possible either, as the early call he'd gotten from Riku had brought such bad news it made his heart sick. Riku's wife had gotten their kids all the way to Idaho, and she was suing for divorce and sole custody. Whatever Kai could do to help his cousin, he was afraid it would not be enough.

And then, there was Maddie. Good God, what was he going to do about her? He had brought her to the island this weekend assuming that she and the family could work everything out, that surely his mother had misunderstood somehow and that Maddie wasn't really *that* clueless.

Evidently, he had been wrong. What Maddie's father was thinking, Kai couldn't imagine. The man had to know that if Maddie was living on Maui, she would surely come back to visit Lana'i. Did he think that the entire population of the island had somehow suffered collective amnesia? Did he think she wouldn't talk to people? Did he think they wouldn't talk to her?

Kai drew in a deep, slow breath. Nobody *had* talked to her. Yet. But that was only because she hadn't been here long, and because his mother and Nana were being so protective. Their quest was clearly hopeless. The perfectly innocent question Sammy had thrown out earlier had proved that. Maddie's family history was no secret. It was going to come up, and when it did, it was going to hurt her. Malaya didn't believe it was Kai's own family's place to make that happen. Kai felt it was worse to let her be blindsided.

It would be fair to say that Malaya had gotten in the last word. At least, hers had been the loudest. Malaya and Nana had their reasons for wanting to keep Kai out of the Westover family's affairs, and he understood why, and how strongly they felt. But he would make his own decision.

They reached a fork in the path, and he watched Maddie deliberate. He knew what she was thinking. She wanted to walk straight ahead down the lava spit they were on, because she liked that view and there was a cool sea arch to their right, and she had always enjoyed walking out where the water wrapped three quarters of the way around the bridge beneath her feet. But he knew she wouldn't go that way now. She was too impatient to get to Pu'u Pehe itself.

Maddie pivoted and turned to the left.

Kai grinned. He stepped up beside Maddie as they walked on the trail along the top of the sheer cliff bordering Shark's Cove. She and Kenny might have joked about throwing each other over the edge back then, but the truth was, they had both made him nervous. Neither kid got high marks in the self-preservation department, and it was a very long way down.

"So, how's your father doing?" he asked, trying his best to make the question sound like idle chitchat. "Is he still working for the state resorts in Kentucky?"

Maddie was watching the dolphins as she walked. The pod was cruising slowly around the far bend toward Manele Harbor and out of view. "He doesn't work for the resorts anymore, per se," she answered, not seeming to find anything unusual in the question, "but he does still work for the state and they still live in Paducah."

"Is he going to be able to come visit you while you're on Maui?" Kai asked.

Maddie frowned slightly. "I'm not sure."

"Have you talked to him lately?" Kai pressed.

She looked at him curiously. "Actually, that was him I was talking to on the phone at the beach just now. Why?"

Kai shrugged. "I wondered what he thought about your seeing us all again, that's all. And if he wanted to do the same sometime."

Maddie's eyes held his. *What do you know that I don't, Kai?*

His heart thudded in his chest. If she asked that question out loud, he was sunk. He wasn't going to lie to her. But damn, this was awkward. It was her father, not him, who should be doing the talking. What was wrong with the man?

"Do you think he'll come visit?" he asked again, before she could speak. "I'm sure my parents and Nana would love to see him." *And have a few choice words with him.*

"I doubt it," Maddie answered, seeming confused. She turned away and looked off down the trail again. "He seems content to put our years on Lana'i behind him. And if that's what works for him, I really can't argue with that, you know? He didn't have the same experience here that I did."

"But..." Kai's mind raced a bit. Was he understanding this right? "You did tell him that you were here, and that you'd seen all of us, didn't you?"

Maddie's forehead furrowed. She did a full stop and faced him. "Why would I *not* tell him that? What's up with you?"

"Ooh!" Gloria shouted. "Humpback spout!"

Maddie whirled. "Where?"

Gloria pointed far out to the southwest, and Kai took a breath and regrouped. Too much stray emotion... he was going to screw this up entirely unless he started thinking more like an attorney and less like the overly sensitive ten-year-old-boy he had been back then.

He looked where Maddie and Gloria were looking. He saw no whale spout.

"Well, crap," Gloria lamented. "It figures. It must have dove down or something."

Maddie started walking again. She took several steps before seeming to remember where the conversation had left off. Then she looked back at Kai. Her gaze was newly anxious, making Kai feel worse than ever. "I didn't get to talk to my dad very long. They were driving somewhere. He's supposed to call me back." Her steps slowed, then stopped altogether. She turned around and looked him directly in the eyes. "Is there something you think he should be telling me?"

Yes, Maddie, Kai longed to say. *There is.* But he could not say yes without explaining everything, because with Maddie there was no in between, there was only *no* or *now.* And although he didn't agree with his mother entirely, he did agree with her on one point: the best way for Maddie to learn the truth was from her father. If Bill Westover had learned only minutes ago that his daughter had not only reconnected with the Nakamas but was planning to continue visiting Lana'i regularly, and if he had promised to call her back, then there was a good chance that Kai's interference would not be necessary.

"There it is!" Gloria shouted, jumping up and down and pointing southwest again.

Maddie whirled and put a hand above her eyes.

She gave up and turned back around faster this time, but Kai was ready. "I just wanted to make sure you told him that everyone in the family remembers you both, and that he shouldn't doubt that he's more than welcome to come visit, too."

Maddie blinked. "Oh."

She looked disappointed. But it was more than that. Deep in her light gray eyes, he glimpsed a simmering brew of angst that yanked at his heartstrings. She knew something wasn't right. She didn't think Kai was lying to her — which in strictly technical terms, he was not — but she knew there was something off between them, nevertheless.

He hated that.

And he would not let it continue. He would give Maddie's father through tonight to make things right, but that was it. The man had had fifteen years already, for God's sake!

Surely Kai could manage to keep Maddie occupied and away from wagging tongues for the rest of the day. That was certainly his family's intention. Gloria was too little to remember it all happening, but even she was aware of the situation Maddie was in now. Gloria was a loose cannon, but maybe if Kai asked for her help...

"Stupid whale," Gloria complained, walking around the two of them to head up the trail first. She nudged Kai's elbow and winked at him covertly. "I think it keeps disappearing just to make me look bad."

Kai lifted an eyebrow, then smiled warmly. There might be hope for his baby sister after all.

Maddie followed Gloria up the trail next, and Kai watched as his childhood best friend's new-and-improved body climbed, her long, muscular legs carrying her shapely torso up the trail of red dirt, every aspect of her figure crafted as if made to order for his own personal tastes. A chicken and egg scenario, perhaps, since a week ago he might have had a difficult time articulating exactly what his personal taste entailed. Now, for better or worse, her perfection was burned into his brain for all eternity.

He was in trouble. Deep, deep trouble.

All around.

Chapter 18

Maddie breathed in deeply of the salty air as the wind whipped her hair about her face. She knew it must look dreadful by now, having not seen a brush since she'd stepped out of the ocean, but she wasn't concerned. She was among friends. Among friends, and standing at her favorite place on earth.

She shrugged out of her flip-flops and wiggled her dirt-caked toes on the bare ground. A few paces in front of her the earth dropped away and the ocean crashed against rocks over a hundred feet below. Beyond her was the blue Pacific. Thousands and thousands of miles of water and whales and fish and sharks and seaweed and giant squid and all sorts of deep and mysterious and unknown things. The ocean was vast and unknowable and infinite, and she was small and wholly insignificant, and for the moment, she liked it that way. It had always helped her put her troubles in perspective.

Just offshore, rising up from the churning whitewater, was her beloved icon of Lana'i, the Sweetheart Rock. She smiled at the slant-topped tower, which seemed impossible to swim out to, much less scale the sheer rocky sides of. Yet somehow, some ancient someone had managed not only to get there, but to build what looked like a burial mound on top of it. The feat had always amazed her, as had that ancient someone's motivation. Kai had made up some pretty clever stories to explain the presence of those rocks, but secretly she preferred the native Hawaiian legend, because despite its macabre nature at least it had some romance.

Maddie's smile went deep. The day had had its ups and downs, but right now, her soul was soaring. "So," she called back over her shoulder, still soaking up the view, "you said they found a woman's bones in there, right?"

Behind her, she heard Kai sigh loudly. "You never give up, do you?"

She laughed out loud. He did remember. And to think she had considered apologizing to him for being dead wrong all those years.

As if.

She turned around, still chuckling. He and Gloria had settled onto some rocks and he was pulling their lunches out of his pack. Maddie felt a flicker of envy as she remembered the small cooler he had loaded into the truck earlier. When they were kids heading off on a day trip, Malaya used to make "rice bowls," which weren't really bowls at all but rice wrapped up in wax paper along with various mystery ingredients. Maddie would always attempt to pack her own lunch, but depending on what she found in her own kitchen on a random Saturday, she could head off with a plastic baggie of dry cereal, a handful of cookies, or nothing at all. And yet, strangely enough, Kai always managed to have an extra rice bowl on hand.

She shrugged off her pack, sat down near them, and pulled out a protein bar and her water bottle. "Here," Kai said, smiling at her. "You don't think Mom would leave you out, do you?"

Maddie looked at the carefully wrapped meal and her eyes nearly teared up on her.

"That's what took me so long to come out of the house earlier," Gloria explained. "Mom had two made up already, and when she saw I was changing to go with you she freaked out. 'I have to make an extra for Maddie!' I swear, she fussed over it for five minutes."

Maddie did tear up. She took the rice bowl from Kai's hand and began to unwrap it with an almost holy reverence. "That's so nice of her," she sputtered.

Both of them were grinning at her with disbelief. "Don't be too grateful till you've tasted it," Kai said good-naturedly, leaning back and stretching his long legs along the ground. "The teriyaki's been around a while."

Maddie took a bite. The sticky cold rice and mystery meat tasted as unappetizing as it ever had. "I love it," she said truthfully. "It's perfect."

Gloria looked skeptical. "You didn't eat stuff like this when you went to the mainland, did you?"

Maddie shook her head. "Didn't exist in Kentucky. Actually, steamed rice doesn't exist in Kentucky. They do know how to barbecue. But everything else is breaded and fried."

"Even, like, vegetables?" Gloria asked.

Maddie chuckled. "*Especially* the vegetables." She shot a glance at Kai. He seemed relaxed, soaking up the sun, his eyes closed. He had always been the quiet kid in their group. But she knew he had always been listening, and she knew he was listening now. Gloria seemed to be enjoying herself, and he appeared to be both surprised and happy about that, but she could sense that he was stressed about something else.

"Did you and your friends come up here much when you were kids?" Maddie asked Gloria, hoping to continue the easy camaraderie their hike seemed to have encouraged between the siblings. "Or take day trips up the mountain?" She nudged the recumbent Kai with her foot. "Those treks were the best, weren't they?"

"We came to the beach," Gloria answered. "We didn't go up in the mountains much. There's nothing to do there, really."

Kai opened his eyes and frowned at his sister.

"Nothing to do!" he and Maddie protested together. Then they looked at each other and shared a smile.

"We had so much fun!" Maddie insisted. "We'd go swinging in the Tarzan trees. We'd take off our shoes and race along the ground barefoot. Or we'd race from tree to tree, pretending the ground was hot lava and you'd burn up if you fell into it. We'd eat our rice bowls in the first couple hours, and then we'd snack all afternoon picking lilikoi and strawberry guava..."

"And you and Sammy would go nuts trying to find the meanest spiders," Kai added dryly.

Maddie's heart warmed anew. Surely most people wouldn't remember so much of what happened when they were in elementary school. She knew she was different, that she always held those memories especially dear because of her situation, but with him...

His brown eyes sparkled at her from behind his dark, curling lashes, and for a second he looked so damned gorgeous she almost forgot who he was again.

"*You* fought spiders?" Gloria said with disgust. "Ew. That is so... like... *Ew.*"

"Oh, it was not," Maddie protested. It was rather a morbid hobby, and she did regret it a bit. But she could hardly admit that now. "Nobody made the spiders fight. They lived for it. And they didn't hurt each other. The loser just ran away."

Kai shook his head at her. "Blood sport," he teased. "You and Sammy the cyclone."

Maddie smirked back at him. Could she help it if she was good at it? If she knew just where to look to find the creepy-looking crab spiders? If she could hold them and watch them move and somehow just sense a winner? The kids used to keep them in matchboxes, and when opponents were found, a "fight" would commence. Some kids would throw the two in a paper cup, but Maddie preferred to draw a ring in the dirt and let them loose. One spider — hers, of course — would take off after the other one, they would spar a little, waving their arms and legs at each other, and then one spider — the other guy's, of course — would scuttle off in shame. Her crowd didn't bet because they never had any money. It was just for fun. And it was fun because she won all the time.

"Sour grapes," Maddie teased back. "Your spiders were such wimps."

He scoffed. The telltale line of disapproval appeared between his eyebrows again. "I did *not* fight spiders, and you know it."

Maddie smiled. No, he had not. He seemed to derive no pleasure from it, and didn't care who knew, either. You couldn't shame Kai when it came to being odd man out. Having a different opinion, doing something his own way. He never gave a crap what was "in."

"Sheesh, Maddie," Gloria persisted. "So far all I hear about you doing when you were a kid is swinging around in the trees, throwing Kenny off cliffs, and fighting spiders with Sammy... didn't you ever do, like, girl stuff? With girls?"

Maddie considered. "No. Not really. Your brother made me promise I wouldn't be a girl."

"I what?" Kai protested loudly.

"Don't you remember?" Maddie insisted. "When we first met you told me you didn't like girls, but you were willing to be my friend because I wasn't like the other ones. And then, on my tenth birthday party when my dad bought ice cream for everybody at the park, Sarah Lu gave me a little plastic pouch with sparkly lip gloss and nail polish in it, and I cooed and said I loved it and you *flipped out* and yelled at me and said that I *promised* I would never turn into a girl."

Gloria cracked up laughing.

"Did I really say that?" Kai asked.

Maddie smirked. "You did. Word for word."

"I deny it," he retorted. Then he cleared his throat loudly. "Anyway, Gloria, the girls in our grade were really 'girly,' for whatever reason. That's why it was always Maddie and the guys."

"That," Maddie conceded, "and the fact that I couldn't jump rope worth crap."

Kai laughed out loud. "Yeah, there was that, too."

Maddie tried to frown at him, but couldn't help laughing herself. She did totally suck at jumping rope, which unfortunately happened to be the rage among all her female classmates. Her early attempts had resulted in several injuries, although none to herself. It was the girls holding the ropes or standing innocently nearby who somehow got walloped.

It was bad.

Ergo, the spiders.

"You people," Gloria said derisively, "were just sad. You did have internet in the nineties, didn't you? Computers? Phones?"

"Yes," Kai retorted. "But we did not all carry around smart phones every minute of the day. We liked being outside. We made our own fun."

Gloria shrugged. "Meh. We have apps for that."

Kai pretended to whack her on the head, and Gloria pretended to flinch. Maddie grinned at them both, then watched as Kai stretched his arms behind his head and closed his eyes against the mid-day sun. She and Kai had become comfortably familiar again, and quickly too, and that unexpected triumph elated her. But at the same time, it presented a problem.

When he had hugged her shoulders earlier, it had seemed so natural and normal that for a second she had thought he was Chad, and she had reacted accordingly. Her friend Chad, whom she had known throughout four years of grad school, was a big guy and had always been a hugger. She hadn't seen him since she'd served as an usher at his and his husband Jim's wedding six months ago, and she didn't know when or if she would ever see him again. But she missed his hugs. Living in Alabama away from her family and with no dating life to speak of, she had craved physical affection more than she cared to admit, and sinking into one of Chad's undemanding bear hugs was a privilege she had dearly enjoyed.

She'd felt completely safe with Chad, but that feeling was a rarity. She hadn't expected to feel the same way with Kai. When men who looked at her the way Kai looked at her put their hands on her — which they did all the time — their fingers felt like alien tentacles. But Kai's touch had felt like a warm blanket straight out of the dryer.

Maddie sighed to herself, long and low. She knew she could trust him. And she hadn't wanted to pull away. But she knew better than to seek affection from a straight male friend. She'd been burned too many times. She would not be accused, *again*, of sending mixed signals, of being a tease. Her signals were not mixed. They were unequivocal. Maybe other girls could get away with flirting a little, touching a little, hugging a little. But she couldn't. Her attempts at affection were always misunderstood, sometimes willfully so. Unless she was certain she wanted more than friendship, she had to stay off that slippery slope altogether.

Which meant no hugging Kai, because it would mess with his head, and he deserved better.

No matter how incredibly good it would feel.

"So, what's on the agenda for the rest of the day, warden?" Gloria asked, poking her still-recumbent brother in the ribs with her elbow as she finished up her lunch and packed away the trash.

Kai opened one eye and shot her an exasperated look, and Maddie studied them both. It sounded like Gloria's key-stealing attempt last night had resulted in a sort of mobile grounding. So, the guilty teen could either sit at home or be chaperoned all day, eh? The perfect punishment. Aki was good at that. Perhaps a little more quality time with her respectable yet fun-loving bro was exactly what Gloria needed.

"Yes," Maddie joined in. "What's next? How much time do we have with the truck?" An idea came to her and she practically bounced with enthusiasm — before she remembered Nana's warnings about bouncing. "I know! Why don't we take a nice long drive out past town? We could head toward the shipwreck first and then drive out to Garden of the Gods and Polihua Beach and just stop here and there and look around at everything!"

"At what?" Gloria protested. "There's like... *nothing* out there!"

"There's no people out there," Maddie corrected. "But there are plants and animals and rocks and trees and sky and fungi and—"

Gloria groaned and rolled her eyes. "Oh, whatever!" She rose and dusted off the seat of her shorts.

"Do you have time?" Maddie asked Kai hopefully. It wasn't a long drive in miles. No drive on Lana'i was. But much of the road wasn't paved, the rough dirt surface was impassable without a four-wheel drive, and it could take forever to bump and rattle all the way down to the northwestern coast of the island and back again.

He smiled at her, but his expression was guarded somehow, and Maddie's gut twisted unexpectedly. She had been trying her best to ignore whatever he was hiding from her, but his eyes kept reminding her, regardless. The guy was terrible at subterfuge — he was far too honest. For that trait he had Aki to thank — or to blame, depending on your point of view. Surely that kind of integrity was a liability to an attorney? She could not look at him without seeing his sympathy for her, and his concern... and the thought of what knowledge might be at the root of those emotions disturbed her.

She didn't want to think about it.

"I'll have to double check with my dad," he answered, getting up. "And I need to make a couple more calls for Riku. But then we can probably work it out."

He held out a hand to Maddie to help her up. It was a perfectly ordinary, chivalrous gesture, and she tried not to make too much of it as she put her hand in his and rose to her feet. She dropped his hand as quickly as possible and, without looking at him, shouldered her pack.

Chapter 19

The afternoon was glorious. Even Gloria enjoyed it, although the childish antics of her older companions had her rolling her eyes so much she finally pleaded a headache and started saying "eye roll" instead. Maddie noticed that once Kai made his phone calls and secured the truck for the afternoon, a good part of the weight he'd been carrying seemed to lift off his shoulders, which buoyed her spirits as well. She tried to convince herself that his earlier distress was all about Riku, and not about her, and she resolved to revel in the remainder of the day like they had never reveled before.

This was a challenge, because as children they'd set the reveling bar high. But today was different, because today they had *wheels*. And although being able to drive himself on the island was nothing new to Kai, Maddie could tell that her own enthusiasm for doing what they couldn't do as kids was contagious.

They began their tour with the island's second resort, the Lodge at Ko'ele, a sprawling Victorian-style estate whose lofty British splendor made a surprise appearance on the hill just outside town. They swung through the circular drive to admire the giant Norfolk Pine and Aki's expert landscaping, then waved at the horses in the nearby pasture and drove on. With music playing and the windows open, they sped along the paved part of the road down toward Shipwreck Beach, laughing and reminiscing about their respective high schools, a topic they decided to stick with after Gloria became an active participant. Maddie was fascinated by the changing landscape around them, which gradually became drier and bleaker as they descended. The high fields and forests turned first to bushes and small trees, then thinned gradually to tufts of yellow grass and black boulders before meeting the ocean at the barren northeast shore. She smiled at the colorful chukar birds that scuttled along the road and twice made Kai stop the truck when she thought she spotted a mouflon sheep.

They made fun of her, of course, for poking around in the bushes looking for nests and for wandering around for twenty minutes on foot tracking what ended up being just another axis deer, but for every complaint they made, she offered more detail about interspecies relationship dynamics, which shut them up nicely. The actual shipwreck visible from the road — an ugly concrete-hulled monstrosity from World War II which didn't wreck at all but was grounded intentionally — held little interest for any of them. After getting a good glimpse of the ocean, they turned around, went back up to the fork near the Lodge, and took the other road to meet the ocean again, this time all the way at the northwest edge of the island.

By the time the truck rolled back into Lana'i City late that afternoon they were all hot, thirsty, banged up from the bumpy journey, and sore in the ribs from laughing so hard. They had run around and joked and shouted and sparred with each other and acted ridiculously goofy, but since they met almost no one else the entire time, Maddie hadn't felt in the least self-conscious, which was a rarity for her these days. And judging from Gloria's flabbergasted reaction, she was certain that acting like a lunatic was even more uncharacteristic for grown-up Kai. The outing was as light-hearted and carefree an afternoon as she could possibly have hoped for, and if every once in a while a little voice in her brain reminded her that she was willfully blocking something unpleasant and worrisome, she had just told it to shut the hell up.

"So, Maddie," Kai said as the truck slowed down on the residential streets. "You think we can do this thing tonight without poisoning everybody?"

She chuckled uncertainly. "Doubtful. But we're committed now."

"Committed to what?" Gloria demanded.

"I told Mom that Maddie and I would handle dinner," Kai answered. "We Maui residents don't want to get reputations as freeloaders, so we're going to buy groceries and cook over at Nana's. We'll let you know when everything's ready."

"Since when can you cook?" Gloria asked.

"I can't," Kai answered.

"What about you?" Gloria asked Maddie.

"I'm a grad student. I eat from cans."

Gloria swore. "Let me out at home. I'll pre-eat."

"Your lack of confidence wounds me," Kai joked.

"Eye roll," Gloria retorted.

Kai let his sister out at their house and drove Maddie on to the market. "Thanks for that," he said, smiling at her.

"For what?"

"For helping to smooth things out between Gloria and me. You don't know it, but this is the best it's been in months. She's pretty much frozen me out ever since the first time I tried to talk to her about Dylan."

"I see," Maddie said thoughtfully. What he could have said that ticked Gloria off so much, she couldn't imagine. But she was happy that he was happy. She was glad she could help the Nakama family in any way at all.

The truck stopped at a crossing and an older couple on the sidewalk waved at Kai. He waved back and so did Maddie, but as the man caught sight of Maddie in the passenger seat his hand dropped to his side. He whispered something into the woman's ear which caused her to look at Maddie, too. As the truck pulled away, the couple continued staring after her.

Maddie's stomach churned. She decided to ignore it.

"So," Kai said brightly, though he was faking it. "What do we need? Ground beef for the burgers. And some cheese slices and buns. What do you need for that Southern potato salad?"

"A real cook," Maddie mumbled, wondering whatever had inspired her earlier confidence. She'd only made Lisa's potato salad once and it wasn't all that good. But she had promised Nana something Southern and although generic potato salad didn't really fit the bill, there was no way Maddie was attempting fried okra. She rattled off what she thought she'd need, Kai parked the truck near the market, and they stepped out.

As they neared the door of the market, Maddie noticed that a group of middle-aged women, a few of which looked vaguely familiar, were watching them from the opposite side of the street. When she looked back at them, the women averted their eyes. One of them attempted a wave at Kai, but he appeared not to notice.

"Hey, Kai," a man greeted as he came out the door of the grocery. He was in his thirties maybe, and he was shepherding two little kids along. "Good to see you!"

"You, too, Kekoa!" Kai returned pleasantly, catching the door and holding it open.

The man's eyes moved from Kai to her, and his smile evaporated. "Oh," he said awkwardly, reaching backward to corral his second child out the door. "Hey, there."

"Hello," Maddie returned. Her heart began to pound.

There was an uneasy silence as the kids dawdled along. A silence during which Kai might be expected to introduce his old pal Maddie. But he didn't. Kekoa and his kids moved on.

Kai tried to catch her eye as she dove past him. "Listen," he whispered. "About—"

"It doesn't matter," Maddie said quickly, darting inside. "I'll get the produce." She grabbed a small basket and headed for the potatoes. Her face was flaming, and she paused briefly by a refrigerator case to try and cool it down.

What the hell?

Maybe it wasn't about her. The dashing and desirable Kai Nakama, Esq. had to be Lana'i's most eligible bachelor. Any woman he brought home was bound to cause a stir. She hadn't gotten any weird looks when she'd come to the market by herself earlier in the week, had she? She'd been walking around the city only this morning, and no one had paid any attention to her. The usual kind of attention, yes. But not *this* kind of attention. These weird, curious, *knowing* stares were something altogether new.

Because they know who you are, now.

Because you're with him. Because the word has spread.

She moved to the end of the aisle and darted around a corner where she couldn't be seen. What was it in their eyes that chilled her so? It wasn't dislike, or unfriendliness, or fear, or resentment... or anything like that. It was... *what?* Embarrassment? Pity?

Women's voices drifted to her from over a dry goods shelf. The conversation was a mix of Pidgin and regular English and probably wouldn't have been difficult for Maddie to follow if she could hear it well. But their voices were hushed and muddled and sometimes barely above a whisper. She heard Kai's name; one of them had just seen him somewhere else in the store. Then she heard her name. They were talking about her. Or were they talking about her mother? *"Lolo,"* one of them said. The Pidgin word for crazy. Or foolish.

Maddie resolved to walk away. She had taken two full steps toward the potatoes when one phrase, painfully easy to understand, floated straight to her ears.

"I'm surprised Kai would want anything to do with her!"

The breath left Maddie's body. She swayed a moment, her chest feeling like a vacuum.

Don't. Think. About. It!

She made a beeline for the vegetables, stocked her basket, and whirled around to bump into Kai.

"Got everything?" he asked.

She looked straight at him, reading his eyes. Not only was he was aware of the wagging tongues, he was as anxious to leave the market as she was. They paid for their groceries and left.

The park was busy late on a Saturday afternoon, and there was no way to drive around it and back to Nana's house without passing by at least a few other people. Maddie didn't recognize any of them, but they all seemed to know Kai. She tried to keep her head down, but she could tell they were staring.

They reached their destination and Kai parked the truck. He tried again to say something, but Maddie cut him off. She hauled her sack of groceries into the house, found Nana's potato peeler, and set herself to work. Nana had voluntarily vacated the premises — perhaps anticipating that if she stayed anywhere within shouting distance, she would get called upon to bail them out in the kitchen. She was probably right. Nana was right about everything.

That's the Maddie I remember, Nana had said about the neglected-looking girl in the picture. *What do you remember, child?* A cagey answer from a cagey lady. A woman who had always declined to speak ill of the dead.

The people of Lana'i City knew something about Maddie. They knew something about her that she herself did not. And as proud as she had always been of being big and bold and brave and fearless — Madalyn Westover, capable of felling annoying lechers with a single blow! — this indefinable thing that she didn't know was scaring the holy crap out of her.

Why?

What was she was so afraid of?

I'm surprised Kai would want anything to do with her!

What had she *done?*

Maddie jumped as Kai's hand appeared in front of her and clasped her gently around the wrist. He leaned up against the sink beside her and caught her eyes. "You're trembling," he said firmly. "And don't deny it."

Maddie opened her mouth to do just that, but she could feel the potato peeler shaking in her grasp, even with his own hand supporting hers. She set both it and the potato down.

"I have no idea what you're thinking," he said. "But..."

"I'm just being paranoid," she said dismissively.

He leaned around in front of her, forcing her to look at him. "No, you're not. You're right. They were talking about you. And about me. It's a small town. It happens. I'm sorry."

He smiled a little, and Maddie's forehead creased with confusion.

He was being truthful with her. Sort of. But not completely.

She gathered her courage and drew in a breath. "Are they talking about my mother?"

He paused, but only for a beat. "Yes."

"I see."

It would only make her feel guilty!

Maddie's hands started shaking again. She could still hear her father's voice outside the door the day her mother had died. She had always heard it, would always hear it. It had plagued her all those dark days in Ohio, and she had kept it tucked away in her memory even in happier times with Lisa and her stepbrothers. She had never forgotten it because somehow, she knew it mattered. That it was connected in some gray and miserable way to the vagueness of her feelings about her mother. Her pain of loss that had never seemed deep enough. The love she had always feared wasn't real enough.

Was it all her fault?

"I wish I could help, Maddie," Kai said with frustration.

He was standing close, but he wasn't touching her. He had even let go of her wrist. All day long, even as they had romped and teased each other, he had been careful not to put his hands on her unnecessarily, much less manhandle her. She had noticed that, and she had appreciated it. He could be a miserable, stinking rat sometimes, but her Kai had also been, and always would be, a sweetheart.

Could he help her? Oh, yes, he most definitely could. Nothing would feel better than a nice warm hug right now. But she wouldn't use him.

She had to get a grip on herself. She had known this reckoning was coming, hadn't she? From the moment she'd looked at her old house she had known it. Known that something was wrong, that her picture of the past was incomplete. She'd been running from it her whole life, but if she wanted Lana'i back, she couldn't run from it anymore. She had to stand up and face it, no matter how horrible it was then and no matter how awful it made her feel now.

It would only make her feel guilty!

No matter what had really killed her mother.

She felt her legs tremble beneath her.

"Maddie?" Kai begged.

He was still keeping his distance, but she could feel his warmth even through the space between them. She could feel it... and she wanted it. Her feet moved involuntarily, closing the hated gap. Her arms wrapped around his waist and she buried her face in his shoulder. His strong arms enfolded her instantly, delivering a firm hug, and the relief she felt was so immense she let out a cry.

You shouldn't!

Too late.

He felt so good. As if the warmth of his own strength and compassion were flowing directly into her veins. She closed her eyes and thought of nothing for a moment, just allowed herself to absorb the goodness of him.

"It's going to be okay, Maddie," he said softly. "I promise. It will. All that's needed here is just a major clearing of the air, that's all. You need to talk to your dad."

Maddie's eyes flew open. She lifted her head and stared at Nana's ancient curtains with pictures of pineapples on them.

Kai knew everything, didn't he? He had known all along. He just didn't want to be the one to tell her. Well, that was fair enough. After all, she didn't want to be the one to hear it. All that mattered was that Kai wouldn't lie to her. If she asked him to tell her the truth right now, he would, wouldn't he?

But she wasn't going to.

So they were good.

Pull away now, Maddie.

Maddie continued staring at the pineapple curtains. *So nice...*

Maddie!

She straightened and pulled away from him, keeping her gaze down. "Thank you," she croaked. She cleared her throat. "And I'm sorry about that." She picked up the potato and peeler again.

"Sorry for what?" he asked, sounding genuinely confused.

"For taking advantage of your good nature," Maddie said, lightening her voice a little. "And masculine charms. Wow. I have a lot of potatoes to peel, here."

She didn't look up, so she couldn't see Kai's expression. But he stood where he was a long time before answering her. "No problem," he said finally, still sounding confused. "I'll start on the burgers."

Maddie skinned potatoes like a madwoman. If Nana's peeler had been sharper, she would have peeled some of her own skin off as well. She needed some time alone, and Kai seemed to sense that. Either that, or he was afraid for his own skin. Whatever his reasoning, he went about his own preparations without trying to engage her, giving her as much space as was physically possible in Nana's small kitchen.

Yet Maddie's eyes followed him covertly, her senses on high alert to his every movement, practically his every breath.

She'd done it, now.

She should never have let herself hug him like that. What had ever made her think she could find him attractive without being attracted to him? She wasn't dead, was she? She had adored the boy. The man was gorgeous. *Duh.*

She was flustered. And the fact that she was flustered irritated the hell out of her. So what if she was attracted to him? Why should that be a problem? She had wanted to be just friends, yes, but there was no reason they *couldn't* be more, if that's what they both wanted. He didn't appear to be otherwise attached. And yet...

And yet the utter, childish nervousness she felt at that prospect was worthy of therapy. Since the tender age of twelve she had been forced to defend herself against constant brushes, bumps, pokes, and grabs. Intrusions of a sexual nature, both physical and verbal, had only escalated as she got older. She was so sickened by inappropriate attention when she was younger that even after she'd matured to the point when it might be appropriate, it held little appeal. Now, at twenty-five, the irony of her predicament was laughable. Every man who looked at her body assumed she came equipped with Olympic-level expertise.

They were wrong.

Maddie fought back a frustrated groan. She had no illusions about Kai's attractiveness to other women and what that meant in terms of his own likely history. If he had any idea of the reality of her own, he would doubtless find her more pathetic than tempting. It was like he was used to racing Ferraris, and she didn't even have her permit.

Ouch.

Just shut up, Maddie!

She dropped the pot of hard-boiled eggs prematurely and it fell into the sink with a clatter.

Kai jumped. "Everything okay?"

"Peachy," Maddie answered. "But only because I was going to break the eggs anyway. How are the burgers coming?"

Kai sighed. "Let's just say that all those times my grandparents had the family over for Sunday dinners in Provo, I'm wishing I'd spent more time watching Grandma cook and less time beating my cousins at ping pong."

Maddie stole another glance at his muscular arms, at the smooth brown skin she'd always found so appealing.

Her "little Kai" had turned out so very, very nicely.

It was a shame she had no idea what to do with him.

Chapter 20

"Kai! Kai, wake up!"

Kai heard his mother's voice and the room around him swam into focus. He was hot. Broiling hot.

"Wake up, now. Everything's okay. You were just having a nightmare, that's all."

Kai struggled to get his bearings. He was half on, half off the couch in his parents' house. The temperature was a thousand degrees. He was dripping with sweat. His heart was racing.

"I'll get a cup of cold water."

His father's voice. Calm, but concerned.

Kai focused his eyes and looked around. Malaya was perched on the edge of the couch beside him. Aki was moving toward the kitchen. Gloria stood at the door to her room. It was dark outside.

"What's going on?" Gloria asked blearily. "What was he yelling about?"

"Just a nightmare," Malaya snapped. "Go back to bed, Gloria."

Kai scrambled to a sitting position. *Dammit*. He'd woken them up. He hadn't had a nightmare like this in over a decade.

Aki returned and placed a cool plastic cup into Kai's sweating palm. Kai raised the drink to his lips, drained it, and gave the cup back to his father. The cold water felt like a healing balm as it chilled his insides. "Thanks, Dad."

"A nightmare about what?" Gloria pestered.

"Go back to bed," Aki repeated firmly.

Gloria frowned, but turned around and closed the door behind her. Not all the way, though. The door was warped, and Kai knew that it was possible to draw it where it appeared to be closed from the middle but still had a gap at the top. You could hear everything that was said that way.

Malaya's eyes remained fixed on Kai as she rose, stepped backward to Gloria's door, pulled it shut with a bang, and returned to her station. "I knew this would happen," she whispered, more to Aki than to Kai.

Aki frowned.

Kai wiped the sweat from his forehead and straightened. "I'm fine,

Mom. It's not a big deal." He would get up, but he doubted he could walk without his legs shaking, and he would prefer his mother not see that. Two more minutes. Then he'd be fine.

He rubbed his face with his hands. How mortifying. To wake up screaming in a pool of sweat when you were ten years old was one thing. To have it happen in your twenties was another. And to have your mother brush your wet bangs from your forehead only added insult to injury.

"I'm so sorry, baby," Malaya nearly wept. "I shouldn't have let you get involved in this."

Kai got up and walked. He wouldn't shake if it killed him. He made it to the front door, turned around, and leaned heavily against it.

"*I am fine,*" he repeated forcefully. "I'm not a kid anymore. It's been on my mind and I haven't been sleeping well. That's it."

Malaya threw a concerned look at Aki. Aki looked gravely back at her.

"We should never have encouraged Maddie to find you," Malaya mumbled miserably. "It was a mistake, her coming back to Lana'i."

"Don't be ridiculous!" Kai said irritably. "You couldn't have stopped her. It wasn't your choice to make!"

"Kai!" Malaya pleaded. "You know I love that girl. We all do. But I'm *your* mother, and *you're* my first priority!"

Kai let out a breath. "I know, Mom," he said, trying to be patient and sound calm even as his pulse still raced and the nightmare visuals still flashed behind his eyeballs. "And I appreciate that. I do. But I don't need to be protected anymore. I had a tough time when I was a kid, yes. But I'm over it. I grew up. I'm good. Maddie is the one who needs your concern now. She never got over it because no one ever gave her the chance!"

Malaya frowned. "Her father did what he thought was best for her."

Aki made a low, rumbling noise in his throat.

Malaya fixed her husband with a resentful look. "It was his decision!" she defended. "We all agreed that at the time, *including* you. Maddie couldn't have taken it all in back then. It would have been too much for her. Even Nana thought so."

"Nana thought, as I did, that it should be explained to her in stages," Aki said. "Over a few days or weeks. Maybe months. But this..."

Kai stood up straight. His legs were fine now. Thinking about Maddie's father made him angry all over again, just like he'd been when he'd gone to bed last night. Perhaps it was that emotion that had brought on the nightmare.

"I think he did what was easiest for *him*," Kai retorted. He took the cup back from his father, poured himself another glass of water, and sat down at the kitchen table.

Malaya and Aki sat down with him.

Kai breathed slowly, working to control his frustration. Bill Westover knew that his daughter was back on Lana'i. He knew that she was staying with the Nakamas and that she had reconnected with Kai. He knew damn well that anyone in Kai's family — or any stranger on the streets — could expose his lies at any time, and yet he had said nothing. He had called Maddie back on the phone during dinner last night, and Kai had been prepared. The timing had been perfect; all the family had been on hand to offer their support. She had disappeared into her room with her cell and Kai had held his breath and waited for the inevitable. And then she had popped out five minutes later lamenting that she had forgotten a key ingredient in the potato salad.

Kai couldn't believe it. Couldn't believe that Bill Westover would take such a chance, expose Maddie to that kind of emotional risk. Kai had even called Nana on the phone from his parents' house later, asking if Maddie had gotten another call. Nana said she hadn't heard any. Maddie was in her room already. Probably asleep.

"I don't believe Bill has any intention of telling her the truth," Kai proclaimed to his parents. "Not now. Not ever. Not if he can get away with it."

Malaya shook her head. "You don't know that. He could have made plans to call her in the morning. It's his business, and his place to do it." She eyed her son intently. "*Not* yours."

Kai held her gaze. He understood that she wanted to protect him. If he had gone through hell in the aftermath of the Westovers' exodus from Lana'i, she had ridden there right along beside him. He was sorry for that.

But on this, she was wrong.

He started to speak, but stopped when his father laid a gentle hand on top of his.

"Malaya," Aki said quietly. "The boy is right. Bill Westover was a kind-hearted man, and I liked him. He was good with people, and he was a hard worker. But he was a coward. He was afraid of conflict. Afraid of any sort of confrontation. Anything that was potentially unpleasant, or hurtful, or messy, he ignored and hoped would go away.

If he's been avoiding this for fifteen years, it's likely he'll go on avoiding it."

Kai threw his father a look of gratitude, and Aki nodded back.

But Malaya only wound herself up tighter. "Well, fine then! Can we not just agree that the woman died from a heart attack and leave it at that?" she exclaimed. "Maddie was fine with that before she came here!"

"That's not an option," Kai argued. "You can't make the whole island lie to her!"

"Nobody has to lie!" Malaya shot back, rising from her chair. "They just have to shut the hell up about it!"

"Malaya," Aki reprimanded softly. "Gloria is listening, I'm sure. As might be others, at this hour."

Malaya sat back down.

"Kai is right," Aki continued. "It would be unkind to Maddie to let her hear it on the street. And that is what would happen. Sooner or later."

"Thank you, Dad," Kai said, exhaling with relief. He had already made up his mind. But having Aki agree with him did wonders to strengthen his resolve. He rose, walked over to where his bag lay on the floor, and rifled through his clothes.

Malaya stood again. "What are you doing?"

"Getting dressed," he answered. "I'm going to Nana's to wake up Maddie and tell her the truth."

"Now?" Malaya protested.

"Mom," Kai retorted, grabbing his jeans and a fresh tee shirt and heading for the bathroom. "I'm not going to let Maddie find out about her mother from some guy walking his dog tomorrow morning. Or some smart-mouthed kid riding his bike past the 'haunted house.' Or from some nosy old woman pretending to need to borrow something from Nana at the crack of dawn."

"Kai," Malaya reasoned. "Surely, after all this time, a couple more hours—"

"Besides," he finished, pulling the door closed behind him. "The stars are out."

Chapter 21

*P*lunk. *Plink.*

Maddie's eyes opened. She stared up at the ceiling of Nana's extra bedroom and felt a sense of deja vu.

Plunk.

She smiled to herself. Then she looked at the time on her phone and groaned. "Are you kidding me?" She rolled herself off the thin mattress and stepped over to clutch at the window sill. She peered out between the open glass louvers and through the screen, hoping that none of the holes therein were big enough to let the next pebble hit her in the face.

The scene that met her eyes in the dim light made her laugh out loud.

"Nakama, you idiot," she giggled. "You could have just reached up and tapped!"

Kai stood on the ground outside her window, his adult face silhouetted not that far below. The boy Kai hadn't a prayer of reaching her old window, but he had snuck out of bed and tossed pebbles at it whenever he couldn't sleep, which had happened a bit too frequently for Maddie's tastes.

"Old habits," he quipped.

Maddie laughed again. "What do you want?"

"Let's go stargazing."

She stared at him with disbelief.

"I'm serious!" he insisted. "It's a beautiful night for it. What, you have something better to do?"

"I always have something better to do!" she retorted. "Sleep!"

"That is *so* boring," he taunted.

How many times had they had this conversation? As far as Maddie could remember, he'd always won. She could never resist a challenge. "Fine!" she replied, feigning peevishness. "I'll meet you out front."

She turned from the window, realizing that she had just had a complete conversation with a man without even thinking about what she was wearing. She glanced down in a panic and was relieved to remember that since the nights were chilly on Lana'i, she'd worn a tee and sleep pants instead of her usual skimpy fare. *Thank goodness.* She ran a brush through her hair, pulled it back with a band, threw on a jacket and shoes, doused herself in insect repellent, and headed for the door. Then she remembered she wasn't alone in the house.

She crept back to the kitchen and looked for something to write a note on. She had just located a pad when she heard a noise from the other bedroom. She walked over and rapped gently on Nana's door in case she was already awake.

A loud sigh echoed from within. "I may be old, child," Nana mumbled. "But I'm not deaf. Just go on out, will you? And tell that grandson of mine I'll be having a word with him in the morning."

Maddie smirked. "Yes, ma'am."

She went out the front door and found Kai leaning against the porch post. "Still fighting that insomnia, huh?" she asked, turning on her flashlight app.

"Put that thing away," he chastised. "I've got my penlight. You can follow me."

Maddie narrowed her eyes at him skeptically. They'd always taken at least one flashlight, unless there was a full moon. Tonight there was none. "You do realize we have to cross a bunch of new streets that didn't use to be there?"

"You afraid of stubbing a toe?" he taunted again.

She set her phone down on the porch, then stepped behind him and gave a playful shove to his shoulders. "Just start moving Nakama. If I fall, you can cushion the blow."

He chuckled, his adult voice deep and wholly appealing, and another ripple of anxiety shot through her. She hadn't just uttered some weird double entendre, had she? Crap, this was complicated. They had so much fun when they were pretending to be kids again... except that pretending could only go so far.

Kai started off down the street as if to pass her old house and follow their traditional route, but after a few steps he hesitated and went the opposite direction. "New plan," he announced.

Maddie couldn't care less which direction he led, but she got the feeling — again — that he was hiding something from her. Was there some reason he didn't want to walk by her old house?

If so, she didn't want to know it.

They made their way uneventfully the few blocks to the "new" edge of town and then plunged into the bushes and weeds beyond.

"This is going to be a shorter trek in the wilderness than it used to be," Kai commented, looking back over his shoulder at the silhouette of the mountains to get his bearings. He forged ahead through a few more clumps of grass and then suddenly, straight ahead, there it was.

The Rock. Or better put, *their* rock. Once located "way out" in the old fields, it now stood a less scandalous couple hundred feet from the nearest new construction. But thanks to the overgrown bushes, it was still well hidden from view.

Kai hustled up to the boulder and leaned against his favorite spot, which was slanted the perfect amount to let him put his head back and see the stars. "Whoa!" he complained, as the once-comfortable "pillow" jabbed him in the back. "It shrunk!"

"Yeah," Maddie laughed. "That's what happened." She'd never been able to lean comfortably against the rock, and hence had wound up either sitting on it or lying on the ground nearby. Tonight she chose to hop up on it, and Kai soon gave up trying to get comfortable leaning and joined her. Indeed, the rock *had* shrunk. They could not both sit on it without their shoulders touching.

But that was okay. The middle of the night was always chilly on Lana'i, and every now and then a cool wind kicked up as well. They sat without speaking for a moment, and as the last of the dogs disturbed by their journey decided to get over it, a silence fell over the field that was near to absolute.

Maddie breathed in deeply of the quiet. How nice.

Kai put his hands behind him, tilted his head back, and began searching the sky. It was big and deep and never-ending, strung with a chaotic splash of sparkly stars.

"Well?" she prompted.

He looked at her questioningly. At least she thought he did. The light was dim, but her eyes were adjusting.

She smirked. "You brought me out here to bore me stiff again, right? Make up all kinds of names for constellations that don't exist or that you can't actually see. Pretending you've actually studied all this stuff. I know the drill. Go ahead."

He smiled at her. At first, it seemed like a playful smile. But then it turned into something horrible. It turned sympathetic. "Maddie," he began earnestly. "I brought you out here because there's something I need to tell you. I wanted to—"

Maddie hopped down off the rock. Her gut twisted and her cheeks flared with heat. "Kai Nakama!" she chastised. "You stinking rat! You tricked me! You got me out here under false pretenses!"

"I'm trying to help you."

"I do not *need* your help," she retorted. "I know what you're doing. You think I need to know all about the past. But I don't. I'm fine with the way things are!"

"It's not a matter of whether or not you hear about it," Kai said sternly. "It's only a matter of *when*. And from who. And how."

Maddie thought about that. Her pulse sped up. She felt like running away.

She decided to go with that.

She turned and started walking toward town.

"My dad told me that your dad was a really nice guy, but that if Bill had one flaw, it was that he couldn't face any situation that was emotionally uncomfortable," Kai called after her. "If there was conflict, or confrontation, if it was going to hurt or even be unpleasant, your father would just turn and walk away."

Maddie's teeth gritted.

"Like a coward," Kai finished.

Dammit! Maddie's feet halted. Her head was so full of hot blood it felt like it would explode. Kai was playing her ego and he knew it and she knew it and she was absolutely one hundred percent powerless to do a thing about it.

Because Madalyn "Tomato-Chan" Westover was *Not A Coward.*

She whirled, stomped back to the rock, and launched herself up on it with so much force she nearly knocked Kai off the other side.

When he resettled himself she was inappropriately close to him, but she didn't care. Aside from the fact that her face was on fire, the rest of her body was cold, and his warmth felt good. "I am not running away from anything," she proclaimed, sounding even to her own ears as though she were trying to convince herself. "Lay it on me, Nakama."

She crossed her arms under her chest, blew out a breath, and waited.

Kai said nothing for a moment.

She shivered.

He sighed. "Maddie," he said, so close she could feel his breath on the side of her neck. "If I put my arms around you, are you going to injure me?"

"No," she replied. "You may proceed."

"Gee, thanks," he said wryly. He squirmed around until he was sitting behind her, then wrapped his arms around her middle. He gave her a friendly squeeze, then laid his chin on top of her shoulder.

"Your mother didn't die of a heart attack," he said slowly. "Your father told you that because he thought it would make it easier for you to deal with. But the truth is, she committed suicide."

Maddie went numb. The blood in her face seemed stuck there, pulsing.

Suicide? But why?

Her mother had *wanted* to leave her.

"Maddie?" Kai whispered.

"I'm fine. How did she do it?"

He didn't answer immediately. His chest was pressed against her back and she could feel his heart pounding. "Do you really want to know?"

"Yes. No. I don't know," she replied, her voice clipped.

The breath Kai released sounded ragged. "You probably should know, because it's likely to come up." He gave her another squeeze. "She hung herself, Maddie. That's why, even today, you may hear kids calling the place you used to live 'the haunted house.'"

Maddie was glad Kai couldn't see her face. She sucked in a breath sharply and tried hard not to make any embarrassing noises. *Oh, God. It couldn't be. Her own mother? But why?*

She left you, Maddie. You weren't worth living for.

"I'm sure your father thought that you were too young to understand about depression," Kai was saying. "He probably thought that you would take it personally, assume there was something wrong with you, that she didn't love you enough."

Did she love you, Maddie? Did she really?

"But of course it wasn't about you, or about your father," Kai continued. "It was about her. It was a mental illness."

Or did you just assume she loved you because Dad kept saying she did?

"Maddie? Are you listening to me?"

She didn't act like she loved you. She didn't even take care of you!

"Maddie!"

"What?" Maddie broke free of his embrace and hopped off the rock again.

"Talk to me," Kai ordered. "What are you thinking?"

"I'm not thinking anything," Maddie snapped.

"Liar."

Her face heated up all over again. How easy it was to drop back into the old patterns... how cathartic it had been to scream and stomp and yell at Kai whenever her crazy childish emotions got the best of her!

"I'm thinking that my mother never loved me, of course!" she answered. "What the hell else am I supposed to think?"

Kai jumped off the rock and stood beside her. "Well, knock it off. You're not a kid now. You know that depression is a mental illness. Your mother was sick, Maddie. The same as if she'd had cancer or diabetes. You *know* that."

Maddie looked away from him. *Depression.* She could remember her mother lying in bed. Sleeping late. Lounging on the couch. Complaining of headaches. Resting. She had smiled at Maddie. Always had kind words. There had been good days here and there, when her mother seemed to have more energy. They might go out together then, or play a bit. But other times Maddie would talk to her and she seemed not even to hear.

You're an idiot.

"I should have known," Maddie murmured.

Kai made a growling noise and stepped in front of her. "Do not try to make this about you," he said forcefully. "She didn't commit suicide *because* of you, and it wasn't *your job* to diagnose and treat her mental illness, either. You were a *child*, Maddie. Look at me." He caught her eyes. "It was not your fault. You could not have done anything to stop it. And beating yourself up about it now will help absolutely nothing."

A stupid idiot.

"I didn't tell you any of this so you could dwell on it — that's exactly what I *don't* think you should do." Kai stopped and ran a hand through his hair, as if suddenly uncertain of himself. "But you have to understand... everyone on the island knows what happened, and eventually someone was bound to—"

"Yeah, I get it," Maddie agreed, cutting him off. "I'm glad you told me. Thanks." She pivoted and looked different directions around the field. She probably looked like she was expecting a bus, but in reality it was just creative fidgeting.

It would only make her feel guilty! Her father's voice taunted her again.

What would make me feel guilty, Dad? she thought. *What made you so sure that I would think Mom committed suicide because of me? Didn't you think that explaining the disease would be enough? Why did you never tell me she had a disease at all? Why have you still not told me to this freakin' day?*

Maddie whirled and faced Kai again. "Did my mother leave a suicide note?"

Kai looked taken aback. "I... I'm not really sure. Nana would know."

Maddie stared at him. The darkness hid a lot, but between the tone of his voice and what she could see of his face, she was pretty sure he was telling the truth. "I see."

"What are you thinking?" he asked.

"I'm thinking lots of things," Maddie answered. And with those words, she realized that her face was no longer hot. She was still angry, but there was no fuel left for the fire. She felt dull, suddenly. Weary.

Kai stood silently a moment, watching her. "Would you like to go back now?" he asked.

Maddie envisioned herself lying in bed, staring at Nana's ceiling. She shook her head.

"Do you... want to cry again?" he suggested.

"No," she said honestly. "I'm too mad for that."

"How about taking a swing at me?" he teased.

She shook her head. *Although if you were here, Dad, we would definitely have some words.* She thought of all the times she had asked her father to tell her more about her mother. Things about their life on Lana'i that she couldn't remember. Things about her mother from before Lana'i. Maddie had been over eighteen and filling out health forms, for God's sake — never once had her father wavered from his insistence that Jill died of "heart disease." Maddie had even gone to the trouble of having her own cholesterol levels checked!

Afraid of uncomfortable emotional confrontation, indeed.

Something rippled along her skin, chilling her. But this sensation was not the wind.

Oh, you don't really want to do your post-doc on the islands, do you? her father had said discouragingly. *It's so expensive there! Your mother and I can't help you anymore, you know. We've got to save for your brothers' educations. Can't you go somewhere closer?*

Her father had never been enthusiastic about her plans to work on Maui. She had thought he didn't want her to go so far away.

Right.

He didn't want her finding out the truth.

Ever.

She felt so cold.

"If there's anything I can do," Kai said patiently. "Just tell me."

Maddie looked up. She had almost forgotten he was standing there. Earnest. Concerned. Her own father wouldn't tell her, her family wouldn't tell her, his family wouldn't tell her... but he would. He had told her because he thought she deserved to know. He had done it decisively, within a mere three days of meeting her again. He'd done it even though the odds were high that she would totally flip out on him. And he had awakened her in the middle of the night to do it.

What a sweetheart.

She could definitely go for another hug. But she would not.

She grabbed his hand and pulled him toward the rock, then she hopped back up on it and gestured for him to follow. Once they were comfortably settled again, she tilted her head back and looked at the sky.

The array of the stars above them was truly stunning. From large and bright to tiny specks, they were strung across an uneven field of blue-black that was wholly dark in some places and washed with a film of milky light in others. An owl hooted from farther away in the fields. Otherwise, the island was silent. The air felt moist with the coming dew.

"Okay," she announced. "Now you can bore me."

Kai chuckled.

She did love that deep, rumbling sound. Not that the old high-pitched snicker hadn't had its charms.

"Excuse me?" he retorted. "Are you saying astronomy is boring?"

"It's not astronomy! You just make stuff up!"

"I did not," he insisted. "Well, maybe I did sometimes. But now I won't." He pointed above their heads. "That's Gemini, the twins. And see there, that's Leo. You always hated Leo."

Maddie choked out a laugh. "I hated Leo? Why would I hate a constellation?"

"How should I know? You just did."

"Okay, fine. I'm sure I had an excellent reason."

"Well, you shouldn't anymore. Look, now it's special, because it has Jupiter appearing right inside it! How cool is that?"

"You do realize I just see a bunch of spots, right?"

"Apply your brain," he ordered. "You can do this. Follow where I'm pointing. First look for the brightest star right off the tip of my finger..."

Maddie settled her head into the crook of his shoulder and pretended to follow instructions. She was pretty sure she'd never actually figured out which stars were supposed to look like a lion back then, either. But when stargazing in a field in the middle of the night in your pajamas, the constellations weren't important.

What mattered was the company you kept.

Chapter 22

Maddie dragged herself to Nana's table the next morning feeling like her skull was packed with wet cotton. She pulled out a chair and fell into it.

She had not slept well.

Nana peered at her over a steaming cup of coffee. "I was going to offer you some guava juice," she said, her voice gravelly. "But now I'm guessing black coffee for you, too."

Maddie nodded.

Nana started to rise, but Maddie waved her off and got up herself. She shuffled over to the counter and poured herself a cup of coffee, then struggled to wake up her brain enough to make Nana a second pot. She managed — thanks to Nana calling out a few corrections, anyway — and collapsed back into her seat with her mug.

"How were the stars?" Nana asked, smirking slightly.

Maddie looked back at her and felt a disturbing urge to cry. She had not succumbed to that urge yet and didn't want to. She was still too damn mad.

"It wasn't that kind of outing," she replied flatly. "Kai told me that my mother killed herself. He was afraid I'd hear it on the streets otherwise. And he was right. I would have."

Nana set her coffee cup down slowly. Her dark eyes met Maddie's squarely, with empathy but not with pity. Nor with apology. She nodded. "I see."

Maddie felt a flicker of annoyance that Nana hadn't been willing to do the deed. Shoot-from-the-hip Nana, who always prided herself on "telling it like it is." Why wouldn't she say anything? It made no sense. But Maddie couldn't stay angry with Nana. Nana always did things — or not — for a reason. And that reason was never cowardice.

Unlike some people.

"My father never told me she was depressed," Maddie explained, aware of the bitterness in her voice and not caring. "Not a hint. All those medical forms he filled out for me while I was growing up... you know, where you have to give your family history? In the mother's column, he'd leave all the mental illness stuff blank, including depression. But he'd always check heart disease. Every time."

Nana made a grumbling noise. She shook her head and took a swig of coffee.

"I don't understand, now, how I could have been so blind," Maddie said with disgust. "I might not have known what depression was *then*, but I learned about it later. And yet I never put it together. It never even occurred to me! How stupid is that?"

Nana set her cup down so forcefully that a bit of dark liquid sloshed out onto the table top. Maddie jumped.

"Now you just stop that kind of talk right now, do you hear?" Nana demanded. "You were a child. I'm no doctor, but if there's one thing I do understand, it's *keiki*. Their world looks different. They think different. They remember different. You didn't see anything wrong with your mama because she was the only mama you ever knew. The way she was, the way your family went about its business — that was your normal, child. And you just accepted it. You were a sunny girl and you didn't go looking to find problems for yourself. As long as you had food and clothes and a roof over your head and Kai to run around with, you were happy." Nana stopped and smiled a little. "Sweet Jesus, child. Half the time you didn't care about the clothes or the roof!"

Maddie felt herself smiling, too. Yeah. She could see that.

"You had no reason *not* to believe what your father told you," Nana continued more sternly. "None. Now when you came back here and maybe remembered a few things you'd forgotten... well, of course you were confused. Maybe they didn't make good sense with the story you'd heard."

Maddie shook her head. "They didn't. But I dismissed them. I didn't want to think about it." She took a swig of coffee and grimaced. It was crazy strong. How did Nana drink this stuff? "I guess that makes me no better than my father."

Nana reached out and laid a wrinkled brown hand over Maddie's pale one. "You are nothing like your father, child. You ask me, your brain was playing tricks on you, fighting with you, because that's what kids' brains do when they've got no other protection. I've seen a whole lot of *keiki* who've been through a whole lot of suffering, and I've watched it happen more times than I can count. They block it out. They put it away. I know it's all the fashion now to make them drag it all out again when they grow up, but you ask me, that's a mistake. The brain knows what it's doing. Sometimes, for the little ones, forgetting is the very best medicine there is."

Maddie considered. "You think I forgot the really bad times?"

Nana shook her head. "No, I think you remember what happened well enough. You just didn't want to think about why it was happening. You blocked out what really hurt you, and that was your mama's not caring — her apathy. But that *was* the depression. You understand what I'm saying, child?"

Maddie's mind flashed to all the times since she'd returned to Lana'i that her instincts had screamed "don't think about that!" It was true, wasn't it? When it came to her feelings about her mother, her inner psyche didn't want to upset the apple cart. It wanted to leave well enough alone.

Too bad that was no longer possible.

She might as well get it all out in the open. Then, with luck, she could pack it all right back up again. "There's something else I'd like to know," she asked.

Nana nodded. But her eyes held a disturbing glimmer of angst.

"Did my mother leave a suicide note?"

Nana didn't answer for a moment. She took another sip of coffee and seemed lost in thought. "She did," she answered finally, setting down the cup again. "And this isn't really my business and never was, but if your dad's not answered you in all these years..."

"Please, Nana," Maddie begged. "He may or may not tell me the truth, even if I can get him to talk to me now."

Nana nodded grimly. "I didn't see the note myself. But Maria did. You remember Maria, my son Rodrigo's wife?"

"Kai's aunt Maria," Maddie nodded, remembering the name now. "She worked with my dad at the resort."

"That's right," Nana agreed. "They divorced years ago, but Maria was a good woman. She got to know your father as well as anybody, and... well, he was a mess when it happened, child. Just a mess. The note sent him into hysterics, and he showed it to Maria and she read it. She tried to help him understand it. To see that it was the depression talking and not the woman he fell in love with." Nana's kind brown eyes sought Maddie's and held them. "I'm guessing that your mother was beyond thinking how her words might make you or your father feel. I'm guessing they made him feel pretty bad. And I'm guessing that if you'd read them back then, they could have messed up your sweet little head pretty bad, too."

The coffee Maddie had swallowed soured instantly in her stomach.

It would only make her feel guilty!

Nana patted Maddie's cold hands. "Don't be too hard on your papa, child," she ordered. "I've wanted to shake the man myself more than once, I won't lie. Drove me crazy how he'd ignore what was right in front of his face, how he could talk a blue streak and never once say what he really meant. But his heart was in the right place. He wanted to protect you from the same awful pain he was feeling. And the guilt. You can't blame him for that now, can you?"

Maddie didn't reply. But she did, suddenly, feel a whole lot more like crying than breaking something.

"He did try to help your mama," Nana continued. "He took her to a doctor on Maui every month, and she saw somebody up at the health center sometimes, too. She was supposed to be taking medication. But when it happened—" She shook her head with a sigh. "It really was a shock. No one saw it coming. That's part of what made it so hard on your father. He thought she was getting better."

"Had she—" Maddie wasn't sure she wanted to ask the question. She decided to get it over with. "Had she ever tried before?"

Nana nodded slowly. "Maria said her first time was what made your father decide to move here. Her doctor on the mainland thought that year-round sunshine might help, and your dad decided right away that that's just what he'd give her."

Now Maddie definitely wanted to cry.

"I know you feel like your father could have handled things better back then," Nana said, her voice gaining an unexpected edge. "And I agree with you on that. None of us were happy about you leaving the way you did. And we didn't care for being told that a 'fresh start' was more important to you than we were, either. But it was your father's decision to make, not ours, and we all agreed to abide by it, although to be honest I wish I hadn't. And as angry as all that makes me now, I can't judge your father, Maddie, and neither should you. The man was a wreck. He was falling apart."

Maddie blinked. "You... agreed... what?"

Nana exhaled, long and loud. "Your father didn't want any long, sobbing goodbyes. He also didn't want us pretending it was all just temporary and promising we'd see you soon — because he knew damn well he was never coming back to Lana'i. There was nothing we could tell you that he didn't think would make things worse, so he just decided your grandparents should take you away and that would be that. He didn't mind if you kept up with Kai and your other friends once you got back to the mainland, but he wanted everyone else —

especially me, even if he didn't say it — to step back and let you get used to depending on your grandparents. The sooner, the better."

"But—" Maddie couldn't finish. There really were no words.

"I know, child," Nana finished for her. Her voice caught. "I'll never forget sitting there in that hotel room, holding you while the tears just rolled down your cheeks, but they had you so drugged up... I'd talk to you but you wouldn't answer me. I've never seen any child before or since who could sleep and cry at the same time like that."

Despite Nana's sadness, her words caused a tiny spark of joy to flicker through the fog of Maddie's brain. "The hotel room?" she breathed. "You came to see me at the resort? After Maria took me there and I asked for you?"

Nana looked back at her with surprise. "Well, of course, child. I had to go back and forth, because Kai was... Well, I went out there twice, but I couldn't tell if you were awake or not. And then once your grandparents got—"

Maddie sprung out of her chair. She threw her arms around Nana's shoulders and fell to her knees as she pulled the older woman into a crushing hug. Then she did cry. "Oh, Nana!" she exclaimed when she could talk again. "I never knew you were there! I thought you didn't come. I wish I'd known. I missed you so much!"

When at last Maddie drew back, she caught Nana surreptitiously wiping tears from the corners of her eyes.

"Sweet Jesus, girl," Nana exclaimed, shaking out her arms, then struggling to her feet. "I think you broke some bones somewhere. I need breakfast. You want some eggs?"

Maddie nodded. "You want help?"

"No!" Nana said forcefully, even as her dark eyes twinkled. "You stay right over there."

Maddie smiled and returned to her chair. She stayed out of Nana's way in the kitchen, grateful that her exuberance did not appear to have caused any actual injury, and the two enjoyed a quiet breakfast with no more talk of the past. By the time they had finished and the dishes were done Maddie felt almost human again.

She accompanied Nana on her usual Sunday morning trek up to Sacred Hearts, then decided to go for a walk around the park. She was drained emotionally, yet at the same time, she felt restless. It was too early to pester any of the Nakamas, but she was glad to find the old man bench fully staffed and open for visitors. She walked up to a chorus of cheerful greetings and settled herself between Mr. Li and Mr.

Kalaw. They had been in the middle of some spirited discussion in Pidgin when she approached, but after she joined them they switched to English. "Well, *Akage-chan*," Mr. Hiraga said with a grin. "We see you have found your old friend again, eh?"

Maddie looked at the uniformly grinning faces around her. *Oh, right.* They had seen her with Kai. She could only imagine what they must be thinking. They had known all along that her mother was neglecting her and that Nana was essentially raising her. They had probably felt sorry for her, spending so much time in the park. Then she had left abruptly under a cloud of drama that was probably good for several years' worth of gossip as well as children's ghost stories, and now she was back looking like — well, what she looked like — and cavorting around with the town's favorite son. Of course they were happy to see her. She was better than a Sunday matinee.

Her head hung a little, but Mr. Kalaw's kind, dark eyes immediately caught hers with a twinkle. "What's this? Something wrong, eh?"

She met his gaze, and both guilt and relief flooded through her. She wasn't being fair. The old men had shown her nothing but kindness long before the drama started, back when she was nothing but an unkempt, pesky little haole girl.

What the hell? She might as well throw it all out there. Maybe she would feel better talking about it. She couldn't possibly say anything these men didn't already know — or at least suspect.

"It's been really nice getting to know Kai again," she answered. "I can see why we had so much fun together when we were kids. But it's been a long weekend. I didn't know until last night that my mother committed suicide. I didn't even know she was depressed. So... I'm still kind of trying to take it all in."

The old men exchanged some not-so-furtive glances. Mr. Hiraga stepped forward. "I'm sorry, *Akage-chan*," he said gently. "But it's best that you know. I'm glad that's what was decided."

Mr. Kalaw nodded. "People think lies protect, but they always end up hurting, in the end."

Old Mr. Li, whom Maddie was not certain could hear well enough to follow the conversation, grabbed her hand. "Kai is a strong boy," he said earnestly, meeting her eyes.

Maddie looked back at him. She felt like she had missed a segue somewhere. But his gaze, albeit cloudy, seemed intentional.

"Your mother's death was very difficult," Mr. Kalaw continued. "Difficult for you and your father. Difficult for Kai and for his family and everyone here. But we move on." He smiled at her warmly. "We are all just happy our pretty Maddie has come back to us."

Mr. Puyat chimed in something in Pidgin. Maddie perked. She had understood him! In essence, the grouchy old goat had chuckled and said, "and Kai is happy she's all grown up and finally got some nice curves on her!"

The other men laughed. Maddie looked straight at Mr. Puyat. He still smelled like fish. "I heard that!" she said accusingly, pointing at him with a grin.

Mr. Puyat, for the first time in recorded history, smiled sheepishly back at her. The other men guffawed with laughter.

Her heart melted.

"Aw, you ignore him," Mr. Yokota said apologetically. "We've got nothing better to do than match-make. Means nothing."

"Speak for yourself," teased Mr. Hiraga. He gave Maddie a wink. "You make a lovely couple, eh?"

Maddie reddened. She was embarrassed because of course she'd had that same thought herself, she was touched because Mr. Puyat had *actually smiled at her*, and yet... something else had been said that worried her.

"You live on Maui now, right? Near where Kai lives?" Mr. Kalaw asked.

Maddie nodded absently. What was it?

Old Mr. Li was still sitting quietly at her side, watching her with a small, knowing smile. *Kai is a strong boy,* he had said.

True enough. But why had he said it? And why had Mr. Kalaw mentioned Kai's name specifically in saying that Jill Westover's death was hard on Maddie's friends here on Lana'i? Kai was a sensitive kid and wouldn't have cared for all the gory talk of hangings and hauntings, that was for sure. He didn't even like to fight spiders! But he was never close to Maddie's mother. Nobody was. Could he have been *that* upset over Maddie's leaving so suddenly, without saying goodbye to him?

She pondered. Surely not. He admitted that he had missed her. But if cared *that* much, he would have written her back!

"You said that my mother's death was hard on Kai," she asked Mr. Kalaw, her pulse speeding up again. "Why? I mean, I'm sure he felt sorry for me, and it was a horrible thing all around. But..."

Maddie's voice trailed off as she watched the men's faces. They were all looking at each other as if they'd gotten caught doing something wrong. No one said a word.

Dammit. And she'd been so certain the secrets were over!

Her face flashed with unwelcome heat... again. She rose to her feet.

"Maddie," Mr. Kalaw said quickly, putting a gentle hand on her arm. "Don't be upset."

"I know there's something you're not telling me," she said with frustration. "Who told you not to tell me? Let me guess. Nana? Malaya?"

Mr. Hiraga smiled apologetically. "You know mothers. Grandmothers. They protect their young. It's nature."

"We feel for you, child," said Mr. Yokota. "But we cannot cross the aunties. Our days are numbered already, you understand?"

"Talk to Kai," Mr. Kalaw urged. "Ask him your questions. But if he chooses not to answer..." He held her gaze. "Respect that."

Maddie fumed. Her first choice, she wanted the record to show, had been *not* to hear any of the truth. But now that she'd been forced to hear some of it, she darn well wanted to hear it all. She wanted it out and exposed and completely air-dried so she could pack it away neatly and forget it again, and she didn't want any loose ends hanging around to remind her of the process. If this mysterious missing piece involved *her* life, she wanted to know about it, and if Kai insisted on keeping it from her — *Kai*, who had forced all this on her in the first place! — they were going to have problems.

Respect that, indeed.

She did, however, respect Mr. Kalaw.

"I'll consider your advice," she told him. "Thank you." She faked a smile and wished all the men a happy Sunday morning.

Then she stomped off toward the Nakama house.

Chapter 23

Kai woke up feeling thick-headed and confused. He was sprawled across the top of his parents' bed, which was odd, because when he had returned in the pre-dawn hours, he had crashed on the couch.

He rubbed his face and sat up. Someone must have woken him up at some point and helped him stumble in here, but he had no memory of it. How much sleep had he managed last night, anyway? Three, four hours? However long he'd slept before the nightmare didn't count. And the last few hours, frankly, hadn't been the most restful either. Thanks to one Miss Madalyn Westover, he might never sleep again.

He exhaled roughly. That wasn't fair. It wasn't her fault. The woman had been doing practically everything in her power *not* to entice him ever since she'd first walked into his office on Maui. Could she help it if that was impossible? If only he'd forced himself to get out more, work a little less, he might have another girlfriend now. But he'd been out of BYU for six months already with nothing to show for it, and the frustration was getting to him.

He didn't like to think of himself as naive. He'd known that the culture shock he would experience in moving between the carefully structured singles world of Provo, Utah and the hookup culture of Maui would be extreme. He knew that finding women to date would be a challenge, that the population of twenty-something females on Maui who lived an LDS lifestyle without actually being LDS would be limited. He had not expected it to be flippin' *non-existent.* He'd accepted the fact that he'd have to settle for a woman who shared only some of his values, and he'd accepted that quickly, but even that pool was no more than a puddle. He'd gotten discouraged, and time had slipped by. Now he'd found Maddie again, and now he was... eager to move things along.

Unfortunately, that traffic signal was still on red.

He groaned aloud and stood up. Enough wallowing in self pity. Maddie had wandered into his office exactly three days ago. Four days ago, he'd been fine. Tonight they would go back to Maui, and this week he would redouble his efforts to meet some new people, date some more. And he'd have his old friend back, too. What was so terrible about that?

Because you want Maddie. And only Maddie.

Kai told himself to shut up. He crossed to the bedroom door and looked out. Neither of his parents appeared to be home. The truck wasn't visible out the front window. Gloria's bedroom door was closed. He grabbed his bag and stepped into the bathroom for a quick shower, then dressed and headed to the kitchen to find some breakfast. At no point did he hear a peep from Gloria's room. In fact, the whole neighborhood seemed unusually quiet.

He plastered a piece of toast with lilikoi jam and caught himself in a sigh. All things considered, Maddie had taken the tough news very well last night, and he knew he'd done the right thing in telling her. Yet this morning, his own dominant emotion was sadness. Yesterday he'd had *fun*. Plain, old-fashioned, whole-hearted fun, more fun than he'd had in ages. He had his Maddie back. Just like when they were kids, she'd been his sunshine. The yang to his yin. Her lively spirit, her snarky smile, her bubbling laugh, her wackiness. Her biting wit, her foolish bravado, and above all, her genuine courage. Always she had challenged his own cautious, resolute nature. Always she had made him feel stronger, more carefree... happier. Now she was back in all her glory, only this time she was all grown up.

And she wanted very much to be his friend again.

But only his friend.

Kai crunched his toast with more force than necessary. He *should* be able to do that. Up until last night, he thought maybe he could. God knew he'd done it enough times before, with enough other girls. But not with Maddie. He wanted her too damn much. The circumstances were beyond frustrating. Maybe if he'd been happily married to someone else when he met her again... But that wasn't the case. If friendship was truly all she wanted — and she had a perfect right to want that — then eventually, he would have to back off.

Which meant that he would lose her as his Maddie. His best bud. His sunshine.

Again.

He sunk his head into his hands. His mother and Nana were wrong. They were being so ridiculously overprotective, so worried that Maddie's return would send him back into the land of his childhood nightmares, back into reliving the events of that one horrible day. What they never really understood, what he was only coming to understand himself now, was that it wasn't that *one day* that had caused his nightmares in the first place. It was all wrapped up with his losing Maddie.

Most likely, it was his fear of losing her again that had brought them back.

Kai rose. His memories of that time were vague. He remembered doctors. He remembered missing school. He remembered horrific nightmares. And he remembered Maddie's letter, and that it marked some kind of turning point. But he couldn't remember a word that she had written, nor why he hadn't answered it. He only remembered that afterwards, he had tried to forget her.

He opened the door to the closet in the main room and pulled out boxes and bags from off the floor and the shelf until he found the one cardboard shoebox he sought. He stuffed everything back into the closet and then brought the shoebox to the kitchen table. He tore off the masking tape, which was marked with his name and a skull and crossbones to ward off would-be trespassers. He had sealed it up when he'd graduated from high school and left for Provo, and he knew it contained some letters from his grandparents and a few others. If he'd kept Maddie's letter, which he was pretty sure he did, it would be in here.

No sooner had he popped the lid than he heard Gloria's bedroom door open. He closed the box again and looked up at her. She was wearing an overlarge tee shirt and yoga pants and looked bedraggled and half asleep, with her hair sticking out in all directions. She returned his look without expression, stumbled to the counter to retrieve an apple banana, then pulled out a chair across the table from him. She fell into it in a slumping position with her knees against the tabletop. She peeled the banana.

"Good morning, Sister," Kai said, enunciating the words perfectly, just to bug her. They had always spoken English, rather than Pidgin, within the Nakama household. Aki's mother, who spoke Japanese to her children but taught English at the local school, had never allowed Pidgin to be spoken in her home, and Aki had followed that tradition with his own children. Of course, all of the Nakamas could and did speak Pidgin in other situations. But the influence of the English teacher in the family lent all of their speech a little more properness than was socially desirable for a kid, and when Kai returned after the additional insult of having been immersed in the affluent suburbia of the mainland, his Lana'ian friends teased him mercilessly about sounding "haolified." He knew they were right; his everyday speech did sound stilted. But he could drop back into Pidgin anytime he wanted to.

"Oh shut, up," Gloria snapped, biting off a piece of banana. She looked around the rest of the house. "Everybody gone?"

Kai nodded. He watched as Gloria slumped some more and fidgeted with her knees against the table. She was seventeen years old. Right now, she looked about twelve. Knowing that for the past couple months his baby sister had been sleeping with a man his age — some jerk who treated her like garbage — made him sick to his soul.

Gloria sat up suddenly. "So?" she asked, her eyes alight with sudden interest. "Tell me what's happening with Maddie. With you and Maddie, that is. Any progress?"

Kai took another bite of his now stone-cold toast. He lacked the energy to berate her for her nosiness. Besides, berating her never worked anyway. "We're just friends."

Gloria's mouth dropped open. She looked genuinely disappointed. "But why?"

He shrugged. "Because that's the way she wants it."

Gloria stared at him. She stared at him a very long time.

"You do know you're perfect for each other, don't you?" she said finally. "Did you know she doesn't even drink? I don't know about the caffeine thing, though. She might—"

"I don't care about that!" Kai interrupted. His voice was ragged. He needed to watch himself. Gloria didn't need to know details.

"Then why aren't you going for it?" Gloria pressed, undeterred. "I watched you yesterday, you know. The two of you together. You think there's not chemistry there? Are you kidding me? I was getting scorched in the back seat! Sparks are flying everywhere and everybody's laughing and everything's great and you had, like, a thousand chances to make a move... and brah, you did *nothing*. Nada. What's up with that?"

"I told you," Kai said heavily. "It's her choice. Not mine."

"She said that?"

Kai hesitated. "Not... in words. But yes, she has."

Gloria gave her head and shoulders a shake. "You know what? There is something seriously wrong with both you people. It's like you're still in the eighth grade or something."

Kai's blood heated. He glared at her.

"Don't just look at me like that! Talk to me!" Gloria demanded. She leaned across the table towards him. "I don't understand you, Kai!

You're obviously into each other. I don't know what her excuse is, but the least you can do is explain yours. You didn't join that church in Utah, you say you don't believe in that stuff, but here you are. Still alone. I don't get it. What are you waiting for? Does it bother you that Maddie's more... *experienced* than you are?"

Kai stood up and whirled away. He did not want to have this conversation with her. Not now, not ever. She was his baby sister, for God's sake! He didn't like talking about his personal life with anyone. It was none of her business. Particularly when her own life was so screwed up that—

He stopped and drew in a breath. Damn, he was a hypocrite. He'd made her personal life his business quick enough, hadn't he? Sat her down and started giving her advice. Nice, safe, big brotherly advice. But he couldn't say it came straight from the heart, could he? In fact, it had come straight from what he remembered of the church's teachings on the importance of chastity before marriage.

Wow.

It had seemed like a good idea at the time.

Crap.

He turned back around and looked at her. Her dark eyes were imploring. Hopeful. *Don't give me a bunch of platitudes that somebody else thinks I need to hear*, she seemed to be begging. *Just talk to me!*

He stepped back to the table and sat down. Whatever he said to her, it could not possibly go worse than the last time. "You want to know what I'm waiting for, Gloria? I'll tell you. I'm waiting for someone who's going to make me happy. Really happy. Deeply happy. Constantly and consistently happy. Not happy for twenty minutes here and a couple hours there with days and weeks of crazy agonizing drama in between. Just *happy*. And I don't just want a couple months of happy, either. I want it all. I want a whole freakin' lifetime of it. And if the price tag is high, if I have to be alone a little longer because I'm waiting for a relationship I'm sure is right rather than screwing around with women I know for a fact will *not* make me happy, that's *my choice*. And yes, Gloria, perfectly normal guys can and do think that way. Not a lot, maybe. But more than you probably think."

He took a breath and studied her. Her eyes were wide. She said nothing.

"You asked about the church," he said more quietly. "I might be too much of a natural skeptic to buy into the whole history of the Nephites and the Lamanites and all the theology that comes with it, but

I can't deny the positive effect the church has had on my grandparents' lives. They're the happiest people I know. Their lives are full of love, and they're always working hard to do good and to make the world a better place. I can't knock that. And I won't knock that."

Gloria was still staring at him. He leaned back in his chair.

"As for Maddie..." he said softly. "Of course there's chemistry. Of course I want more. And I'm not giving up on her, not yet. But I'm not going to push her, either. Ever. She's been pushed all her life and she's got a right to be sick of it. If she's interested, she can let me know."

He paused.

The silence in the room was deafening. Gloria seemed disturbed.

"I'm not judging you, Gloria," he said. "Or anyone else. But I won't apologize for doing things my own way, either."

"I get it," she said defensively, rising. She lowered her eyes, threw her banana peel in the trash can, and walked off into her bedroom.

She started banging around behind her door, and Kai choked down the rest of his limp toast. He pushed off the lid of the shoebox and looked inside. The stack of letters and papers he was hoping to find was right on top and he pulled it out, all the while keeping an anxious eye on Gloria's room. He felt sure he'd upset her again, although in what way this time, he wasn't sure. He only knew her reaction was different.

In a matter of minutes she reappeared wearing street clothes. Her hair looked magically back to normal. She headed for the front door.

Kai stood up and moved after her. He had no idea if he was doing or saying the right thing, but at least she was listening, so it was now or possibly never. "Gloria?" he asked.

She opened the door, then turned and looked at him. "Yeah?"

"Does Dylan make you happy?"

He watched as a miniscule smile lifted one corner of her mouth. Then, abruptly, she let out a sound somewhere between a scoff and a snort.

"Dylan's an asshole," she replied.

Chapter 24

Maddie walked between the towering Cook Island pines of the park and on into the residential streets. The sun was shining brightly already. It would be a warm day. She passed a cluster of teenaged boys she didn't know, and although ordinarily she would tense up at the prospect of catcalls, she knew she had nothing to worry about on Lana'i. The boys would think she was a tourist, and Lana'ians were savvy enough to know that happy tourists meant a happy economy. They might stare at her, but unlike teens elsewhere or even tourists at the resorts, the local boys wouldn't pester her, they would just smile at her and walk on by.

They smiled at her and walked on by.

Another swell of moisture rose behind her eyes, and she sucked in a sharp breath to staunch it. She wasn't starting that again. She had cried all she was going to cry today. She just had to beat this one last puzzle-piece out of Kai, and then all the revelations would be over with and she could go back to loving this little island without being afraid again.

She turned a corner toward the Nakama house and was surprised to see Gloria walking toward her, staring down at a phone.

"Hey," Maddie greeted, wondering if the girl was still supposed to be under house arrest. "Where are you headed?"

"Just out for a walk," Gloria replied cheerfully, pocketing the phone. "And you?"

Maddie hesitated. "I'm... well, I'm on my way to your house, I guess."

"Cool. See you later." Gloria passed her and walked on.

Maddie stopped, feeling uneasy. She was fairly certain that Gloria had been grounded all weekend. Possibly for the rest of her life. But was it her business?

"Oh, by the way, Maddie," Gloria called out suddenly.

Maddie swung around.

"He's not the most obvious about it, but Kai's really into you. And... just my personal opinion... but you could do worse, you know."

Maddie blinked. Where was *this* coming from? She pretended a skeptical look. "I seem to recall you telling me that he was a prig."

Gloria looked thoughtful. "Well, yeah. He is. Technically, I mean. But that word is a little harsh. It's more like he can be kind of lame sometimes, but in an adorable sort of way, you know?"

Maddie had no response to that. Gloria shrugged at her and resumed walking.

"Gloria?" Maddie called, worrying all over again. The girl was definitely acting weird, and if she was sneaking out to see Dylan while the rest of the family slept, all hell was going to break loose — with Maddie as co-conspirator.

Gloria turned around and looked at her while continuing to walk backwards.

"You're not going to see Dylan, are you?" Maddie pleaded.

Gloria cracked a grin. "Who?"

Maddie was confused. "*Dylan*," she said louder.

"Oh, him," Gloria said, still grinning. She waved a dismissive hand. "I broke up with him *seconds* ago." She laughed out loud, turned her back, and strutted off.

Maddie stared after her. She wanted to be hopeful about the truth of that statement, but she was far too perplexed. Why, oh why, did everyone have to talk in riddles this morning?

The Nakama house was quiet as she approached. The truck was gone and there were no signs of life. She jogged up to the front door and knocked. In a few seconds, Kai opened it.

She could not get used to the sight of him. Still.

All it took was a couple hours of not seeing him — heck, even twenty minutes and a change of clothes — and her brain did a total reset. He was so unexpectedly tall, and mature-looking, and aggravatingly handsome... it made her nuts, especially when she was annoyed with him, which she reminded herself that she was. "Good morning," she said tersely.

"Good morning," he returned.

Maddie tensed. The stiffness of her greeting had been entirely put-on, but his was not. When she'd left him last night they'd seemed okay with one another, albeit emotionally exhausted. This morning, in addition to looking tired, his beautiful brown eyes seemed almost wary.

"I'm upset with you," she announced, throwing a playful edge into her voice.

He opened the door for her. "Yeah? So what else is new?"

She grinned at him. To her relief, he grinned back.

"How are you?" he asked. "Did you get any sleep?"

"No. Did you?"

Kai shook his head. He waved her over to the couch and pushed a bunch of stuff off the edge of it and onto the floor. She sat down first, and he perched himself at the couch's opposite end. Maddie studied him thoughtfully. She marveled again at his "gentlemanly" behavior and wondered if his later upbringing in Utah had been responsible. For his sister to label him as a prig for being courteous and considerate was grossly unfair, to be sure. But at the current moment, his body language went past polite. He was being standoffish.

"I talked to Nana," she began, not knowing what she wanted to say. "She filled in some of the blanks for me."

Kai nodded. "That's good. Do you feel any better?"

Maddie considered. "In a way. I found out that she came to see me at the resort, while I was waiting for my grandparents. I never knew that. I asked for her, but I didn't think she came."

Kai was quiet for a moment. "That's awful. I'm sorry."

Maddie felt a pang in her middle. She could tell from his expression that he understood. That he cared. But how could he care about her hurt feelings over missing Nana, and not understand how much it hurt that he had never answered her letter? How could he care enough to tell her that her mother committed suicide, but then leave out some other dark secret at the same time? She didn't get it.

"I went to see the old men this morning," she continued. "I told them I knew about my mother, and Mr. Li said something strange. He said that you were 'a strong boy.'" She watched Kai's face carefully. "Now, what would he mean by that? Why would he say it? And what is it that Nana and Malaya don't want you or anyone else to tell me?"

Kai looked stricken. Practically green. He rose abruptly and turned away.

"Kai?" she rose and followed him into the kitchen.

She watched as he picked up an empty cup from the counter, filled it with water from the sink, and drank. He had drained a third of it before he looked at her again. "You want anything?" he asked, gesturing to the fridge.

"Just an answer," she said calmly.

His reaction worried her. Kai was nothing if not a straight arrow. Whatever he wasn't telling her, it bothered him deeply.

"Maddie," he said, his voice quiet. "Last night I told you everything that has to do with you. The rest of it really doesn't. It only has to do with me. My mom and Nana — it's me they're worried about. They shouldn't, because I'm fine. But that's what all the mystery's about. I promise, no one's trying to keep you in the dark for any reason other than to spare me."

Maddie stared. He looked so vulnerable all of a sudden that she felt a primal urge to vault herself across the kitchen, throw her arms around his neck, and hold him. But she was able to restrain herself. Because he was definitely putting distance between them this morning.

"I see," she answered.

"I do think we should probably talk about it," he continued quietly. "Just get it all out in the open so that we can put it behind us both once and for all. If you think you're up to that. I didn't want to lay it all on you last night. Hearing about your mother seemed like enough for one sitting."

Maddie felt a trembling sensation well up in her arms again, but she willed it back down. *No.* She had already faced the worst of it. Whatever this was, she could handle it.

"Okay," she agreed.

Kai smiled at her, but it was a small, sad smile. A smile that worried her. "We should take a walk somewhere," he suggested. "I don't want Gloria to overhear. Maybe we could pack some food? Head up the mountain?"

Maddie envisioned herself swinging from the Tarzan trees. Her mood brightened and she was about to smile when she realized that she had completely forgotten about Kai's sister. "Was Gloria supposed to stay here?" she asked. "Because I ran into her down the—"

Her explanation was cut short by the crunching sound of the Nakamas' truck rolling up on the gravel outside. Malaya parked and jogged quickly through the front door. "Hey, Maddie. Listen, Kai, I've got to get up to the marina. If you want the truck today, you'll have to drop me off."

Kai put down his cup. "Sure. Just let me get my shoes on. Maddie, you want to come?"

She nodded in agreement.

"Where's Gloria?" Malaya asked, looking through the girl's open bedroom door.

"Was she not supposed to leave the house at all?" Kai asked.

Malaya drew in a breath and threw back her shoulders, instantly mom-scary again. Maddie felt herself mentally shrink two feet and suspected that Kai was doing the same. *"Kai!"* Malaya bellowed. "You told us last night you would keep an eye on her!"

"I'm sorry," he apologized quickly. "We had a good talk this morning, and she went outside afterwards, but I didn't think—"

"Malaya?" Maddie broke in. She tried to remind herself that she wasn't eight years old anymore, but an angry Malaya could scare the crap out of anybody. "I ran into Gloria just now, down the street. She said she was going for a walk. And she also said... although I can't be a hundred percent sure she wasn't joking... but she *said* that she had just broken up with Dylan."

Malaya's dark eyes widened to saucers. She mumbled something in a language Maddie guessed was Filipino.

"Maddie," Kai said breathlessly, stepping forward. "Are you sure?"

"No," she answered. "I'm not sure she broke up with him. But I am sure she told me she did."

Malaya's perfectly shaped lips broke into a radiant smile. "I'll *take it,* Maddie girl! I'll take it! Hallelujah!" She turned to Kai. "What did you say to her?"

Kai looked flabbergasted. "I... I can't believe it was anything I said."

Malaya looked at her phone, then dodged into the bathroom. "You can tell me on the way. I'm going to be late!"

Maddie waited in the kitchen while Kai put on his shoes, and when her eyes alighted on a gold baseball batter figurine sitting on the kitchen table, she cried out with glee. "Your MVP award! Fourth grade Little League. Geez, you worshipped this thing! You practically had a shrine going," she teased.

The trophy was sitting next to a shoebox along with a stack of envelopes, and on top of the stack was a letter addressed to Kai in pretty cursive handwriting. The return sticker had a picture of an angel and was printed with the name of Stan and Amy Ford with an address in Provo, Utah. Maddie looked at the postmark. December 10, 2001 — the time of her own first Christmas back on the mainland. She pushed the letter aside and looked further down the stack. More letters from Stan and Amy. Dozens of them.

Malaya came out of the bathroom and hustled toward the door. "Let's go!"

"Maddie?" Kai called.

"Sorry." She hastened to follow the two of them outside, then jumped into the back seat of the truck.

So, Kai's grandparents had written him letters. So what?

That didn't mean he had written them back.

Get over it.

Malaya drove the truck, which put Maddie's nerves on a razor edge. Malaya's subconscious driving was hazardous at the best of times, and the tour guide was even more distracted than usual. She wanted Kai to spill every detail of his conversation with Gloria, and the more he kept respectfully insisting that the details were private, the more agitated his mother became. Maddie kept a death grip on the passenger door in the back seat as the red dust flew and the truck narrowly avoided head-ons with three Cook Island pines and a rental jeep. Kai wouldn't budge, however, and Malaya finally gave up and decided she would just assume the good news to be true. After all, what could be the harm in thinking positively for *one* sunny Sunday?

They reached the Manele boat harbor in a frighteningly short time, and Malaya turned into the parking lot. She pulled up next to one of the tour vans and hopped out in a flash. "Van's not supposed to be here," she explained, shaking her head. "And I've got to pick up some people at the airport. Thanks, Kai. See you later!"

She started up the van and disappeared in yet another cloud of red dust. Kai got out of the truck and walked around to the driver side. Maddie stayed where she was. She was thinking.

After a moment, Kai looked back over his shoulder at her. "Am I supposed to drive you around like this? Because it feels kind of weird."

"I saw that stack of letters from your grandparents," she replied, not listening. "They obviously put some effort into keeping up with you while you were growing up. Did they call, too?"

Kai was quiet for a moment. He looked like he didn't want to answer. But he did. "Yes, maybe once a month or so. But calls were more expensive back then. And talking on the phone could be awkward. I didn't know them all that well. But my grandfather used to make crossword puzzles for me. And then I would make puzzles for him. And my grandmother would encourage me to write stories for her. It was easier for me than trying to talk about school and day-to-day things."

He shut the engine off. "You want to take a walk around the marina maybe? Now that we're here?"

He wrote back to his grandparents.

A weight settled in Maddie's stomach.

Why does it matter? she screamed at herself.

"Sure," she answered, unbuckling her seatbelt.

They stepped out of the truck and began walking across the grassy picnic area toward the boat docks. Kai's phone rang, and he pulled it out of his shorts pocket.

"It's my dad," he explained.

"No problem," Maddie replied, secretly relieved. A flash of blue, black, and white had caught her eye. "I have birds to watch."

The small flock of birds swooped over the tourist family at the picnic tables and lighted in a cluster of trees farther away. Maddie followed, catching up to the birds on the lawn near the barbecue pavilion. "Hello, Java sparrows," she greeted. She had seen the species many times when she was a child, but then she hadn't known what to call them. "And my old Kentucky cardinal. How's it going?" She smirked at the solid red, crested bird that pecked in the grass along with the sparrows. A few feet away from it, another cardinal also hunted for food.

"Now, you're a little more interesting," Maddie complimented, admiring how its own red head was set off from its dark wings by a bright white breast and neck collar. The two cardinals hopped closer together suddenly, and Maddie studied them with a wry expression. When the volcano that was to become the island of Lana'i had first popped out of the ocean, there was no bird life on it — all the species had come from somewhere else, at some later point in time. She happened to know that both these species had settled on the island in just the last hundred years. One from the Eastern United States and one from South America. To her, the Brazilian Cardinal was wonderfully exotic while the Kentucky bird was a bore. But the birds didn't see it that way, did they? As far as they were concerned, they were both Hawaiian.

Maddie looked up. Kai was far away in the parking lot, still talking on the phone. Another flash of interesting feathers fluttered across her field of vision. Pale yellow, a soft olive brown... perhaps a Japanese bush warbler?

Kai would have to catch up with her. She followed the bird past the pavilion and into the forest as it flitted from tree to tree. She wished she had her binoculars. Regardless, as she moved quietly through the thick woods, listening closely to the mingled tunes of a variety of unseen birds overhead, her spirits lifted. She always felt soothed when she was alone with nature. Even if "nature" meant camping out in the Humpty in the boondocks of Lee County, Alabama in ninety-eight degree heat and two hundred percent humidity trying to trap one feral cat eaten up with fleas and ear mites. Even then. Nature was her home.

Could she help it if this particular room of the house was her favorite? Warm and slightly breezy, with dappled sun shining through the gently waving mesquite trees, with just a hint of sea salt on the air?

She had long since lost the warbler she'd been tracking, but the forest was full of other birds, and she kept moving. When she heard an odd sound she couldn't identify, she stopped. It was a strange sort of popping sound. And then... was that a moan?

Whoops.

Maddie froze. Perhaps she had approached a little too quietly. She was not the only person who appreciated the romantic beauty of the forest, and the couple who had arrived before her had taken their appreciation to another level. They were leaning against a fallen tree trunk, wrapped in each other's arms and thoroughly enjoying what they thought was their privacy.

Maddie began a covert retreat, then froze again. *Wait.* She knew that head of hair! It was Ben the boat captain, who had brought her to Lana'i on the catamaran. Her heart fell, and the sick feeling she'd just gotten rid of came back again. Ben was married. What the hell was he doing hiding out in the woods making out with some skinny brunette in the middle of a Sunday afternoon? She could have sworn he wasn't the cheating type. When he talked about his wife, he had sounded like a man who was genuinely in love. And he hadn't flirted with Maddie *at all.* Was she losing all sense of judgment? And furthermore, if he was the cheating type, why *hadn't* he hit on her?

She turned and started walking back out of the woods, not caring whether the couple heard her or not. She emerged into the open to see Kai near the pavilion, obviously searching for her. When their eyes met, he hurried over.

"Good news," he announced happily. "My dad says Riku's headed to the mainland tomorrow. The family got enough money together for the ticket and the lawyer. He's going to take leave from work here and look for a temporary job out there until he can get custody straightened out."

Maddie smiled warmly. "That is good news. Excellent work, Nakama."

He shook his head. "I didn't do anything. I don't have any money. But a whole lot of people gave all that they could afford. It's such a relief that Riku has a good lawyer on his side. I really don't think he'll lose those kids, now."

"You did help him, Kai," Maddie repeated. "You got him a lawyer in the middle of Idaho, didn't you? What are the odds he could have made that connection this fast if you hadn't located another BYU grad?"

Kai's smile was crafty. "I told you the LDS community was a wonderful thing. But that's not all the good news. My dad had a talk with Gloria. She told him she *did* break up with Dylan! She wouldn't explain, though. All she said was that she figured she could do better. And he said that she actually seemed to be in a really good mood."

Maddie grinned broadly. "I'm sure she's happy to be rid of him. And the conflict." Her smile turned into a smirk. "Told ya."

"Yes, you did." Kai smiled back at her, and Maddie had the feeling that she should be happy. She *was* happy, for Riku and for Gloria and for the whole Nakama family. But the various rotten feelings that had been gnawing at her all morning were gnawing worse than ever now, thanks to the disturbing spectacle she'd just been forced to witness.

Why, oh why, did Ben the boat captain have to be sucking face with some other woman when he had a perfectly nice lawyer-wife at home on Maui? Was there no male human on the face of the earth who could be trusted when it came to sex?

Damn, it was getting hot.

She tugged at the neckline of her jacket, fanning it to bring in a breeze. The woods had been cooler, but she was standing in the sun now, and the temperature was climbing. She pulled down her zipper an inch, but couldn't lower it any farther. She'd packed for the weekend at the end of a laundry cycle and was down to her last shirt. It was perfectly decent, of course, but the scooped neck caused problems. It showed a hint of collarbone and cleavage both, and though she'd had no choice but to pack it, she knew she should keep her jacket on around Kai.

"Are you hot?" he asked.

She stared at him. It was a stupid question. He had beads of sweat on his own forehead, didn't he? And he was wearing a perfectly comfortable lightweight tee shirt. A shirt which, she couldn't help but notice, fit his nicely shaped torso like a glove. "Of course I'm hot," she said testily. "It's a hot day."

"Then why don't you take that jacket off?"

Maddie's temper flared. Partly because she was hot, partly because she was mad at Ben the boat captain, and partly because Kai was looking at her with that ten-year-old-boy, smugly superior, what-you're-doing-isn't-logical-and-I-know-better expression that had always made her blood boil. "Excuse me?"

Her tone was snippy, caustic. She sounded ten years old herself and she fully expected "polite adult Kai" to recoil and apologize.

Maybe it was the heat. Maybe something had been eating at him all morning, too. Whatever the reason, polite adult Kai disappeared wherever civil grown-up Maddie had gone, and obnoxious know-it-all kid Kai took his place.

"You said you were hot!" he snapped back at her. "I said take your jacket off! How complicated is that?"

Maddie fumed. "I *can't* take it off!"

"Why not?"

"You know perfectly well why not!"

"Because all men are animals who can't possibly control themselves?"

"You said it; I didn't!"

"Well, it's not true!" he decreed.

"Says you!" she sneered.

"Well, I ought to know!"

"Yeah?"

"Yeah!"

Maddie's next words died on her lips as a crackling of brush drew her attention to the edge of the woods. The previously caught-in-the-act couple stepped out from the trees a few yards away. The woman stared straight at Kai.

He looked back at her with an expression of pure horror. "Hello, Haley."

Chapter 25

"Hello." The woman stepped closer to them both, a sly smile playing on her lips. She was tall and somehow commanding in presence, despite her casual dress. Her long brown hair was unstyled and she wore little makeup, but her intelligent green eyes gave her a businesslike demeanor, nevertheless. Ben followed behind her, and as his gaze came to rest on Maddie, his own friendly hazel eyes lit up.

"Maddie!" he greeted cheerfully. "How's Lana'i treating you? Is it everything you'd hoped?"

Maddie looked back at him in confusion, but only for a second. His *wife's* name was Haley! A surge of relief swept through her, and she smiled broadly back at him. "It's been great. Thanks."

Ben turned to look at Kai, and his brow furrowed. "We've met, haven't we?"

Kai extended a hand. "Kai Nakama. I work at EarthDefense. You came by the office a couple months ago."

"Oh, right!" Ben enthused, returning a hearty handshake.

"Kai grew up here on Lana'i," Haley explained to her husband. Even as the couple stood, undoubtedly aware that they had been caught necking like teenagers, Haley leaned against her husband's side, and he snaked out a long arm and wrapped it around her thin waist.

"Is that so?" Ben replied, looking back at his wife. "Well, so did Maddie! She's the ecologist I told you about. The one who's going to single-handedly save the monk seals from toxo!"

"So that was you?" Haley asked, smiling at Maddie and shaking her hand with a grip every bit as firm as a man's. "Nice to meet you." She looked from Maddie to Kai, then back again, her keen gaze missing nothing. "Let me guess. Childhood sweethearts?"

"No," Kai said quickly.

Maddie glared at him. "You said that awful fast."

"Well, we weren't, were we?" he defended. "We were friends."

Maddie looked at Haley. "I only lived here until I was ten. Kai still had cooties then. Plus he was a shrimp."

She looked sideways to find Kai glaring at her. She chuckled playfully, and he grinned back.

"Kai Nakama," Haley accused. "You've been holding out on me. I thought I recognized your voice when I was coming out of the woods, but I didn't believe it was you, because I couldn't believe you would ever use that tone with a woman."

Kai looked horrified all over again. "You mean, bickering like a fifth grader?"

"I said the tone, not the words," Haley explained. "You were arguing with Maddie like she was an equal. No kid gloves. No pedestal. No worry that you were offending some delicate female sensibilities that demanded special treatment."

"Ha!" Maddie scoffed. "As if!"

Haley grinned at that. Kai still looked horrified.

"All I'm saying is," Haley continued lightly, "I may have less pro bono work ahead of me than I thought. All you have to do is channel the little boy who used to *like* arguing with this little girl — back when you didn't give a damn whether she was a girl or not."

"Oo-kay!" Ben said good-naturedly, lifting his arm to circle his wife around the shoulders and pull her away. "Enough shop talk. It's a weekend."

"Hey, who was talking about toxo?" Haley protested with a grin, twisting in his grasp.

In response, Ben swept her off her feet. "You want to go back in the woods?" he asked playfully.

"We never got the mesquite!" she reminded.

"Oh, right." Ben set her back down and cast a glance toward the picnic area. "Our passengers," he explained to Kai and Maddie, tilting his head that direction. "We brought her sister's family up for the day — they're headed back to the mainland tomorrow." He turned back to his wife. "You think they're going to miss us soon?"

Haley laughed. "I think they missed us ten minutes ago."

Ben sighed. "Better go."

He and Haley waved goodbye to Maddie and Kai and headed off.

"That," Kai said slowly when the couple was out of earshot, "was *not* the same Haley I see at the office."

Maddie studied him. "Sounds like she could say the same thing." The beads of sweat on Kai's forehead had turned into rivulets. Not only had the encounter been tense for him, but they had been standing in the sun the entire time. Maddie's own bangs were plastered to her forehead and underneath the accursed jacket sweat was now running down her front and back like a river. Lana'i was almost never this hot in January.

Kai studied her too, then exhaled heavily. "Come over here." He led her a few feet away to a patch of shade, then stopped again.

"Maddie," he began uncertainly. "It's none of my business. I grant you that, okay? But you really can take that stupid jacket off. You shouldn't have to wear it. It's ridiculous."

Maddie bristled. This again? "You're right. It *is* none of your business."

"So call it a justice issue, okay?" he pleaded. "I know you think I'm obsessing, here..."

He paused a moment, as if deciding whether or not to go on. Maddie found herself hoping that he would, if only out of curiosity. Kai was no control freak. Why did he even care what she wore?

"Maddie," he began again, his voice softer. "The truth is, all this frumpy stuff you've been covering up with... it makes me crazy, and I can't stand to watch it anymore. But not for the reason you probably think. This isn't the single guy in me talking, it's the crusader. You just... happened to hit on an issue that's bugged me for years now."

He held her gaze. "You have a right to wear normal, comfortable clothes like any other woman. You have a right to wear makeup and dress any way that makes you feel good about yourself. If men choose to harass you, and we both know that some will, that's a consequence you'll have to deal with. But the blame is *theirs*. Not yours."

Maddie's eyebrows lifted. That was hardly what she expected him to say.

He sighed and looked away. "At BYU there was a dress code. Girls weren't supposed to wear anything sleeveless, or low-cut, or any dress above the knee. Forget shorts or even capris. It was supposed to be helpful to all concerned. Not that the guys weren't still held responsible for their own behavior. They were. But the idea was that the girls should cooperate by providing as little distraction as possible."

Dress code? Maddie never had gotten around to looking up that mysterious BYU behavioral honor code. How intrusive was it, exactly? She made a mental note to check it out as soon as she could get a signal.

"I always hated it," Kai continued. "I felt like it gave men no credit and sent women the wrong message at the same time. And watching you walk around this weekend dressed like a potato and swimming in a man's tee shirt is like the worst part of BYU all over again."

"Well excuse me for not providing more entertaining visuals,"

Maddie said sarcastically, albeit with a smile. Thinking about Kai's spending the last seven years unable to see his classmates' bare shoulders amused her greatly.

"The problem with a dress code like that," Kai continued, his voice irritated, "is the subtext of the message it sends to women. Namely, that having an attractive body is a crime. I see that same attitude in you, Maddie, even though I doubt you'll admit it. I bet every time you wear something that makes you look good, you feel like you're doing something wrong."

"I do not!" she protested immediately.

He threw her a look.

She withered a little. Was he right? Because if he was, that would really tick her off.

"You know rationally in your brain that you're not at fault when men approach you," Kai continued. "But there's some part of you that still feels responsible."

Maddie's teeth clenched.

"I can see it because I remember how you used to be," he pressed. "You couldn't care less what you wore or how you looked. You were such a free spirit. Hair flying. Not a care. And now you're about to faint from heat exhaustion because you're too afraid to take off that damned jacket."

Maddie growled. "I am not *afraid*."

"Then what?"

"I am being *considerate!*" Maddie said rudely.

"Well, cut it out!" Kai shot back. "You think you're not desirable with the jacket on? I've got news for you — you're ridiculously sexy no matter what. The incremental difference isn't worth your suffering."

Maddie said nothing. She could think of nothing to say.

Kai blew out a breath. He studied her a moment. "I don't blame you for being afraid. Men can be jerks. And you're absolutely right that the more gorgeous you look, the more attention you'll attract and probably the more trouble you'll invite."

"I am not afraid of... *that*," Maddie insisted. "I can handle myself just fine, and you know it. You've seen it. I just get tired of doing it!"

Kai's dark eyes held hers. "If that's the real reason you feel like you have to hide yourself, then fine."

Maddie's ire sparked again. *Stinking know-it-all!* "What do you mean 'the real reason?' What do you think 'the real reason' is?"

"I already told you," he answered. "I think you're afraid of feeling guilty."

Maddie faltered a little. Could he be right? She really, *really* hated it when he was right.

He lifted his arms as if to touch her, then thought better of it and dropped them again. "Do you remember when we would swing on the Tarzan trees, and everybody said you were the best?" he asked.

"I was *The King*," Maddie corrected.

"Yes, well," he replied. "Do you also remember that I never fell? Never hurt myself? Not once? Whereas *you* got banged up and bruised all the time? I could make the case that I should be the king."

Maddie snorted. "You never got three feet off the ground, you wuss! I was the one out there climbing the tallest trees and taking off on all the longest vines!"

"Right," Kai agreed. "Because *you* weren't afraid of falling."

Maddie sucked in a breath. Her little Kai had indeed turned into a lawyer, darn him. And she was pretty sure she had walked straight into his trap.

"I know you're brave, Maddie. Bruises and banged up shins have never scared you. But feeling guilty gets to you. It gets to you like nothing else does."

He took a step back. "Now, how about instead of that walk in the sun, we drive over to the beach and cool off instead? And just so we're perfectly clear, you do not have to wear that jacket for my benefit. You are free to look and feel as gorgeous as you want, and I promise to control myself. If anybody else is rude to you, I'll give him the stink eye and you can *bus' hees ala-alas*. Okay?"

Maddie felt something inside herself crumble. She could see what Kai was doing. Both things he was doing. First off, he was going out of his way *not* to say that as long as they were together, other men were unlikely to bother her anyway. But they both knew that was the case. He could be eighty-three years old and toting oxygen, and if he was male and not flagrantly gay, his mere presence would deter far more pests than her own cold stare and well-developed biceps ever could. That fact was annoying and humiliating, but true, and Kai seemed to know she would perceive it that way. He could so easily have played the macho card, making a show of defending her, protecting her. The fact that he did not made her want to rip off his sweat-stained shirt and pounce on him.

Oh, my.

Judging from the way he'd been looking at her lately, if she did anything like that, she would get far more action than she bargained for. Which brought her to the second thing he was doing for her. He was inviting her to be more physically comfortable, even if her comfort came at his own expense. She'd given him no indication that she wanted a romantic relationship, and she was certain now that he would make no move in that direction unless she did so first. Which was sweet. And commendable.

But also unsustainable. Which was almost certainly why he had been putting extra distance between them this morning.

She had seen it happen so many times. With all the nicest guys. They were her friends as long as the relationship showed some chance of developing, but once convinced her feelings would never change, they politely disappeared. The defections had always aggravated her, but looking at Kai now, she felt an unaccustomed jolt of sympathy for the men. If their roles were reversed, would she act any differently?

Probably not. But it didn't matter. Her Kai would not be defecting anywhere.

She smiled back at him, and the lust in his dark eyes shone through, strong and unmistakable. Another unwelcome tremor of nervousness coursed through her, and she sighed to herself with disappointment. *Madalyn Westover: Tarzan brave!*

Right. She supposed she *was* afraid of feeling guilty. The intangibles in life had always been the most fearsome.

"The beach sounds good," she agreed.

"Let's go, then," he said, leading her back towards the truck. "We can have our talk there."

He made an attempt to sound light-hearted, but Maddie could tell that he dreaded whatever he still had to tell her as much as she dreaded hearing it.

Last night he had held her while they talked. She didn't think she'd be so lucky today.

Unless...

Unless she could get a grip on herself and get over feeling like such an ignorant babe in the woods beside him. So what if they had always been equals before? In everything?

They reached the truck and opened the doors. It was two hundred thousand degrees inside.

Kai's eyes flickered over Maddie as he started up the engine and turned on the AC. He looked distinctly hopeful.

Her mind flooded with images of countless girls and women taking one look at those gorgeous eyes of his, those broad shoulders and strong limbs, and offering themselves like candy.

Her stomach flip-flopped.

She left the jacket on.

Chapter 26

Kai looked out over the crowded beach lot with chagrin. So much for finding a private stretch of sand to wade along. They had to find water somewhere. Maddie would clearly die of heat stroke before she'd take that damned jacket off.

He didn't understand it. It couldn't be that she didn't trust him. He knew she did.

It must be just one more way of saying *no*.

"Why don't we walk up and check out the *keiki* pools?" he suggested as he parked, trying not to think about it. "We've got a bunch of old shoes in the back of the truck." He had his usual sandals on, but he had noticed that — not expecting to wind up at the beach — she was wearing a decent pair of running shoes.

Maddie threw him a skeptical look. Her red hair was limp and her skin was shiny with sweat and he hated her jacket with an abiding passion and she still looked ridiculously, incredibly desirable. "Whose old shoes?" she asked, pulling up a foot. "Unless they're yours, I'm out of luck. You seriously think these dogs could fit in any other Nakama family footwear?"

Kai looked, but not at her shoe size. Her perfectly formed ankle and sexy calf were way more interesting. "We'll figure something out," he assured, recognizing that she had a point; the rest of his family did have small feet. But trying to walk barefoot on lava rock and coral was a recipe for pain and suffering.

They got out of the truck. Maddie pulled out her phone, cooed over having a good signal, and headed off to get a quick drink from the water fountain. Kai fished around in the truck bed and found a pair of men's sandals he suspected might be Dylan's. *Perfect.* When Maddie was done with them, he would throw them away.

He leaned against the front of the truck to await Maddie's return. She wandered back through the trees with excruciating slowness, her face buried in her phone. When she was about ten feet away she stopped, looked up, and stared at him wide-eyed. Her expression made his heart skip. She gave him one of the most brilliant smiles he'd ever seen.

"Um... Did you find me any shoes?" she asked.

Kai swallowed. She gave him a smile like that, then asked about shoes? "Yeah," he replied. "Try these." He held out the sandals.

Maddie stepped over and took them, smiling at him all the while. Her gray eyes sparkled knowingly, and her lips drew into a grin.

What the hell?

She walked around and sat down on the passenger seat to switch her shoes. In a few seconds she reappeared with the sandals on. "Ready!" she said with enthusiasm.

Kai stood up. She was no longer wearing the jacket. She was wearing an excruciatingly form-fitting yellow cotton shirt which dipped low at the neck, revealing an expanse of perfectly delicious skin and fantastical curves straight from heaven. Or hell, depending on your perspective.

He was aware that he was staring.

Maddie smiled at him. "It's your own fault, Nakama," she said wryly.

Kai forced himself to blink normally. "More comfortable now?"

"Much," she said with enthusiasm. "In fact, I've never felt better. Let's go!" She took a step forward, swung her arms, and bounced a little.

Kai sucked in a breath and followed.

Maybe that BYU dress code had its good points.

They walked through the picnic area and on across the sand to the trailhead. With his eyes glued to her form ahead of him, he had to concentrate to keep focus. He had promised to tell her the whole unpleasant story, and he was going to get it over with right now.

They reached the *keiki* pools, and he was relieved to find no one else in the immediate area. They walked down the steps and out on the lava rock across the maze of tide pools until they found a cool, private spot where they could wade or sit and dangle their feet in the water.

Concentrating was a difficult task with this newly uninhibited version of Maddie before him. Not only had she taken her jacket off, she had rolled her Bermuda shorts halfway up her thighs. At some point along their trek she had unbraided her hair, and at this very moment she was combing through it with her fingers while she splashed her toes in the water like a friggin' mermaid.

He indulged himself in another long, unabashed viewing of her person, and she acknowledged his interest with a sly grin. He shook himself. He didn't know what had brought about her change of heart with regard to covering up, but as long as the traffic signal stayed on red, his own situation remained unaltered. If he had half a brain, he would have waited to give the wear-what-you-want speech till five minutes before the ferry docked. But they were here now. And he still had "the unpleasantness" to deal with.

"Maddie," he began tiredly. "You know I don't want to talk about this. I wish we could spend the rest of the day goofing off and acting like kids again, just like yesterday. But you need to know that... Well, your mother's death was difficult for me, too, as it turned out."

Maddie stopped splashing. "So I understand," she said softly. "But why, Kai?"

He blew out a breath. The images were coming back. He had hoped they wouldn't, but if it was going to happen, he'd just have to power through it. That was okay. He'd be fine.

"You remember, the afternoon it happened, you didn't go straight home from school, right?"

Maddie nodded. "I went to Christina's house to work on a project," she said. "Your Aunt Maria came and got me there."

"You didn't think that project was going to take very long," Kai reminded, a detail she had no doubt forgotten, but which was emblazoned on his own memory. "You and I had planned to meet afterwards and hang out. I waited around at Nana's, but you didn't show up, and I decided to walk down and wait out in front of your house instead."

Maddie drew in a breath sharply. "Oh, Kai," she said in a whisper. "No."

Kai's heart pounded. She didn't need to know the details. It would serve no purpose, other than to give her nightmares of her own.

"I'm afraid so." He caught her eyes. "It was me who found your mother that day, Maddie."

Not right away, as it turned out. No, and that was part of the nightmare too, wasn't it? For at least fifteen minutes he'd sat on the Westovers' front step, wondering what the odd creaking noise was that came from her living room window whenever the wind kicked up. It had taken him a long time to get bored enough to peer through the glass louvers and try to find out. If it were anyone else's house, he would have knocked on the door right away, but Maddie's mother was strange, and he didn't want to bother her. Jill Westover wasn't unkind, but she was unhelpful, and he knew that even if she did bother to get up and answer the door, she would have no more idea where her daughter was than he did.

The glass louvers had been tilted down, and he couldn't see clearly into the middle of the room. But he could see something that disturbed him. He saw a cup on the floor. And a book. And a splash of bright red.

His ten-year-old heart had begun to race then. *Maddie? Mrs. Westover?* Was someone hurt? He had knocked on the door. No answer. He had pounded on it harder.

"Kai?" Maddie said gently. She had materialized at his side. He could feel her warmth. "You don't have to relive it again for my sake. I can tell it was bad. I'm sorry. I'm so, so sorry you had to go through that."

He had put his hand on the doorknob and found it open, as he knew he would. Hardly anybody locked their doors in the middle of the day on Lana'i. *Mrs. Westover?* He had stepped in and turned around and with that one action he had seen it all. She had hung herself with the aid of a scarf, a light fixture, and a coffee table, and she'd done it many hours before. All of which was more than enough to horrify him, even if she had not been his best friend's mother. But no, there was more, because hanging had not been Jill Westover's preference. Her first attempt had been to slit both her wrists and her neck with a kitchen knife, and while those wild swipes were not sufficient to render her unconscious, much less end her life, the picture they painted in the small living room had been more than gruesome enough to batter his young mind.

"That must have been awful for you," Maddie whispered.

Her face was close to his. Her hair was loose and flowing about her cheeks. She'd grown up to be so amazingly lovely. But she was a beautiful girl, too, in her way. How Jill Westover could be so far gone as to look at her daughter and never *see* her had always amazed him. What amazed him more, what appalled him even now, was what would have happened if he *hadn't* walked into the Westovers' living room that day. Maddie's mother had to know — as she was pulling out that knife and tying on that scarf and kicking away that table — that there was a damn good chance her cheerful little girl would be the first one home.

Kai took a step back and cleared his throat. "It was awful," he admitted. "And I didn't handle it the greatest. I had nightmares for a while. I had trouble sleeping, and I missed some school. My family had a hard time of it, too, because they were worried about me." He tried to smile. "We all got through it, of course. But you can see why my mom and Nana, as happy as they were to see you, had their reservations about *my* seeing you. They were afraid of what it might dredge up again."

"But you're okay, aren't you?" Maddie asked anxiously.

Kai hesitated. "I'm fine."

Her shoulders slumped. "You're such a liar."

Dammit. How was he ever going to make it in negotiations?

"Kai!" Maddie protested. "Talk to me! What's going on with you?"

"I had one nightmare, okay?" he admitted. "Last night. But it wasn't because I can't handle gore. I mean—" He looked up at her, mortified. He hadn't meant to say it like that.

"Don't," she insisted. "I understand. What are you trying to say?"

Kai bit his lip. He ran his hands through his hair. There. His catalog of procrastinating gestures was exhausted. "After I... found your mother, I went to Nana's house, and then somebody took me home. I guess I was close to hysterical. A doctor came to the house and gave me some kind of sedative. God only knows what it was — I didn't know up from down for a long time."

Maddie let out a huff. "I think we had the same doctor. I'm sorry. Go on."

He met her eyes again. This was the hard part. Especially now. "I was so mixed up about everything. Disoriented. I still think the drugs that doctor gave me had a lot to do with that. I remember that I wanted to see you. I was worried about you. I kept imagining you walking in on that same scene, even though everyone explained to me that it didn't happen that way, that you never saw what I saw. Still, I had nightmares where it was you instead of me."

"Oh, Kai," Maddie's soft, sweet voice threatened to undo him, tempting him to grab onto her and not let go. The sun on his face and arms was hot, but the water around his feet was cool and soothing. Waves splashed on the rocks and the sound of people playing on the beach drifted around the bend, but hidden in their little pool he felt as if they were alone.

She moved closer to him. Her side pressed against his. Her shoulder. Her hip. Her curves. He took another step back.

"And then everything got worse," he continued. "Because everyone started lying to me. And I knew that they were lying. I kept asking to see you and they kept giving me excuses why I couldn't. You weren't feeling well, you were taking a little vacation on Maui. Stuff like that. I think that was the worst part — being lied to by everyone I loved. I couldn't understand why they were doing it, and I started getting paranoid and coming up with all kinds of crazy theories. For whatever reason, the one that made the most sense to me was that you were dead, too. You had died along with your mother, and now my whole family was in some conspiracy to keep the bad news from me."

Maddie kept inching closer to him as he talked, and he kept backing away from her. But eventually he backed into the wall of the tide pool. He sucked in a breath as Maddie wrapped her arms around his waist, cuddled into his side, and laid her head on his shoulder.

Holy hell. She was trying to comfort him. The irony.

Kai realized he was holding his arm stiffly away from her, and he wrapped it around her shoulders and gave her a squeeze. He could do this.

"I don't know how long it was before they decided to tell me the truth," he continued. "But eventually they did tell me that you had gone back to Ohio with your grandparents — and that you were never coming back. They said they were sorry for lying and that they had delayed telling me only because they didn't want to upset me any more than I was already upset. But the damage was done. In my mind you were gone forever either way, and the nightmares kept coming. Sometimes I even dreamed..." He paused a second, then finished roughly. "Sometimes it wasn't your mother I saw hanging in those nightmares, Maddie. Sometimes, it was you."

Maddie raised her head. Her eyes were moist, her face flooded with misery. "I'm so sorry," she breathed. "I had no idea. No one ever told me any of that. It makes me heartsick. Surely my father—"

Kai shook his head. "Don't blame your father. He didn't know anything about what was happening with me, and it wasn't like he didn't have enough of his own grief to deal with." He looked at her. He lifted a hand and brushed a strand of red-gold hair across her temple and behind her ear. "This may all be new to you, Maddie, but I've had a long time to think about it. And while I know that from our perspective it seems like the adults in the situation totally screwed up and made both our lives miserable, it really wasn't that simple. Your dad didn't understand how close we were, much less how close you were to Nana and the rest of my family. And my family was following a therapist's advice; my dad and Nana in particular weren't happy about the lies but they genuinely believed at the time that they were doing what was best for me."

Maddie stiffened. "That's charitable of you. And I hope that someday soon I can make a similar statement about my dad, saying that I've forgiven him for cutting me off from everyone on Lana'i and then for lying to me my entire freakin' life. That I understand he was grieving then, that he made the best decisions he could, and that just because he isn't the bravest person in the world doesn't mean he doesn't love me." Her voice lowered to a growl. "But I'm pretty sure I'm going to have to call him up and yell at him first."

Kai chuckled with relief. He wrapped both his arms around her and held her tight. "You're going to be fine, Maddie," he assured, resting his cheek on top of her gorgeous red head. "And I'm already fine. I told you that. It's in the past now."

He wanted to keep on holding her. But she seemed tense. He loosened his hold, and she took a step back and studied his face. "Did you miss me, Kai?" she asked quietly. "Aside from being concerned that I was dead, I mean. And aside from worrying that I was okay. On a day to day basis, as time went on... did you miss my company?"

Kai's heart skipped a beat. He was missing her company right now. He wanted to feel her body next to his. "Of course I did. I told you that. I missed you very much."

"Then why didn't you answer my letter?"

Her gray eyes swam with torment. *That damned letter of hers. Again.* So he was right. His failure to reply had meant more to her than she let on. She'd probably been nursing a grudge over the stupid thing this entire time. And she probably had no more idea of what she'd actually written than he'd had.

"I know you were confused and an emotional wreck," she said tremulously, "and I feel bad even asking about it, now. But I can't help but wonder, if you were worried about me, didn't my letter help? I mean, at least it should have proved to you that I was alive and well! Even if we knew we'd probably never see each other again, it would still have been fun to be pen pals. I thought so, and I thought you would, too. I was so sure of it!"

Her face was earnest; her eyes were drowning with hurt. Kai started to reach out towards her, but she immediately drew back.

"I saw all those letters from your grandparents!" she cried, her voice catching. "And I knew then that I hadn't been wrong. Maybe most boys your age wouldn't want to write letters, but *you* would. You would have loved to do dumb stuff like make puzzles for each other and write stories and tell jokes. I was so excited about that! It was the only thing that kept me going for weeks! But you didn't answer me, Kai! Nothing!

Never!"

"Maddie, stop!" Kai commanded as her voice began to break. "You were *not* wrong, okay?" He reached into the back pocket of his shorts and pulled out the envelope he'd stashed there this morning. He knew he'd need to show it to her. Thank God he'd never thrown it away.

"Here," he said, pulling out the single sheet of stationery and extending it to her. "This is your letter, Maddie. The letter you sent to me. Read it."

Chapter 27

Maddie looked down at the small sheet of paper. It had sepia-toned roses around the edges. Filched from her grandmother's roll-top desk, no doubt. Lines of large, ghastly print clearly recognizable as her own ran slantwise across the page in blue ink. She reached out with unsteady fingers and took the letter from Kai's hand.

> *Dear Kai,*
>
> *You miserable stinking rat! Why didn't you come and say goodbye? I hate Ohio. It is SO cold here. EVERYTHING is either BROWN or GRAY. I miss the ocean and everyone is mean. I want to come back but Dad says no. I think I might get a job there someday though. But I'm mad at Nana too cause she didn't come see me either and I hate it here. And I'm mad because nobody asked me if I wanted to stay and I think I could have found somewhere to sleep and I would have been fine. And if you had said something I could have stayed with you but NO you just let them take me and so I'm mad at you too now.*
> *You better answer me!*
>
> *M*

The letter fell from Maddie's hands. It drifted onto the surface of the water and rested there a moment before, slowly, the saltwater began to seep through. Kai leaned down to rescue it, but Maddie stopped his arm with her hand.

"No," she ordered. "Let the damn thing sink."

Her stomach felt like she'd been sucker punched. A shiver rocked her shoulders. Was that truly what she had written?

"I swear to God, Kai," she said miserably, "I had no idea I wrote such an awful thing. If you'd asked me before I saw that, I would have guessed that I waxed nostalgic about our walks up to the Sweetheart Rock, confessed how much I missed you, and sent you a cryptogram with the names of the constellations."

She wasn't looking at him, but she heard him chuckle. "Yeah, that would have been fun," he said warmly.

She turned to face him, her stomach still aching. "I'm sorry, Kai. So, so sorry."

He shook his head. "I didn't show you that to make you feel bad, Maddie. You'd just lost your mother and been ripped away from your home and half the people you loved. You were at least as messed up in the head as I was. The letter was obviously just a venting mechanism. You had no idea what you were doing, certainly no idea what effect it might have on me."

Maddie thought she might be sick. "I can't even begin to think what effect it had on you," she murmured, lowering her head again. "First you thought I was dead, then you found out I was alive but gone forever, then you get a letter from the undead bitching and moaning that I'm miserable and it's all *your* fault? Oh, my God, Kai."

She expected him to put his arms around her. She wanted him to put his arms around her. But he didn't.

She straightened her spine and looked up at him. "What I wrote in that letter was horrible. Unforgivably horrible. And what's worse is that I've been mad at you ever since for not answering me. Whether I admitted it to myself or not, I took your not answering to mean that our friendship didn't matter as much to you as it did to me. And that it probably never had."

Kai's dark eyes held her gaze, and Maddie's still-sick stomach got butterflies. He was so damned gorgeous. No man should have lashes like that.

"I didn't answer the letter because I had no clue what to write back to you," he replied. "Really, Maddie, what *could* I write? I was a mess. There was no good news. I had no control over anything that happened to you or would happen to you, or anything that was happening to me. I thought you were really mad at me and I had no idea what to say in my defense to make things better."

"I was mad," Maddie said miserably. "But I wasn't *mad* mad."

Kai smiled at her. "I know that. Now. And I would have understood it then, too, if I'd been in a better place. But I wasn't. Like I said, I was a mess. And so were you. If we'd both been in a better place — if your dad had gotten some great job offer on the mainland and you'd moved away like any other kid moves away, we could have been pen pals and it would have been great. I'd probably have three shoeboxes full of letters, all from you, back home in my parents' closet right now."

Maddie felt the clenching in her gut slowly ease up a little. Her eyes moistened anew and she felt herself grinning. "I don't think Malaya would like that."

Kai grinned back. "What? Me writing to you, or me trying to store a bunch of extra boxes in her closets?"

Maddie considered. "I'm hoping just the last part."

"My family adores you, and you know it," Kai said gently. "They always have. And they're all very glad to welcome you back again."

Maddie met his eyes and smiled at him. A warmth spread through her middle, and she began to feel better. Truly better. At long last, everything about her departure from Lana'i and the miserable months that followed made sense. It was not a pretty picture, or a simple one. But it was clear, and it was real. And it was solid.

She was going to get past it. And the future would be just fine.

She lifted a hand and raised it to his temple. The long, glossy locks of his boyhood were cut shorter now, but she indulged herself in running her fingers through the black curls over his ear. He stood perfectly still, regarding her curiously.

Her heart soared. Straight from high school to BYU. Seven years living under an honor code *with no extramarital sex allowed*. Six months on Maui, working all the time. He'd even said that the LDS lifestyle suited him! And how many times had Gloria hinted at the same?

And yet, what had Madalyn The-World's-Most-Spectacular-Hypocrite Westover done the second she'd laid eyes on that amazingly gorgeous face and totally hot body of his? She had assumed he must have slept with a million women, because of course why *wouldn't* he if he was good-looking enough to have girls falling all over him every day of his life?

Oh, the irony. Someday she would tell him about it, and he would have a good laugh.

But not right now. Right now, she was going to do absolutely nothing but enjoy the rest of the afternoon on her favorite island with her favorite guy. No pressure. No fear. No nervousness.

Just fun.

"I suppose we really shouldn't litter," she said lightly, stepping away from him. She squatted down in the water and leaned out to scoop up the remnants of her letter from the sandy bottom. *Oh, darn.* Her shirt front got wet. She stuffed the soggy mess of paper in her shorts pocket, then climbed out of the pool. She stood on a rock ledge and stretched, readjusting her clingy shirt. "I can't remember it ever getting this hot in January before, can you?"

She stole a glance at his face, and it was all she could do not to laugh. The water in the pool around him might as well be steaming. "You want to take a dip? I can get wet in these clothes. I don't care." She grinned at him. "We can cap off our day with an hour at the launderette." She arched her back, lifted her hands above her head, and shook out her hair.

"Maddie!" Kai said in a strange, strangled voice.

She fought back a grin. "What?"

"Nothing," he said brusquely. He climbed up on the rocks and walked toward her. Maddie walked away until she reached the deep pool by the steps. "So, what do you say, Nakama?" she teased. "Shall we jump in? Clothes and all?"

His expression was all over the place. He looked frustrated, and conflicted, and completely incapable of taking his eyes off her.

Maddie jumped in.

Kai jumped in after her.

She laughed as the splash he made doused her hair and plastered it to her face. The pool they were standing in was only waist deep, but she lifted her feet and treaded water for a moment, soaking her torso and letting her hair fan out behind her.

Kai's gaze could set the water on fire.

She got her feet back under her again and took a step closer to him. It was time to put him out of his misery. And herself, too.

His rib cage heaved with uneven breaths. His dark, beautiful eyes swam with torment. "Maddie," he said in a whisper. "If you want to be just friends, that's fine. I'll *always* be your friend. But—"

Maddie moved forward, silencing him on the "but" by placing her hands on his chest, then sliding them up over his shoulders. Slowly, she pressed the rest of her body against his until they were standing nose to nose. "Well, see," she whispered back. "Here's the thing. I've decided I don't want to be just friends anymore. So if *you're* feeling guilty about lusting over this super hot bod of mine, you really shouldn't." She grinned at him wickedly. "I certainly don't feel bad about lusting over yours."

He stared back at her in surprise, but only for a second. In the next second, he pulled her against him so tightly she almost lost her breath. And in the second after that, he released her just enough to lean down and touch his lips to hers. It was a soft kiss, tender and undemanding, but she could feel the pent-up heat inside him as his every muscle shuddered with restraint.

Oh, yeah, she thought happily, *this would be fine*. She buried her head in the curve of his shoulder, hugged him soundly, and then let herself relax. She could feel his heart beating next to hers: pounding with excitement, in perfect sync.

Whatever had she been so worried about? If it hadn't felt right before, it was only because the relationship wasn't right. There was nothing wrong with *her*.

A seabird flew screaming over their heads. Children's voices echoed up from lower on the trail, unfortunate omens that their privacy was soon to meet an end. The cool water of the tide pool lapped gently at their waists.

"Kai?" she whispered.

"Yes?"

How she loved that deep, adult voice of his!

"We had a lot of fun when we were kids."

"Yes, we did," Kai agreed. He lifted a hand, began to caress the small of her back. Tentative, affectionate.

Nice.

Maddie pulled up her head and smiled at him. "I'm thinking we could have a whole lot more fun, now that we're both grown up."

He smiled back at her, his brown eyes sparkling like the stars he loved so much.

"Definitely," he replied.

About Lana'i

Unlike Madalyn Westover, I did not grow up on Lana'i (nor has anyone ever asked me if I was a model). Like Maddie, however, I did spend several delightful hours at the Lana'i Culture and Heritage Center (www.lanaichc.org), which is a wonderful resource for anyone interested in learning more about the people and history of this enchanting island. I am indebted to everyone I met who was willing to share their personal experiences of growing up on Lana'i, especially Mikala Enfield, who tolerated my endless list of bizarre questions with admirable humor. Any mistakes or misrepresentations with regard to island life and lore are entirely the fault of my own brain and not of the people with whom I spoke.

An art gallery is portrayed in the novel as being located next to Dole Park in Lana'i City, and in fact there is a real gallery in just this location. At the Mike Carroll Art Gallery (http://mikecarrollgallery.com) you can view a variety of prints and paintings of the island, as well as browse through offerings by local artists.

My EarthDefense legal team and the firm they work for is fictional, but the concept is based on a worthy nonprofit organization called Earthjustice, whose motto is "Because the earth needs a good lawyer." If you share Ben Parker's passion for the natural world, you should definitely check them out! (http://earthjustice.org)

Any people and events in this book associated with the "Resort at Manele Bay" and the "Lodge at Ko'ele" are entirely fictional. There are two very real Four Seasons resorts on the island however; as well as the historic Hotel Lana'i, which was built in 1923 to lodge executives of the Dole Plantation. Both have their charms, if you're ever so lucky as to visit Lana'i yourself. But even if you never get there in body, I hope this book has taken you there in spirit.

About the Author

USA-Today bestselling novelist and playwright Edie Claire was first published in mystery in 1999 by the New American Library division of Penguin Putnam. In 2002 she began publishing award-winning contemporary romances with Warner Books, and in 2008 two of her comedies for the stage were published by Baker's Plays (now Samuel French). In 2009 she began publishing independently, continuing her original Leigh Koslow Mystery series and adding new works of romantic women's fiction, young adult fiction, and humor.

Under the banner of Stackhouse Press, Edie has now published over 25 titles including digital, print, audio, and foreign translations. Her works are distributed worldwide, with her first contemporary romance, *Long Time Coming*, exceeding two million downloads. She has received multiple "Top Pick" designations from *Romantic Times Magazine* and received both the "Reader's Choice Award" from *Road To Romance* and the "Perfect 10 Award" from *Romance Reviews Today*.

A former veterinarian and childbirth educator, Edie is a happily married mother of three who currently resides in Pennsylvania. She enjoys gardening and wildlife-watching and dreams of becoming a snowbird.

Books & Plays by Edie Claire

Romantic Fiction

Pacific Horizons
Alaskan Dawn
Leaving Lana'i
Maui Winds
Glacier Blooming
Tofino Storm (2020)

Fated Loves
Long Time Coming
Meant To Be
Borrowed Time

Hawaiian Shadows
Wraith
Empath
Lokahi
The Warning

Leigh Koslow Mysteries

Never Buried
Never Sorry
Never Preach Past Noon
Never Kissed Goodnight
Never Tease a Siamese
Never Con a Corgi

Never Haunt a Historian
Never Thwart a Thespian
Never Steal a Cockatiel
Never Mess With Mistletoe
Never Murder a Birder
Never Nag Your Neighbor

Women's Fiction

The Mud Sisters

Humor

Work, Blondes. Work!

Comedic Stage Plays

Scary Drama I
See You in Bells

Made in the USA
Middletown, DE
08 July 2021